The Perry C

The Perry Gene

By Nelson Brooks

The Perry Gene

Prologue

A body takes around two seconds to plummet forty feet, conscious or unconscious. Wind resistance will have some impact on the speed, but weather conditions will not make a perceptible difference to the time it takes to fall. The thin, persistent rain of 2 a.m. merely followed the body down from the top of the Victorian railway arch to the ground behind the grey industrial bins below. There was no traffic or railway noise nearby so early in the morning, just the distant backdrop of the City; emergency sirens and a deep base beat.

The skull had been cleaved as it hit the side of the bin near the end of its descent. Now as the cooling body lay on the ground, the blood began to pool. The rain did little to wash away the stain. A thick red trail had been smeared upon the metal as the body came to a rest and it was this that would alert an early morning cyclist to the corpse five hours later. Across the road, a London pub was dark and silent; if a body falls in the City when nobody sees it, does it make a sound?

The Perry Gene

1. Adenine

The Perry Gene

Chapter 1

Billy had for ten years been a creature of habit who demanded routine; both his saviour and nemesis, his crutch was about to be kicked away. At 8.30am he was walking towards the door to collect the newly delivered post, as he did every day of the week except Sunday. This is not some Alice in Wonderland idealised world, it's just that Billy lived near the start of the round and his postman, generally Frank unless he was on holiday, was punctual and reliable. In fact, Billy was so old school, he still left out a Christmas box; it is what his Father would have done. Would have because he had died when Billy was eleven. That had left him alone with Mother - Rachel Perry - who had dragged him up kicking and screaming for the next few years, neither sportsman nor scholar, not liked or disliked, just a smaller version of his Father.

When his Mother got the initial diagnosis of cancer, Billy was seventeen. She clung on with a will of iron for the next four years, possibly just to make sure her offspring was sufficiently prepared for the world. Or more likely in an act of sheer belligerence and bloody-mindedness. Whatever the reason it had left Billy stunted in some way. His social skills were poor, his friends were few and far between. He descended, especially toward the end, into the landscape of routine where his only escape was the world of books, especially detective novels; a trait he inherited from his Father, much to his Mother's distaste.

In the end, Billy found his place in the world, installing and servicing fruit machines in pubs and clubs across South London. He had established his own business with the proceeds from his parent's estate, and he still occupied the two up two down his parents had purchased when they first got married. It was neat, tidy, easy to keep clean and fairly low maintenance. It also held the ghost of his Mother in every nook and cranny. Each vase, or china ornament, souvenirs that Billy barely remembered, lay in exactly the same positions as they had done when they carried her out of the door in a box. Billy was convinced he could sometimes hear her shuffle across the bedroom floor above.

It was Monday; the post having just arrived, kicked off a sequence of synchronised events. Before going to the front door, Billy pressed down on the toaster and having filled the kettle two cups full, pushed the switch to boil. His collection and subsequent sorting of the post took the required two minutes and thirteen seconds for the kettle to boil and the toast to pop up. The letters would need to be sorted in size order, then if the same size, into colours. He knew ninety-five percent of the mail that arrived because he had now been performing this routine for nearly ten years. He recognised circulars, tax documents, bank statements and begging letters (a line from Mother). Every now and then junk mail would invade the letter rack and it was given short shrift. But today, Billy was thrown. He had a manila envelope, not buff, not white; it looked official, like a summons or a fine. It had private and confidential printed on the top and a return address on the back. He stared at it, willing it to open of its own accord. As he stood there, he swayed gently, the movement involuntary. His eyes fell on the porcelain cow, evidence of Mother, just as he brushed it with the envelope, the paper catching on the ragged ear. It had been chipped many years ago in another careless accident.

The Perry Gene

Suddenly Billy was a teenager again and Mother was sitting at the kitchen table ruling from her throne. He worked out his approximate age based on how rough his Mother looked at that moment. The plastic mask hung across her face and a small portable oxygen tank sat beside her. This was near the end; a time as darkly impenetrable to Billy's memory as any. By that point, he was already starting to show signs of the psychosis that was to follow. The thing that had brought him back to this time was the porcelain cow, still intact at that point, but as if foretelling the future, he had knocked it onto the floor then and the ear had chipped. Even in her weakened state, Mother removed the face mask and bellowed at him; the harridan never far from the surface. She bullied and cajoled her son. She wanted to mould him, as she knew she didn't have long. He needed to be better than his useless Father, a man who she may have once loved, but who she had long since learned to despise for leaving her so soon. Rachel was a bitter woman and Billy felt every ounce of her resentment daily. He sensed himself being sucked in this wormhole into the past until suddenly his reverie was broken by the shattering of porcelain on the ground. It may have survived the fall all those years ago, but now it lay in a myriad of bovine shards across the kitchen floor.

Five minutes later, when he had cleaned up the mess, he realised his routine was gone. The toast was cold and the water was too lukewarm for proper tea, (another affectation of Mother). Ten years ago, this would have sent him into some form of paralysis, unable to move due to the constant analysis and reanalysis of the situation. Even five years ago, he would have been unsettled for the whole day. But now at just over thirty-one years of age, Billy had his condition under control, and he took these little moments of difference in his stride.

Knowing that he now built sufficient time into his day for these unavoidable interruptions, he reboiled the kettle but decided the toast would do. Selecting the Marmite from the table and placing it next to the already cold toast, he opened the bank statement that had just been delivered and scanned the balance. He knew what the number would be but the checking was everything. All the while he was looking at the stranger, the outlier; the sand in the oyster that might become a pearl; the manila envelope. He stared at it from the corner of his eye to see if it would reveal some secret when it thought it was unwatched. No, it just sat there, inscrutably goading him. He got up and went over to the kettle, picked up his breakfast mug and poured boiling water on to the tea bag. Waiting the requisite forty seconds, he took out the bag and returned to the table.

Spreading the selected topping on his toast, he sat and wondered whether he would pluck up the courage to open the envelope this morning or wait until the normality of the day had calmed him down. Every moment of normality a calming influence. The classical music helped; the rhythms and patterns of the Baroque chamber music giving the air substance around him. He did not listen to the radio, the adverts wound him tighter than a spring. He had tried Classic FM, but that phase lasted no more than an hour. He also toyed with Radio 3, but the unpredictability of the styles caused him angst. Modern sound landscapes would drive him to distraction.   Even Eric Sarte was difficult to bear as he found the discordant undertones as hard on the ear as Avant Garde Jazz. No, he thought, the evening was the time to open the envelope, as he crunched his toast and slurped at the mug of tea.

Staring around the room, there was no sign of clutter or a single item out of place.   Billy lived alone for a reason.   Yes, there had been a girl or two along the way, nothing long term. They noticed his sullen moods in the home and generally left shortly afterwards, unaware of the ghosts that watched on. Billy was no looker, but he was not ugly either.   Spending your work life in pubs and clubs certainly put you in view of many potential mates, and he would often bump into them when he was sober and they were well on their way to not being so. He could be charming and by this time no longer socially awkward. His memory, possibly due to his OCD-like symptoms or to his affection for Sherlock Holmes and the Mind palace, was impeccable.   He could tell long and detailed anecdotes, not his own you understand, but those he had salvaged from his work.   He was a good listener; on many occasions, five minutes interacting with a drunken ramble had given him a fine story to tell again later.   The problem with Billy was not when he was out, but rather when he returned home. The house was Rachel's sanctuary, her sanctum Sanctorum; a point made very often by Doctor Miles, Billy's Counsellor.

'Billy, you have lived alone in that place ten years now, time to move out and see the world' was the latest proclamation. 'You have come on in leaps and bounds with the therapy, you are a fully functioning adult now with barely a trace of the issues you first exhibited when your Mother died. But now, that house is holding you back, you need to escape, break free, and spread your wings. No wonder you scare away any woman who ever finds herself there. You are tied to the past and you need a change.' And so, it went on, Doctor Miles would cajole, coerce, and even try more direct approaches to Billy to get him to take the final step. The damage done by his dying Mother was so close to being buried, Doctor Miles could sense it, but Billy needed that final push.

With breakfast finished, he broke with routine for a moment to clear up the broken shards of china. Wrapping them carefully in newspaper, he put them in the bin, just like she would have done if his or his Father's carelessness ever got the better of her. He then got back on track; washed the plate and cup, put them on the drainer and went to clean his teeth. The routine had been drummed into him through years of parental persuasion. He had the cleanest teeth on the street but the weirdest mind his punters used to say. Punters, there was a great sign, of all the environments you would not expect Billy to thrive within was pubs and social clubs. But somehow the culture, the nuances, his observation skills gave him an advantage when it came to both negotiating and navigating his way through drunks, drugs, drop outs and the occasional rival firm. He looked and sounded like a local in a way that would have horrified his Mother and satisfied his Father. He was his own man, but somehow Doctor Miles was right, every time he returned to the house, it was like putting on his Mother's dressing gown. She was right back there, bossing him about and controlling him.

The Perry Gene

Teeth done, he picked up the keys to his car and headed for the lock-up to collect his works-van and supplies for the day ahead. The last thing he did before double checking the alarm was set and the door was bolted was to stare across the room at the manila envelope. It was still there and would be waiting for him on his return later that evening. He popped the lock on the car, an ageing Ford Focus, and checking the mirrors were aligned and the car out of gear, fitted his seat belt before starting the engine and heading off.

The drive to the lock-up was all of ten minutes. Billy never considered it living above the shop but just close enough in case the alarm went off at night and he had to be called out. It had happened a couple of times before and the Police were very quick to inform the key holder. Being in a partly industrial, partly residential area as most of South London is these days, there were enough sensitive ears to consider and the law didn't hang about. But on this bright and chilly February morning, the lock-up under the clichéd railway arches was just as he had left it the night before. Sensibly it was wide enough to drive his car in before removing the van, which prevented the need for either a twice daily swap over or on-street parking. It wasn't an unsafe area but the amount of graffiti it regularly attracted meant he wasn't going to trust his car to it.

Inside the arch was a set of workbenches, an old desktop computer he used for enquiries, two locked cupboards of spare parts and diagnostic equipment and then a set of six machines which he could swap out when one of the current ones was damaged or needed an upgrade. Billy's business covered the old and the new. The fun and the money as he called it. The fun was in the form of video games that made a steady income wherever they went. They would never light up the world, but they were good little earners. The money came in the form of high-end fruit machines. Admittedly most of the work Billy did was the maintenance of other people's machines for a retainer but having his own kit in the field could be quite lucrative if he popped by regularly enough to check cash floats and collect any deposits that were not recycled. He even got alerts on his phone to make it easier. Over the last few years, he had built up a good base and he had twenty machines in the field of his own, while servicing a further seventy or so for three major firms. One was a chain of local pubs and the other two were nightclubs. The odd thing was, Billy never played and never gambled. You could say the kid in the sweet shop concept, but that wasn't it. It just didn't appeal. Billy set up the machines and knew the odds. When Ian Dury sang about the jackpot being in the handle of a normal fruit machine, Billy knew this was not the case. It was in the jumper setting on the rear of the circuit board. Years of set ups had told him how he should configure each machine, based on the clientele. You needed to be careful, too low a jackpot-setting and you were out of pocket, too high and some drunken thug would put his fist or head through the screen in frustration.

With his inspection of the premises complete, Billy consulted the desk diary and checked on his jobs for the day. He was sure he knew what they were already, but his habitual creature stalked him internally and he played along. Three pubs before lunch, a sticking wheel at one where he would try and convince the manager to go for an upgrade, for which he got commission, and then after a quick bite of lunch he would do a tour of four clubs. They opened later based on the late-night nature of their business hours. His tool box was already in the van but he put a spare wheel for the machine in the back in case the sales patter failed him and got in to drive off. Some Vivaldi came on his playlist and he smiled as the first bars of an oboe concerto filled the cab of the van. He pulled up outside and closed the gates before applying the lock. As he checked everything was secured, he stared, as if the concentration gave him x-ray vision, through the door, thinking the manila envelope may now sit there on the bench having followed him. He was conscious of the change to his routine which unnerved him slightly. It was like being watched but in reverse. When your entire day was one giant game of spot the difference, you were never happy until you had found all the seven or eight advertised variations. But getting back in the cab, the music washed over him, and he popped the satnav on to warn him of the traffic cameras. He knew the route and stuck to the limits religiously, however forewarned is forearmed.

As he pulled to the end of the street and prepared to enter the flow of traffic, he heard a siren. Police, ambulance, no both, their piercing screech beating with the lack of synchronisation, a most unpleasant row for him to experience. Suddenly from around the corner came first a police car then an ambulance on the wrong side of the road to avoid the traffic. This section was one of the few places you could cross the railway that ran into London Bridge and so it was a commuter cut through and a back-streets rat run when the main roads snarled up. Straight under the bridge the road turned hard right and disappeared along the line of the railway towards Southwark and Borough. Billy looked to pull out into the now blocked traffic when he heard the siren getting louder again. No, it was coming from a different direction, no wait two directions. A car shot past his view the other side of the bridge and a second car again came around the stationary vehicles. Three cars and an ambulance to one incident, this early in the day, this was no run of the mill traffic stop or donut run. Something big was happening. Billy sat for a moment and thought about it, but then realised he needed to get back on schedule. What with the letter that morning, if he was not careful his day was going to slip away from him.

Finally, he found a polite driver in the queuing traffic, so he managed to get out of the junction and head off in the opposite direction from the action. The noise of the sirens produced that familiar Doppler Effect until stopping after a minute or so. Billy didn't really give it any more thought. What happened outside his world was almost another planet, which was the way he liked it. He didn't care for the news or current affairs. Politics didn't really interest him and celebrity left him cold. All those people who changed partners almost like he changed oil in the van that was not for him. He just got on with his life, his work, seeing Doctor Miles once a month and building up a little something for a rainy day. He knew it was the right thing to do, Mother had said so, but for the life of him, he had no idea what he wanted to do when the rain came; irrespective of how much he had saved for it.

The Perry Gene

Chapter 2

To say the morning passed without incident would be something of an understatement as Billy was more used to routine than the average man in a van. His first jobs went well, two standard service checks and a replacement coin unit, as he suspected.   He still couldn't convince the miser that ran the Three Cockerels to part with his hard-earned cash and replace the ageing machine. Still, Billy knew as he worked on him that the opportunity was there, it was just a matter of time and the continual planting of seeds.   That was Billy all over, slow and methodical, not stupid, just precise and planned. Doctor Miles insisted he needed more variation to try and break the cycles that were built into his life, but the harder he pushed the more Billy seemed to resist.   The best thing Doctor Miles had managed to do in the last year was to hold alternate sessions at the house.   He saw Billy lighten noticeably away from it, which confirmed in his own mind this was the key to the problem.   But how was he going to get Billy to move out of the house he had grown up in? Initially, his memories were happy; chess and crime novels with his Father, but from the age of eleven, all that changed. This was the place he had learnt the news of his Father's illness and subsequent death, then finally where he had nursed his Mother as she grew weaker and died.   She would not move into a hospice even at the end, just doggedly stuck to her own bed and coughed her way straight into the grave, with just a small detour via the funeral directors.

Even in death she had him in her vice like grip.   Billy and his Mother had got into a routine of visiting the family plot shortly after his Father's untimely departure from this life. She organised a twin grave at the time so she would be near her husband after she died. Billy, although not prone to family analysis, thought this was uncharacteristically romantic for a woman who barely showed love or affection above the scale of a peck on the cheek. When she became noticeably ill towards the end, the visits to lay flowers grew more frequent and there was an unspoken promise being solicited that this behaviour would continue after her passing. Doctor Miles knew that everywhere Billy turned, his Mother had laid traps and waited even in death for him to topple right in. She had said things to him as she lay dying. Undertakings were extracted, behaviours programmed. When she finally passed away, his breakdown was engineered to follow. He never knew what drove her to be the way she was, and frankly after all this time, he did not care. She had seemed angry in the world for as long as he could remember and when he Father was no longer there, it was only Billy left to bear the brunt.

The beauty about being Billy was, that unless Doctor Miles laboured a point and got him to accept it and restate it, he was oblivious to such subterfuge. If he ever broke the mould, and got away from the traps, he would be a man without emotional artifice. Oh yes, he could spin a yarn while showing off merchandise, this was a learned skill. He took a Saturday job working on machines in an arcade to bring in extra cash a couple of years after his Father died, so he saw how the game was played. Over the years, he had developed his own patois, his own style, but still those early lessons were key to the way he now was. He knew, as if living the life of the song 'The Gambler', when to hold, fold, walk away and most definitely when to run. It was this healthy sense of self preservation and knowing not to over stretch himself, a classic character flaw of South London Wannabes, which had kept his head quite literally on his shoulders. He wasn't sure if this was something to thank his Mother for, or just a side effect of her regime.

Billy tried to rotate the pubs so that he finished at a different one for lunch on his regular visits. This way he could show he was willing to give a little back, pick a cheap enough lunch and also ingratiate himself with the man or woman who was paying the bills. Today, without much in the way of a travel plan, he had ended his morning shift at around two with lunch and a pint of lager in the Flag & Staff. It was a proper South London boozer which lay on the road parallel with the railway lines into London Bridge, about a quarter mile out from the station. This also made it about a mile from Billy's lock-up which was ideal for a restock after lunch and to drop off broken parts.

The Flag & Staff was typical of the pubs built in the fifties to replace the bombed-out shells left by our careless German cousins during the war. There were green ceramic tiles on the walls, stripped planks on the floor to which your shoes stuck at certain times of day, and the overpowering smell of bleach from scrubbing if you arrived too early in the morning. But to its credit it was independent and was run by a fierce landlady by the name of Shirley. She was a widow having lost her husband, the original landlord, in a pub brawl where a knife was drawn, sometime in the middle of the 90's. Although initially untrusting of Billy, he had been providing a quality service to the pub for over seven years now and so Shirley took the time to chat to him when he came in. She was a great one for gossip and liked to be a bit of a flirt, but she also had the annoying habit of finding potential dates for Billy, which had already proved to be a mistake on more than one occasion.

Billy smiled at her as he walked in, shouted across his order of food, the pie of the day, and took a detour via a bookshelf by the bar where he dropped off two detective novels. He didn't like to keep books once he had read them and gave them to the pub for their charity shelf.   Once he had discarded the books he headed directly to two slot machines in the corner.   They were reasonably new models which he had acquired for Shirley so they were still in the 'earning money for old rope' phase of their life cycle.   This meant Billy knew they needed little more than a health check and a quick clean.   Twenty minutes later he was putting away his diagnostic equipment and toolkit when the steaming plate was delivered to the bar.

'Grub's up Billy' yelled Shirley from behind the bar, as she deposited the plate where he would always sit. 'Lager as usual right' she chirped, 'a man of routine is our Billy', her voice softened and reduced in volume as he crossed the room and settled on the stool.

'Thanks Shirley', Billy said as he picked up the salt and pepper and shook both at the same time, one in each hand.

'How many times do I have to say, try the bloody food first before you season it. I swear you do that out of habit. How do you know it's not too salty already?'

The Perry Gene

'Shirley, you never put enough salt in the shepherd's pie, it always needs seasoning.' Billy said between mouthfuls of steaming meat and mash.

'You never know, today could be the day I actually put some in, you really should try, and call me Shirl for Christ's sake. How many years have we known each other?'

'Seven' Billy said absent mindedly.

'It was a rhetorical question, I keep asking you to call me Shirl as everybody else does, why can't you? You're not scared of me, are you?' she picked up a knife from the bar and simulated the shower scene from Psycho. 'Reep Reep Reep' she said and mimed tearing the shower curtain.

'Shirley, the only thing that worries me about you apart from your cooking is your acting, so no I'm not scared of you. It's just I was introduced to you as Shirley and that's the way my mind works'. He took a long drink of his beer emptying maybe a third of the glass. 'That first lug is always the best'.

'On the subject of death' she said thumbing the edge of the blunt knife and wiping it clean before putting it back in the cutlery draw, 'you missed the excitement this morning'.

'Oh yeah, what was that then?' Billy sat back and belched quietly as the gas got the better of him. Shirley pulled a face and shook her head in disgust.

'Billy, I thought you were a gentleman.'

The Perry Gene

'I am, I always say thank you to a girl afterwards' and he pulled the most ridiculous grin showing way too many pearly white teeth.

'Listen shark boy, stop acting like Jack the Lad and listen to me.' She walked to the other end of the room and pulled up the hatch of the bar. She passed through and came close up so she could talk more discretely to Billy, without the other three remaining drinkers hearing.

'We had a jumper this morning, landed over there on the pavement' she pointed across the road to the railway arches.

'This morning? What time?' Billy now thought back to the sirens and the overzealous police drivers.

'He must 'ave jumped in the wee small hours as nobody seemed to 'ave seen anything. Some cyclist coming to work stumbled upon him when he went to lock-up his bike before going into the arches.   Rather a lot of strawberry jam, from what I heard.'

'Jumper you say? That's a bit odd, isn't it?' Billy got off his stool and walked to the window. From that angle, he could just about see the top of the raised railway above the arches.   It was only about thirty-five or forty feet. Also, how would somebody get up on the railway?   We all hear of trespass, but that generally tended to be at ground level.   Billy did not like puzzles and now this was bothering him.   He carried on looking up at the parapet as if transfixed.

'Billy, come and finish your lunch eh, it's getting cold.   What are you looking at, he jumped down, he didn't fly up?' Shirley walked across and linked her arm through his and made a huge show for the other customers of walking him back to his seat while performing something that looked passably like the Lambeth Walk. Under her breath she was singing. 'Any evening, any day, if you go down Lambeth, la la la la la, doing the Lambeth Walk'. As she nestled Billy back on this stool she concluded 'Hey'.

Billy ate the rest of his plate of food in silence, stopping to swig his pint in increments; he was deep in thought. When he had finished, he took the plate down to the serving hatch on the bar where it needed to go through to the kitchen.

'Penny for them Billy' Shirley said as he looked vacantly on.

'Mother used to say that' he said and looked at her. 'Didn't understand it then, don't bloody well understand it now.' With this he saluted Shirley as he always did and picking up his toolset headed for the van. As he walked through the door, Shirley called after him.

'That's another quid for the swear box next time you come in. Every time you mention that Mother of yours. You know the rules?'. The rest of Shirley's curse against her was lost to Billy as the door swung closed behind him. She couldn't help being just a bit protective of Billy, people got that way about him as he was so genuine. Shirley would see the impact on him, when she heard the stories of his upbringing. She knew the damage 'that woman' did before she died.

After a quick stop at the arches for parts, Billy hit the road again and managed to get snarled up in the start of the rush hour. All the time going through his mind was the jumper. Billy loved puzzles because it was a way of bringing order from chaos. It reminded him of playing chess with his Father and the logical thought processes and progression involved; B followed A, which was followed C. He played it back over and over, running a mental picture of a man falling and flailing. It was like a broken TV with no sound. As hard as Billy thought about it, like banging the TV on the side, he could not hear what was happening, but he could see it again and again. Then the sound finally came, but it was not from the image but from a car horn. Billy looked up and the light was green but he was not moving. He had become so engrossed in the image that he had lost track of reality. This had not happened in a long while, although it was something that occurred a lot in the years following the breakdown. At first the doctors suspected epilepsy, a petit mal, but it was proved not to be. It was the old axiom of analysis paralysis; he would literally get stuck in a mental loop process and needed external stimuli to break out of it.

Checking the traffic, he pulled away to the sound of yet more horns, in the direction of the last of his three stops of the late afternoon and early evening. He was due to finish his day at the casino, they had high end machines which they certainly were not going to purchase off Billy, but they still needed maintenance and servicing. Billy knew the door staff, the croupiers and the bar tenders. It would have proved useful if he ever wanted to go for a night in a club or in the casino, but it wasn't really his style. In all honesty, the gig paid well but he preferred the honest boozers and Shirley and her dying ilk of independent publicans; what was once the lifeblood of the city. These days there were more chains, more wine bars and more Russians. Billy steered clear of the latter, as his sixth sense told him a short-term profit could turn into long time pain and he was not in the market for that. He simply wanted an easy life and to be able to get on his way.

The casino work completed, it was nearly eight o'clock as Billy pointed his van in the direction of the lock-up. He was now ten miles away from it, but the rush hour traffic had dissipated like spring fog so he did the journey in just under half an hour. Swapping vehicles, he locked up and made for home. The house was dark, but then again, who would be home? Doctor Miles had suggested setting timers on the lights, but Mother would never have gone for that. 'What a waste of electricity' he could hear her saying. He stared at the darkened windows and for a moment swore he could see her standing there watching him, but no, it was just the net curtain catching the breeze.

With all the excitement of the day concerning the jumper, the manila envelope had slipped Billy's mind. This was something of a miracle; Doctor Miles would be impressed and he would need to mention it on his next visit. Before going in, Billy took a small notebook out of his inside jacket pocket and wrote down a note of what to relay to his counsellor during his next scheduled appointment. This was all part of the routine, although the entries had become less over the years as his dependence had reduced.

Unlocking the front door, Billy turned on the light and there it was, propped up on the sideboard next to the world of tasteless tat that was a constant reminder of the life he had never escaped. He locked the door, hung up his coat, grabbed a tin of beer from the fridge, no glass, popped the ring pull and took a long draw.

'Now for you my oddity' he said as he sat in the chair at the table and ran his finger along the flap of the envelope to open it. He was so gentle doing this it was if he was a bomb technician looking for wires. In reality, he was looking for clues while all the time his mind was processing. He saw a return address as he turned it in his hands, but who was it from? Once open, he put the can of beer down and withdrew a single sheet of good quality vellum notepaper. He knew quality as Mother had keep decent paper for writing serious letters.

'People recognise quality' she would say. Billy didn't know about that but he knew this was a serious letter. He unfolded it and read the address at the top of the page. It was just outside the City walls at Holborn (he checked to see it matched the return address on the back, a standard Billy reaction). The legal firm on the letter head was 'Jeeves & Jarvis, Est. 1847'; very serious. The letter was an invitation to contact them for a formal meeting. The reference on the paper was not one he recognised, neither was the person it was about. It referred to the estate of one Elspeth Perry. That was odd, considered Billy, I don't know an Elspeth, but Perry is *my* name. This must be mistake he thought and putting the letter back into the envelope he decided to give them a call in the morning to straighten things out. He replaced the manila envelope on the sideboard, put a tin of soup on to boil and carried on swigging from his can. The victory of not using a glass would have driven his Mother to distraction.   Billy smiled at this little act of rebellion.   It was one of a number that had started to show themselves, nurtured at every turn by Doctor Miles.

The Perry Gene

Chapter 3

Billy was neither a lark nor an owl. His chosen profession meant he needed to work slightly later than most but that meant starting later too. He tried on most days not to be on regular visits outside the hours of 9 to 7. This allowed him to rise at a comfortable time, the same time to be precise, and it meant he was not in a rush to get to bed. After finishing his soup and bread, he had a second can of beer, flicked through the free newspaper, and decided to switch on the PlayStation. He only played two types of games, car chases and shoot 'em ups. He was currently on the latter working his way through a sniping game. He liked to immerse himself for a couple of hours at a time, shooting and strafing his way through a World War Two scenario. He was good as he had an eye for careful precision and stealth, not just mindless gun toting. In fact, when the alarms were triggered, he tended to get flustered and find himself back at the last save point, trying to find the trip switch he had missed. His evenings would tend to alternate between this escapism on screen and reading his beloved detective novels. When he came across a passage which was well written, he would read it aloud, as he had done all those years ago as a child. However, now there was no audience to appreciate it.

After a couple of hours, he used the remote to turn off the Plasma, put the controller onto charge and switched off the lights before climbing the stairs. Nothing seemed odd to Billy, but he still turned left to the single bedroom at the top of the stairs and not right to the double room which was once his Mother and Father's. His room was adequate and although he had lost some items over the years, it still showed clear evidence of his childhood and the stains from BlueTac that had been used on teenage posters. These days there were a few modern prints on display, mainly IKEA as Billy was no expert, but the underlying wall was still visible. One day he knew it would need to be repainted, but there was no rush. It was part of Doctor Miles' plan, that and emptying his Mother's room.

He kept that room locked and only went in there once a month to run a Hoover around, less than Mother would have accepted, but it was not as if there was any mess being created now she was gone. It was just part of Billy's routine. The bedding got changed every few months, in case of guests that he knew would never come. He was an only child; all family were now dead and none of his acquaintances were what you would call the 'come and stay for the weekend' type. He had drinking partners that he knew from the pubs he worked in, a few school friends that had never got away from the area and his Sunday morning football league. This was Billy's great release; not playing, but refereeing. It was ideal, all the fitness, but none of the camaraderie. He got to exercise the rule book, which he could recite, and did if required, whenever any indiscretion occurred. In fact, this was another area that had helped with Billy 'coming out of his cave' as Doctor Miles would say. Rachel had built that dark cave and Billy struggled every day when her magnetic influence would pull him back towards it. In all honestly, he probably kept the room locked in the end as a way of keeping her influence contained. One day, he would be brave enough to empty the wardrobe of her clothes as she had done with all his

Father's things.   One day, but not today. No today, he had yet again turned left into his childhood room.   He set his alarm, checked his phone for work messages, of which there were none, and turned off the bed-side lamp. Moonlight shone through the window and in the distance the train wheels could be heard squealing as they took the late-night revellers home.   The City sung him its lullaby and he obediently went straight to sleep.

*

Tuesday morning started as it did on all weekdays with the 7am alarm.   Billy pulled on his running gear, looked out the window to check the weather conditions and saw there was no need for a rain top.   It was one of those winter into early spring days when the city sky was on fire.   It was cold and crisp, but dry and bright.   Billy was no gym Nazi, but he tried to get in a run three times a week as this meant his Sunday matches were a pleasure not a chore in terms of fitness.   His run was just three miles, but he managed this in under twenty minutes, including some bench-based stretches in the park at the half way point. It was enough to keep him in a reasonable physical state, without the need for protein supplements or even more importantly a gym membership.   Mother would never have approved of that vast expense every month.

Getting back from his run he showered, stuck his running gearing to wash and looked at his diary of the day ahead.   Billy had found over the years there were a few advantages to his obsession regarding detail and one of them was diary planning.   He was never late, he left time to get to appointments, which was probably one of the reasons the publicans and club owners liked him so much. He was literally as punctual as a Swiss watch, unfortunately most of the time he was also wound as tightly as one. Scanning the day ahead he noticed not much booked for after lunch. It sometimes worked that way, the maintenance routines for the machines came in cycles and that meant at times there were quiet patches. During these periods, he would do the books, engage in a bit of upselling, and carry out repairs on the machines he had in the lock-up. He was cannibalising a couple for parts and they were already in a fairly stripped-down state. He would occasionally pick up a broken machine from eBay and either repair it or scrap it after harvesting valuable spare parts. It gave him instant inventory and meant he could charge for new parts but used 'pre-loved' ones as he called them. He had seen that slogan outside a bike shop once and liked it so much he took it on board as his own; but not in front of the customers. They didn't need to know how much love their 'new ' parts had seen before.

Finishing his breakfast (Tuesday; marmalade on the toast) he reflected on the mysterious letter be had received the previous day and retrieved it from the sideboard. He thought he would give the Solicitors a call. He was disappointed to get a recorded message saying they did not open until 9.30. 'Bloody hell', Billy thought, 'someone that starts later than me.' With this thought he collected his keys, pushed the letter into his jacket pocket and locked up before jumping in his car. His diary had shown three pub visits, two before lunch and one after, so when he got to the lock-up he tinkered on his graveyard machines for a while before making for his first appointment. In the van with the music playing he felt a rustle in his pocket and remembered the letter, so before driving off he took out his mobile and tried the Solicitors again. This time he got a human voice on the third ring.

'Good morning, Jeeves and Jarvis, how can I help you?' came the efficient greeting.

'Yeah, this is Billy Perry, I got a letter about somebody called Elspeth, but I don't know any Elspeth, so I think you made a mistake' Billy blurted out before really thinking it through.

'Sorry sir, this is a big office, did your letter have a reference on it?' Billy scanned the paper and read out the code, which could have been hieroglyphics for all he knew.

'Oh, yes sir, just found you on the computer, one of Mr Transon's cases, would you be able to come this afternoon, Mr Transon is free after 3pm?'

'But you've made a mistake, I don't know a'

'Mr Perry' the voice interrupted', 'sorry to stop you but your file shows a connection and it would be very worthwhile you coming to see us, could you make 3?'

'Where are you exactly?'

'Just off High Holborn, near the start of the meat market, do you know it?' Billy ran through the map book in his head, 'Yeah I know it, but 3 will be tight, what about 4?'

'Ok, we will see you then, last appointment of the day.' With that the line went dead.

The Perry Gene

'Start at 9.30, finish at 4.30, I got to change jobs' Billy said out loud. Putting his phone away and tucking the letter back into his jacket, he re-started the van, drove out of the lock-up, and then onto to his first appointment.

There were two ways he could go to his first job of the day at the Plasterer's Arms, left or right out of the street. He looked around, saw the traffic was clear and then his thoughts sank back to the previous morning and the sirens. As both routes were much the same in time, he turned left under the bridge followed the railway track for half a mile or so. By taking this decision, his route took him past Shirley's pub and the site of yesterday's jumper. As he nearer the location, he slowed, even though there was nothing to see, but just enough to get a toot from the car behind who obviously did not appreciate rubber-necking or in fact any form of slow driving. As he passed the Flag & Staff, he thought about his next visit there in a week and how he would have to find out if Shirley knew any more gossip. She was a true old school publican in terms of her network and loved to share what she knew. 'Well,' Billy thought, 'time to test her skills.'

*

The morning passed without incident and Billy deliberately got to his last appointment early so he would not be late to get into the City. This was much to the surprise of the manager who didn't expect to see him until after the lunch rush.

'Normally set my watch by you I can Billy, what's occurring?' Steve said as Billy started to work on the rear panel of the machine.

The Perry Gene

'Got an appointment in town this afternoon that came up at the last minute, but I didn't want to let you down by having to cancel.' Billy spoke not to Steve but to the back of the machine. After two years in the role, Steve was still new to the pub in Billy's mind and he didn't think he could trust him. Billy thought back to a piece of work he was doing on a machine in the bar some eight months ago. He had overheard Steve talking about him when he came back from the toilet.

'He's not exactly the sharpest tool in the box, is he?' Steve was saying to the barmaid. She saw Billy across Steve's shoulder and caught his eye. The message was clear, stay out of this.

'We have known Billy a bit longer than you Steve. He is a gentleman and straight.' Steve had looked out of the window at this point and the barmaid winked at Billy. Billy smiled in response and got down behind the machine to continue working. He could still just make out the conversation.

'Straight, no, I reckon he's celibate. He ain't getting any, I can tell.'

'I bet you can' she laughed 'probably from personal experience.' With this he growled something and walked off. Billy peered out from behind the machine and blew her a kiss in thanks before getting back on with his work.

Billy looked like he was daydreaming as he recalled this run in. Steve still didn't know Billy had overheard and Billy was aware that he now had the power in their relationship. Billy was determined that business was business but to keep Steve at arm's length.

'You sick or something? What sort of last-minute appointment? You got some virulent disease I should know about?   Maybe you got the Big C?'

'Leave him alone Steve' one of the barmaids said, 'don't joke about shit like that.   Billy, you just ignore him love.   I hope you got a nice little liaison going on with a lady friend.   Steve's just jealous as he can't pull his own weight, let alone a decent bird.'

'Ain't you got work to do Debbie' sneered Steve at the barmaid, but she just stared at him and continued to dry the hot glasses from the dishwasher. During this exchange, Billy kept his head down and continued his routine. Since nobody was paying him any attention Steve wandered off to talk to a customer, leaving Billy to get on.   Billy knew how to deal with bullies, he was a past master now. When he looked at Steve, his mind flashed back to his Mother and he shudder, but then caught himself and got back to the job in hand.

The maintenance of the machine took just over half an hour as one of the tumblers was sticking and Billy needed to take it apart to clean out the contacts. Once reassembled it ran like new.   Billy had a real gift with his hands, there wasn't much he couldn't turn to and make work, which often came in handy at the pubs when something broke. It had started with just the mechanics and electric needs of the old machines in the arcade, but along the way Billy had also picked up some electronics and basic computer skills. He had earned a good reputation which of course got him repeat business and the occasional extra machine sale. Once he closed up his box, he went to get the barmaid to sign the maintenance log to show he had completed the work.

'Go on Billy, is it a girl?' Debbie gently teased him, 'or a boy, I am open minded. In fact,' she looked down at her chest encouraging him to 'very open minded.'

'No Debbie, just got to see a solicitor, but don't tell Steve. I don't mind you knowing but he will just take the piss again.'

'Secret's safe with me love' and she gave a peck on the cheek as he left.

*

After driving back to the lock-up, Billy swapped vehicles and drove home to get a quick shower and change. He was not dirty, but he wanted to look smart for whatever this Solicitor had to say and he never put on clean clothes without a shower. This was another throw back to his Mother and he often felt her presence at times like this; something akin to the school monitor or prefect, ensuring the rules were adhered to. He walked out the front door and up to the local bus stop. The commuters who came into town were all about the train and tubes and cabs. The real Londoners used the buses. They were cheap and they went where you wanted to go, not a mile or two away. They ran late into the night and they were mostly safe unless you were careless about where you went on your own. Billy made it over to Holborn in just over thirty minutes, as there was not a lot of traffic since the rush hour had not started to wind up yet. True to form he arrived at the address twenty minutes early; which would have allowed for one missed bus or connection. It was not a massive office, built as it was into what looked like a row of four Victorian or Edwardian houses knocked through; a very London solicitor look.

When he got to the front door, he pressed the intercom button and waited.

The Perry Gene

There was a camera pointing at him and after a few seconds the sound of a metallic buzzing while the solenoid released. Billy was thinking to himself how that mechanism worked inside the door, mentally tracing the wires back and imaging a slender finger with a deep red painted nail on the end pressing it. When he walked into reception, the girl behind the large marble desk was in her late-twenties, slightly plain looking but professionally dressed; beyond that Billy paid little attention to her as was his way in strange settings. She pointed to some chairs and continued with her phone call. Billy got the feeling, even though she was reasonably young like him, she could be prickly and wanted to show him who was boss. When she finally got off the phone, it was almost the top of the hour.

'Mr Transon is waiting in his office at the top of the stairs; first on the left.' She said as she removed the headset. Billy walked up the narrow staircase and looked at the wallpaper. It wasn't the best quality and the paintwork could do with a touch up. He brushed the banister with his hand; it was thick and glossy, like too many layers. It felt like years of touch-ups adding to what came before. He knew it needed to be stripped down back to the bare timber and he pulled his hand away as it felt all wrong. Billy turned the corner and there on the left, the first door had Mr Transon's name and credentials on it. He knocked and waited, he could hear the shuffling of papers inside.

'Come in' came the muffled response through the door. Billy pushed the door open and entered. 'Mr Perry, I presume, please take a seat'

The Perry Gene

'There's been some sort of mistake, I don't know any Elspeth' Billy blurted out. He stood and did not take the seat he had been offered.

'Mr Perry, the fact that you don't know Elspeth does not mean she did not know you, please do take a seat, we have quite a lot to go through and I doubt we will get it all done today.' Billy took the seat and slipped his coat off his shoulders.

'So, who is she?' Billy glared into Transon's eyes daring him to be wrong.

'Billy, may I call you Billy? Billy, Elspeth was your Aunt. She died recently and she made you the sole beneficiary of her estate.'

'I don't have an Aunt. My mum had a brother but he died in his teens in the army. My dad was an only child, so I don't get it'

'Billy, your dad was not an only child. He had a sister and apparently, there was some falling out many years ago. They never spoke again and your Aunt never married. But for reasons best known only to her, she kept an eye on you. I don't know why she never made contact, I guess after your Mother died, she assumed you wouldn't want to hear anything bad about her. Anyway, she became ill and spent her last few months in a sort of hospice, but she was mentally as bright as a button and very astute financially.'

'How do you know all this then?'

'Billy, I was her Solicitor for the nearly thirty years.' Billy sat frozen for a few moments. He could feel the waves of change washing over him like a rough ocean. This is how the panic started. Suddenly nothing was for certain and it scared him. He felt the breakers getting bigger and he grew nauseous. Transon sat back for some thirty seconds and let Billy try to assimilate the news. Billy knew he had to remember his lessons, the way Doctor Miles had taught him. He imagined a piece of drift wood and he clung on. The harder he clung to the wood the more the waves would begin to calm until eventually the sea became a placid mill pond.

'She told me that you have some issues; something resembling OCD?' Billy looked up, once more in control.

'You make it sound like she was spying on me.'

'Elspeth Perry had no children of her own and you were in fact her only living relative. She was a woman of considerable means and she was estranged from you, her nephew, due to a falling out with his Mother, can you blame her? She kept an eye out. I should mention, she is the reason Gordon Miles is your counsellor, she pulled strings to get you the best.'

'Doctor Miles? I can't see how that could be.' Billy stopped and thought for a second, he was struggling to cope. 'Hang on, what do you mean considerable means? When people say, *an old lady dies in a sort of hospice,* you expect maybe a few dodgy bits of pottery and a vase. Is there more to it than that?' A huge smile broke out across Transon's face.

'Billy, if you fancy expanding your business, now would be a good time. The cash and shares are worth over half a million, there's a small house which I would advise you to sell to cover the death duties and then there is the apartment.'

The Perry Gene

'An apartment?'

'Flat, apartment, call it what you want. And you have a sitting tenant; so guaranteed income.'

'A sitting tenant, what is that some dodgy low rent one up from a squat somewhere?'

'No Billy, it a two-bed duplex apartment in Butlers Wharf by Tower Bridge, somewhere in the region of one and a half million pounds in value. She bought it when she worked in the City, but when her heath failed, she let it and moved back to the house. So, in summary, even after death duties you are going to be a wealthy man.' Billy was about to let go of the plank and allow the waters to wash over him when he realised Transon had come around the desk with a glass of water. 'Drink this, calm yourself down. Your Aunt and her premature death could be the making of you. I have also taken the liberty of informing Gordon Miles that you will need a session later this week, so clear your diary for a day.' Transon walked over to the door and opened it. 'You ok to get home? Book a day to see me next week to go through the first transfers. If you have no objections, I will offer my services to you as your ongoing representation.' Billy just nodded, got up, slipped his coat on and shook Transon's hand. 'Get a cab Billy, just this once, you are probably in shock. I will get my secretary to contact you when the news has sunk in a little. Until then, I suggest you keep this to yourself as you are likely to become very popular otherwise.'

Billy felt like he floated down the stairs but when his hand hit the slick

The Perry Gene

paint and the overly thick glossiness touched his skin, the spell was broken. Had he just imagined the last twenty minutes? No, in his hand was bundle of documents and in front of him was the doorway to a new life. As he passed reception the queen bee had buzzed off for the night to the hive. He stepped into the street and hailed the first cab he could find, firstly checking he had enough cash for the fare.

The Perry Gene

Chapter 4

Billy woke on Wednesday morning feeling less than perfect.   He had a low grinding headache from one too many beers.   After getting home in the taxi, he had made a meal and then grabbed the first of several tins of beer.   As he ate and drank, he mulled over the meeting with Transon and the existence of Elspeth Perry.   Even now he thought it was some kind of giant hoax and during the course of the evening, one beer slipped down after another.   In the end it was nearly midnight when we woke up in the armchair still cradling a half empty can and realised he needed his bed.   Although being Billy this still meant pouring the beer down the sink, washing out the can and putting it in the recycling bin to leave everything tidy.

The hangover, which was unusual for Billy, did not settle his mood. Transon had said that he had no need to make any decisions immediately, but it left him thinking.   For a while now he had considered getting in some help as the business had grown and had potential for even more.   He had Pete, an old mate from his arcade youth, to pick up the occasional calls if he was too busy. They were not really rivals as such, as their territories did not directly overlap and their skillsets were pretty much matched which helped when looking at each other's machines. This was particularly important if there had been power cuts or surges in an area.   Billy thought if the opportunity to grow was there, and now he might have some money for new kit, he had better start looking for something more permanent staff wise.

The Perry Gene

The other thing on Billy's mind was Doctor Miles. He had known him for ten years now and it was only with his help that Billy had managed to drag himself out of the black place he'd ended up in after his Mother had died. It had taken until now to really get a feel for how much damage he had suffered at her hands. It was tricky one, because he realised, he loved her and hated her all at the same time. She was the person who was there for him when growing up. She had held on to life through sheer force of will at the end. Although he was not sure if this was to make sure he grew up the way she wanted or simply to torment him. When she died, she had left all she had to him. However, her routines, her sayings, her constant bullying and neediness had triggered something in Billy that he had been trying to break out of ever since. She would hound him daily to complete his chores. She watched the clock and lived by it, insisting he did the same too. On the surface, she would say this was her way to make sure he could survive on his own, but he knew there was more to it than that; well he did now. She was a bully, she took out petty acts of vengeance on him. Possibly it was related to the cancer, but more likely she was just cruel. Angry at the hand that life had dealt her and Billy was the only outlet for frustrations once Billy's Father was dead. Through Doctor Miles' sessions he had come to understand the power and control his Mother had exerted. It seemed like a switch had been flicked deep inside his mind which turned mild OCD into something debilitating and suffocating. The thing was, now he was aware that Doctor Miles had more going on in the background and he needed to know the full story.

The Perry Gene

*

It was mid-morning and Billy had already visited two pubs on a busy day when he got a message on his mobile from Doctor Miles' assistant Sally.

'Friday Morning 10am for 1 hour, are you free Billy?'

He had been dealing with Sally for almost as long as he had with Doctor Miles and she knew now that fact and dates were all that Billy wanted; there was never idle chit chat or greetings. Even though he had his diary in his head, he took the book from his bag and confirmed he was free, which also meant blocking out travelling time either side as the doctor was twenty minutes away by car.

'Friday Morning 10am for 1 hour, check.'   Was his clear and functional reply.   Right he thought, time to find out what Doctor Miles knows about my prodigal Aunt.   Going back to his diary, he turned to the back pages which were left intentionally blank for note making. He wrote 'questions' and underlined it.   He then began to jot down notes on what he thought he could find out from the meeting.   He didn't know how much would be revealed, but he didn't want to forget anything.   Not seeing the Doctor that often any more, he now knew that preparation was essential and this was likely to be the most important session he would have with his counsellor in many years.

During Wednesday, he also contacted Transon's secretary, or PA, he was not sure what the difference was, but it was likely to cost a few pounds more an hour to speak to the latter.   He organised a follow-up meeting for a week after their initial consultation. According to Transon, this would allow Billy to get his head around the situation and for Transon to start preparing transfer papers and drawing up plans for what Billy needed to put in place going forward.   In the same way that he was curious about Doctor Miles, he now wanted to find out what Transon knew about his Aunt.   What had caused a split within the family so bad that he had never even heard of her?   How did she have so much money?   Billy was no church mouse, but the money his Mother had was mostly from his Father's death policies and likewise Billy had inherited a little more from his Mother.   However, a flat worth over a million, shares, cash and another house elsewhere, this was not in the same league.   Was she a professional person, a doctor, a lawyer, a manager in some big company? Billy knew he had more questions than answers, and the people who could help him were Transon and Doctor Miles.

*

Friday morning was always a bit of a treat in the Perry household, the austerity toast for the rest of the week was replaced with bacon and eggs.   Billy's dad had liked a glass of ale after work on a Friday and this was part of his Mother's routine to prepare him. They were not a religious family so there was none of that fish on Friday rhetoric going on.   Billy washed his two rashers and two fried eggs down with a large mug of tea and went not to the lock-up but to the offices of Doctor Gordon Miles, which were based just outside Lewisham.

As he drove through the outskirts of the town, he saw how much the place had changed in the ten years he had been coming here.   Initially his visits were always on the bus as it had taken a year of therapy alone just to get Billy back behind the wheel of a car.   He would shake uncontrollably and then sit there waiting to pull into traffic, rigid and unable to decide when to go.   Doctor Miles had told him it was a combination of chemistry in his amygdala and the ghost of his Mother.   Over the years, the description of the aforementioned parent had become more colourful as the doctor realised just how much damage had been done. Now as he looked out over the more gentrified landscape of designer flats and glass office buildings, he thought back over some of those meetings with a new light.   On the passenger seat next to him lay his diary.   It was now brimming with questions and Billy was fired up to start asking them.

'Morning Billy' said Sally as he walked into the small office.   She had the voice reminiscent of a mouse and Billy supposed this was meant to keep the patients calm. It was not at all clinical; the modern décor had been an unchanging constant even when the office moved thirty yards down the road to its present location. It was a comfort to see the constancy in the surroundings when he visited the good doctor.   He now knew this was designed to put clients at their ease.   There was TV running BBC news 24 with the sound turned off but subtitles scrolling. Billy however was not taking it in.

'Morning Sally' he said checking the time on his watch and seeing he was the regulation five minutes early, 'is he...'

'Ready for you?' she interrupted, 'Yes, he figured you would be keen to start today.   You know the way'.   With this Billy walked down the corridor and knocked on the Doctor's door.

'Come in Billy' came the friendly voice of Gordon Miles through the door.   Rather like Mr Transon's receptionist, what you heard was not what you saw.   With the door still firmly shut there was the sound of a very softly spoken man who was potentially studious and maybe wore small tortoiseshell national health glasses.   However, when the door opened Billy saw the familiar frame of his Consultant, who was pretty much the stature of a prop forward. He was over six feet tall and about 16 stone of muscle. He kept fit but also this was a personal defence shield. In the early days of clinical practice, he could double up as a very effective orderly when it came to restraining unruly patients. Not that this had ever been the case with Billy, who was placid to a point of catatonia in their initial meetings.   Billy sat down in the chair that had been left in front of the desk behind which sat the giant.   'How are you Billy, I hear the cat is finally out of the bag.'

'You knew, all along?   Why didn't you say something?'

'Elspeth asked me not to.   The falling out between her and your parents was very dramatic, she didn't want to rake over old wounds while you were still not yourself.   Ideally, she would have introduced herself to you in a year or two's time when I thought you would be ready for the shock, but the cancer rather made that idea a non-starter. It was a highly invasive strain, but she also decided you should not see another family member die from the disease in front of you.   Elspeth was many things, she was a very strong woman and her profession could make her hard-nosed, but she was never cruel. What she did for you these last ten years was done through duty but also love for the last remaining member of her family.'

The Perry Gene

'What happened, why was there a split? I don't get why she was never mentioned.' Billy rubbed his cheek and screwed his face up as if doing so would make the whole situation clearer somehow.

'Not even I know all the details, but it had to do with your Grandfather and Grandmother. There was a car crash. Your Grandfather died instantly, but your Grandmother went to intensive care and was put on a ventilator initially. Elspeth was away on business in the Far East and almost impossible to get hold of, there were no mobiles or even pagers then. When she returned, she found out that your Father and Mother had agreed to turn off of the life support machine. They had both been cremated at the same time four days after the accident. There was no body for Elspeth to see, just ashes to be scattered. It was not normal for bodies to be cremated in the Perry family but your Mother had insisted on it and your Father let her have her own way. An almighty row ensued when Elspeth discovered what had happened and as far as I know they never spoke again. Your grandparent's estate was not big but it was split up by Transon and that was when he first started working for your Aunt. The doctor stopped, sat back in his chair, and crossed one leg over the other. He drank from a bottle of water while Billy stared into the middle distance. Twice Billy went to speak, but the words would not form. He had no memory of this, he didn't know the timing, but had certainly not met his grandparents. He now wondered why they had never been mentioned. Finally, on the third attempt, Billy managed to get his mental train back on the rails.

'Ok, so that was then, and how did you get involved? Mr Transon suggested that Elspeth organised it.'

'It was all open and above board, I assure you. After your Mother died, your condition for that first month was almost a catatonic stupor following your breakdown. You were admitted into hospital and Elspeth saw you a couple of times, but never made herself known to you. She knew you needed help and she did some research. She found me through a medical research paper I had written on higher level cognitive dysfunction and the role of nature versus nurture. In the paper I had put forward some ideas for therapeutic interventions, but they were all untried. She found me and suggested she had the perfect patient. We needed each other. The approaches I took with you formed the basis of my life's work to this point. You my dear boy are patient zero. Some of your peers have made even better progress than you along the way, but mostly because they changed their circumstances. You keep living in that bloody house. Every time you go back there in the evening she chips away at you again. Elspeth knew it and wanted to move you but that would then reveal her hand, so we played a waiting game. A game she unfortunately lost.' He took another swig from his water and left Billy to ponder for a moment.

'And now, what happens?' Billy asked.

'Well that all depends on you. Will you move? You now have the house and the flat as well as your parent's house. The problem is the flat has a tenant on a long term let and the house is too far away for your business, so in the short term, you would be best to move out into somewhere local as quickly as is practical.'

'I like it at home' Billy said slowly and clearly.

'No, you don't Billy.   You go back there under sufferance of that woman.' The doctor raised his voice and then toned it down again.   He knew every issue Billy exhibited had one and only one cause, his Mother.

'You always say that. She wasn't all bad' but something in his voice lacked conviction and Doctor Gordon Miles knew what he had suspected for nearly a year: Billy finally understood and accepted the truth. What was needed now was the catalyst to make him walk away from his old life.   Elspeth had done the work and prepared the ground well.   Now Gordon simply had to provide the final push.   Not today, but this was a Churcillian moment, *'the beginning of the end.'*

'Let's do a couple of exercises and then leave it for today. I think you have enough going on in your head for now.'

'No' said Billy, opening his diary to the last few pages. 'I have questions that need answering.' Gordon smiled, the worm may have started to turn, he thought to himself.

'Ok, fire away.'

*

For Billy, Friday afternoon was busy, as was often the case. A couple of last minute pieces of work as machines with faults needed to be working for Friday and Saturday nights.   He finished at the second of his casinos at 9 and called it a week.   The van was left in the lock-up and Saturday was a day for a run, a decent meal out and a few beers watching the afternoon or early evening football unfold.   He did not really support one team, partly as it caused havoc with his sense of fair play when being a referee, but mostly because he loved the game; often more than the people who participated.   A decent game between two positive teams was a thing of beauty and Billy liked to watch a flowing match.   A referee who knew how to overlook things for the betterment of the game, like giving the advantage, was much more fun to see.   When you got a bunch of divers and skivers it used to make his blood boil as it rankled with the way he liked to see the game played.   It was much the same on a Sunday when he was in charge. The move into Sunday refereeing was an odd bi-product of his counselling with Doctor Miles.   When his Mother was still alive, his one release in the week two hours of five aside football on a Wednesday evening. But after his collapse he never really got back the desire to take part in team sports.   A couple of years later, once he was starting to integrate back into the real world, his counsellor had asked him to play a match with a local hospital team.   When he got there, he was not required, but they were short of referee. He took to it like a duck to water.   It was not more than four weeks later that Gordon found him a coaching course (paid for secretly in the background by Elspeth as his guardian angel) and when he got his qualification, he went straight into the Sunday league scene.   The referees and assistants, were not the most sociable bunch which was no great loss to Billy, but his encyclopaedic knowledge and love of rules and strong sense of fair play, gave him a natural flair for it.

On this particular Sunday morning, it was cold and wet. Billy was unperturbed by this, he was in his element. He quite often ran into players who drank in pubs where he had machines. They were never going to be friends that was for sure, but the longer he ran first the line and then matches, the more the nodding acquaintances grew. This was ideal for him, just a distanced mutual respect, none of that mates buying each other pints down the pub. In and out of each other's houses, going on tour together; none of that appealed.

Today he was in charge and the match got off to a brisk start, but it was not more than five minutes before he had to pull a yellow card from his pocket. Getting the player to turn he took his number and put it in the book. This was going to get dirty if they had started this early. He remembered these two teams of old. There was a great deal of inter-school rivalry, as they were a couple of ex-pupil teams. Men who frankly didn't give a stuff about their old school but had fond memories of those rucks every year at the end of term. One school descending on the other's gates at closing time. All the small kids stuck inside. All the young men fighting and the young girls drooling. So, ten or fifteen years later, here they were. There were no school gates, no jumpers for goal posts but a lot of pent up aggression for a cause they never cared for in the first place. It was only going to get uglier. But it made Billy think back to something Transon has said when they met. 'Don't tell anyone yet'. Billy looked around; at the players, the assistant, and the supporters, then thought to himself, 'who the hell would I tell?'

2. Guanine

The Perry Gene

Chapter 5

'When you said I had a sitting tenant, I naturally assumed that he would be a sitting, paying tenant Mr Transon.' Billy held the phone to his ear, the proper way; none of that holding the mobile in the air as if you were speaking on some reality TV programme, he really hated that.

'Sorry Billy, shall we start this conversation again and this time with the assumption I know as much as you?' Transon was getting used to Billy's little ways by now and to be honest he was very much growing on him. Billy had taken to his new responsibilities and assets in a business-like manner. The more paperwork Transon introduced the better Billy became at it. As they cleared out and transferred the rest of Elspeth's estate, Transon saw Billy start to grow and change. It was like he thrived on it and something had been holding him back. There were some details of Elspeth's life that were still a mystery to both, but slowly and surely the mist was beginning to clear. This exchange was like many others over the three months that had passed. Billy would ring up, already half way through a piece of logic that he would not have previously shared with Transon, and ask a question expecting him to know the answer immediately.

'My lodger, a Mr C. Deville, swanky address in Butler's Wharf, and after my Aunt's untimely demise, *my* address. Well Mr Deville does not seem too keen on paying any rent. I sent the paperwork to transfer the monthly payments from Elspeth's bank account to the new one we set up for rent. Two months later, it is still empty.

The Perry Gene

'Have you tried to call him, I have his number here in the files?' Over the phone, Billy could hear the shuffling of paper and the sound of pages turning.

'I have his number, you gave it to me with the apartment details. I tried phoning and I got nothing. It just continues to ring. I tried the mobile you had as well and that just goes dead, like it's been disconnected. What do I do next? If he won't pay, do I need to evict him or something?' Transon was smiling. This was the new Billy. Very quickly turning to practical matters, even though at this point, he did not know much about them. Everybody who came into Billy's path and heard the story would start to give him advice. Landlords, barmaids and punters alike, all little Barrack Room Lawyers.

'Billy, first let's talk to him, there might be some reason. We don't just go about evicting people in this country, that is a last resort and it's not like you are needing to use the place immediately. Maybe he saw the forms and thought it was a scam of some kind. You have heard of those Nigerian Oil-well cons? You have a part share in an oil well, but you need to send a release fee. He might have thought it was a scam and thrown the paperwork away.'

'So why not answer messages? Why the dead mobile?'

'I don't know Billy, away for work, dropped his mobile in the river, changed contract? There could be any number of reasons why as you well know. Have you tried going around there?'

'I didn't know if I was allowed. Besides which, I don't have keys or anything and there is a gate.'

The Perry Gene

'Which means you have been around, but could not get past security, hence this call. In fact, I would hazard a guess you are there right now, am I right?'

'I may have wandered past this morning on my way to an appointment, it's not a crime, is it?'

'Ok Billy, enough of the smart bugger.   Come and get the keys and go and see if you can raise him by knocking on the door.   But if you intend to go in, please take a third party with you.   I don't want you getting into trouble for trespass. Rent or no rent, he is still a legal tenant.'

'Ok Mr Transon, I will be over later this morning.   Shall I grab the keys from your secretary?'

'Billy, my assistant hates that as you well know.   Secretaries went out with the mullet and glam rock.   Jenny will have the keys for you, so be nice to her.' With this Billy hung up the phone and returned to staring at the locked entry door of the apartment complex.   He had already tried the buzzer.   He had not seen anybody come or go that he could tailgate for the thirty minutes he had sat there.   The takeaway coffee he was nestling was now half drunk and cold.   He dropped it in a nearby bin and walked in the direction of his car. He wouldn't bother with public transport today as at eleven in the morning the trip to Transon's office would be quicker under his own steam.

He parked around the corner from the solicitor's office, having found a cheap little place for short term use, then he walked up to the door and heard the buzzer go on the latch before he pressed a button or even looked at the camera.

The Perry Gene

Jenny was expecting him and therefore Billy was going to get a roasting or a teasing; it was generally one of the other.

Over the months since their initial meeting, Billy had been a regular at Transon's office and although he remained distant to begin, it did not take long for him to strike up a bit of banter with Jenny the PA, Receptionist, and general factotum. She was not at all the stern authoritarian he had first taken her for, but quick witted and playful. She was tall, which he had not noticed at first until she stood up from behind her desk. She was not anorexic, but healthy looking and had fabulous long brown hair. In fact, Billy started to think she was quite attractive however he had made the cardinal error on their third meeting of calling her Transon's 'secretary'. That had gone down like a lead balloon and so from that day, Billy had been more careful and Jenny had been pricklier at times. Slowly they had got to a point where there was a good level of friendly conversation and gossip and Billy looked forward to catching up with her.

'How's your love life Billy?' This was the opening gambit as he walked into the office. The place had a nice feel of familiarity to him now. As it was June, there was bright sunshine streaming through the vertical blinds and the dust motes danced from the air driven by the closing door. The office was hot and Billy was tempted to remove his jacket, but he did not consider he would be there long enough.

'In truth Jenny, I think we share the same sexual fantasy.'

'Really lover boy, and what's that?' She stopped her normally incessant touch typing and looked up at him.

'That we have a partner of course.' He laughed and walked towards her desk.

'You are a cheeky sod, I will have you know I get my share.' She reached into her desk drawer. 'Is this what you came for?' She pulled out a set of keys and an electronic fob.

'Yes thanks, is there any key code? I saw a number pad on the wall outside.'

'No, apparently that is for visitors. The key fob should get you in.' Jenny handed the keys over to him but could not help dragging her thumb along his hand seductively as she did so. 'You never know when you might need a new flat mate' she smiled and winked at him. At that point as distracted as he was by his missing lodger, he couldn't help thinking how nice her green eyes looked when she stared at him.

'Aren't you supposed to be kept away from customers by the Hippocratic Oath or something?' he pulled his hand back in mock horror.

'That's doctors you Muppet. Go on away with you and hound your lodger or whatever he is.' She waved her hand like she was royalty dismissing a servant.

'You'll miss me when I'm gone.'

'I've missed you before, but next time I'll aim better. See you later Billy.' And with this he raised his hand and headed for the door.

It took twenty minutes to get from the office back to Butler's Wharf as traffic was still light. The tourists had not yet arrived in their droves and school had not broken up. He returned to the same meter he had used for the car previously and walked the three hundred yards back to the front door of the complex. Before going further, he stopped and looked around. This was not his neighbourhood and yet he now owned property there. He felt just a little queasy for a moment. In the old days, the dark days, he would have shrunk back from proceeding further. Cold and confused, his condition would have stopped him from entering the building. He would have seen the layers of concrete and chrome, marble and glass and run to the hills. But that was the old Billy and through Elspeth, he was realising he was slowing morphing into something, but as yet not complete – nor was he sure what he would become.

He gave the buzzer one more go and held it for thirty seconds or so. After getting no response he took the key fob and pressed it against the door plate. A pronounced click sounded and Billy pushed the door, which moved freely and smoothly. 'Step one, entry obtained' he thought. Across the lobby was a lift, he pressed the button and after thirty seconds the metal doors slid open. Using the fob again he activated the lift and it took him to the third floor, which was also the top. Emerging from the lift he could see two doors, one to his left and one right. The one to the right was the door number he sought. He took a step forward and knocked on it. Not a sound apart from his own breathing and the distant traffic below. He knocked one more time and was about to try the key when the door of the flat behind him opened.

'Can I help you darling?' came a voice like a kitten purring at a fireside. The *ah* in darling elongated like an art school debutant.

'I am looking for Mr Deville.   Have you seen him?'

'Not for a while, and who might I ask are you?'

'I am Billy, I am his landlord.'

'Really?   Elspeth's Billy? Surely not.'

'You knew my Aunt?'

'Yes, for several years.   We both moved in the complex when they were first built, she only moved out when she got ill.   How is she? We lost touch when she moved away.' Now the darling's voice was far more subdued, unsure, even hesitant.

'She passed away, nearly four months ago. I only found out about her after she died. I didn't even know she existed.'

'Such a sad case darling. I am sorry to hear about her passing, she was a real force of nature.'

'I am beginning to find that out. Anyway, sorry to be rude but when was the last time you saw Mr Deville?   I need to speak to him about the rent as he appears not to be paying.'

'I think you will find he is exempt from paying the rent.'

'What do you mean?'

'Well if you want to speak to him, you are going to need a medium.'

'A medium what?' Billy looked genuinely mystified.

'You know, someone who can speak to the dead.   Mr Deville, Chris I should say, killed himself.   He has been gone three months now.' She was beginning to well up.   There were tears forming in her eyes, they had not started to fall down her cheeks as she dabbed them away, but they had already attacked her mascara, and her eyes now resembled a panda's.

'Did you know him well? He had been here what, six months?'

'Oh yes, I knew him very well, it was a hell of a shock when he died as he just did not seem the type. We regularly would enjoy a bottle of wine together in the evening. He was some sort of local government officer or civil servant. But he also had a side line in writing. Something to do with academic or technical books. It was beyond me really, but he was good company.'

'So, is his stuff still in the flat?'

'I'm afraid so, I had no idea who his next of kin was and after the police had finished their enquiries, I assumed someone would turn up. But nobody ever did. '

'So, nobody has been in here in three months? That might explain the mail and phone calls being ignored.' The last part more to himself than to her. He turned his back on her and opened first the mortice lock and then the Yale. As he turned the Yale he pushed and the door ground slowly open. It was obviously held up by the amount of mail just inside on the floor.

'We only brought the proper mail up from the pigeon hole and posted it through, not junk.' The voice over his shoulder chimed in. Billy stopped for a minute wedging the door open with his foot and turned back to her.

'Did he kill himself in the flat?' Billy felt queasy at the thought. A stranger's body might have lain here undisturbed for some time. He would have to fumigate the place just to get over it.   He heard loads of stories about pensioners who had died at home from the guys he chatted to in the pubs.   The stories went that they were not found for months, and that the bodies were only discovered when the smell alerted the neighbours. He guessed they were mostly apocryphal, but there had to be truth in it somewhere.

'No darling, silly bugger he was…' she stopped and caught her breath, 'he threw himself off the railway line down below London Bridge somewhere. We heard about it on the news that night but it took a day or so before we found out it was him.   Had no ID on him.   Such an odd way to go for such a lovely man.' Her eyes were now watery again and she was staring off into the distance. Billy stood there and knew, without a doubt, what day his tenant died; the same day he got the letter about Elspeth. What were the chances, his lodger dying, across the road from the pub, the reason for the Police sirens that morning? Suddenly it became too much to process and Billy knew he had to get into the apartment and be on his own.

Turning his back on her, Billy mumbled a goodbye and pushed on into the flat. He stopped, closed his eyes and waited thirty seconds to try and regain his composure. He was surprised after such a short time that he was already feeling ok.   His recovery times from these episodes were getting shorter.   He looked around and tried to get his bearings. The terms of tenancy he had seen showed it was let with fixtures and fittings, but he had no idea without going through the paperwork with a fine-tooth comb what belonged to Elspeth and what formed the estate of the seemingly late Chris Deville.   He would have to speak to Transon about it. Maybe he knew someone, he appeared to be like the legal version of an East End fixer. He knew a man for just about every little job that needed doing and frankly his charges were not exorbitant. Walking through the strange room he saw a set of stairs going up to a second floor where he guessed the bedrooms and bathrooms were. On this lower level was a kitchen diner, a cloakroom and a lounge with the most amazing picture window overlooking the Tower of London and Tower Bridge. In front of the window was a long couch which must have given a spectacular view to relax to. There were several book shelves, a large desk and a flat screen TV with a games console (which Billy guessed did not belong to his Aunt). The place looked lived in, as if someone had popped out expecting to come back later, but never returning.

'Bloody hell Elspeth, you knew how to live,' he spoke aloud and whistled through his teeth. Everything carried with it a thin sheen of dust. This would be next on the list of things to do, get a cleaner in once Deville's possessions were removed. He would call Transon when he got back to the house later. He had no urge to sit down right now as it felt like the place had dead man's skin in its dust.

Continuing his tour, he noted two double bedrooms upstairs, both with ensuite bathrooms at the back. This place really was a bit of a palace. The common thing about all the rooms was that they had one or two blown up photographs in beautiful but elegant frames. Mostly in black and white, and not of your usual twee subjects like landscapes or a man holding a baby against his naked chest. No, these were stark, telling stories. War torn landscapes, screaming children, sweat shop bodies and all manner of other harsh realities of life. 'How could you live in a place with such horror on the walls?' he thought. But they were captivating in some way, each one a masterpiece. Billy thought he would ask Transon about them when the inventory was reviewed. Right now, he decided with the combination of dead Aunt and dead tenant, what he needed more than anything else was a drink. He took a few minutes to sort through the mail which was piled behind the door which included his letter requesting the rent changes and a couple if final demands for the Electricity and Water Rates. He piled up anything that looked like it needed further investigation and binned the rest.

As he left the apartment, he locked the door and was about to call the lift when the neighbour reappeared. The blotched mascara was gone and a fresh coat of war paint had been applied. She was not an unattractive woman, late forties, or early fifties he would have thought, and well preserved. The sort of lady who loved to lunch as well as spending time with a personal trainer at the gym. She was around five feet nine inches tall and had startling green eyes with dark brown hair, (which Billy suspected had more help from a bottle than Mother Nature). She was dressed in tight white denim jeans and a top that had a clever way of fighting gravity while exposing what could best be described as an ample bosom.

'How was it in there darling, ghastly? I did have a key but could not face going in after he was gone.'

The Perry Gene

'You had a key?' Billy was a little taken aback by this.

'Just for emergencies you understand' she blurted out a little too quickly. 'In case he was away and something happened. Not that I ever used it.' Her face had gone a little red at this point and she looked away.

'I didn't catch your name by the way. Miss...'

'Carruthers, Mrs Carruthers. But Julia to you Billy, we are all friends here. Will you be getting a new lodger or taking up where you Aunt left off? She was quite the social butterfly when she was in town.'

'Mrs Carruthers'

'Julia'

'Julia, what did my Aunt do? How did she pay for all this?'

'You don't know? Did nobody fill you in? She was photo journalist who ended up becoming famous in the world of investigative journalism. She was quite the superstar in her field. Did you see the pictures on the wall?'

'Were they hers?'

'Yes. she broke several major stories including being one of the first people to highlight far Eastern Sweat shops and child labour. God only know how she stayed in one piece. She covered three wars and endless visits to the African bush for both Ivory and military dictatorships. She made her money afterwards from the pictures. She had gallery openings and everything. When the luvvies turned up here it was as camp as a row of pink tents inside. But she didn't really like the celebrity bit and so she took a step back and went into semi-retirement. It should have been then she settled down and had fun, but that's when she got ill. It was so unfair; just so desperately unfair.'

'It looks like I have a bit of reading up to do on my family.'

'She had an agent, your lawyer man should know, I guess you are using him, Tran-something. I met him once when he came around to sign some papers.'

'Transon? Yes, he now represents me. He is rather useful. It looks like I have a few things to talk to him about. He has never mentioned any of this.'

'I think when she got ill she just wanted to put it behind her. She was always sad about you. Never said much directly, but you know when something is niggling a person. She would never be drawn on the details; she would just change the subject.' Billy pressed the lift button.

'Are you off already? I thought you might like a little drinkie after this, I know I could do with one.'

'No, I am driving and I now need to get Transon working on a few things. I will see you again soon I've no doubt.' The lift door opened and he stepped inside. Turning to face her he pressed the button for ground.

'I look forward to it' and she turned her back wiggling her bottom towards the door of her apartment.

Emerging from the lift and opening the outer door, Billy punched in the short cut to Transon's office in his phone. After three rings Jenny answered.

The Perry Gene

'Hello Billy, I have your number in the system now. Did you find him?'

'Hello Jenny, yes and no.   Is Mr Transon available? I need to chat about a couple of things.'   Billy stopped and looked up at the front of the flat and worked out which one was his.   He felt like whistling all over again.

'Sorry Billy he's with a client, I can get him to call you.   What do you mean yes and no?' in the background the tapping of the keyboard continued as she talked.

'I know roughly speaking where he is, but he won't be paying the rent anymore.'

'Stop being cryptic, has he done a runner on you?'

'No, he's dead. Topped himself according to the neighbour.' The typing stopped at that point.

'Oh, my God. Seriously? You're not winding me up?   What am I saying? This is Billy, of course you're not. Shit.' There was silence for a moment as she was thinking.

'You still there?'

'Yes, sorry, it's not what I was expecting exactly.   Are you ok? After your Aunt and everything another death is not what you need.'

'When I thought that he had passed away in the flat I freaked a bit, but then once I heard how he died I just found it one of the weirdest coincidences.'

'What is?'

The Perry Gene

'The day your letter arrived, there were police cars and sirens when I left the lock-up that morning. It appears a strong possibility that my ex-tenant was the jumper who landed opposite a pub I service the machines for. I was there that lunchtime.'

'You're right, that is bloody weird if it's true. You fancy a drink later and you can tell me more? His nibs will be free at 4 if you want to see him in person and we could grab a glass of wine afterwards.'

'That sounds like a plan. See you then'. Billy hung up the phone. He would need his new assistant to take one of the afternoon jobs as he now needed to get the car home in order to travel up to town for 4pm. Pete had joined him full time six weeks before as Billy had been able to put more machines in place after his recent cash injection. It couldn't have been better timing for Pete in the end, as he was struggling with some awkward customers and a rival firm moving into this area. Billy would call Pete and juggle his schedule. Suddenly changes like this were becoming easier for Billy and his mind stepped up from neutral into first gear. He pressed the speed dial for Pete and explained the situation. Once he had closed the phone and slipped it back into his pocket, he took one final look at the front of the block. As he turned to go, he saw Julia in her window at the front. She was watching him. Next to her was a thick set guy in his mid to late fifties, dressed in a suit. He was also watching Billy, intently.

The Perry Gene

Chapter 6

Billy walked into Transon's office dead on the dot of four. He had waited in reception and passed a rather more sedate exchange with Jenny than usual, although she made it clear she wanted all the gory details later. Many things had changed in Billy's life over the past three months and this was reflected in a radical shift in character and growth in confidence. However, his punctuality never altered. His eye for detail and his propensity for planning were still qualities that made Billy who he was.

'Sit down Billy, I guess you have had a bit of a shock today?' Transon pointed towards the chair as Billy entered the room. 'Coffee, Tea, Water?' He got up and walked around the desk to a long shelf with a built-in fridge underneath. Opening it he got a can of diet Coke out for himself, which was his late afternoon treat. Billy shook his head, he couldn't stand the diet stuff, only full fat.

'Bottle of water would be good please' he responded to the original question having turned down the sugarless offering. 'I have a few questions.' Billy was staring at Transon as he walked around the room to his desk. He had the early onset stoop of a man too long behind a desk. Billy guessed late fifties, maybe even early sixties. His hair, which was impressively intact, was no longer the dark brown of youth, but now sported greying at the temples. His skin was good, but he had the pallor of a man who never saw enough sun. His weight suggested that he may not have stuck to the diet Coke over the years or he was at least using it to compensate for an otherwise higher than required calorie intake.

Transon had known Elspeth for nearly thirty years and yet had not shared any of the details of her work at the time of their first or subsequent meetings. Billy needed to know why, but that could wait, first there was the late Mr Deville to address. Billy allowed Transon to drop back into his chair and pull it into his desk. His standard pose when listening to Billy over the months was to temple his fingers and listen with his eyes closed. He adopted this pose and nodded his head to suggest Billy should begin.

'We can talk about how much you knew Elspeth later, but first, let's start with Mr Deville. I should say the late Mr Deville. How comes you didn't know he was dead? I thought you were taking care of my affairs' Billy fidgeted in his chair. He didn't want to be rude to Transon who had treated him very fairly up to this point, but he did feel he had been somewhat blindsided by the whole affair as of six hours ago.

'Billy, first off, I am a solicitor and not a bloody clairvoyant. How was I supposed to know? Elspeth had a private tenancy agreement with him. Yes, I brokered the deal and set up the contract, but other than that, Mr Deville and I had never met or corresponded. He was a prompt payer and Elspeth never had any issues to complain about. Besides in the last few months, I think she had other things on her mind.' Transon went silent. Billy looked at him and realised he was genuinely upset.

The Perry Gene

'Was there something going on with you and my Aunt? Or do you get this upset about all your clients?' As ever the old Billy was never that far from the surface and this sort of 'bull in a china shop' approach should have come with a copyright warning.

'No, nothing like that.' Transon looked hurt now. 'Although we did have the occasional drink and I was invited to a few social gatherings, I was not your Aunt's type. I did try to initiate something more once, but she made it clear she saw me as a friend and nothing else. I was hurt then but you couldn't know Elspeth and stay angry with her for long. She was just a ball of energy. You get lot of your traits from her, well the good ones. She was organised, punctual, clever, and industrious. I see more of that in you now I know you better, other things may come in time.'

'Like what?' Billy was now interested in this little window that was being opened into both his family and his own personality.

'Fierce loyalty. When you were part of Elspeth's circle of people she cared about, then you got a great deal of love and respect in equal measures. I'll give you an example. There was a cameraman who she worked with out in the bush on her first ivory story. Ten years afterwards, he was killed by poachers. Elspeth set up a trust fund to make sure his daughter could finish school and that his wife had enough money to bring her up. The little girl, Gaia, is now at university in Cape town, mostly thanks to Elspeth.' Transon stopped, swigged from the diet Coke can (a habit that Billy hated, use a glass his Mother would have said). He was silent for a moment as if thinking of something.

The Perry Gene

'And you see this in me?' Billy seemed confused.

'Not yet perhaps, but you are changing, becoming much more of the Billy you are going to be in the future.   That though, is Gordon's territory not mine.'   Putting the can down, he lifted his finger as if to count off. 'That's another thing about her; she had a very well-developed sense of right and wrong.   She championed the underdog and hated the oppressor.   Most of her journalistic work portrayed that.   Let's see if any of that comes out in you as well.   You saw the pictures at the apartment I take it?'

'Yes, I was a bit perturbed to start with but I must say, after a very short time, you can really appreciate the power.   Julia, the neighbour, said that Elspeth had displayed at galleries before?'

'Displayed no, she had her own exhibitions on several occasions.   She used them to raise awareness for her causes.   The money was good, but half of it went back to the folks she met in the East and in Africa. Elspeth knew the true value of money, this is something I hope you arrive at in your end time. You are still living to your old means.'

'Just give me a bit of time. Having this money, it's strange, almost decadent; it's not really me. Also, I'm a bit confused as to what belonged to her and what was Mr Deville's left in the apartment.   Are you able to do a couple of things for me?   Firstly, can you get his stuff removed based on the inventory and then secondly arrange to have the place cleaned.   I was freaked out when I walked in there.'

The Perry Gene

'Yes, Jenny mentioned you thought he had died there.   In fact, his suicide appears to be a bit of a puzzler.   In between your call earlier and now, I did a bit of digging; friends in low places and all that.   There seemed to be a lot of confusion as to how it all happened.'

'I was there, later that morning, across the road at the pub.   I didn't get it.'

'Jenny didn't mention that bit, but then she can be a bit secretive where your conversations are concerned. How do you mean you were there?   And what don't you get?' Transon went back into listening pose, it was as though nothing went in unless he was truly prepared for it.

'I was servicing the machines at one of my regular pubs that lunchtime, but I had heard the sirens that morning when I left the lock-up. Now what I mean is that two things don't look right.   Maybe I am watching too many detective programmes on TV or reading too many crime novels, but firstly how did he get up there? It's a railway line, it must be close to forty feet up and access is limited.   He must have come down the track some way. Why jump there?'

'That's interesting, nobody mentioned that in the police report, but you said two things.'

'The height. Forty feet is not high enough to die from unless you are unlucky.   It's broken leg territory.   Now, if I was going to top myself, I would make sure.   I would want at least a hundred feet.   Plenty of places in London to do that from.'

The Perry Gene

'I am not sure I shouldn't be more concerned about how much thought you have given this Billy.' Transon was half smirking when he said this and Billy was a little annoyed by it.

'Ok, Mr Know It All.   If he was so intent on killing himself, why not simply jump out of the apartment window?   It is higher than the railway line.' Transon stopped smirking and looked at Billy.

'Say that again.'

'The apartment, Elspeth's apartment, *my* apartment.   Straight drop from the balcony onto the concrete below is more than forty feet.   Why go for a jog across town when you can literally jump out of your own window?' Billy sat back in the chair crossed his legs, templed his fingers and aped Transon's listening pose. 'So, Sherlock, what do you think?' Transon sat back in his chair, noticed what Billy was doing and changed his pose.   He gave Billy a stare, encouraging him to stop having fun at his expense.   He wrote a note on his desk pad and circled it

'I think I might like to introduce you to a couple of friends of mine who would be very interested in your observations.   They are, or I should say were, in the law enforcement sphere of operations. That's how I found out about the report.   Not exactly Old Bill, but Ex. They have connections and funny that you should mention Sherlock, they have been known to do a bit of Consulting.' As he said the word, he made inverted comma in the air around it. 'I will reach out to them and let you know if and when they might like a word.'

The Perry Gene

'Ok, in the meantime while you are busy doing a very passable Diana Ross impression.' Transon looked for confused for a second, 'Reaching out? Anyway, can you also put me in touch with Elspeth's agent? Julia said there was someone who looked after the art side of her life.'

'Oh yes, Xavier, you are going to love Xavier. I will write down his email address and number. He was to expect a call at some point.' Transon started to jot down a name on a card. He then looked up while opening a rolodex to complete the details as Billy started to speak.

'On that subject, I am getting a little bored with the drip feeding.'

'Sorry?'

'You and Doctor Miles. Carrying on Elspeth's legacy, slowly revealing more and more about her. You first told me you knew very little, so did he. Now I find you knew her very well. Even wanted to be more than friends. I'm capable of hearing the whole story now, so please starting treating me like an adult.'

'Easy Billy. Gordon was the one in charge of bringing you up to speed and making sure this did not overwhelm you. He didn't want you put back in the hospital with another breakdown.' Billy winced, those words that he tried not to react to, but they made him feel like a freak, a failure, a loser. But even now he knew he was stronger than ever and more capable of coping than any time in his life. He could feel the mental shackles dropping off and he wanted to remove the last few ties that bound him to the world his Mother had created.

The Perry Gene

'In hindsight, you might have done a better job if you had not let me find out my tenant had killed himself without any warning.' Billy got up and paced the room. He grabbed his left wrist with his right hand. It was a control move he'd learned from Doctor Miles, but when he realised he was doing it, he let go immediately as if his hand were on fire or even a foreign object not under his own control. He stopped, looked back at Transon who appeared horrified, as if the Genie was about to pop out of the bottle. But quite the opposite, Billy was now putting it back of his own accord. 'Look I'm sorry Mr Transon, that wasn't nice and you didn't deserve it. I know you have done right by me all this time and I should treat you accordingly. It's just frustration talking.'

'Apology accepted Billy and to be honest Gordon is a touch frustrated too. I phoned him earlier and he almost lost it when he thought you might be hurting. You were his first patient for this therapy programme. Patient zero with zero patience he used to call you. He has built up real affection for you over the years, like a big brother, and he only wants the best for you. He will make some time to see you in the next few days if you want to talk about what happens next.'

'Ok, I will give him a call.' Billy sat back down in the chair.

'So,' Transon paused as if not wanting to broach the subject, 'what happens now?'

'Sorry, I don't follow.'

'Well, we talked about you moving. Now you could sell your old house and move into the apartment. Start enjoying Elspeth's legacy.'

The Perry Gene

'I'm not sure yet.   It's a big move leaving home. And, I am not sure about being where a dead man lived.'

'As opposed to at home where your two dead parents lived and the ghost of your Mother still comes around for tea and cakes.' Billy looked up, caught Transon's eye and then the two of them broke into a smile.   The smile became a laugh, Billy knew it was true.   Elspeth and Deville had offered him the perfect escape from his own personal nightmare, the shadow of his Mother on every wall and floor.

'I will talk it through with Doctor Miles but I am making no decisions now.   Maybe I will feel different when his stuff is gone and the place is clean.'

'Well, give me a call if you need me to start sorting out buyers and such for the house.'   With that he handed the card for Xavier to Billy as they both stood and shook hands. As he walked to the door Transon spoke over his shoulder. 'And don't get her too drunk this evening, she has work tomorrow.' Billy waved a hand goodbye without turning around.

Billy descended the stairs, not even bothering now about the paint which had disturbed him so much on that first visit. He walked up to Jenny's desk and stood still for a moment while she was rummaging in her drawer for something.

'Are you trying to look down my top Billy Perry?' she trilled without even looking up. Billy shuffled from one foot to the other before responding.

'Did you want me to?' he then took two steps back from the desk as she rose quickly with a ruler to slap him.

The Perry Gene

'Cheeky bugger.' She was glowing with a smile though, this was pretty standard now. Jenny was as much part of Billy's development as Transon or Doctor Miles. She had started to be more flirtatious with him and as she stood there, she twirled a lock of her hair through her fingers and even began to blush a little. Billy knew hundreds of people through work, but very few got near him. Partly this was the way he liked it, but also, he used to be very intense. He was hard to be with for a long period. The first night Jenny had dragged him out for a drink with the girls, he had lasted half an hour before crying off. But over the months, these nights had become more frequent and less crowded. Jenny's friends still saw the old Billy, but she saw what he was turning into. Some of the traits his Mother instilled into him made him something of an anachronism; but he was delightful with it. He would hold doors open and curb his language around Jenny. He would be gallant and courteous. He also didn't try it on with her after one drink which was refreshing in the City bars she frequented. In many ways, she wished he would try something, a girl could feel unwanted. The strange thing Jenny found was that not only was Billy changing but she was changing too. Maybe it was just because being treated well was unusual, maybe she was learning to expect more. She had gone on a few dates over the previous couple of months but they had not lasted beyond the first hour before she had walked away. She may not want Billy per se, but she knew now she wanted someone more Billy-like, whatever that was. Honesty appeared to be contagious around him and she liked the person she saw in the mirror better for it.

The Perry Gene

'You need time to put on your war paint or are you fit to go?' Billy saw the look on her face, somewhere between Dervish and hurt puppy. 'Oh, come on, you know I am joking, you look as lovely as ever. Where do you fancy, one of your usual haunts?' He saw her soften at this and he knew he had her back on side.

'I thought we might try somewhere quieter so we can talk; it's been a big day for you. What about the Hand and Shears over the back of Smithfield's?'

'I don't know it, but I am happy to be led like a horse to water.'

'Or a lamb to the slaughter?' she smirked.

'His nibs says I have to get you back early as it's a school night, otherwise you turn into a pumpkin.' She turned to face him confused, grabbed his arm and dragged him towards the door.

'You didn't do a lot of Disney films as a child, did you? The coach turns back to a pumpkin, Cinderella loses a shoe.'

'Mother wasn't keen on Disney, thought he looked like a nonce. Besides from what I remember Mr Transon saying, the last time you were out drinking past midnight you lost both your shoes.' She punched him playfully on the arm.

'I didn't lose them, I just left them in a nightclub.' With this literal parting blow they walked out of the door and into the street. 'Besides, you could always make sure I am home by midnight by taking me back there yourself.'

The Perry Gene

The walk to the bar took about twenty minutes and most of the journey was spent with Jenny recounting stories about some of the less savoury clients who came to see Transon. She was probably the least private personal assistant ever, but Billy figured much of this was for his benefit and not something she shared with everyone. When they entered the bar, he got her a G and T and a pint for himself. It was early enough for them to get a table at the back of the snug.

'How's Pete working out now he is full time?' she asked in between sipping her drink through a garish green straw. 'You knew him before from what I remember?'

'I've known him on and off for about fifteen years; from the old days of the arcade. We lost touch for a while, while I was, ill.' Billy paused, he knew Jenny knew bits and pieces, but he was not sure how much. He was not even sure yet how much of the truth he knew himself. Another thing to bring up with the good doctor when they got to meet next. 'Yes, he's good, but I'm not sure he is going to be enough if I keep using your boss's expansion plans. We are already getting stretched again. Not a bad place to be though.'

'And what about you, William Perry, what's next for you?'

'Billy Perry' His face went blank without expression, like he was chanting a mantra. She thought at any moment he was going to read out his address and phone number, like a well-practised boy scout.

'I know but your name is William, it's just an expression. You know.'

'Old habits' he said and his face softened. He was still not back in the room mentally.

'Where do you go to?' she reached down and took his hand and looked into his eyes.

'Don't start singing Peter Sarstedt, they have no license here.' With this she cuffed him gently round the head with her free hand.

'Now, shall we try that again? When you go away at times like that where do you go?'   She looked at him and waited silently for him to answer.

'I am back in the kitchen, five, seven, nine, the age is irrelevant; I'm small and looking into her face. I am repeating my name and she is glaring at me.   I don't know what I have done wrong, but I know there will be a belt or a slap. How can she still do this now?'

'You know my boss and your doctor want you to move?   How about your Aunt's lovely apartment, now it's available?'

'He asked that earlier, so did Julia.'

'Who is Julia?' her attention suddenly focused on him with a glare.

'It's ok, she's just the cougar who lives in the apartment across the hall from Elspeth's. I still struggle calling it mine.' He stopped for a second and looked up into her face. 'Everybody seems to have plans for me or to tell me what to do and I am done with that now.' There were tiny globules of water forming in Billy's eyes and Jenny looked away worried about what she had caused. 'Sorry' he said 'that wasn't directed at you. I just need a bit of time for things to settle down and then I can decide.   I will chat to Doctor Miles in the next few days, take on board what he has to say and then make my mind up.'

He turned away briefly and wiped his eyes. She unlatched her hand.

'You want another?'

'Yes' he said, 'but let's go somewhere a little livelier. This place is like a morgue.' She looked at him surprised, as he normally preferred quieter places. 'I've been around too much death lately and now I want a bit of life. There's a band on at one of my pubs, if you fancy? Maybe a bit of food before?   I will even stick you in a cab later so your boss is happy tomorrow.'

'Are you alright Billy?' She looked at him with concern.

'I wasn't, but I have the feeling I will be - and soon.'   With that comment they grabbed their jackets and bags and headed for the door.

The Perry Gene

Chapter 7

Billy looked around Doctor Miles' office. On the wall were shelves full of books. There were more than on his last visit; not that he deliberately counted, but the inside of the treatment room, even after the move, had not changed much over the ten years of their relationship. It had just grown progressively more crowded. The folders of papers were augmented now by published volumes by the good doctor. His theories at first and then case studies (suitably anonymised) but he knew none of the material was about him. He was the first and one of the hardest to crack according to their later conversations. Before Elspeth's appearance in his life, he knew Doctor Miles was getting frustrated that elements of Billy's character seemed unable to be broken down whatever he tried. But the progress since had been very much improved and Doctor Miles wondered how much longer his services would be required. He knew that a move from the house to the apartment was the ultimate bridge that had to be crossed. The last lay lines of his Mother's influence could finally be earthed. But could he convince Billy it was right thing to do?

'Billy, how have you been since our last chat?' Dr Miles paced, he was never still when the real work began. In his mind, he brought energy into play when moving.

'You know I wish sometimes when we do this you would sit down. It is the most distracting thing when I am trying to bare my inner most demons to you.' Billy followed him around the room with his eyes until the last word and the pacing stopped. Dr Miles looked at him in the face.

The Perry Gene

'Really? You find this distracting? You never said.' The good doctor looked hurt as if his favourite toy had been taken away and replaced with a brush and shovel. 'But I have been doing this the entire time we have worked together. Don't you find it calms you?'

'No Doctor Miles, I find it distracting, re: my previous comment. Can you sit down? We need to talk.' The doctor looked confused and moved back to his desk where he took a chair. This was new, Billy was taking the lead, showing control of their interaction. 'That's better, now can you stay there and listen to me for a moment?' He nodded in agreement but said nothing. 'I guess you have spoken to Transon and you know the story of my tenant?' He nodded again almost afraid to speak as it might break the spell. 'Ok, you can speak now.' Billy crossed his legs and waved his arms like a conductor gesturing for the orchestra to start playing.

'Well, yes, I have spoken to him and I do know about.... Mr Deville, that's correct, isn't it?' Billy nodded this time.

'So, you know my circumstances have changed. I have some decisions to make.' Billy stopped and the doctor had started smiling. 'You're loving this, aren't you? You think finally you are going to get your own way and I will move out. Your therapeutic master plan will come into play and I will be cured of all the ills of the Mother.'

'Well you have to admit it's a change from the sins of the Father.' The Doctor stopped smiling and let his face go more neutral. 'Yes, I will be honest I see this as an opportunity not an issue.'

The Perry Gene

'Not to Chris Deville it wasn't.'

'Chris? Not Mr Deville?'

'Julia introduced him as Chris, this is no medical breakthrough; three months has not made me *normal* whatever you decide that is.' The doctor opened his hands in a show of deference. Billy nodded his head and continued. 'Ok so thanks to Chris's' he emphasised the word '*demise*, I now have lost a cash-cow but gained a new residential option. Having been there, I accept that it is a nice place. I'm not sure I will fit in with the locals based on what it's worth, but I think I can give it a trial; once his stuff is gone and it is cleaned.' Doctor Miles tried desperately to hold a smile inside. He knew now that his work here would be complete just as soon as Billy got away from his old family house. He was different already, but there was still real change going to happen.

'Mr Transon also said you wanted no more drip feeding, is that correct?'

'Look at you two, *as thick as thieves*! Lucky I'm not paranoid, or have you got a pill for that?'

'Bit harsh, Billy, you know I do not condone pills as nobody really gets better, they just stay the same.'

'Yeah alright, but I think now I need to know the whole story. No more leaving bits out. It's like trying to play Tetris with Elspeth's life. I need to know it all.'

'Ok, when she was ill towards the end, I worked with her on a dossier. A 'who am I', if you will. She, however, was a story teller herself, remember that.   She told tales with her pictures. She tugged on heart strings to raise awareness.   This is who she wants you to think she was.   I am not saying it is lies, just that she helped to build it; don't expect it to be warts and all. She was no saint.' Doctor Miles handed over a folder he had taken from the drawer.

'But she was no sinner either.   She appears to have cared for me when nobody else was there.'

'Don't get me wrong Billy, without her, you would have ended up institutionalised by all accounts.   Yes, she was your guardian angel, but I am simply saying there are two sides to the coin.' With this the doctor let go of the folder he had handed to Billy and withdrew his hand.   'And now?'

'Now, I am going to take some time away from the two of you and get my head around this whole thing. The flat, the house, the money, it's a lot to take in and it was not how I was raised. Once the apartment is clean in a few days, I am going to take my stuff from the house. Transon will then get a team in to prep it for sale.   I am sure they will hear my Mother's soul screaming abuse at them, but I least I won't have to.   I think they will be safe though. She was always a lousy shot when she threw things.   I can't see that her ghost will be any better.' Billy got up to go, reached for the door handle, but stopped and turned.

'I don't think we are done yet Doctor Miles, but I think to misquote your favourite Churchill saying, we have reached the *beginning of the end.*'

'Come back and see me in a month' Doctor Miles said, but by this time he was speaking to Billy's back and the closing door.   After a couple of minutes, he buzzed his PA. 'Can you please book Billy in for a follow up in a month?'

'Too late' said a young and classless voice. 'He has already booked a session on his way out. It's in six weeks' time.'

'Thank you.' He released the button of the intercom, sat back in his chair, and smiled.

*

It took Transon slightly longer than he had originally suggested to get the flat cleared of Deville's belongings and to then have it cleaned.   He knew that cleanliness was one of those things that had set Billy off in the past, (another issue from his Mother) and so he wanted to make the transition as painless as possible.   Billy, trying desperately to cling to the routine of his old life and maintain his new and expanded client base, left it until the following Saturday to remove the few possessions that he was taking from the house to the apartment. There were decisions to make and all this change still weighed heavily on his mind.   He knew choices he made now would impact his life going forward so he did not want to make them in haste. Even what would appear to be trivial choices later, needed to be made now, such as what furniture would be kept. Transon's clean-up crew has left the bed frames, cupboards, and sofas in the apartment.   However, Transon had intervened when it came to the mattresses and replaced them so that Billy would not be freaked-out.

One of the bonuses of the apartment had come with the discovery of his own parking space in the subterranean garage which was freed up when

The Perry Gene

Deville's car had been removed by Transon's men. Pulling in he figured out the easiest way into the building, slowly seeking the routine that would make this transition more possible. There was a lift all the way to the top floor from the garage, but he decided to take the stairs. His fitness was important and with the gap in the football season for the summer recess he needed to do a bit more to keep in shape. Luckily, he discovered a small gym which he noticed as he exited the garage and entered the stairwell. This would be a great fall back to running outside when the weather was bad. Still he wondered about all those people in January who joined a gym and never used it; the thought drew a smile as he passed.

Emerging from the top floor, he saw the now familiar front door to the flat. He undid the first lock while balancing a backpack on his shoulder and pulling a wheeled suitcase. As he turned the key on the Yale lock he heard the door behind him open.

'Oh, you came back darling.' He could hear Julia's soft shoes or slippers sliding across the polished floor. 'And it looks like you are moving in. Bravo dear boy, it's been too quiet around here, about time we brought some life back to the penthouse.' At this she went silent as if she had realised the callousness of her comment. Billy pushed the door open and wedged it with his case. He turned to face her and was surprised to realise she looked sad and slightly lost. But as she saw him looking at her, her face changed as if she had literally painted on a smile. 'Will you be moving in on your own or are you bringing a little friend?'

The Perry Gene

'Sorry, I'm not sure I...' Billy stopped. Was she flirting with him? He had her down as a cougar from their first meeting but he hadn't thought her attention was previously directed at him; now he felt the high-powered spotlight of her focus; she drew closer. He could now hear her breathing, there was slight rasp to it.

'I mean is there a Mrs Perry or some darling waif that you are sheltering from the harsh realities of London life? These apartments are rather large to be rattling around on one's own. Chris certainly liked company.' And there it was, the unmistakable reference to his previous tenant, and maybe more. Was he reading between the lines; adding two and two and making five? Only time would tell, for now he just wanted to get away from her and get into the space he had to learn to cope with.

'No, it's just me. I've got a few things to move in and then I have to sort out the house. I'll be gone for a while. Maybe I will catch up with you later. I think you said you have been here since it was built? Is it just you or is there a Mr Julia?' Billy pushed the case into the room and dropped the backpack on top of it while he waited for her to respond. This had allowed him to make a little more of a gap between them. His personal space was still not something that he liked to be invaded.

'Oh, you are a naughty one, asking after my marital status. Yes, unfortunately there is my sourpuss of a husband Tony. You should come around and meet him next time we have drinks. He is a little gruff but deep down he has a heart of tin.'

The Perry Gene

'You mean gold?' Billy took his keys out of the lock and placed them in his pocket. He turned to her looking for a response.

'I know what I mean darling.' With this she air kissed him and walked back towards her door. 'You know where I am if you need a spoonful of sugar etc.' With this she closed the door behind her.

Billy entered the flat, awkwardly pushing the large suitcase over the deep pile carpet in the entrance way. He dropped the backpack on the desk and flopped onto the freshly cleaned sofa. Transon's crew has done a good job and he could see how things were both tidier and more sparsely arranged than his last visit. The desk, bookshelves and the sofa he now sat on were the only surviving furniture on this level. The sofa had been arranged to look across the open plan area into the kitchen dining room when seated, presumably for guests to chat to the chef. On his first visit, Billy had spun it round to point towards the floor to ceiling picture window, which looked out at the Thames and the two towers of the bridge. It was the perfect position to sit and think from. He had a number of issues to resolve, not least of which was where he was going to sleep. He needed help getting Elspeth's place to be more like his own home. Knowing he had nothing else to do for the rest of the day, other than settling in and moving more of his life in, he thought about who might be able to help. He opened his mobile and looked at the pathetically short list of contacts. Ninety percent were work related or numbers of pubs and clubs. He also had Pete, his one-man workforce (who was already asking for more help), Transon, Doctor Miles and Jenny. He had no idea what Jenny did on Saturdays; he thought that she possibly slept in and dealt with the excesses of Friday night, but he dialled her number anyway. No answer and it went to voicemail.

'Hi' Billy said awkwardly, not quite prepared for leaving a message. After a short pause, he continued 'Hi, it's Billy, Billy Perry. Sorry to bother you, not sure what you are up to today, but wondered if you fancied looking at the apartment. Ok, well, try and catch you later.   Sorry to have bothered you.' Billy finished the call and sat looking at the phone.   'Very Cool' he thought sarcastically to himself. 'She must think I am a complete loser now.' He sat for another minute looking out at the river and then realised he had to empty his car of boxes and then do another trip to the house to move the things he wanted. He would put them all in the lounge until he figured out where he wanted to sleep.   Two bedrooms, the choice presented him with problem.   A new flat meant new rules. He would be fine once he got his head around it, but right now all he could see was questions.   At the bottom of the pile of questions was Elspeth and of course the mysterious Chris Deville. He needed a list, things were always better with a list.   It had the soothing and calming effect of bringing order to his mind. He decided that he would get the house cleared of what he was taking and then sit down and start to make sense of the mess he had made in the room with his newly deposited belongings.

He was in the car on the way back to the apartment with the second load of boxes, (there was more coming than he originally envisaged) when his mobile rang.   He saw the number was Jenny's but he knew the rule on phones while driving so he let it go to voicemail.   When he pulled back into his parking space, he tried to call his voicemail but there was no signal downstairs. He took two boxes, locked the car, and entered the lift. Fitness was one thing but with all this fetching and carrying there was a limit.

He moved swiftly to the door and having left the Mortice unlocked deliberately, he slipped through his front door before Julia had a chance to emerge and engage in conversation. Billy was not antisocial, but he was already feeling Julia was someone who needed to be controlled and kept at arms-length. He remembered that he must get the spare key back from her as well. There was no way that would have been allowed in the tenancy agreement, he was thinking.

Once the door was shut and the walls of his new castle were back in place, he put the boxes down and tried the voicemail again.

'Hi Billy, Billy Perry' giggles in the background 'I'm sorry mate, but you need to work on your phone manner. I'm just having a bit of fun with you. Any who. Sorry to have missed you. You have never called at a weekend before, in fact I was thinking you must hibernate as it is normally radio silence outside the working week. I was in the hairdressers in case you were wondering, not making wild passionate love to the milkman.' More giggles over the line 'Fat chance of that. You can't even find a milkman these days. Sorry, digressing. If you still want company, then bell me back. I am, if not free, fairly cheap, and completely available this weekend. The world is my lobster.' Billy ended the call and stared at the phone. The faintest blush of colour rose in his cheeks. After a few moments, he called her back.

The Perry Gene

'Hi Jenny, nice to get hold of you and not the machine this time, those things kind of freak me out. So, based on your voicemail, I am guessing you are available. I wondered if you would like to come over and help me sort out the apartment?'

'Billy, let me get this straight. You rang me for help.   Are you calling me under false pretences?   I only work office hours.'

'No, nothing like that, I just need a bit of help planning...'

'Billy, I'm joking. I'm flattered you called.   I would love to come around and check out your new bachelor pad. What time do you want me?'

'Well, I've moved all the stuff I'm going to now, so I will be here for the rest of the day.   Just come when you are ready.   You know the address, right?'

'I think I can find it, based on what I do.   See you in a while, do you need anything?'

'Not that I can think of, we can grab some food out later if you are hungry.   I don't think I want to inflict my cooking on your, at this point.   It is a bit basic.'

'Ok then, bye Billy.' The line went dead and Billy put the phone back in his pocket.   He thought the best use of his time was to unload the kitchen items and food that he had brought with him.   It took him quite a while as he positioned and repositioned the tea, coffee, sugar and mugs.   He was vacillating.   He would firstly move them to look as much like the house layout as possible and then he would swap them to be completely different.   He went through this pattern three times taking over half an hour and was finally interrupted by a buzzer. He realised it was the door from downstairs. Jenny must have literally left straight away and headed over. He had seen the intercom by the front door of the flat so he walked over and pressed the speak button and the release.

'Push and come up to the top floor Jenny'

'Ok Billy, see you in a minute.'

Billy stood by the door with it closed but with his eye to the spy hole. He didn't want to enter a discussion with Julia or have her quiz Jenny. As Jenny came out of the lift, he opened the door and beckoned her over. He put his finger to his lips and although she gave him a stare, she came over and walked inside. As he was closing the door, he thought he saw movement across the hall. Now he knew that Julia was keeping watch and he would have to simply be wary in future if he didn't want to get caught.

'What's all that about? Am I a dirty little secret or something?' Jenny had a touch of irritation in her voice.

'You remember the cougar I mentioned?'

'Julie?'

'Julia, Darling. Well anyway I think she is watching my door or something. Every time I have come to the flat so far, she has appeared as I reach my door, or I exit the lift. She can't just sit there watching, can she?' Billy now had an image of Julia on a stool at the spyhole of her door watching for Billy to return.

'Webcam, that's what I would do…if I was a mad crazy stalker that is. You sure it is just not the new place getting to you?'

'I'm not imagining it. Anyway, thanks for coming. As you can see, I have unpacked the kitchen.' From within her bag, Jenny pulled out a bottle of white wine. She stopped for a second and took in her surroundings.

'Bloody hell, Billy, Billy Perry, did you land on your feet. What did you Aunt do, bank jobs? This place is gorgeous.' Jenny wandered over to the windows and took a look out both East and West to examine the view. 'A-maz-ing.' She strolled back over to the kitchen holding out a bottle. 'Well be a love and pop that in the fridge for later. It's a house warming present.' Billy gave her a peck on the cheek in thanks, took the bottle and opened the fridge door. Jenny looked over his shoulder and smiled at the contents. 'Have you been shopping yet? There is nothing in there but milk and beer.'

'I told you my cooking skills are a little basic. Mostly soup and beans.'

'Yes, I remember you saying, well this should come in handy too. I was going to give it to you next time you came in the office, but since you called.' Out of her bag, whose capacity Billy was now starting to marvel at, she pulled a thick cookbook.

'Everybody eats Italian and Jamie is so easy it should get you started.'

'That is really nice of you, thanks.'

'Billy' he was about to answer but she stopped him 'we are friends, would you agree?'

The Perry Gene

'Yes' Billy fidgeted on the spot unsure of where this was going.

'Can you call me Jen then? Jenny is fine for work, my actual name is Jennifer but not even mum uses it, but my friends call me Jen.'

'I don't know.' Billy looked frustrated and perplexed. 'It's the condition, Doctor Miles now makes fun of it to make me aware, but people get trapped in my head with the first name I am introduced to them by. I know Doctor Miles' name and Mr Transon's, but I feel blocked when I try to use them. But I will try and work on it. I feel different already being here now. Going back to the old house this morning felt like I was slipping down a steep slope into a dark valley. I swear every time I go back that Mother is there watching and criticising.'

'Don't go all Bates Motel on me Billy. As long as we are friends then use what you are comfortable with, but if you were to call me Jen it would really make me see you as friend much more than one of my boss's clients.'

'Ok, as I say I will try.'

'So, I can see a pile of boxes, bedding, and clothes in the middle of the room, what do you need me for? Is it my muscles?'

'No, I don't need you to do any physical work, I need help with something else.'

'This isn't a cheap way to get me into your bedroom, is it?' Jenny smiled and felt warm flush rise up her face, forgetting that it was something that she had actually thought about before coming.

'In a way, yes.' Now Billy was smiling.

The Perry Gene

'In a way? What do you mean?' The flush was now fully up her face. She could feel herself getting hot and her heart beginning to beat faster.

'I can't decide which bedroom to have as mine and you know the issues I have with too much analysis. Well I thought if you came over then you could pick my room for me and save me days of brain strain.'

'Are you serious, you want me to pick a room? Not to ravish me?'

'Yes, to pick, I am not sure I know you well enough for ravishing yet, can we take a rain check on that?' He turned to face her as he said this and gave her a massive smile.

'Rain check, you are a cheeky bugger Billy, Billy Perry.' The flush began to subside as she walked over and gave him a huge hug. 'As I said earlier, I am flattered you called and as a mate I am happy to help you in any way I can. I know what a big deal this is for you. Although they don't say it too, I think my boss and your doctor are impressed with how you are coping. In fact, coping is the wrong word. You're thriving from what I can see. Now do you want me to go up on an own and then come down and tell you?' Billy nodded his head. With this she detached herself and walked through the door. Billy sat back down on the sofa to wait.

About five minutes later, he heard her feet descending the stairs. As she rounded the corner he stood.

'Well, what do you think? Did you pick?'

'Easy tiger. First off, aren't you a lucky boy, this place is amazing. Now in terms of bedrooms, the one on the left has far more cupboard space, a better view and is not sharing an external wall with a neighbour, in case they, or you, are noisy at night.' Billy scowled a little at that.

'Thank you, that has helped me so much.'

'You would have got there in the end. So, you need help putting this stuff away?'

'No, I will do it later, now I know where it's going.'

'The pictures on the wall and all the books on the shelves; they're hers aren't they; your Aunt's I mean.' Jenny went over to the main bookshelves in the lounge. She ran her finger down the spine of several as she read them under her breath.

'Yes, there were part of the fittings she left when she let it.'

'Quite a mixture, but some nice pieces here. All well bound and in good condition. They must be worth a bit, you are lucky the lodger didn't damage them or flog them. The inventory I saw just mentioned bookshelves and books (various) so you would never know. I think with the cancer being so advanced your Aunt moved out quickly.'

'I guess. On my set of tasks for the day is the creation of a list of things I need to find out about and she is number one. Closely followed by Chris Deville.'

'You have a task on your task list to create a list. Come on Billy, live a little. Enjoy your new space for a moment.' She didn't turn but continue to scan the contents of the bookshelf.

The Perry Gene

'This is important to me Jenny. It is like a door has been opened onto a whole new world. A world that's full of chaos. My only way to deal with chaos is to order it and for that I need to find out more.' Billy stopped for a moment, not even sure he had thought of it in those terms before.

Jenny had stopped scanning the shelf and was examining one book without a title on the spine. She pulled it out and opened it. From where he stood, Billy couldn't make out exactly what it was, but he could see it was hand written.

'Well my friend, this may help. It's a diary.'

'My Aunt's diary, oh that will be useful.'

'Not your Aunt's Billy, Chris Deville's.' Jenny handed him the book and went to the window to look out over the Thames.

Chapter 8

It took Billy less than a week to decide on what to do next. He loved his new living space and once he got his few possessions integrated with the remains of Elspeth's belongings, he knew he was never going back to the house. He didn't know if it was a trick of all that glass overlooking the river or something deeper. He felt lighter in the flat, like a great weight had been lifted. The whole world seemed brighter and the thought of going back to the house to pick up his few remaining possessions left him feeling physically cold. Maybe the doctor had been right all along.

He spoke to Jenny every couple of days either by phone or through text. He had always found text a comfortable medium. You got to prepare what you were going to say beforehand and then press when happy, but he was starting to like speaking to her too. He didn't really think anything romantic was going on, but he had precious few people in his life and now he felt he had someone special and genuine he could rely on. She had asked a couple of times about the diary, but it sat on the shelf, exactly where Jenny had taken it from and where Billy had put it straight back. He needed time to spend on it and there were other priorities.

On Friday morning Billy rang Transon to ask him about selling the house. Jenny as ever picked up the phone as his trusty Assistant.

'Hi Billy, how's it hanging lover boy. You christened your new pad yet? It must be a real magnet.' Her enthusiasm was unbounded, which Billy loved. She was always positive; sarcastic, but encouragingly effervescent.

'Morning Jenny' there was a short pause 's.sorry, morning Jen.' Billy spoke slowly as if under great effort. He had used Jen on text a couple of times but had not managed to call her it before out loud.

'Wow Billy, you managed it. Jen. You must be settling in. His nibs is free if you want a word, shall I put you through? Do you want me to tell him what it's about?'

'Yes please, I want to talk to him about selling the house.'

'Hallelujah. You know that apartment is amazing and it's just what you need for a new start. You need a lodger?' She was as ever giggling in the background. She loved to rib him and the more they saw each other the more she relaxed with him. 'Don't answer, I'm just having fun. Connecting you, hold the line please' she said aping a telephone switchboard operator from the 1950's with cut glass diction.   After a few seconds, while Jenny obviously explained the situation to Transon, he came on the line.

'Billy, good morning.   I hope you're well.   Jenny said you wanted to speak about the house.   Have you come to a decision?'

'Yes, I like the new place and frankly I think my mind rather likes being away from the house.   It is a hell of a place. Not quite what I am used to, but amazing how quickly you can get settled.' The sentence trailed off as if Billy had another train of thought.

'Without ghosts?' Transon proffered.

'Yes' Billy said with a large exhale 'without her.   My Father never haunted me. I still miss him, but I was young and so the memories are not as clear as they should be.'

'Sounds like Gordon territory to me. Maybe getting to know Elspeth will help you to find out more about your dad.   They were brother and sister after all.' The line went quiet for a little while. 'You still there, Billy?'

'Yes, sorry, just thinking. So, the house, as you say let's stick to your territory. Two things, what do I need to do to kick off a sale, I've never done this before.   Second, I need to clear it of her possessions.   I have taken everything I want from it now.'

'If you are happy for me to continue to represent you on this, then I will get the house put on the market as soon as possible.   Just leave it to me. However, I would suggest the following.   That house does not look like it's had much in the way of decoration in twenty years. When I get a clearance specialist to empty it, I could get a decorator in and give it a once over in every room. Make it neutral colours, it will help with the sale.'

'Mr Transon, you know more about my affairs than anyone. If I can't trust you to do this then I am a little bit buggered. So far, your advice has been spot on. Please go ahead and put it in motion.'

'Ok, consider it done. On another subject, how is Pete working out in the business?'

'We have never been busier. The cash we used to buy the new machines means he is fully occupied and he is now talking about us needing to take on someone else. Maybe an apprentice?'

'Great idea. You want me to explore the options for a grant?'

'You serious?'

'Yes, Apprenticeships are important these days. You might as well get all you are entitled to by employing and training someone. The grant goes to the company anyway.'

'Ok, if you could look into it for me, I will see if Pete had anyone in mind. He might know another machine rat like we were.'

'Anything else you need Billy?'

'Were your friends going to be in touch about Chris Deville?'

'They have been out of town, but you should hear something this weekend or early next week.'

The Perry Gene

'Ok, thanks for all this Mr Transon. Not sure what I would do with you.'

'Just be nice to my Assistant and we will call it quits. Well that and pay your bill on time. Bye Billy.' Transon chuckled as he closed the call.
Billy had a full day with calls and catching up on jobs that Pete had completed. They went over the schedule for the week ahead and Pete reiterated his appeal for more help.

'Pete, I had a word with Mr. Transon and we have a compromise for you. How do you fancy an apprentice?' Billy was sitting at the desk in the lock-up and playing with the schedule of work with his back to Pete.

'Not sure that's going to cut it Billy. It would take ages to train someone up and they won't be able to work independently for a while. I guess you think the wages will be lower though?' He sounded in a huff and the last comment was spat out with a bit more venom than he really intended. 'Sorry Billy, I know that's not your way, you see me right, but I wonder if they will cut the mustard.' Billy stopped what he was doing and gave Pete his full attention.

'If I could clone you I would, which is why I mention an apprentice. Look, both of us are machine rats. We spent a lot of time in the arcades as kids, doing the Saturday job, once we are old enough to pull a wage. We knew the machines. We need someone like that. Why don't you reach out to your contacts and see who is coming of age as it were?' Billy stopped and let the information sink in.

The Perry Gene

'You know what boss, that's not a bad idea. You been getting all this advice from that solicitor guy?' Pete seemed somewhat more engaged now and was starting to get visibly excited.

'No, you cheeky sod it was my idea. I have OCD not some form of low IQ.' Billy was smiling at this. Pete had seen him before and after the breakdown, but never at his worst; at his lowest ebb. The almost catatonic Billy, laying in a hospital bed, lacking any animation.

'Ok, I will get onto it over the weekend. Have a scoot around some of the arcades and slot shops.'

'Feel free to tout for business while you're there.' Billy turned and got back on with the scheduler.

'Doesn't that put us back to square one then, too busy?'

'Then we hire someone else. It's how business works my son.'

'Oh, my God, Billy Perry is now Arthur Daley.'

'Get on with your work, Serf.'

'Yesum boss.' Billy turned up the background music on the computer. Pete had been anti classical in the first week, but since he heard him humming a melody from the Water Music the other day, he figured he might have a convert on his hands.

*

It was Friday evening and nearly 10pm by the time Billy had eaten and cleared up. He was going to have just one beer with some music on and watch the river. This had now become a regular event in the evening. The ebb and flow of the tides and traffic were as soothing to him as his beloved classic playlists.

He put his feet up on the sofa and was going to turn off the lamp as he often did,

when the diary in the bookshelf caught his eye.

'Ok, I think I am ready for you now' he said out loud. He got up and

took the book out of its place between the leather-bound hardbacks and

instinctively sniffed it. He didn't know why. It just seemed to be the thing to

do, as if it held clues. Dust, or strong aftershave; a woman's perfume. Those

were the things his beloved detective books would have highlighted, but no, he

just smelt paper, cheap paper. He even ran his tongue gently across the leaves

(trying not to get a paper cut), but it tasted vile and he wished he hadn't. He

popped the ring on his beer to remove the taste and walked back to the sofa.

Sitting down, he angled the reading lamp at the book and opened the first page.

After about fifteen minutes, he realised this was not a work of Booker

Prize fiction or Pulitzer prose. It was mundane and petty. It started a little while

before Chris had moved into the apartment. There were a few bits of interest

to Billy on Chris' impressions of Elspeth. Forceful and ferocious were just two

of the adjectives starting in F. It was not a tirade, but you could tell he was not

a fan. Billy guessed at that point Chris had no idea she was ill and in pain.

This could have been a factor in her behaviour, which Billy had learned from

Transon and Doctor Miles was harsh at times, but eminently fair and generally

affable. As he got into the last two months of the book, the entries became a lot

more cryptic. There were the usual laundry lists of events and people, but

there were continual references to people by letters. J being the most prevalent. Apparently, he had spent a lot of time with J and not just chatting and drinking tea. It was dawning on Billy that his initial suspicions about why Julia would have a key to the apartment might well have been right. They were having if not an affair then regular contact which was probably sex. The more he read, the more he realised this was the case.

Evening with J. T out with his dubious buddies leaving the lovely lady alone. In theory, she came around for a drink and to look for a recipe. What happened in the kitchen was more Heston than Roux. Definitely chemistry not cooking! It was lucky he was out, that girl has a pair of lungs on her.

When it came to a month before Chris's death, the tone changed again and now Billy realised this was a three can night, at least. Firstly, it said that 'J' was being needy and wanting more of him. He also mentioned hearing the odd argument between the couple next door through the walls. Although it never stated a connection directly, the diary left little to the imagination on the subject of J's identity. Finally, a few entries later, Deville finished the affair and Julia was obviously very upset as she went off in tears.

God knows what happened last night, but I heard the lovebirds pecking at each other again. It ended in an almighty row and she was bawling her eyes out and not for the first time. Since we stopped I have come back and found her in the flat three times waiting for me. She won't give the key back. She seems to think we can pick things up again, but I now realise she is almost as psychotic as he is. I've seen him peering through the window a few times. I don't think he knows, at least I hope not. That man is dangerous.

The entries that mentioned 'J' coming to the flat stopped after that point, although Chris seemed to think she was still coming into the flat when he wasn't there, although again there was no mention of proof.

Came home tonight and I could smell her perfume. She wasn't there but she had been for a while. There was a wine glass in the dishwasher and when I went upstairs the drawers had been riffled. God knows what she is after. I should get the locks changed but I don't want Elspeth finding out. Let's see if it calms down on its own first.

The diary recorded that when Chris saw Tony in the stairwell or the car park below, the mood was frostier than usual. Chris had stated earlier that he didn't like Tony and that he thought him a bit of a thug. But now there was something else. He wondered if Tony had worked it out and that was the cause of the arguments. Maybe it was Tony that had been in the flat searching?

The Perry Gene

The entries become a little sparse and back to mundane things until a week passed and Chris saw J in the lift.

Things got awkward today. I saw J in the lift and she started on about getting back together. When I said no, the silly bitch threatened to tell Tony. I got out of there as quickly as possible. I climbed into my car in the garage and as I tried to drive away she suddenly appeared. She lay across the car and started to lift her top to tempt me. I revved the engine and as she got off I slowly pulled away. She began ranting and raving, thumping the roof as I went by. I saw her in the rear-view crying and screaming. Let's hope she can take a hint. I don't want to have to move.

The entries for the next few days were just Chris getting back on with his life and catching up with friends he had not seen much while he had been distracted by J. But the following Saturday a more sinister tone appeared.

Saw J today in the entry hall. She was collecting the post in what looked like a dressing gown and wearing sunglasses. The big old American movie actor type. She acknowledged me, but would not face me. Her voice didn't sound quite right, it was quiet and muffled. I took her by the shoulders and turned her round so I could look into her face to try and at least get a civil conversation going after her ranting of a

week ago.   That was when I saw it, the bruises beneath the glasses.
She had one hell of a shiner in her right eye and her jaw looked
swollen. I asked her about it, but she said she had walked into a
cupboard. When I pressed her, she told me to leave her alone, saying I
had already done enough damage. I left it at that, collected my post
and said no more. Later that evening I heard another row, something
that had become almost customary when Tony came in from wherever
Tony went.

Billy read on with fascination.   The next few days did not mention J
again but rather trivialities of Chris' life. Some new girl that he was chatting to
and was going to bring back to the flat as soon he got the opportunity. 'God only
knows who he was writing this for' thought Billy. What struck Billy more than
anything was the general good mood throughout the diary.   How could he
equate this with a man who killed himself shortly afterwards?   It just didn't
make sense.

The final entry was dated the evening before Chris died and it
mentioned a run in with Tony in the car park. Chris had written a fair amount on
this and it had obviously shaken him. It seems he had come home from work
and parked only to find when he got out that Tony appeared from the stairwell
door and came towards him.

He warned me off going near his wife. Warned is a polite word for it.
He was like a thing possessed.   I had to push him away as he was

trying to intimidate me with his physical presence. I denied it all of course, but apparently, she had told him about the affair when I had broken up with her, out of spite, after a few drinks. He had gone crazy and it was then he gave her the black eye I think. So, he made it clear, stay away or I would regret it. To be honest I am already regretting it. The crazy cougar was fun for a while, but who needs this sort of hassle. There are plenty more fish in the typing pool. Time to stay away from this lunatic pair for a while. I told him maybe he should stay away from me and that if there was any more trouble like this I would report him and the black eye that he had given his wife. I thought that had worked as he went quiet for a moment. He then walked up to me nose to nose and asked me who the fuck I thought he was... word for word. At this point I walked away and left him to it. Crazy old man.

Billy saw that the next day Chris had an appointment for drinks in the evening with friends, but there were no more entries. He didn't know if this was significant, but he knew the police would not have seen this. He thought maybe Mr. Transon's friends might be interested. They had left a message during the week. It turns out they were a pair of ex-policemen who now did a little bit of private investigative work whilst researching a series of books on gangland crime in London. They were keen to meet up with him. He decided to contact them in the morning and call Jen to tell her about the diary contents. However, he looked at the clock and realised it was now one in the morning and he was suddenly incredibly tired. He put the diary back in its slot on the bookshelf, *everything in its place* as his Mother would say, and went up to bed. On his phone, there were two texts from Jen from 3 and 2 hours before.

Text: 'You busy tomorrow?   Fancy a catch up?'

Text: 'You ignoring me?   Or you got a hot date?'

Billy knew it was late, but it would bug him if he didn't reply.   These things were part of his psyche and he didn't like to leave conversations unfinished.

Text: 'Sorry I didn't see your text, was reading. Yes, tomorrow would be great.   I have something to show you.'

Billy went into the bathroom and cleaned his teeth, two minutes with the electric brush waiting for it to tell him the time was up with the different buzz pattern. When he returned to the bedroom the message indicator was flashing on his phone again.

Text: 'See you tomorrow lover boy - Muah'

What was she still doing up he thought, but then smiled at the fact she had replied.

*

Saturday morning came a little too quickly for Billy as the late-night reading of the diary had left him unable to sleep.   He used to have terrible insomnia when he first left the hospital.   This was linked with his inability to switch off and his mania for analysis.   But over the years he had found ways to calm himself down.   Little routines, the occasional beer, but not too many.   Addictive personalities like his had to watch for things like that; his doctor had warned him. But this was different. Suddenly all his thoughts of Chris Deville and his untimely death were back to the fore. This was not just his imagination or the plot of one of his crime novels. Chris Deville seems to have befallen a grave injustice and Billy needed to understand why.

He made himself a coffee aware that Jen would not be over for a while. He had a text from her to say that she would be there after her Saturday hair appointment. Maybe she was more a creature of habit than she realised. That amused Billy, in that people were adding contours to his life, while all the time he was flattening their curves in return.

He took his coffee and went to the sofa to watch the world go by. He was deeply concentrating on a Russian pleasure cruiser exiting the port of London under the currently open Tower Bridge, when the phone rang.

'Billy Perry, how can I help?' A far cry from his first timid responses on the phone

'Mr Perry, I am Roger North, I believe our mutual acquaintance George Transon mentioned I might call. My partner Jerry and I would like to have a little chat with you.'

'Yes, Mr Transon said you would call, but he was all a bit mysterious about what it was you actually did. He said something about journalism and the Police.'

'Well Mr Perry, Billy isn't it, may I call you Billy?'

'I would prefer it, I have never really been a Mr Perry.'

'Quite so. Well Jerry and I wondered if we could take you for a late lunch tomorrow. I know there is no football, but I guess you will not be up that early?'

'Ok, where?'

'Shall we say the Boot and Flogger down on Bankside? 2.30? It will be quieter after the lunch rush and we can get a little room to chat.'

'Yup, that works for me. I know where that is. And you will explain what this is all about then?'

'Yes Billy. See you then.' The phone went dead. Billy proceeded to perform the latest trick that he had learned and programmed the number into his mobile phone.

*

Billy was woken from his slumber by the buzzer going on the outside door of the apartment. He was still tired from the night before and he had drifted off on the sofa. Looking at the clock two hours had gone past. When the buzzer went again he came to fully and saw he had missed a call on this mobile. He got up and went to the door release and pressed the button. Speaking into the intercom he mumbled an apology and to come up. Opening the door, he looked out blearily towards the lift. However, the calling of the lift has obviously alerted Julia and he had now lost the element of surprise when leaving the flat. She was looking across the hall at him.

'Hello stranger, haven't seen much of you. I was starting to think you were avoiding little old me.'

'Not at all Julia, just busy with work and catching up with some reading.'

'Oh really, anything interesting?' As she spoke the lift went ping and the doors opened. Jen walked out, she had dressed up a little more sexily than her Saturday clothes the week before. Julia gave her daggers. 'Oh, lovely Billy, you have a little friend.'

'You must be Julia.' Jen said as she glared for a second before making a big deal of giving Billy a hug and kisses on each cheek.

'You were saying about reading Billy?'

'Yes, some interesting material that Chris left in the flat.' Julia looked at him with a slightly perplexed expression.

'Terrible hand writing Billy said to me on the phone. I've come to check it out myself.' Jenny looked at her with a smile as after a few seconds the penny dropped.

'Oh Julia, any chance I can grab that spare key back at some time? It is a pain having to let Jen in when she comes around, I thought it would be easier to let her have one herself.' Jenny turned and looked at Billy with a face full of surprise, but Billy winked and she got it.

'Oh of course darling, it was only for emergencies anyway. I will pop it round later when you are less busy. Toodle pip.' With this Julia turned and closed the door of her apartment behind her.

'Billy, you are a bit of a fast worker all of a sudden' Jenny said as they got in the flat and Billy closed the door.

The Perry Gene

'Sorry Jen, I'm not getting that far advanced. I needed her to give me the key back and I also wanted her to think we are an item so she stays away. I think she is a very unhealthy person to know.' Jenny looked slightly disappointed at this and Billy saw it in her face. 'Jen, you are welcome to the key as you are one of my few friends. I'm just not about to make a move on you, that's all.'

'Not sure if I should be flattered or offended. However, I am more intrigued about what you meant about her being unhealthy?' Billy gave her the diary.

'Go sit down and have a read from the start. I will get you a cup of coffee and practice my culinary skills. If you get bored, we can go out, but I think once you get started, I have time to cook you a meal.' Billy walked into the kitchen and opened his new book at the first recipe. He got out the scales, then hit the button on his new coffee machine. After it had whirred away for a minute or so he took the steaming mug over to Jenny. She was by this time already engrossed in the diary.

The Perry Gene

Chapter 9

The next morning found Billy with something of a thick head. Jenny had finally left at about 11.30 in a cab. Things were progressing very nicely with her, but he was not yet ready for anything else new to be happening in his life; change was still something he could only handle so much of at once. He guessed it was a little bit to her disappointment from her reaction. He would have even suggested she stay in the spare room, but he was yet to acquire any bedding, (something she had promised to help with in the near future).

Billy knew he was meeting the journalists for lunch, but what he needed now was to clear his head and obtain a little bit of normality back to the day. The other thing that helped with both his fitness and his concentration was running. He donned an old tee-shirt, Nike running shorts, (the ones with the pocket for his door key) and pulled on his trainers. It was warm enough that he didn't need another layer on his legs or his top. He opened the door and was making for the stairs when Julia appeared.

'Oh, I do like a man in shorts Billy, you off for a run?'

'Yeah, need to clear my head from the second bottle of wine last night.'

'Your little friend not running with you or have you left her back in bed; you naughty boy.'

'She didn't stay Julia, she left late last night.'

'You really are a naughty boy aren't you, having your fun, then sending her home. I shall have to watch you.'

'Julia I'm not like that.'

The Perry Gene

'It's ok Billy, I am just having fun' Julia interrupted. 'I have yours keys here. I didn't want to disturb you last night when you had company.' She walked over to him and handed him the set of keys. He opened his door and threw them inside to collect later. In the meantime, she had pressed the lift button and when the doors opened she beckoned him inside. 'You coming with me Billy?'

'I was going to use the stairs.'

'It's quite safe. I won't bite. Unless you ask really nicely.' She smiled and suddenly all Billy could think of were those nature programmes about predators and their prey. He got into the lift deciding he would have to face it out.

'So, where you off to now?'

'Popping out to get the papers.' She reached across him and pressed the button for street level. As her hand came away from the button she ran it down his arm and squeezed his bicep. 'You obviously work out. Do you go to the gym or just run?' As the door to the lift closed Billy thought he saw movement at the door to Julia's flat. He was focusing on the now closed doors; as the lift started to descend, so did her hand. She ran it over his buttock and squeezed. 'I do love good hard glutes'. Billy pulled her hand away and held it firm.

'I don't think your husband would like you doing this Julia. We don't need any more accidents do we.' She tried to pull her hand away as Billy said this, but he held firm. He looked at her and saw the message had hit home as she had gone white in the face. She then looked away from him as the lift reached the ground floor.

'I am not sure what you mean Billy. I am just being my usual friendly self. Anyway, you should meet him, my husband, he a bit gruff but he's not so bad really.'

'I will bear that in mind. Anyway, enjoy your Sunday.' Billy went to leave the lift but she grabbed his hand back and pulled him to her.

'No parting kiss?' She reached forward and kissed each cheek lightly as if they were ladies who lunch. 'Have a fabulous run darling. Keep working on those buns for me.' Billy grimaced and got out of the lift. He would normally have stretched before he started to jog but decided under the circumstances that a swift exit was the best policy.

*

Billy had been busy with the flat move recently and had not made enough time for exercise. During the off-season for football, he needed to keep his fitness up and longer runs were a great way to do this. He ran three miles up the river until he was past Westminster and almost at Battersea. The landmarks of London were solid and reassuring. He turned and took the inland route when he reached the MI6 building so beloved of Londoners. It had such a high profile due to the Bond movies that now the irony of our spy headquarters being a tourist attraction was not lost on many.

For once Billy was not running a pre-planned route, but rather going with the flow. He had been getting better at being spontaneous of late and the recently acquired additional business had drawn him to new parts of London that he now explored. According to Doctor Miles going 'off piste' like this was good for his psyche but this morning he was also unsettled by the interaction with Julia and needed some time to get his head straight before venturing back home. He found his way through to Elephant and Castle with all the disastrous roadworks; he never drove this way these days, too much hassle. In his mind, although he was running without a plan, his route home would now take him via the Flag & Staff. When he arrived outside the pub, he stopped and crossed the road to where Chris Deville had fallen, nearly four months before. He stretched his calves, his hamstrings and went up and down on his toes while he looked up at the railway line above.

'What made you go up there?' he said aloud.

'Billy, what you up to?' he heard shouted at him from across the road. The voice was pure South London. He turned to see Shirley, fag in the corner of her mouth returning from the paper shop, laden down with two carrier bags. Billy jogged across the road. 'I almost didn't recognise you with your clothes off' she smirked at him. 'You wanna coffee? On the 'ouse.'

'Better not Shirley, I need to get back and take a shower. I will catch up with you on Wednesday if that's Ok with you?'

'Yeah that's good for me Billy. What were you up to over there?'

'Just curious about the jumper. It turns out he was my tenant and I didn't even know it.'

'No way, shit Billy, that is spooky.'

'Yes well, got to shoot, see you later.' With this he started to run along the road that ran down the railway line. He crossed under one of the bridges and made his way back to the apartment.

Luckily when he emerged from the top of the stairs outside his door there was no sign of Julia. He figured it was the lift call bell she was hearing and using to track his movements. He decided he would take the stairs as much as possible now. It was time to treat himself to a long hot bath and a think. He put some Grieg on the MP3 player and waited until the bathroom filled with steam. Jen was right he thought, this was the better bedroom as his ensuite had a bath and a shower.

*

Billy left the apartment with plenty of time to walk to the Boot and Flogger where he was meeting Roger North and his associate Jerry. As of yet, he did not know quite what to expect, but Transon seemed to be a good judge of character generally and Roger had sounded reasonable on the phone. Billy knew the Boot by reputation rather than professionally as the place had history in the brewing trade and did not like anything electronic to ruin the ambience, so there were no slot machines. When he walked in, he looked around to see if the two guys were obvious. Around the room, he saw a few lunches that were winding down over dessert wines and coffee. The bar man whom Billy had dealt with previously when touting for business looked up and gestured to him.

'Billy, the guys are in the snug around the corner, they are expecting you.' Billy thanked him with a nod of his head and wandered around the back.

The Perry Gene

The first thing he saw was what his detective books would have called a couple of guys who looked like *very heavy wallpaper*. He didn't know which one which was, but they could have been cut from the same cloth. Short cropped, grey thinning hair, polo shirts, chinos and what looked suspiciously like steel toe-cap boots. Billy guessed they were steel toe-capped as he had once tried to protect his feet from damage when lifting machines around. Personally, he couldn't get on with them and had abandoned the idea of wearing them, but he certainly recognised the design.

'I'm Roger' said the first one getting up and offering his hand 'and this is Jerry. Can I get you a pint?'

'Whatever's good, I'm not that familiar with the draft beer in this place' said Billy trying not to give too much away until he got the lay of the land. He moved towards Jerry to shake his hand but Jerry just looked at him. 'So, you're the silent partner then?' Jerry pointed to the chair opposite and grunted. It wasn't clear what he said, but it was crystal what he meant. Billy sat down and waited for Roger to arrive back with a pint of bitter a few minutes later.

'I see you two are getting along famously' said Roger laughing at the silence. 'I should explain a bit before we start. I think George Transon told you what we do, well as I mentioned on the phone, we are also both ex-serving police officers with the Met. We were partners until we both retired a few years back. We both got good pensions, but we decided we wanted to top up our earnings a bit so we do freelance writing and we are putting a series of books together on the local gangland scene from the seventies up to the modern day.   A kind of *what happened after the Krays* if you like. We also do a little bit of private investigation work when we are asked to help out by *acquaintances*.' Billy almost saw the quotation marks hang in the air around the word acquaintances but decided not to push the point.

'I've got to ask, with Jerry and you working together, I am guessing he was bad cop all the time?' With this Jerry cursed again under his breath,

'Don't be so sure, it's all an act with our Jerry.   He is the real writer here, I'm just the public face.   He also has a plus 120 IQ so don't be fooled by the gruffness, it's a great act that goes a long way.' With this Jerry gave a look conveying daggers to Roger.

'Big mouth' he grumbled at Roger.

'Shsh Jerry we need Billy to share, not to be scared.' With this Roger sat down and let Billy have a long draw on his beer before he started. 'We understand you have some information or at least suspicions about the death of Chris Deville, am I correct?'

'It makes no sense.   He jumps from a height that was unlikely to kill him outright, from a place he could not get to easily.   But more importantly, the apartment he lived in, my Aunt's and now my apartment, has a balcony he could have jumped from that is higher than the railway line beneath which he was found.   Why would you trek across town to kill yourself and take the chance of just being crippled?' Roger was focusing on Billy, but Jerry was taking notes in a little book.

The Perry Gene

'That is a very interesting notion, but have you a better idea?' Jerry did not look up from the book, but he was obviously considering the options.

'He was taken up there and pushed or thrown off.' Billy realised he had raised his voice a little too much as he spoke and looked around to see if he had been noticed, but it was not the sort of pub where people listened in.

'But the same argument applies, how could the person who allegedly did this be sure that he would die? If Mr Deville lived, he would be a witness.' Silence descended on the table.   Billy took another long slug of ale.   There was now less than a quarter left in the glass.

'Unless he was dead already' said Billy after a few more seconds.

'George said you liked detective books, you sure you're not a conspiracy theorist as well?' said Jerry suddenly changing his persona. It went quiet again for a minute.

'Unless of course he had just been shagging someone else's wife.' Jerry and Roger both put down their pints which they had previously picked up in sync with each other. They stared at Billy.

'I found a diary in the apartment. It's in code, but he obviously wasn't very bright as he used the woman's first initial as a reference to her name from what I can gather. There is a very flirty cougar living across the hall of the building.'

'So why would this be relevant?' enquired Jerry.

'Well, after he broke it off, she ended up with a black eye and he thought the husband had slapped her around.' Billy tried on his best East End Patois.

'Easy mate, let's try to stick to what we know.'

'He said in the diary there was lots of arguing with her and her husband and then a few days later he saw her in dark glasses which didn't quite cover the bruising up completely. She says she walked into a door, from what he has written.'

'And I certainly know she is the flirty type as she has already tried it on with me, but I'm managing to keep her at arm's length. She even tried to grope me in the lift today.'

'What's her name, and what about the husband, you actually met him?'

'No, but I saw him staring at me one day out of the window when I first visited the apartment. She is Julia Carruthers and her husband is...'

'Tony?' proffered Roger.

'Yes, that's right, how the hell do you know?' Billy looked confused.

'Billy, keep away from her. She may be a cougar, but he's definitely trouble.'

'What do you mean? Is there something I should know?' Billy suddenly looked rather concerned. This was exacerbated by the fact that Jerry had stopped writing and was now looking at Billy, making eye contact for the first time.

'He has a history of *bad things* happening around him.'

The Perry Gene

'Would you care to expand on *bad things*? Am I living next door to Hannibal Lechter or a Kray triplet?'

'Nothing proved, no actual record or not at least while we were still in the job. But it's a name that keeps coming up. He was close to bankrupt in the early nineties from what I understand, clung by his fingertips; but from what I hear, there may be blood under his fingernails. Since then we have heard a variety of things. Property deals that happened at knock down prices. Tenants forcibly evicted, and there was that poor sod who had his hands nailed to the floor.' Roger interjected.

'Roger that is not helpful and unproven. Billy, just keep out of both of their ways until we know more of what is going on. It's probably all just coincidence. We may be jumping to conclusions.'

'A bit like poor Chris Deville, except he didn't jump.' Billy said. He drained his pint and looked at the two of them. 'Do you want a refill?'

'Yes please' said Roger 'I would like you to tell us a little more about the diary.'

'That's lucky' said Billy, producing the book from his inside pocket like a magician pulling a rabbit from a hat. 'I thought this might come in handy. You can read it now and take it away if it helps, but I would like it back please.' Billy handed over the notebook to Jerry, now he realised that he was the brains of the operation. He took their empty glasses to the bar and ordered refills. Taking two journeys back with the three pints, he sat down again. Jerry was now engrossed in the diary, but Roger was looking at him as if deep in thought.

The Perry Gene

'We met her a few times you know.' Roger said quietly to Billy.

'Who, Julia?' Billy appeared confused at the turn of conversation.

'No, Elspeth. Nice lady, forceful, strong, tenacious. She would have made a good copper. I think Jerry had the hots for her. He likes the strong, intelligent type. Me, I'm a little less cerebral, more into heavenly bodies than heavenly minds.'

'How did you meet her? I want to find out about her as I never knew she existed, let alone got to know her.'

'George Transon introduced us. We knew him through professional connections, but over the years we got friendly with him as he has a useful network. When Jerry and I decided to start researching and writing books after leaving the force, he set up a meet with her. She gave us some advice and told us some war stories. In this case, literally war stories. Places she had been, people she had met. Not something she bragged about, but just matter of fact. Her life had been in danger more times than your average spy. She had managed to piss off Warlords, Poachers, child labour gang masters and more. She had some interesting scars to prove it too, or so she told us.' Jerry was reading the diary but looked up and nodded sagely on the subject of Elspeth. 'Happy to talk to you about what we know, but if you need more detail you need to speak to her agent chap.'

'Xavier?'

'Yup, that's the one. A typical arty-farty type. He will love a bit of fresh meat and the chance to gossip. But he will also know about you. Elspeth had a tight little circle of people she trusted. We were not inner circle so we just saw a glimpse of what she was like. Yeah, speak to Xavier, you got his details?'

'Yes, Mr Transon gave them to me.'

'You know he prefers *George* to Mr Transon, right? He has been watching you for a few years now. He did a lot more for Elspeth than your average solicitor. He was her eyes and ears on your affairs. He has actually taken on some of here protective instincts about you.'

'It's my condition, it makes it hard to change.'

'Billy, apart from you straightening the table mats every five minutes, I haven't seen any sign of this so-called condition you are supposed to be afflicted with.'

'Don't tell me Mr Transon told you? Well to be honest, it is so much better than it used to be, Doctor Miles says I am almost fixed.'

'That makes you sound like a neutered cat. Billy, you are just a quiet guy with good observational skills and a need for order. Maybe you are already more *fixed* than the average man in the street. Just think about it. If you had not brought it up, we would not have thought anything was particularly wrong with Mr Deville's sad demise.' Billy sat and thought on this while he took a drink of beer.

'Billy, I will make a copy of this and then drop it back to you in a few days, you ok with that?' Jerry was holding up the already well-thumbed diary. He had been making notes while Roger had been talking.

'Yeah, fine, as I say, as long as I get it back. Are we all done here now?'

'Yup, I think so. Just remember what we said' Roger pulled in close to speak a little more quietly. 'Don't tell anyone about this conversation that you don't trust. Don't go near this Julia character and watch your back with Tony Carruthers.' As Billy began to rise, Roger put out his hand to shake Billy's. Jerry put down the book and rose as well.

'Keep your head down and keep in touch. You have our details.' Billy walked out of the pub into the dull grey of the afternoon. It was now damp as a light rain had started to fall. He stopped underneath the railway bridge and checked his phone for messages, there were two texts and three missed calls, all from the same number. Jenny obviously wanted a catch up. He scanned the text and listened to a voice mail. The theme was consistent, I am bored, where are you? The last one was twenty minutes ago, so he dialled the number and she answered on the second ring.

'Hi Billy, have you had lunch?'

'Just liquid, could use some food.'

'You want to come to my place, or meet me somewhere?'

'Let's meet. You know a good pub near you serving food?'

'Is my cooking not good enough for you?' came the reply, which from the tone you could tell she was stifling a giggle.

'Just trying to make it easy, besides, had a couple of beers and I fancy a couple more.'

The Perry Gene

'We had better stick close to yours then, in case I need to pour you back home, something on the river?'

'Too many tourists.   You know the Goldsmiths?'

'Yes, that's about midway.   Done.   See you there in twenty? Mine's a glass of chilled white.'

'I will make it a bottle with a straw. See ya' he rang off and turned on his heel, pulled his collar up from the rain and started in the direction of the pub. As he did so, the sun came out in the West of the city.   He looked around, he knew there must be a rainbow somewhere.   It was just that he was damned if he could find it right now.

3. Cytosine

The Perry Gene

Chapter 10

Although Billy took a shine to Roger and Jerry almost immediately, their concerns did not make him feel threatened or intimidated by Julia's husband. Yes, they were ex-detectives who knew their stuff, but it was almost possible there had been exaggeration in the tales. Also, Tony was older now and appeared to be a legitimate business man, how dangerous could he be? Billy had yet not even met the man, although several times now he had seen him in the window of the apartment when returning from a run. He knew, however, the easiest way to stay out of trouble was to remove himself from the attentions of Julia. As he had now worked out, if he used the stairs there was no tell-tale ring from the lift call bell announcing his arrival. There were cameras on the front entrance, but not when approaching through the carpark. He also realised that if he arrived back at the apartment from the road behind, he would not alert them to his presence. It became like a game; how little could they see of Billy.

With the business of moving in to the apartment now completed, Billy was getting used to the new location and how it impacted his day. His commute to the lock-up was a little longer, but other than that, he just learned a few new back doubles and where the speed cameras were located. Transon had asked why he didn't buy a new car and get rid of the old Focus, but Billy felt he still had to retain some ties to his past at this point and besides a car was just a workhorse. He could not get excited about Porsches and Ferraris, they were just not him. Well, at least for now.

The Perry Gene

Over the next couple of months, Billy picked up his friendship with Jenny and they saw each other socially at least once a week. Billy was not yet ready for anything romantic, but he was enjoying having a friend around who he could chat to, even confide in. Jenny for her part was patient and growing very fond of Billy, but on one occasion after a liquid Saturday lunch and an afternoon of pub hopping, she did let her frustrations be known.

'Billy, do you like me?' she said as she stared at the TV screen above the bar showing athletics. They were sitting on high barstools in a little sports pub in Greenwich that Billy wanted to try.

'Of course, I like you, we're mates' Billy said as he tried to catch the barman's eye to signal the need for a refill.

'No, I mean really like, as in physically.' She turned to him, grabbed his shoulder and pulled him around on the stool. It was a little clumsy as both she and her seat were well lubricated. 'I am asking if you fancy me.' He looked her in the face trying to steady the stool from spinning around.

'You are an attractive girl Jen, what's not to like?' Billy would rather not be having this conversation as he was not ready for anything serious, and certainly not here. However, he knew their friendship had the potential to be something much more and he just wanted to take it easy. He guessed what had been going on in her mind for a couple of weeks, but now after a few drinks it was spilling out.

'So why haven't you tried it on? We have a lot of fun together, I think, don't we?'

The Perry Gene

'Yes Jen, we do. I like you. You have become a real friend and I don't have many of those.'

'Friend, is that it?' Jenny had previously had quite a few relationships, but they tended to start and end rather explosively. This waiting game was making her think that Billy was not interested. 'Nothing more?'

'I would hope so eventually, but I need to take things slowly as so much has changed and I take time to process these things. I know I don't have all the issues that I used to, but still you have to agree it's a lot to take in.'

'So, there's nobody else? No little barmaid in one of your pubs giving you special service while you are servicing the machines? Or maybe you like that Julia woman. You call her a cougar, but you might secretly like that sort of thing. Like a replacement, Mother figure.' Jenny suddenly stopped. Her rambling had taken her down a path into a dead-end and now she knew she had inadvertently crossed the line. Billy's face screwed up and he looked away for a moment. 'Oh God, I'm sorry.' He turned back to her and took a deep breath.

'It's ok Jen. I know you didn't mean that. You are starting to realise what my Mother did to me. I'm in no way ever looking to replace that. And no, to answer your other question, there is no flirty barmaid or club hostess. I am just a little slow to get going. If you want more than just friendship, which I must say is pretty nice at this point, then you need to give me time.'

'Don't you have needs?' She put her hand on his thigh and softly squeezed his leg. He gently removed it and got off his stool. Standing in front of her, he put his arms around her and have her a gentle peck on the cheek.

'Yes, I guess, I don't really think about it.'

'You're not a virgin, are you?'

'Jen, I'm thirty-one and not a monk.   There have been girls.'

'How many?'

'A small number.   Anyway, there have been girls as I was saying, but it didn't seem to go anywhere after the first time.   They would come back to mine and get freaked out.   The sex wasn't great, more like drunken fumbles, so what's to miss?'   He pulled her closer to him and gave her an enormous bear hug until one of the vertebrae in her spine cracked.

'Ok Billy, you win, but don't hang around too long.   I might get another offer.'

'It's a risk I'm going to have to take.' She did not look pleased as he said this. 'But I hope you don't find anyone else soon.' With this the look disappeared and she smiled again. 'Weren't you getting another drink?' They returned to their stools and the moment was lost.

*

A number came up on Billy's phone as a missed call.   He did not recognise it. He also noticed he had voicemail, so he dialled up to get his message.

'Billy dear boy.   At last.   I have been waiting for years to meet you. Oh sorry, I hate these things.   This is Xavier.   I've been in New York and I'm now back, would you like to meet up and talk about your Aunt?   I understand from your messages you are keen to ask some questions. Well, let me know, TTFN darling.'   The voice sounded bubbly, playful, and even slightly manic.   But nothing about it concerned Billy.   It was now just another new face in his life.   Just another personality to assimilate. 'You wouldn't know me Mother', he thought to himself.

Billy was very keen to find out about Elspeth but felt a little moral support would be helpful. He also knew that a little guidance in these new situations was not a bad idea.   Going through his head were the usual three suspects: Jenny, Transon and Doctor Miles.   He guessed the latter two already knew about Elspeth and were not going to add much value, but Jenny was different.   She asked obvious and subtle questions in ways that sometimes he didn't understand. She was a person who could go from the mundane with a conversation about washing up, to a thought-provoking comment concerning the homeless on the streets. Billy didn't know if this was normal, or abnormal behaviour, who the hell was he to judge?   He just knew the more time he spent around Jen, the more she both calmed and intrigued him.   She was becoming more than just an acquaintance and yet there was still that question of physicality he had get his head around.   Maybe because she worked for Transon and he still had that official view of her from the first day in the office. Their recent chats, which were becoming more frequent, had forced lots of ideas to percolate in his head.

'Morning Jen, how is the world of work?' Billy spoke into the phone and waited for Jen's lilting tones to wash over him.   He knew she took half an hour for an early lunch, to eat a sandwich or a salad at her desk.   She had worked for Transon for about eight years now, starting as just an office junior straight out of college, but as Transon had relied on her more, her role in the firm had grown and now she had three girls who worked for her providing secretarial support for the twenty-five lawyers in the firm.

'Afternoon Billy' she corrected 'it's after twelve you know.' Billy looked at his watch. He was so focused on work that morning, he had not noticed how late it was. He stopped and thought. This was weird, time used to rule his life, every minute was allocated with room left in for contingencies. Now, not all of a sudden but gradually, he had become able to work and focus on problems so intently that the clock became an irrelevance. He reached for the notebook which was inside his jacket pocket. He opened it up at the last entry to write a question for Doctor Miles. He looked at the last line and realised he had not written down a new question for nearly five weeks. He used to raise five to ten issues a day in the period after the breakdown. Even a year ago, his session with Doctor Miles always began with ten or twenty questions about the world and Billy's place in it. What did this mean, just one question to ask, what was happening to him? 'Are you still there Billy, you're not offended, are you? Or sulking?'

'Sorry Jen, a little moment of clarity, I'll explain later. You free this evening?'

'For what Billy, you going to whisk me off my feet and take to Rome or Paris?'

'How does Hoxton sound?'

The Perry Gene

'Better than my flat on a Wednesday evening. Why Hoxton?' In the background, the beat of the keyboard stopped. She was obviously intrigued.

'That guy Xavier got in touch and when I phoned him back he suggested I meet him at this gallery he is promoting in Hoxton. Modern art of some description.'

'If you want to meet up with him, won't I get in the way?'

'I said I might bring a friend and he was fine with it. In terms of friends, I don't think that Pete is much into art and so I am kind of stuck with you.' Billy knew this would generate mock righteous indignation, but Jenny went for broke.

'Oh, you really are Billy no mates aren't you.' She was giggling when she said it.

'Touché. Shall we settle for Billy two mates including you?' He got back what he deserved; he loved this sort of sparring with her. Even Doctor Miles had said there was something different in the way he was speaking and thinking. Billy had the secret suspicion that Jen was good for him in several ways.

'Billy, I would love to accompany you to Hoxton. What time and where?'

'You ok if I pick you up from work and we can grab a glass of something first? I might like to pick your brains about what to ask. I am more than a little nervous about this.'

The Perry Gene

'Ok, I've got some paperwork to do for his nibs tonight, so is 5.30 good for you?'

'Perfect, I said we would meet him at seven.   See you then.'

'Laters, lover boy.' The connection was cut and Billy went back to cleaning the machine assembly with a small hoover to remove two years' worth of dust.   He still loved the intricate work on the circuit boards. It provided a focus.   A locus of calm in a world which was changing rapidly.

*

Billy and Jen had found a small wine bar at the top of Shoreditch High Street. It was one of the City's most rapidly changing and hotly contested neighbourhoods. In all honesty, you needed to be an estate agent to be able to define where the boundaries lay.   The correct postcode could add fifty thousand pounds to a property's worth. They had a glass of wine each and sat on stools in the window to people watch. Billy still had his tendencies to be early to avoid being late.   Jenny was getting a free drink and night away from her flat, so she was happy.   Billy stared at the world going by for a while, lost in a place of too many questions and not enough answers.   Not the over analysis of old but the conundrums brought by his new life.   His dead lodger, his Aunt, his growing business, his new friend, and his potentially dangerous neighbours. He was a million miles away when Jenny spoke.

'Billy, come back, you are somewhere else right now.' Billy snapped out of his thought process and smiled at her.

The Perry Gene

'Sorry, just lots of things to think about. Sometimes it all seems a bit too much. All these extra things going on and all because of someone I never met, or at least knowingly met.'

'You sound sad.' Jenny reached across for his shoulder but changed direction and took his hand. Not sexual or flirty, but gentle and friendly.

'I suppose I am a bit. Elspeth sounds like quite a woman. Yet one more thing my Mother seems to have screwed up for me. 'He shrugged, took a drink, and squeezed Jenny's hand before letting go. 'Anyway, enough of that, we have the lovely Xavier to meet.'

'You said he seemed rather excited to be meeting you. Just his personality or do you think he wants something?'

'Sorry, what do you mean?'

'Well this guy is obviously well connected and loaded. You leave him a voice mail and suddenly he comes back to you and wants to meet up immediately he is back in the country. Bit too eager, isn't he?'

'Is it me? Is it something in my upbringing that I am missing?'

'What do you mean?'

'Well how comes everyone else sees ulterior motives?' He looked like a petulant child and Jenny got a flash in her head of what it must be like for him. All those years, almost crippled by the condition his Mother had forced upon him. She reached across and this time rather than holding his hand, she cupped his face in her hands and kissed him on the forehead.

The Perry Gene

'I'm sorry Billy. I sometimes forget that you are the definition of nice guy.'

'I get it when people are acting awful, you might think the worst, it's just that we haven't even met him and you are already predicting that he has a motive. I suppose it just doesn't cross my mind. You may be right, but I guess he can't be all that bad if Elspeth trusted him, surely Mr Transon or Doctor Miles would have warned me?'

'You are probably right Billy.' Looking at her watch she saw it was ten minutes to seven. 'Come on, drink up, we should be there on time at least.' She drained the last of the white wine and picked up her bags to go. Billy pushed the stools back under the window ledge, took the glasses to the bar, for which he got an approving nod from the staff and walked towards the door. He held it open for Jenny and then as walked through onto the street; her on the inside away from traffic. She slipped her arm through his and they headed for the gallery.

It was only a five-minute walk and as Billy had looked it up the web, he had the location embedded in the map in his head. They arrived at, what for Hoxton, was the closest thing to a cliché. It was a coffee shop that trebled as a wine bar and exhibition space for local artists. Currently around the walls were grimy black and white photographs of the colour graffiti that exists around the streets of the East End. It was beautiful when you saw it in the flesh and large in scale, but these pictures somehow robbed it of its glory. It was as if the artist had sucked out every bit of joy from the art and replaced it with the dull black and white of stark contrasts. Billy scanned the room and was about to walk to the bar to get a drink when he heard a voice from a booth in the corner.

'Billy Perry?' Billy turned around and saw a bird with very strange plumage. The man who he assumed must be Xavier was in his late thirties and dressed somewhere between a peacock and an advert for the Hawaiian tourist board. He beckoned Billy over and then spied Jenny behind him.

'Bring your little friend you with you, I don't bite.'

'Not unless we asked you too, I guess?' offered Jenny.

'Oh, she's a feisty one. No love, not even if you asked, but I might make an exception for him.'

'I'm guessing you are Xavier? Is that a first or last name? Or maybe a catch phrase?' Billy offered in retort but continued to walk over and shook the proffered hand.

'Oh, I can see we are going to get on like a house on fire.' Xavier smiled through the whitest teeth that Billy had ever seen. All white that is, apart from one Gold replacement at the back of his mouth. 'Come sit down, I have champagne, I imagine that is acceptable? Michael' he called to the bartender 'one more glass please.' He had obviously not thought Billy would come with someone. 'You're not quite what I was expecting.'

'Good or bad?'

'Just different' Xavier took the glass from the scurrying barman and filled it up carefully without wasting the bubbles. He then filled the other glass and gave it to Jenny as she sat down. Finally, he topped himself up before sitting in the space between them, not across the table which would have seemed more obvious to Billy. 'And you are?' he asked turning to Jenny.

'My client's legal team' said Jenny without missing a beat.

'I knew I recognised you. You work for George, don't you?'

'I've never met you before in my life. How do you know that?'

'Oh, I have my little ways.' He smirked. 'I am just teasing. I spoke to George before coming over to see how things were with Billy. I know his past and I didn't know what to expect. I have been representing Elspeth for over eight years, so you have been quite the topic of conversation in that time.' He looked wistfully in the distance. 'Yes, I was there when she started to take the art world a little more seriously and then Ker pow. Anyway, enough of that. Firstly, I understand you want some background. Well I am the font of knowledge about her artistic tendencies. Fire away.' Billy was wondering up to this point if Xavier needed to breathe as he just didn't stop talking for an instant.

Over the next thirty minutes, including the break for Xavier to order a second bottle as this one appeared to *have a hole in it*, Xavier answered questions about Elspeth. They had first met through a colleague of hers at work when she started to think she was too old for being chased by War Lords and sweat shop owners. Billy found each question led to an intricate story about Elspeth, often with Xavier in a very complimentary or even starring role. Billy didn't feel he was learning about his Aunt as much as hearing a whole bunch of theatrically recounted anecdotes. He wanted to know about her work and her life.   He wanted to know about her and the falling out.   He wanted to see the woman he could barely picture through the fog of time and the cloak of death.

'You're the last Perry now Billy.   And may I say, a very wealthy one.   I assume you have seen her studio? 'Billy looked blankly at Xavier.   'Well she used to have a place she rented for working on her pictures. It had a dark room and everything.'

'I think Mr Transon would have said something by now if that was the case, don't you?' Billy was starting to feel like he was being drip fed again.

'The studio was disposed of when she got ill.   I know that much as I worked on some of the paperwork for Mr Transon.' Jenny added, as she realised she was now in a position of knowledge.   In this arena, knowledge was power.

'But what about her work?   She had projects she was working on. And her cameras?   Her equipment, what happened to that?' Xavier was becoming more animated.   He reached out to Jenny and put his hand on her shoulder.   'Tell me what you know young lady.' Xavier twisted Jenny's body around a little so he could look straight into her eyes.   His own face took an a kind of manic look.

'I am guessing that it all went into storage.   I know that's where most of her possessions are.' Jenny was looking at Billy. Billy was frowning.

'What's that bloody song about being the last to know?   I thought there wasn't much on display in Elspeth's house, but I guessed it had been put in boxes or she lived minimally. Mr Transon never mentioned it.' At this point,

The Perry Gene

Xavier started to clap his hands together in a way that resembled a demented seal.

'You know what this means don't you? I was right all along. We can do one more show of her work. Maybe a collection of old and new works. A posthumous retrospective. All the luvvies will flock.'

'Billy, I'm not saying I told you so, but do you smell a rat with an ulterior motive?' Jenny whispered in Billy's ear.

'Yes, but more importantly, I have a way back into my Aunt's life' he replied. Xavier was on his way back at the bar, already calling out an order ahead of him for shots. His celebration had started and would now run for a while. This was potentially Christmas, Easter and birthday rolled into one for him. Billy looked away and moved towards the window. Jenny ignored Xavier and was more concerned with the slump in Billy's shoulders. She caught him up and walked in front of him to make eye contact and saw huge silent tears rolling down his face. At that moment, she did the only thing she thought would help. She kissed him softly on the lips and wrapped her arms around him. He didn't make a sound, just continued to make her face wet as the tears rolled down his cheeks. Jenny had never seen Billy cry before, but then again, neither had Transon or Gordon Miles. Even in the bad times of the breakdown, tears never flowed. Now it felt as if a giant kink in the pipework had been cleared, many years of loss began to flow, and it was ten minutes or more before it stopped. Jenny did quite know what to do, but she turned her back on Xavier and put her arms around Billy. She hugged him for what seemed like ages, but he did not reciprocate, his mind was reeling and he could not take any more input at this time. There was a moment when Billy felt the water rushing over him again, but he focused on his breathing and took his time to come back to the world. He felt this was not going to be the last surprise he would have to face in the future.

The Perry Gene

Chapter 11

To say that Xavier was excitable was an understatement. Billy received no less than two phone calls and five texts each day for the next week. During this time, Xavier pressed for more information about the pictures and Billy got into a quid pro quo arrangement whereby he received snippets of information about his Aunt in exchange. Of course, what Xavier initially wanted was confirmation of the contents of the storage unit. Billy did not have time to go until the weekend, so until that point, nobody knew what awaited them.

On the Saturday morning, once he had had his morning run and a large coffee, Billy left the apartment in search of Elspeth and in a very real sense, in search of his place in the world. Jenny had laid into her boss the morning after the meeting with Xavier, to such an extent that he had got a bit annoyed with her. There were comments made about knowing her place, but Transon was also kicking himself for not mentioning the storage unit to Billy. After Elspeth was diagnosed and she knew it was only going to end one way, she researched storage units in the town nearest to her house as she was moving back there. Everything was packed away neatly and protected in bubble wrap. Her photographs may have existed only as digital files these days, but she had many framed enlargements and quite a bit of equipment.

Billy picked up Jenny from her regular Saturday morning hair-appointment and they drove the thirty-eight miles to the storage company. Walking into the 'U-Store' unit on the outskirts of Dorking, Billy cracked open the door, turned on the light and marvelled at the number of packages in front of him, each marked up with a bar-coded sticker to identify them. The air felt cold but fresh; these were modern units, well-lit and ventilated. It was not the dusty and damp, half dark Aladdin's cave of *Silence of the Lambs* or the untidy jumble sale of some *Storage Wars* episode. This was precisely ordered and tidy, labelled and efficient. He felt a bit foolish that he had brought a rubberised torch with him, the way you see the Police do in the movies.

Jenny followed him into the room, which was about twelve by six feet and maybe eight feet tall. The walls were bright yellow and metallic. In the ceiling were two neon strip lights that were covered with wire mesh grills to stop them being damaged. Jenny whistled through her teeth.

'Billy, do you think by any chance your sense of orderliness is genetic?' Jenny put her arm around his shoulder and stared at the labelled packages. It looked like Christmas has been wrapped up by someone who only had access to brown paper.

'Where do we start?' said Billy looking slightly overawed by the sight. He had been quiet on the journey down to Dorking. Jenny assumed that he was struggling with the day ahead and the not knowing what he might find. She picked up a manifest that was hanging on the wall. It ran to eight or nine pages of fine print, with one line for each item stored.

'Well we could do the traditional thing and fumble around in the dark, or we could simply read the storage manifest' she said handing it to Billy with a huge smile. Jenny knew that organisation was one of her strengths and being here now was how she could help Billy most.

The Perry Gene

'What would I do without you Jen?' he said quietly as he began to scan the document.

'I am rather more interested in what you intend to do with me Billy, but this is probably not the time or the place.' With this she reached up and pecked him on the cheek. Jen sat herself down on the desktop that was on one side of the room and waited for Billy's next move. He was slowly reading the manifest and had got to the third page when he yelped. He read out the number under his breath and started to look for two packages on the middle shelf unit next to the desk. 'What's got your interest Billy?'

'Her computer is here. In fact, her desktop and laptop. This is the road into her art and her life, if I'm lucky.' Billy moved a couple of small items out of the way and then lifted a large box off the shelf. 'Ok, that's the desktop, now just got to find EP367A45.' He continued to look at the boxes on the shelf and failed to see Jenny pick up a much smaller package from the end of the desk.

'Did you say A45?' She picked up the package and held it up for his inspection.

'That's it Jen, you're a genius.' He took the package from her and laid it on the box containing the desktop computer. He went back to scanning the list. After about a minute, he found one more item of interest on the last but one page. 'Can you help me find EP367A73 please? I'm not sure how big it will be, but it says it is stored on shelf 11.' Both of them moved to the larger racking unit on the right of the room. Shelf 11 was about Billy's chest height.

The Perry Gene

He and Jenny started from opposite ends and within thirty seconds she had pulled out a medium sized box that bore the correct label.

'Eureka' she screeched in triumph at finding what he wanted. It made her feel good to be here, now, helping this complex and sometimes vulnerable man. She knew he needed help but more importantly she was aware how attracted to him she was becoming. 'Do I get a prize?' She handed the package over and faced him with her lips puckered up.

'Lunch?' He teased. She pulled a face, but then Billy reached down and kissed her on the lips. 'Thank you.'

'Oh, it was nothing, just a bit of filing. It's what I do you know.'

'No, thank you. Thank you for being here; here for me. Thank you for helping.' He kissed her again. This time it lasted a little longer and now with her free hand she gently ran her fingers through his hair. After a few more seconds, they disengaged and she was left with a silly grin on her face.

'Nice to see there is some passion below the surface Billy boy.' She pulled the trolley they had borrowed over and went to pick up the smaller of the boxes.

'You know what they say, still waters run deep.'

'Billy, you must be deeper than the Marianas Trench for it to take this long.' But all the time she said this she was smiling. 'I think you mentioned lunch?' He lifted the two computer boxes on the trolley, closed and locked the doors and took the manifest with him so he could make a copy. He started to wheel the trolley towards the exit and the security desk. 'Xavier will be having kittens by now you know. I wonder how long before he calls you?'

'Already had two texts.' Billy said as he signed out and wheeled the trolley through the door.

'Aren't you going to call him back?' Jenny seemed a little unsure of Billy's mood.

'Terrible reception in these storage places. Let's let him stew for a while. Shylock will have his pound of flesh but only when I am good and ready.'

'You know Billy; I may have got you wrong. I think you are developing a devious and mischievous streak.' As they reached the car, he hit the remote control and opened the boot so he could load the boxes.

'I'm just fed up with everybody trying to lead me around. It wasn't so bad with Doctor Miles and your boss, but now this Xavier character. It about time I took control.

'Good for you Billy, now on the subject of food, since you mentioned it.'

'How do you fancy a fry up? I know a couple of good pubs that do an all-day breakfast on the way back into town'

'Done.' With this Jenny pushed the trolley back to the front desk from where they had borrowed it, while Billy got in and started the car. Although it had a few miles on the clock, the fact that it was Billy's meant it was pristine inside and was regularly cleaned. He still could not bear disorder, so it was lucky that when Jenny got in and unwrapped a sweet, she put the paper in her pocket. She noticed at this point Billy was staring at her.

'Something I said or did?' she said to him.

'Nothing bad. I just appreciate tidy people.' She looked around and the put her hand into her pocket and pulled out the wrapper. He nodded and started the engine.

'My mumma dragged me up proppa' she said imitating a bad cockney accent.

'Well your Mother did a better job than mine from what I have seen so far' he said in a very matter of fact way.

'I'm sorry Billy, I didn't mean anything.'

'Jen, stop. I'm not who I was ten years ago. I'm not even who I was when you met me six months ago. I'm changing. But more importantly, don't imagine every time you or someone else makes a comment I'm being destroyed mentally. I know you are a lot more caring than the work persona of Miss Efficiency and Miss Bossy Boots would suggest. I like you as my friend because you are a good person. You don't need to walk on egg shells all the time with me. Firstly, it's messy and secondly, I'm not a fan of omelettes.' Before pulling off, he flashed her a smile and she put her arms around his arm and gave it a squeeze. 'And now, to the food.'

Billy put on the CD player and out came the strains of Rachmaninov. Still classical, but Billy was stretching himself now. Trying different things; food, music, books. Every new step seemed to speed his progress. He needed to see Doctor Miles to discuss it, but he was not sure for how much longer that would be the case.

*

They were back at the apartment two hours later, having devoured most of a pig in a variety of forms over breakfast. Billy had finished his, but as the portion size was massive in the pub, Jenny had wimped out in the end and left a third of it on the plate. Retiring injured she'd called it, in other words stopping before she exploded. Billy took two trips to get the boxes and a bit of shopping up to the apartment from the garage. On the second trip, he knew he had obviously snagged Julia's trip wire because when they reached the top floor she was standing on the threshold of her apartment.

'Hello stranger, I was starting to think you were avoiding me' Julia said and then stopped as she saw Jenny walk out of the stairwell behind him. 'Oh, back again, like a proper little couple,'

'Well what can I say Mrs Carruthers, it's my pheromones apparently, she can't resist.' Jenny knew this was her cue to kiss the back of his neck.

'Oh ok' Julia was knocked off her stride and didn't appear to have a comeback for a second. As Billy pushed open the latched door and went to go in, she countered. 'Don't be a stranger, you know where I am if you need a cup of sugar or something.'

'Jules' came a muffled voice from the back of the opposite apartment. She looked shocked and then a wave of something between embarrassment and fear drifted across her face. She regained her composure and smiled.

The Perry Gene

'HMV as I like to call him.' Billy stopped and looked back at her, perplexed.

'His Master's Voice Billy' Jenny said and pushed him through the open door 'like the record company.   You know with the little yapping dog.'   With this line, she stared back at Julia, smiled and then closed the apartment door.

'I never knew that's what it meant, but I have to say with lines like that you certainly know *How to Win Friends and Influence People*.' He smirked at his own comment and carried the box into the lounge.

'Billy, firstly, she annoys me by the fact she is omnipresent when you come home.   You've had to try to avoid her; that's just not right.   Secondly, you suspect she is dangerous to know because of her thug of a husband. Thirdly, I might be a tiny bit jealous.' Jenny switched the kettle on and got two mugs out of the cupboard. She knew where everything was by now as she had helped Billy get most of the place into some sort of order.   'Coffee or tea?'

'Coffee please.' Billy was opening the larger of the boxes and pulling out a flat screen, keyboard, mouse and the base unit of a computer. He carefully wired it up on a small desk he had installed against the far wall. He knew if he put it near the window, he would just stare at the passing river traffic.   After a few minutes, Jen walked over and handed him a cup. 'The moment of truth' said Billy as he plugged in the lead and switched on. There was the inevitable whirring noise from inside in the base unit and numbers started to flash across the screen. After about thirty second the machine displayed a password prompt and Elspeth's username with picture.   It was not the usual sort of photo one expected to see when logging in.   It was not some screen snap taken with the on-board camera of a laptop or from a mobile phone, but a very professional looking portrait with Elspeth smiling.   Like the Mona Lisa, the word Billy would have used for it was enigmatic.   It was a knowing smile, a powerful and controlled piece of publicity.   The image must have been taken about ten years before based on the age she appeared to be in the picture.   She had a little grey showing in her hair, and her skin had obviously seen a fair amount of sun.   It was the face of someone practical, not vain. Billy knew if she took this much trouble with the picture for her computer then she really must have been an interesting person to get to know. 'Hello Auntie' whispered Billy. He finally had the opportunity to see his mysterious benefactor up close and personal and he hoped the revelations did not end with just her picture.

'Yes, that's the Elspeth Perry I have seen on occasions. Are you impressed, surprised, intrigued?' said Jenny from behind his shoulder.

'I guess so. Sorry, yes. All of the above I suppose.'

'Have you not seen a picture before?' Jenny put her arms around him and snuggled into his side, realising this was a far bigger moment than she had thought.

'No, nobody has given me a picture yet and for some reason it did not occur to me to ask.   There were no pictures of her at the house.   I don't suppose there was any reason for your boss to have images.   From this photo alone, I get the feeling she liked to control her image if not her identity as well.'

'So, password?'

The Perry Gene

'Well I'm damned if I know. What about your boss, is he liable to?'

'I suppose he might, they were closer than your average client. What about any Post It notes or note books?'

'I will have a look through the other boxes. Any chance you know Transon's out of hours contact details? I would love to look at this today.'

'I will give him a call. He won't be happy but for you I think he will be ok at being disturbed.' Jenny walked off to the kitchen and pulled her phone out of her bag and punched in a number. While waiting for it to ring, she took her mug of coffee and sat on the sofa looking at the river. She was starting to see why Billy found this so addictive. It was fascinating and yet relaxing all at the same time. It occurred to her that she might be picking up some of Billy's traits and that made her smile. She had decided a while ago, it wasn't someone Billy-like she wanted now, but Billy. She heard a voice answering the phone but Billy could only hear one side.

'Hello Mr Transon, I am so sorry to disturb you on a Saturday but Billy asked me to call.' There was a short pause then she continued 'yes, Billy Perry, who else? Want? He wants to know if you have the passwords to Elspeth's computers. He has collected them from the storage unit but he can't get in to them.'

'You don't? Ok, thanks for that. Again, sorry to disturb you at the weekend, see you Monday.' She closed the phone. 'Sorry Billy as you heard, no luck on that.

The Perry Gene

'My other option is to ask Pete.   He is a wiz with these things and probably has a way of breaking into it.'   Billy opened up his phone and tried to call Pete, but it went to voicemail so he started to type in a text message.   He still disliked answering machines and used them as little as possible.   As he was typing, the phone started to ring, it was Xavier. 'I'll say one thing for that man, he is persistent.'

'Who's that?' asked Jenny.

'Xavier.   Let's see what he wants, as if I don't know.' Billy answered the phone and put it on speaker so Jenny could listen in. 'Good afternoon Xavier, you know, it might have been the booze, but I never did get to the bottom of your name the other night, is it your first name?'

'Billy, you darling boy, lovely to finally speak to you. I thought you were screening my calls.'

'No signal at the storage unit and only just got back to the apartment after driving.   Sorry I missed you.'

'No problem at all. So, do tell, what did you find?   Is it a small goldmine? Are there lots of brown paper packages tied up with string?'

'Don't tell me, I think I know what your favourite things are.   Yes, if you are asking, I did see lots of equipment, large wrapped packages that looked like picture frames and some family photos. Oh yes, and I have her computers. Desktop and laptop.'

'Oh... My... God.' Xavier almost squealed down the phone. 'Have you looked at the computers?   There should be a complete digital archive of her work on there and somewhere online there is a backup of her pictures. She was very careful and technically very canny for an artist.'

'Well we have plugged them in, but not looked yet.'

'Why ever not? Billy, the world awaits your Aunt's final exhibition.'

'We don't know the password.' Billy looked embarrassed when he said that. Jenny smiled at him as if to reassure. 'Any ideas what it might be?'

'Oh, you do so need Xavier in your life Billy.'

'I normally try not to associate with people who refer to themselves in the third person.'

'Suit yourself darling, but I think you need what I have.'

'I'm almost afraid to ask' Billy said. At this Jenny stifled a laugh and walked over to the window so that the microphone would not pick her up.'

'I have the password, I watched her type it in many times. I also know that you are 31-years-old right now Billy.'

'That's correct, but what has that got to do with it.'

'Billy, you were her biggest project for the last ten years. She wanted to make you whole again after the breakdown. She devoted a huge amount of time and energy to making sure you were helped and healed. If she hadn't died you would have probably met her by now.'

'I'm still failing to see the relevance of...' Billy's words were lost as Xavier spoke over him.

'It's your name and your year of birth. Big B, illy and the year 1984, try that.' Billy walked over to the computer and laid the phone on the desk. He carefully typed the instructed password. After a few seconds, the login screen disappeared and Billy was sitting looking at the desktop of Elspeth's screen. 'I assume with the silence that it worked then?'

'Yes Xavier. I'm in.   Is the laptop the same?'

'I am pretty sure it is yes. So, what do I get in return, what's my prize for being so helpful?'

'Is there something specific you are after, or do you just generally want access to her pictures?'

'The packages in storage.   You mentioned frames. I would like to know what is there.   Before Elspeth got ill, she agreed on one final exhibition of her work. She was preparing it when she went off the radar and it was not until she was close to death that I managed to get in contact with her.   I would like to see a list of what is stored there and to understand how close she was to getting the exhibition finished.   I will need to work out a location for it and start the preparations.'

'Don't you need my permission?'

'Well I assumed you would want the world to see your Aunt's work one last time?'

'Try not to assume with me Xavier, it is not my default mode of operation.'

'Billy, I just helped you. Don't go all funny on me now.'   Jenny, having stifled her giggles, walked back over to the desk.

The Perry Gene

'Xavier, let him have some time to process it all, you know he needs to handle change slowly.' Jenny looked at Billy who was now frowning at her. She put her finger to his lips and pointed to the phone. Billy got the hint and pressed the mute bottom. 'He doesn't need to know you are better now, this will buy you some time to think. But you need to offer him something to keep him off your back for a few days. What about the manifest?' Billy unmuted the phone.

'Xavier, I noticed a scanner in the computer box. How about I scan in the manifest from the warehouse and email it to you? It will give you a chance to see what Elspeth had already had framed; I assume you knew her work well?' Jenny gave Billy an appreciative thumbs-up.

'But of course, and that would be very helpful darling, you still have my details on my card I assume? Sorry, you said not to assume, but you know what I mean.'

'Yes, I have it here somewhere.' Billy fished into his wallet and pulled out the card he had been given. On it, he read Xavier, just the one-word name again. Below it read 'Art and Literary Agent' with a slightly dubious quote in Latin, his phone number and email. Billy read out the email to Xavier for him to confirm. After he did this Billy continued 'So, even your business card only has one name, you weren't born Xavier, what's the story?'

'I was born Peter Smithson' came a now much more macho and less flamboyant voice from the phone 'but you need to stand out in this game. So, more years ago than I care to mention, I buried *Peter* and Ta-dah' the flamboyance returned to his voice 'Xavier was born. But if you ever tell anyone my real name, I will be very upset with you. Elspeth knew, but she also appreciated an artiste.'

'Your secret is safe with us Xavier; I will email you later. Goodbye.' With this Billy hung up the phone, pulled up a chair and opened the file browser on the computer.

The Perry Gene

Chapter 12

Billy now had a project.   Looking through the computer took up most of his non-working hours over the next two weeks.   It was as much as Jenny could do to drag him out to dinner one evening.   This was what Billy was built for; searching.   His meticulous manner made the whole process a series of logical tasks.   As far as her work was concerned, Elspeth had been as organised as Billy and it started to make him wonder if some of his traits were indeed genetic.   Her photographs had been filed into folders on the computer and on day three of his searching he found the index she had created.   It had dates, titles and background information.   She had also rather helpfully included details of the exhibitions she had held previously and had quite a lot of the pre-work completed for the final exhibition that Xavier was so desperate to organise. This fact made it a little easier to deal with Xavier as Billy now knew that this was something that Elspeth had wanted, not a fanciful idea created to top up the peacock's coffers.   In a way, this added a certain amount of pressure to Billy. This was a way to do something for the person who had done so much for him in secret.   All those years watching and waiting, planning, and praying for the day that she could reveal herself to him and re-enter his life.   There was a moment of sadness that washed over Billy as he thought about her not seeing the finished article.   But then he snapped back realising the best way he could honour her memory was to keep a tight rein on Xavier.

The Perry Gene

'Ok', Billy said to Xavier as they met for lunch the following Saturday, 'you can go ahead and start planning the exhibition. Do you know where you want to hold it?'

'Well that depends, how much money do you have?' There was a mischievous glint in Xavier's eye.

'Money, you mean this thing is going to cost me?' Billy sat back from his plate and reached for his glass. The condensation from the cold, crisp wine ran down the stem as he took a sip. 'Aren't these things self-financing? How do you make money from it?'

'All good questions Billy. Firstly, you will sell off the framed prints which will make you some money back. Generally, you would create them as limited-edition prints and have them numbered so that it increases the value. Part of the deal is that they stay on the wall until after the exhibition is over, let's say two weeks. We would obviously have to pay to staff the gallery unless you want to do it yourself. And then of course we would do a press and critics' night. This must be catered for, which means booze.'

'That sounds like a lot of money to me. By the way, you have still not told me what's in it for you.' Billy was playing with the food on his plate, moving it around as he became less comfortable with where the conversation was going.

'If we do this right, we price the pieces up so that if you sell 50% of them, you break even. For me, I get twenty percent of all sales, but for that you get my organisational prowess and my art world contacts. But to be honest, a retrospective of Elspeth Perry will sell itself. '

'So, how much?'

'About ten thousand should be enough for me to get the ball rolling on a modest little affair somewhere grimy but arty. If you want something more West End, then it will be double that. If you are ok to leave it to me, I could shortlist five places and then meet again to decide, possibly with a visit to each.'

'How soon?' Billy put down his knife and fork as he knew Elspeth's money was just sitting in the account. The fact was that he still felt awkward spending it. It was all very unreal and it took some getting used to. Gordon and Jen had been nagging him that he should start to use the money or even live a little. He was almost earning more in interest than he was spending, and he felt to himself this was a small amount to say goodbye to his Aunt.

'If we moved quickly, we could have the thing up and running in six weeks. From the files you sent me, it looked like Elspeth had already done the hard work. She has had ninety percent of the photographs framed and stored down in that unit. There are only two things I would change.' Xavier pushed his plate away and reached for the bottle of wine in the ice bucket. He topped up his glass and offered some to Billy but he held up his hand as he still had enough in his glass and he struggled a bit with lunchtime drinking. He was meant to see Jenny later and wanted to be awake.

'What two things?' Billy asked as he took a drink from the glass of water on the table.

The Perry Gene

'Well firstly I would like to add a few of her older prints to show where she came from so that it is not all new. I want it to be the story of her photographic career. We could use some of her older war footage and the pieces from the sweatshops.'

'Ok, to be honest, you are the expert in this area, so I need to leave the selection to you. I am surprised that this sort of thing would sell, but since you have done this with her before, you have a far better idea of what works.' Billy watched Xavier's face. He was now getting the measure of the man and he knew there was something else coming, which was more major than the addition of some older pictures. 'Come on, spit it out. You said two things and the second one has got you very much wound up. 'A big smile had broken out across Xavier's face and he put his glass down so that he could reach across the table and take Billy's hands.

'You know, there is more of Elspeth in you than you realise. She was a great reader of people and always knew when I had a card to play. Ok, here is my idea. I need some additional photographs in the exhibition.'

'But I said you had carte blanche to pick from her catalogue, what else do you need?'

'Oh, I need more than that, the photographs I'm after have not been taken yet.'

'Sorry, you lost me, please don't tell me this is some sort of afterlife thing or spiritualism.'

'No Billy, nothing like that. I want you to use Elspeth's cameras.'

'And do what?'

'I want you to take the pictures of her biography. I tell you this is gold dust. You want to know more about your Aunt and I want photographs of the important places in her life to include in the exhibition. The idea of her long-lost nephew coming back into her life and providing the missing pieces of her lifetime puzzle is just delicious. It will add an extra interest level to the exhibition and you never know, if you are any good, it might give you a new outlet.'

'I might be terrible.' Billy offered, without giving anything away to Xavier.

'Have a look at her photographs, get a feel for her style, or if you are not comfortable with that, just do your own thing. If they are truly rubbish we will rethink, but personally, Elspeth's life newly seen through the eyes of her Nephew and the lens of her own camera works for me.'

'Agreed,' said Billy 'give me a list of what you suggest and I will give it a go.'

'You are going to have to do some digging; where she was born, school, first job etc. You might even find something about your grandparents. You never met them, did you?'

'No.' Billy was suddenly lost in thought. He knew that their death had been the catalyst for his parent's estrangement from Elspeth. Did Xavier know this too? Just for a moment, he wanted to have more information about his own family than anyone else. 'No, they died when I was too young to have known them.   All right, I can dig, and Elspeth's computers help tremendously. The laptop has a lot more useful stuff on it, but as you say, I still have spade work to do.'   Billy picked up his glass and emptied it.   He beckoned the waiter for the bill.

*

Jenny arrived at the apartment at about six.   She let herself in with the emergency key that Billy had secured from Julia.   He was happy about Jenny having a key as he knew he could trust her and it was also good for another key to be in existence in case he ever got locked out, (although to be fair that was unlikely with Billy). She walked into the room and could hear the heavy breathing of a good lunch followed by peaceful slumber.   She smiled because she was pleased he was resting.   He worked hard on both the computer and the laptop with a thirst for knowledge.   Billy's sleep patterns had gone out of the window and she found herself receiving texts from him at one and two in the morning as he finally turned in and realised he hadn't responded to a question or prompt from her.

She filled the kettle and switched it on.   She had a bottle of wine with her but fancied seeing how Billy was before opening it. She walked to look out at the river, the sun was still quite high and the city glittered like an ornate chandelier; the sunlight bouncing off of the steel and glass.   The view from the window not only showed the Bridge and Tower, but also the Mayoral building and several of those iconic structures now so in the public consciousness that they had their own names.   She looked across at the Cheese Grater, Lloyds,

The Perry Gene

The Gherkin and the Walkie-Talkie. From this angle the Shard was out of view, but it dominated the skyline on the south of the river. She heard the kettle come to the boil behind her and the automatic switch clicked off. With the click, Billy stirred in his sleep. Jenny walked over to him and kissed him on the head. He came to and saw her there, but the sleep still paralysed his speech and movement.

'Hello sleepy head, did Billy boy need a nap? You Jet-Set millionaires, I don't know, the life you lead.' Jenny spoke slowly and softly. She looked around the flat; there was still no obvious signs of Billy splurging with his new found wealth. She was ribbing him, but in this state, still dozy after sofa sleep, he was an unfairly easy target. 'Do you want a coffee?'

'What time is it?' He looked around the room bleary eyed.

'Just gone six. How long have you been asleep? Did you have a big session with Xavier?'

'I got back about four and just shut my eyes for five minutes. We only had a bottle of wine between us, I think I'm just tired. Yes please, to the coffee, I need to wake up if we are going out.'

'You have been hitting that computer quite hard this week from your texts. You haven't been in bed before one any night and mostly it's been after two. Candles are only meant to burn at one end Billy. If you don't want to go out tonight we can just stay in or I can even go and leave you to get some rest. There is always tomorrow.'

'On that subject, do you fancy a drive tomorrow?   I want to go back to the storage unit and pick up a couple of things.   I have also been doing some searching this week and need to follow up some stuff.'

'Searching for what?'

'Elspeth.   I reached out to those two ex-coppers to see what they could find out about Elspeth's early life and it's lucky I did.'

'Why is that?   Don't tell me there is even more wealth coming your way Croesus?' she brought two coffees over in mugs, slipped off her shoes and sat on the sofa at the opposite end from him with her legs tucked under her.

'Oi, you know I never went looking for any of this.'

'I know Billy, you are a good man, I'm just winding you up, so why lucky?'

'Well, apart from wanting to know more about her, things got a bit interesting with Xavier today. He is very excited about setting up the exhibition, but he has had an idea to make it more representative of her life.   He wants to add some older photographs from her early work to create a timeline. Xavier thinks it will be a good idea to be able to show the development of her work.'

'Ok, that makes sense, but I don't quite see...'

'...the connection?' interrupted Billy, 'Well he wants me to use Elspeth's cameras to take biographical photographs of the milestones in her life. He has suggested that I start with the house she was born in, her school, the office she worked at in Fleet Street when she did her first bits of photojournalism; before it was even called that. That way there is a link between the past, present and future.'

'That's clever, Xavier certainly had his eye on the prize.   But, and just supposing this for a second; what happens if you are crap with a camera?   You have never really studied it or taken a load of photos, have you?'

'I would say it's all pie in the sky, genetics will not cover this, except for one thing.'

'Which is? Honestly Billy, this is worse than pulling teeth. Spit it out man.'

'Easy, *Miss Impatient*.   Anyway, during my therapy in the first year, I was so obsessed with order and things changing when I was not looking that Doctor Miles got me to take photographs.   It was like playing spot the ball with my own life.   As I got better, it was something I stopped needing to do, but it got me to a pretty good standard with the mechanics of photography, so I would say this idea is not as daft as it sounds.   Could even be a new career, you never know. Obviously, I said none of this to Xavier, as I like to keep a few secrets.'

'That sounds wise. So, what happens next?'

'I want to go get the rest of the camera equipment and a picture from storage.'

'What picture?'

'I want one of Elspeth in this room.   There is a self-portrait she took. I want it here in the apartment, like she is here with us.'

The Perry Gene

'Billy is that wise? You know the issues you had with the presence of your Mother at your old house. You told me how much it used to affect you. Why do you want it here?'

'Firstly, Elspeth is a positive thing in my life unlike my Mother. I want her to be remembered here for everything she achieved and did for me. Secondly, I want to look at how she took pictures so I can try and do her justice for the exhibition.'

'That's certainly a smart idea Billy. I like it. Let's go in the morning to get the bits and pieces.'

'There's more, but I will tell you over dinner.'

'Now, are you sure you're up for it?'

'Much better now.' Billy got up and realised he could do with freshening up before going out. 'You ok if I take a quick shower and change?'

'Take your time, I might open the wine.' Jenny got up and walked over to the kitchen, took a chilled bottle out of the fridge and replaced it with the one she had brought with her. Taking a glass from the cupboard she unscrewed the bottle and poured a large measure. 'Actually, skip that, don't take too long, I'm starving'. Billy broke into a half jog as he headed for the stairs.

'Fifteen minutes' tops' he said as he took the stairs two at a time. Jenny returned to her previous position on the couch and pointed the remote control towards the stereo. What came out could have been anything randomly on Billy's classical playlist but it was jazz. Nothing Avant Garde, just soft saxophone in the foreground. Jenny was aware that she was starting to appreciate Billy's classical choices in her own time, but she didn't realise he had added some jazz to his list. She settled back into the big cushions and was drifting away on the river when she heard a sliding noise over by the door. She got up to investigate and found an envelope pushed underneath. On the front it just had the word *Billy* written in a beautiful calligraphy style. She picked it up and propped it against the wine bottle on the counter.

When Billy came down, fourteen minutes later (he was still punctual, that would never change), he saw the envelope on the kitchen top. It was a strange letter and made him flashback to the day the manila envelope arrived at his old home. An envelope that changed his life, introduced him to the foreign world of Elspeth Perry and of course enabled him to meet Jenny. But this was different, it just had his first name on it.

'Where did this come from, you started buying me cards now? It's a slippery slope you know.' Billy looked around to see Jenny and found her gazing out to the river. 'Are you impressed I added the Miles David by the way? I know you like it and I guess my music must get a bit samey for you sometimes.'

'Billy the music is heavenly, but did you just get it for me?'

'Not just you, also a little bit of expanding my repertoire. Jazz still has its limits with me. You know, where they forget there's a tune? I was saying, what's with the card?'

'Sorry, I was Miles away, see what I did there?' She got up from the chair and beamed a smile at him, a full beam smile that trapped Billy like a rabbit. 'It wasn't me, it got pushed under the door.' Billy walked back over to the counter and used a knife to make a slit in the envelope. He pulled out a card from inside, opened it and started to read.

'Houston, we might have a problem; beep' he said in a strange impression of a NASA astronaut.

'Why, who's it from' Jenny walked over to look. Billy handed her the card. After a few seconds, she looked up. 'Yes, I can see what you mean.' The card was an invitation to a soiree at Julia and Tony's the following Saturday. Drinks and things on sticks or something like that but posher. 'I'm guessing it's not just you, there will be others there, judging by the way it's worded.'

'Yes, but, do we want to spend the evening with the psycho and his cougar wife?'

'Who said anything about *We*?' Jenny handed the card back to Billy.

'Did you not see the Billy and *guest*? And we need to RSVP. Roger North suggested we kept them at arm's length. I don't think this is what he had in mind.'

'We need to think about this a little more. Let's get out to dinner. You wanted to tell me something else about tomorrow and after that we can formulate a plan.'

'Right, let's grab dinner, but can we please get out of here without bumping into Julia or she'll put us on the spot. We can use the stairs.' Billy quietly opened the apartment door and they half crept and half ran to the stair-well and didn't speak until they got outside.

The Perry Gene

Chapter 13

'How do you know where to start?' Jenny asked as Billy pulled into the storage depot. It was just gone midday on Sunday. After dinner, the night before, they'd had a nightcap and then Billy put Jenny in a taxi home; much to her annoyance. She was getting keener and Billy knew she was only going to have so much patience. As it had been a long week, Billy slept in until nine and then had a run before going to fetch the van from the lock-up. He drove over to pick up Jenny for the drive out of town. On the way to Dorking, he added a little more detail to the sketchy plans from the night before. They were going to pick up the cameras and a few more personal effects that Billy wanted to examine. The journey back into town would then take them via a couple of places Billy needed to see.

'Well for a start, you know that Doctor Miles put together a dossier on Elspeth with her help before she died?'

'No Billy, that is one of those details you conveniently forgot to tell me.' Jenny sounded slightly miffed with him, although the creeping hangover could also be the cause of her being off balance today.

'I thought I had said, sorry. One of the things I was always guilty of was thinking everybody knew what I knew. I probably played a conversation with you about this in my head and sometimes that can make the imaginary real for me.' Billy was reversing the van into a parking space near the door to the unit.

The Perry Gene

'Any other conversations you have had with me that I should know about?' Jenny was no longer frowning, but as usual found the world of Billy both frustrating and amusing at the same time. Yes, he could be hard work sometimes, but then who wasn't? She decided she might as well have a bit of fun back. 'Any proposals on one knee or offers to stay for the night?' With this, Billy stopped backing up the van, half in and half out of the parking bay. He looked across at her, partly surprised but almost trying to work out if she was serious. At the same time, he knew that conversations of many types had been played out in his mind over the last few months. Those of recent weeks had been more personal in nature. 'It's Ok Billy, I'm just having fun.' Jenny undid her seat belt and kissed him on the cheek. 'You keep your fantasies to yourself; for now.' Billy smiled again and as the moment had passed, finished parking the van.

It took no more than twenty minutes to collect the three boxes and twenty framed prints that Xavier had identified by their names and coded references. Billy wanted to drop them off at an office Xavier had mentioned he used so that he could start to pull together the contents of the exhibition. Once they had signed out of the building, they sat back down in the van and Billy took a slip of paper out of his pocket on which a series of letters and numbers was scrawled.

'You leaving yourself coded messages now Billy? Perry, Billy Perry, licenced to thrill.' Jenny made the shape of a gun with her fingers and started to hum the James Bond theme. Billy waited until she had finished and raised his eyebrows to her in an act of showing patience with her having fun.

'Some spy you would make.' Billy said as he took the Satnav from the dashboard of the van. 'It's a postcode.' Entering the code, he hit the button to plan route. As the machine calculated, he waited until it had finished and given a journey time of fifty minutes. 'Roll up for the magical mystery tour. Belt up Jen.' Billy chuckled as he put his own seat belt on.

'So, half an hour later, I will try again. How do you know where to start looking? Where did you get the postcode from and what bloody dossier?' Jenny pulled the belt across her chest. 'Or are you just trying to restrain me?' She twisted the belt around her wrists briefly in an imitation of manacles. When Billy turned his head side ways to look at her, she realised he was not in a playful mood.

'Which question do you want me to answer first, or shall I just go for all four at once?' Jenny screeched in mock frustration and put her head in hands or a few seconds. 'Sorry; let me have a go at them all as you have been incredibly patient with me today. We are going to find my grandparents' house, which is where both Elspeth and my Father were born. Doctor Miles worked with Elspeth on pulling together some information about her for my benefit before she died. She knew by then that she would never meet me and both she and the good Doctor thought that another death from cancer might set my recovery back. Additionally, I got North and South to do a bit of digging for me and I am amassing a fair amount of information on my grandparents. From the address in the dossier, I looked up the postcode so that we could go and see first-hand. Although the cameras we picked up today will not be charged, I already had one from our first visit, which is in the bag beside you.'

'So, we are taking a trip into the past to see if you can find your grandparents' house? At the same time, you are looking to take photographs for the exhibition.'

'Yup, that's about it, anything else?'

'Well yes, you didn't comment on the bondage' Billy looked across at her and saw her eyes were full of devilment. It was as if they had suddenly grown in size as she looked at him and waited for an answer. Billy processed five or six separate responses but realised they ranged from smutty to sleazy and figured verbal restraint was in order at this point.

'Not now.' Jenny looked deflated and was going to say something else but Billy continued 'But not never.' With this, he reached across and kissed her. Not just a peck or a gentle brush on the lips, but rough and hungrily. He put his hand in her long hair and pulled at it while they kissed deeply. After nearly a minute, he pulled away. 'Now, are you ready to set off?'

'Oh yes Billy. I am pretty much ready to go anywhere with you now; although I might suggest some other places later.' She sat back in her seat smiling. Billy put the van into gear and pulled out of the car park.

'Lewisham here we come.'

'You do know how to spoil a girl Billy, Billy Perry.' Jenny Smiled as she repeated his name. 'Take me away from all this; take me to Lewisham.'

The Perry Gene

*

The conversation on the journey was Spartan to say the least; Billy was now back into the land of family connections and all things Perry. Jenny sat quietly and pondered the change in Billy regarding the kiss. In fact, the most audible voice for the entire journey was the Satnav that for some bizarre reason was set to a Northern Irish accent, which started to grate after a while. The background music was by Philip Glass and Billy focused on it. He was a more modern composer who wrote subtly changing melodic sequences; these calmed Billy and generally, much improved his mood. This was another surprise to Billy as previously he had not been able to listen to any twentieth century classical composers. They had always been too chaotic for his orderly mind.

Eventually, as they entered the outskirts of Catford and started the slow crawl through Lewisham to their destination, Billy realised how much he appreciated the short cuts around his own neighbourhood. He could see cars disappearing down side streets only to reappear five minutes later, 200 yards ahead of him. Not knowing about short cuts like that was slowly winding him up again.

'Is it much further?' Jenny asked idly as she watched the world of South East London slide by.

'Well, I will give you credit for at least not asking *Are we there yet?*' Billy looked at the Satnav. 'Sorry, I am getting a bit bored of this traffic too. According to the Irishman, about a mile to go.'

The Perry Gene

'I am getting a bit stiff. Stretching my legs would be good. What's the name of the street?'

'Sunning Hill Road, based on the contents of the dossier.'

'That's a strange way to put it. Surely, it is that or it is not. Do you doubt it?'

'Just something that Doctor Miles said. He implied that Elspeth liked to tell a story and that the dossier may be more of what she wanted me to see. But then again, he could be wrong. At the end, I believe she was in a lot of pain and the fact she worked on information for me, a set of breadcrumbs if you will, says a lot. I don't think a dying woman in agony would waste her time; she sounded too practical for that.'

'You sound like you are starting to get a handle on Elspeth.'

'It's like doing a bloody jigsaw puzzle without a picture and having the bits provided by rival manufacturers. It just feels to me like everyone has a spin or an angle. I'm worried I could just be being paranoid now.'

'Billy, you are not getting paranoid, you are just showing signs of normality and being human. I can't imagine what you had to cope with in your head ten years ago, but what you have dealt with in six months and what it has done to you is nothing short of miraculous. You are a very different person from the one who first walked into our offices half a year ago.'

'Different good I hope?'

'Different good you know! Stop fishing, that's my job.' She paused and her face broke into a broad smile. 'Are we there yet?' Billy roared with laughter.

'If you ask for the toilet next, I swear I'm throwing you out; while moving.' Billy flicked the indicator to turn right. 'Anyway, we're here.' Once the traffic had passed, he turned into the road. 'See if you can find number twelve. I don't know what side it's on.' Jenny started to count the number almost under her breath.

'Over on the right Billy, but I don't know where you are going to park.' She scanned the street and almost in unison, they yelled and pointed to a place big enough for the van. 'So, what do you want to do now you're here? I don't think you can just take snapshots unless you ask first. If the owner sees you, they might get funny.'

'Time to play knock down Ginger I think.'

'You wouldn't?'

'No, I wouldn't, but I did as a kid.' Billy grabbed the small camera case and they both got out. He locked the van and they crossed the road before walking the fifty yards back to the house. Billy could hear voices inside. 'Well here goes nothing.' He rang the bell and stood back. There was an increase in the volume of the conversation inside making Billy think they had heard. Eventually there was the sound of shuffling feet. The door opened but only on a chain.

The Perry Gene

'Yes, what do you want? I'm not buying anything and I won't vote for your party, whatever lies you tell.' The voice belonged to a man who must have been pushing seventy.

'I am not selling or trying to get anything from you. I just want to ask your permission to take some photographs of your house. '

'Why?'

'Well I'm led to believe my grandparents lived here many years ago and I am trying to track down a little family history. If I am right, my Father and my Aunt were both born in this house.'

'You sure you're not after anything? That sounds like a load of old cobblers. Hold on. Mavis, Mavis, you got a minute, can you come to the door? My wife has a better memory than me. Now what did you say their names were?' Billy could hear a much slower shuffle approaching. From the sound of the walking pattern, Billy thought either a Zimmer frame or walking stick.

'Perry, Mr and Mrs Perry. I am Billy, their grandson.'

'Mavis, what was the name of the couple we bought the house from?'

'I believe they died in a car crash, so maybe I made a mistake?' said Billy, suddenly thinking he was on Elspeth's wild goose chase. As he said this, the door shut. He thought he had blown his chance and that he would be returning to the drawing board. Maybe Elspeth was making up stories. Suddenly the door reopened, a similarly aged but slightly frail looking woman had replaced the old man. Billy was right; a stick supported her on her right-hand side.

'Sorry about my husband dear, but you need to be careful these days. When you said about the car crash, I knew you weren't making it up. Nobody around here knows that detail to have been able to tell you. Come in, have some tea and tell me what you want to know'

'That is very kind, I'm Billy and this is Jenny, my…' Billy stopped and looked at Jenny 'my girlfriend I suppose.'

'Mavis, welcome to the wonderful world of Billy, yes we would love a cup of tea, thank you.' Jenny kissed him on the cheek as they walked in.

*

Thirty minutes later, and on the second cup of tea, Mavis had given a thorough background to the story of buying the house, which was by then vacant possession. They never met the people who owned it, but they knew from their solicitor that it belonged to a married couple who had died in a car crash. Fred, Mavis's husband, tried to add in his own comments from time to time, but a withering or knowing look from Mavis soon had him off to make more tea. Billy took it all in, learning about the house more than about his grandparents, but at least now, he was beginning to understand a little about their lives. It still did not quite explain the schism in the family. Mavis was filling in a few bits of detail about the two children, his Father and Aunt, when Billy suddenly realised that she should have been in unchartered territory. How could she know about his Grandparents if she bought their house after they died?

The Perry Gene

'Sorry, you were saying about my Father and Aunt growing up here, but you never met them. Do you mind me asking how you know?' Billy did not want it to sound like a cross examination, but he also needed to get any information while he could. Mavis and Fred were no spring chickens.

'Well we didn't live here when they were alive, but when we moved in we heard a lot of the stories from the other neighbours. Oh, I know people love to gossip, but the folks who lived either side of the house in number ten and in fourteen knew them well. They had both seen your Father and Aunt grow up. There were many stories about your Aunt especially. It turns out she was more of a Tomboy than your Father. He was very bookish, always sat reading somewhere, whereas she was a free spirit. '

'Well, I consider myself lucky to have come at this time Mavis, thank you. You could be the last remaining link to them, and to think I may never have heard these stories otherwise' said Billy.

'Well not quite the last link.'

'What do you mean?' Billy put his cup down and focused on Mavis.

'There is old Mrs Granger. She'll be going on what, ninety-three now?' Fred walked back into the room with a tray containing four more mugs of tea. 'Mrs Granger Fred, how old, ninety-three?' Fred nodded sagely.

'Who is Mrs Granger if you don't mind me asking?' Billy took the tea from the tray offered by Fred and sat back down on the sofa, but he perched forward on the edge. He was not sure of what to make of this information.

The Perry Gene

'I said before that the folks at number fourteen and number ten were here before us. Well the Crouches died ten years ago. They were number ten, nice couple, passed away within six months of each other.'

'And Mrs Granger?' Billy leaned towards Mavis so far that he almost tipped off the seat.

'Well she lost Mr Granger to Emphysema when he was still in his late sixties. A forty a day when he was in his prime. However, Mrs Granger lives on. She was a head-mistress; very strict. Used to teach piano to the local kids to make a bit of pin money.'

'And what happened to her, where is she now?'

'Well about three years ago, the house got too much for her. She had no kids to look after her. We did what we could but as you can see, we are getting on ourselves. Anyway, the council decided it was best for everyone if she was put in a home so that she could be looked after properly.' Billy was about to burst. Was there someone still alive that had known his grandparents? Could she fill him in about his Father and his Aunt's childhood? He tried to slow his breathing; Jenny was looking at him, seeing the state he was getting into and willing him to calm down. She reached across and took his hand to offer support.

'Do you know where she is Mavis?'

'I should bloody well hope so; we go to visit her once a week. It's a bus journey of about twenty minutes out to Erith. Nice place, warden controlled, own room, day room for cards. To be honest, I think we are eyeing it up for ourselves when the time is right.' Mavis reached up and took Fred's hand.   Almost comforting, but also aware of their own situation.

'Do you think she would talk to me?   Would you give me the address? Please.'

'Billy, I will write it down, but let us speak to her first on our next visit. We go on a Wednesday because that's the day we pick up our pension from the post office machine.'

'Right then, I will plan to go and see her next Saturday if that would be convenient.   I will leave you contact details in case of any problems. Now back to the reason we first showed up at your door.   Do you mind if we take a couple of pictures of the house? '

'You snap away love.   But finish your tea first.' Billy and Jenny drank their tea in silence and listened while Mavis continued to tell them stories about their time in the house.

After another twenty minutes, Billy got up to make his goodbyes and to say thank you to their hosts.   He quickly popped out into their rear garden, not much more than a postage stamp, but a place to start.   He knew about taking pictures technically but was still unsure about how his style would be, compared to Elspeth's.   Whereas she took action shots, his instruction was to obtain pictures of buildings.   However, it occurred to him that this house, probably built in the twenties, was no spring chicken.   It had seen better times, and he guessed that Fred and Mavis now struggled to do much in the way of maintenance.   He took snaps that captured the house as a whole; no holds barred, the decay was clear. The leaking guttering, the moss on the sheltered side of the roof, the stained paving slabs. He was taking pictures for about ten minutes when Jenny came out.

'Oi, David Bailey, don't forget the front.'

'Yeah, alright, this is trial and error you know.'

'Get a picture of Fred and Mavis while you're at it, they have been lovely and it would be a nice thing to do.' Billy again saw something very gentle and giving about Jenny that you only had to be around her for a while, away from work, to see. Billy walked around the side of the house, took a couple of pictures of the front and then knocked on the front door again. Mavis was already there opening it, so he assumed Jenny had said something.

'I'm ready for my close-up Mr DeMille,' she said in a patchy American accent. Fred was more of a curmudgeon but Billy could see the affection with which he held her. He took five pictures with the two of them together.

'If they come out ok, I will get you a print.'

'You can always email them,' said Fred. Billy looked perplexed.

'We're seventy years old, not one hundred and seventy. We have grandchildren all over the place and we use Skype a lot.' Mavis chirped.

'I've got the details,' Jenny added, 'come on boyfriend.' She took Billy's hand and dragged him towards the van. As they got inside, the elderly couple were still watching. 'We're going to be waved off, let's get moving so they are not on the doorstep all day.' Billy put on his seat belt, did not bother checking with the mirror, started the engine and pulled out, as there was no traffic. Jenny waved to Fred and Mavis on the way past. At the end of the road, Billy pulled out right and up Loampit Vale towards the city.

'Billy; girlfriend I suppose?' Jenny dug her fingertips into his ribs.

'What? It just never occurred to me how I would introduce you before. I was not sure how best to describe us. Friends seems a bit odd. I said girlfriend and then I suppose I, well...' Billy stumbled on the words.

'Panicked? Come on Billy let us get something straight from this day forward. You don't grab a girl and kiss her the way you did to me in the car park without being more than just friends. We have been pussy footing around this for a while, and I know you have issues, but it's time we're at least honest with each other, if not quite the rest of the world.'

'I'm good with that. I really enjoy your company and you make me smile. It's not like you don't already have a key!' He stifled a laugh.

'Oi, I'm not easy I will have you know.' She faked annoyance.

'No, my darling girl, you are anything but easy, but I think you are worth it.' When they pulled up to the lights, he plugged the address of Xavier's office into the Satnav and it started to dole out instructions. Jenny put the MP3 player on and selected Charlie Parker. It was her idea of driving music. Not so much the sound but more the fact that in London when driving, there was always the chance you would have to give someone 'the bird' as the American's would say. Billy was gloriously oblivious to this and simply drank in the sound. They drove silently save the voice of the relentless tyrant of the Six Counties with each new navigational instruction.

The Perry Gene

Chapter 14

On the Sunday night after dropping the pictures off, Billy and Jenny had a couple of decisions to make. Firstly, what to do about the party with Billy's dubious neighbours.   Billy was adamant that it was just a few drinks and there would be other people around so what harm could it do? Jenny was less convinced.

'Look Billy, North and South said to avoid them.' She had used this expression several times now when talking about the two ex-police officers. Usually Jenny grinned at the inherent humour of their names, but when Tony and Julia where the topic of conversation she was a lot more serious.   'You know she has the hots for you.   I would say anything young with a pulse, but she has already made a pass at you on more than one occasion.   Then on top of this you have Bermondsey's answer to the building mafia, who you already suspect of nefarious actions and possibly being complicit in the death of your ex-tenant. Why risk it?'

'That was very impressive.   Learned counsel makes a good argument. I like nefarious especially.'

'Don't take the piss Billy, I'm serious.   I see some of the seedier clients my boss has had over the years and I hear some scary stories. If the *boys in blue rinse* think it is a good idea to stay away, then why not stay away?'

'I need to meet Tony and ask some questions.   In a social setting we will be safe and the cougar won't be able to try anything with you there.   Also, don't you want to see who else he invites? Aren't you at all curious?   I'm betting it will be rich locals from the area, not down and out thugs from his day job.'

'What's this *we*?   I never agreed.'

'Well, you are my *girlfriend*.   It's going to look a little odd if I turn up without you. '

'I see; you have a point there.   We don't want to give the old cougar any reason to think you are available, or worse still, interested.'

'So, you will come?' Billy waved the invitation in front of her, 'it does say RSVP, so we really should Respondez.'

'Ok, but any sign of trouble and we leave, deal?'

'Deal. We will have a big day on Saturday then.   Are you free all day or just the evening?'

'I have nothing on, but I thought you were busy going to see this old lady?'

'Mrs Granger, yes, assuming that once Fred and Mavis talk to her, she is happy with the idea, I want to go on Saturday morning.   But I want you to come with me if you don't mind.'

'Are you sure this isn't something you would rather do on your own? It might be upsetting.   What if she knows details about your grandparents' death?'

'I am hoping she does.   North and South have provided me with a bit of background on the crash from newspaper clippings of the time, but it's a few column inches, nothing detailed.'

The Perry Gene

'You can collect me on the way if I am getting my directions correct?'

'Yes, that will be fine, then we can grab some food while we are out. We should have plenty of time to talk to her before coming back for the party.'

I will drop a card through their door tomorrow night after work to accept then.

And with that the subject was closed.

*

Billy received an email from Mavis on Wednesday afternoon saying that Mrs Granger would be happy to see them on Saturday, although it did suggest she drifted in an out a little. Mavis was more euphemistic about it, but the point was made loud and clear; the old lady was not as with it as she had once been. Billy thought that anything was better than nothing and felt he was fortunate someone was still alive who could remember the family he never knew. With a little gentle prompting from Jenny, he had sent flowers to Mavis to say thank you. He figured that if Mavis was happy then Fred would be too.

The rest of the week was spent back to back with work. Now there were going to be three of them in the company, once Pete had found his new apprentice, Billy decided he wanted to make the whole outfit a little more professional. He and Jenny worked on a logo for the company that would be recognisable and help to spread the word to increase business. He visited a local printer and got stationery made up and then to a workwear outfitter to order polo shirts with the new logo on the chest and the name on the sleeve with a website address. He thought phone numbers would be a bit naff, but this was a more modern and subtle form of advertising. Pete was not convinced when he was told about the new uniform, but when Billy explained he got on board.

'I'm not asking you to do anything I am not prepared to do myself. I will be wearing the shirt going forward whenever I am on a job. If you don't like polo shirts, I'm happy to have some normal shirts or even tee-shirts made up. You can wear what you like below the waist, jeans, chinos, combats, I am easy. But I want us to be recognisable as a company. This way when you find your new apprentice, he will come into a professional looking organisation.'

'Alright, I get it and yes, it actually sounds like a good idea. But no bloody MacDonald's style badges with stars on.' Pete was smiling when he said this and Billy knew he was on board. As business had picked up and Billy had been distracted by events elsewhere, Pete had become both key to the operation and had also continued to grow a friend. Billy trusted Pete with everything, and he knew that his business was in safe hands. Safe and strangely large hands, in fact it was the only real physical difference between the two of them. Same hair, same eyes, almost as if the arcades were breeding some kind of clones in secret. In fact, since Billy was going to lead by example and wearing the company shirt, he hoped that it would not make telling them apart even harder for the clients to distinguish them. They already got confused occasionally by people they met on their newer contracts.

'Have you done anything worth a star yet today? Come on,' Billy clapped his hands, 'chop chop. Time is money and all that. I have got seven pubs to work at today, so I will head off now. If you fancy a pint and a catch up, we could do beers after work on Friday?' Billy walked off to get in the car. He realised if things carried on like this he would need another van. He thought to himself, *better make sure this new guy can drive.* He was going to mention it to Pete, but he figured it could wait until Friday and he was running a little behind on his schedule. Being Billy, he would skip lunch to make up.

*

On Saturday morning, Billy was slow to rise. The clock-watching automaton of six months ago was slowly disappearing as the new Billy emerged. Part of this was a change in him, but part of it was the effort required to juggle all of the things he now had going on in his life. The business was growing from strength to strength as word of his steadily growing empire spread in the landlord community. His fairness and reliability won him a lot of respect in what was often both a cutthroat and fly-by-night profession. He had a couple of rival firms approaching him about working together so as not to overlap or undercut. He was holding them at bay at this point, but once Pete got his new help Billy might have time to do more in that area. He realised as much from working with Xavier on the exhibition as he did from his day to day job, that networking was everything these days. He knew he also had to do something with his website. Design was not his strong point, so it was currently very basic. He thought it might be something to give the apprentice to do when he joined.

Xavier was also keeping him busy. He had called Billy on Wednesday and as Billy was flat out during the day, he had shown up at the apartment that evening to discuss plans.   This being Xavier, it was neither a quick nor sober affair.   Billy could just about keep the jester in the box, but at the same time, Xavier seemed to be seeing something in Billy that he liked.

'Are you sure you never met Elspeth?' he asked at one point.

'Looking at the timelines, the split happened when I was between one and two.   She did visit the hospital after my breakdown' Xavier had looked away at that point, as if uncomfortable, 'but I was in no state to know anyone at that time.   And it's ok, I can see that look on your face, I don't mind talking about it.   Doctor Miles thinks it is good for me.   Anyway, why do you ask?'

'Well you know the whole nature versus nurture thing?'

'Not exactly, go on.'

'Well there is lot of debate about whether it is your genes or your environment that impact the way you act and think.   The more times I meet you, the more convinced I am that there is something in it.   Especially now we are planning this event together.'

'You mean you trying to railroad me into getting your own way?'

'There it is again!   That comment is pure Elspeth.   I am seeing more and more of her mannerisms in you.'

'Really? How odd.   Anything else?'

'Gestures, your approach to business, your inquisitiveness.   That's what made her a good journalist and photographer in the end.'   Xavier left the comment there and moved onto other business but the seed was sown.

The Perry Gene

Billy spent the rest of the week pondering this. His mind drifted back to the neatness of the storage unit. Was it pure Billy, or maybe, just maybe it was really pure Elspeth? As he slowly slipped the shackles imposed on him by his domineering Mother, he wondered what lay underneath and where it came from. Maybe Xavier was right; it was possible that he had something of the makeup of Elspeth, she was his Father's Sister after all. Now on Saturday morning as he rose late from his bed, he considered what else Mrs Granger might reveal when they met.

He showered, dressed and then rather than make breakfast, he texted Jenny to see if she wanted to eat on the way or on their return. Within a minute he got a response that she would love to eat first, so he grabbed his keys and headed for the stairs. As he opened his front door, Tony and Julia were emerging from the lift, loaded down with carrier bags. He guessed provisions for the evening ahead.

'You look like you've got a load of work to do before this evening' said Billy. 'You must be Tony' he went to shake hands but realised there was not one to spare. 'Sorry I can see you're weighed down there. We can chat later. What time do you want us?' Tony half smiled but he was not giving much away or even acting as if he wanted Billy there.

'*Us* darling, I thought it would, just be you?' Julia oozed charm in such a Hollywood manner.

'Oh, I'm sorry, I assumed you were inviting us as a couple. Did I not RSVP for two?' He paused for a second to let the comment sink in, but continued before she could respond. 'You've met my girlfriend Jenny before?' Billy pressed the lift call button again as the doors had shut and he wanted to get away from this awkward moment.

'But of course, both you and Jenny are invited' said Tony in a slightly stilted way. Julia did not look happy, but Tony seemed to at least relax a little. Maybe he was happy that his wife could not flirt so much if Jenny was in the room. 'See you at 7.30 for 8? There will be at least eight of us at the moment, but you never know until the night who might turn up.'

'Ok, thanks, we will see you then.' He pressed the button for the basement and felt the relief wash over him as the doors clanged shut.

*

He picked Jenny up at her place just after eleven and reprogrammed the Satnav with the address of the home. As he was not sure of traffic, he thought it best to get out to Erith first and eat there so that they would not be late for their arranged meeting with Mrs Granger. Mavis had offered to be there, but apparently the old lady was happy to meet Billy without her, so they had agreed a time of 2pm on the phone.

As they pulled into the outskirts of the town, Billy saw a large pub with a carpark which didn't look terribly busy.

'You think this place will work?' Billy asked Jenny.

'Looks good to me. It's a pub, an all-day breakfast, we're not looking for Michelin Stars, and this place should be fine.' Billy parked and they walked into the pub. It was almost empty and Billy found himself wondering where the punters were for the cars in the carpark. He guessed they might have been left there the night before after a few beers. They chose a table by the window and ordered some food from the bar. Billy got an orange juice and lemonade and Jenny had a Coke.

'So, do you know what you are going to ask her?' Jenny said and took a slurp of her Coke noisily through a straw. Billy gave her a look as if to say *how old are you*, but then realised this would have been his Mother's reaction and smiled.

'Lots of questions have gone through my head, but it's difficult as I have no idea what she knows, if that doesn't sound too odd.' Billy looked over his shoulder to see their two breakfasts appearing from the kitchen. 'That was quick, they must have it on a hot plate.' The barmaid laid the food down and disappeared to get some ketchup and mustard. 'Anything she can tell me about the accident and about my Father and Aunt, I guess. Mavis said she was there at the time and implied she knew my grandparents well. She might know more details of what happened, she might not. At this point, I don't even know how long they were neighbours.'

'Well take your time with her. She is likely to be frail and she might even be a bit senile. She is in a home after all.'

'Mavis said she was only there for her physical health. She told me she thought that most of the time Mrs Granger was really switched on. She spends a lot of time doing crossword puzzles and jigsaws to keep her brain active. Let's see how well it works. By the way, I meant to say, I finally met Tony and I think I may have upset Julia.'

'When and how? As long as you haven't upset Tony we should be fine.'

'They were coming out of the lift when I left. I asked about what time we were expected and Julia made a big deal about thinking it was just me coming.'

'Oh, so do I get out of it now? You know I was never keen.'

'No, I said you were my girlfriend and Tony made it clear you were welcome. I get the feeling he was relieved you were coming so that Julia doesn't get out of hand,'

'So close. I almost got away.' She smiled and made a small gesture of forming a tiny gap between her thumb and finger and looking though it at him. She then stopped and squeezed his hand. 'But I do like you referring to me as your girlfriend again now. It feels like you have finally come out of denial.'

'Behave you. I also told Pete. I am proud to be with you. In fact, I wondered if you wanted to stay at mine tonight.' Billy could feel the blood rising in his cheeks as he got a little red.

'You planning to have your wicked way with me?' Jenny knew Billy felt awkward with the way that had come out and now he was on the back foot she was going to milk the situation for all the humour she could.

'It's not like that. Look there are two beds. I just wondered about you staying. No funny business.'

The Perry Gene

'Let's get one thing straight Mister, if I'm staying, it's not in the bloody spare room. I have been waiting for you patiently to move this relationship on a little further. Sex isn't the only thing that happens in bed. We can just sleep if that's what you want, but I think it's a step in the right direction and it stops you spending a fortune on late night taxis, which you have been very sweet doing lately by the way.' She reached across the table and gave him a kiss on the cheek and then went to sit back down. Before she could move, Billy grabbed her and pulled her closer to kiss her properly. Once he let her go she settled back into her seat. 'Can we drop past my place on the way and put some things in a bag?'

'Wow, talk about me being a quick worker, you planning on moving in?' It was now Billy's turn to have some fun.

'Easy Tiger, just a change of clothes, a toothbrush and washbag.' The grin on her face revealed she was happy with the concept though. Billy walked over to the bar to order two coffees as they still had over an hour to kill before their appointment at the home. He waited as the lady used the complex coffee machine that seemed to be ubiquitous in every pub these days. He turned to see Jenny watching him, or more importantly staring at his rear. She put her hands up to signify she had been caught, causing Billy to shake his head mockingly and then to tut. Finally, he roared with laughter and then collected the two coffees from the bar before returning to the table.

*

The Perry Gene

As planned, it was only a few minutes' drive to the home and having got the post code entered in to the Satnav, Billy found it easily. Fortunately, there was also visitor's parking, so the usual issues of where to put the car went away. He pulled into the space, shut off the engine and exhaled.

'You ready for this?' She asked him as he went to open the door. 'You sure you want me to come with you?'

'To answer in order, no I'm not sure I'm ready and yes I do want you there. You were great with Fred and Mavis, you seemed to know how to deal with them. I have not spent a lot of time around old people. Besides, you are becoming a big part of my life and it feels good having you here.' Billy reached over and gave her a soft kiss on the cheek before opening his door and getting out. Jenny got out of the car and walked around to join him. She took his hand and as they walked together up to the front door of the big Victorian house it was opened by a lady in dark blue nurse's uniform.

'Mr Perry, I presume?'

'Yes, Billy Perry' said Billy 'and this is my girlfriend Jenny. Is Mrs Granger available still?'

'Oh yes, she has not stopped talking about getting a new visitor since Mavis was here on Wednesday. She is in the day room; I'll show you.' The Sister guided them through the ground floor of the converted sprawling Victorian pile. The first thing that struck Billy was the smell. He couldn't put his finger on it, was it disinfectant or something more lingering coming from the slowly ageing bodies? He felt strangely nauseous and he realised nobody in his family had got old.   He had so little experience of this.   For his grandparents it was a car crash.   His parents and his Aunt all falling foul of terminal illnesses and premature deaths.   It made him wonder about Xavier's comments about nature and nurture.   He had never spent time considering his future before, but now he wondered, how many turns of the calendar did he have in front of him?   He looked across at Jenny for support and she seemed equally uncomfortable.   When she saw him looking she produced a weak smile, but it seemed false which was unusual from his experience of her. He guessed it was something he should ask her afterwards.

They finally entered a large and well-lit glass extension to the building. Sunlight poured into the room through net curtains.   In the far corner there was a large flat screen television showing the horse racing.   Several male residents were watching and holding newspapers, some heavily marked up. The Sister showed them to the opposite corner where sitting on her own was probably the oldest woman Billy had ever seen.   She was tiny and her arms were thin.   She looked like she would snap in a strong wind.   Billy imagined having to get up close and listen while she whispered her truths but when she saw them, a broad smile broke across her face and she spoke in a powerful voice.

'You must be Elspeth's boy, Billy?' she reached out to shake his hand and then Jenny's.

'I'm Jenny, Billy's girlfriend' she said as if to legitimise her presence.

'Oh, I know who you are young lady.   Mavis has a keen eye for detail, she told me all about you two.   In her day, Mavis was a lovely little artist;

mostly pen and ink. That eye for detail never left her, she got you to a T. And you Billy, I think I would have known you, you have the same bone structure as Elspeth. There's something else. The eyes, I think you have her eyes. She was quite the looker when she was young.'

'Don't I have anything of my Father?' Billy was not quite sure how genetics worked. This felt part history, part science lesson.

'Not much. I would say you got your grandparents' traits, but they skipped a generation in your Father. Not such a bad thing. They were like chalk and cheese you know, Elspeth and Thomas. Her strong and outgoing, him quiet and bookish. Even before the crash, once he had met your Mother, your Father was already becoming a stranger. We saw lots of Elspeth when she came back from her assignments, unlike your Father. Once he met that woman we didn't see much of them again.'

'What about me? Did you ever meet me?' Billy was now transfixed. In front of him sat the Svengali of his family history. A snake charmer with his life story. You wanted to look away in case you heard bad things, but you knew you had to watch even if the snake ended up biting you.

'Twice as I recall. When you were a babe in arms, maybe only a month old you were brought around to meet your grandparents. And then one more time, just before the crash. You were walking, but I don't think you were two at that point.' She stopped and her eyes drifted to the ceiling. After a few seconds, she continued. 'A bright blue sailor suit, that's what your Mother had dressed you in. You looked so smart, but you were not allowed to play. Even then she was controlling and wanted you to be kept clean.' She looked around and spotted a large folder. 'Hand me that will you.' Billy picked up the aged and weighty tome. She opened it up about half way through to where a book mark had been placed. It revealed black and white photographs. There were three pictures of a street party. From the bunting Billy could see it was a major event, but he couldn't place the date. 'Queen's Coronation in case you are wondering. 1953. See the couple at the end in their late thirties?'

'Yes, is that my grandparents?'

'No, that's my husband and me. Look three seats down, the slightly older couple; that's your Grandmother and opposite your Grandfather. And so, guess who the two children are you see next to them?'

'Elspeth and my Father?'

'That's right.' Billy looked at the picture, trying to get a feel for the scene. His grandparents seemed happy. His Aunt had something about her even then. Billy did a quick mental calculation; his Aunt would have been about eight and his Father six. He could see a spark in her, whereas his Father just looked bored. 'And do you know what is even more strange?'

'No, go on. It appears to be a day for strange news.'

'Your Grandfather took the picture.'

'But you said he was in it?'

'Timers on cameras are not new. It was your Grandfather who initially had the interest in photography that got Elspeth hooked. He was so proud of her and what she became. Sorry to say, I don't think the same could be said of your Father and his choices in life.'

'Would you mind if a borrowed a couple of these pictures? We are putting together a final exhibition of Elspeth's work and this would be amazing to use.'

'Billy, I left the whole album out for you. I have others, but when I am gone I have nobody left who will want them. Mavis told me quite a bit when she came and I am happy to help in any way.' Mrs Granger sipped at the slowly cooling tea that had been brought to her. For all her strength of voice, she suddenly looked tired. It was as if the effort of recalling the past had somehow weakened her. The Sister came over.

'I think she needs her rest now. Can you wrap it up quickly please?'

'Its fine Sister,' the old lady said 'we're done for today, but Billy and Jenny will come back with more questions in future I feel. Just don't leave it too long dears, none of us are getting any younger.' Billy reached out to shake her hand, but Jenny bent over and gave her a gentle hug and kissed her on both cheeks.

'Thank you for helping Billy with this, it means a lot.' Billy then followed suit and goodbyes said, they were shown out of the room and back to the car park. Billy carried the precious cargo, like some holy relic.

'Back to your place for a change of clothes?' Billy asked Jenny as he started the car.

'Yes, that would be good.' She replied.   Billy thought she seemed quiet.

'You ok, you didn't look that comfortable in there?'

'I have spent enough time in places like that with my grandparents, they are not how I would want to finish my life.' Billy didn't respond, but as he drove off, his mind returned to his own mortality and his family's history of ill-health.   Maybe there were advantages to that in the end.

The Perry Gene

Chapter 15

Billy was surprised at how quickly a little bag could be packed as he waited outside Jenny's flat. Earlier that morning was the first time he even seen the outside but he was not quite ready to go in yet. It appeared that she was not ready for that step either as she promised it would not take long and left him in the car with a peck on the cheek. The only thing that surprised Billy was how large a *little* bag could be, and he suspected the majority of the contents may have already been prepared, just in case. When she appeared at the car door, she was carrying a back pack that Billy would have taken up Kilimanjaro or perhaps on a gap year to Thailand. Jenny smiled self-consciously as she put it on the back seat.

'When I suggested staying the night, I didn't know you were moving in' Billy said gently. He wanted her to know he was joking and not having second thoughts. Jenny looked relieved and appreciated him making the awkward moment easier.

'Girls have *things* Billy. That's how we roll. Besides you wouldn't want me showing you up tonight, would you?'

'I am sure you will look lovely. Shall we head straight back to the apartment or do you want to stop for a drink first?' Billy, still wearing his seat belt, started the car and pressed the home button the Satnav. Funny how the apartment had rapidly become home and the family house when mentioned was now relegated to being his Mother's house. Not Mother and Father's, just Mother's. It was now on the market and since Mr Transon had engaged the house clearance and decorations teams, Billy had not been back. Jenny had asked him about it, possibly intrigued to see where he grew up, but when Billy did not take the hint, she guessed he needed to stay away.

'Let's drop the car off at the apartment and go for a walk along the river. I would like you to myself for a while before I have to share you with the crowd. This whole girlfriend thing is still rather new and it feels like the test drive has gone well. Maybe we need to spend a little time on our own running up a few miles.'

'There are a couple of galleries on the South Bank under the Oxo Tower which are normally open. We could go and have a look and I might get some ideas as to how Xavier is going to run this exhibition. Afterwards we can grab a glass of wine or a snack before we have to get ready. You sure you're still happy with this?'

'Well after King Tony gave his consent earlier, I don't think we have a choice. Once you are granted a royal audience, you have to attend' Jenny smirked and looked at Billy. She realised he was not going to pull away from the kerb until she did her seatbelt up. They looked directly at each other for a moment and then she aped the movements of a gunslinger; hand going to her hip showing she was the fastest draw in the South; South London in this case. He saw the humour and laughed as she blew imaginary smoke from her fingertips. With this act of compliance complete, Billy signalled and pulled out into the traffic for the ten-minute journey back to the apartment.

The Perry Gene

When they arrived, they parked in the garage and called the lift. Billy figured he was safe from Julia's advances while accompanied by his new talisman. Besides she would be busy preparing for the party. As they exited the lift outside the apartment he realised how wrong he could be. Standing there, fiddling with a piece of paper she was attaching to the door, was Julia.

'Hello my Darlings. Excited about tonight? Oh Sweetie, you look divine. Such an effort you have made' the barbed comments directed to Jenny who was still in her jeans and tee-shirt. Jenny impressed Billy with the way she handled herself. He knew she was a professional at dealing with people quite often not at that their best. *Let's face it* she had said, *you don't see a solicitor when things are going well.*

'Just my old rags I put on to help Billy run errands. I have my dress hanging in the wardrobe inside' was Jenny instant reply. 'No point your boyfriend having all that extra wardrobe space and not using it, is there.' Billy liked the retort and was about to shepherd Jenny away when Julia responded.

'I didn't realise you were using any. You are a fast worker Billy. Well I can't keep chatting all afternoon, I have things to put on plates and glasses to polish. See you two later.' With this she disappeared through the doorway shutting it behind her, leaving Billy and Jenny in silence. They looked at each other and Billy opened the apartment door. Closing it behind him he turned to Jenny.

'What was that comment all about? '

'Which one, I try not to listen to what she has to say.' Jenny started to carry the backpack up the stairs to the bedroom.

'Commenting on whether you had clothes in my wardrobes. How would she know if you were using any? I thought it was an odd thing to comment on. It implied she had been inside snooping, but she can't get in, so how can have done?'

'Billy, she is just trying to play mind games. She is hacked off that you have a girlfriend and that she can't get her claws into you. I think you are lucky to have me based on your theory of what happened to Chris Deville.' Billy ran up the stairs after her and wrapped his arms around her.

'I am starting to realise I am lucky to have you for lots of reasons.'

'I don't want to be picky but you have not *had* me at all yet; don't leave it too long to rectify that please.' He kissed her on the back of her neck and lifted the backpack from her shoulder. Taking her hand, he led the rest of the way up the final few stairs and into his bedroom.

'I think the gallery can wait until later, don't you?' Billy dropped the backpack unceremoniously onto the chair and drew in close to kiss Jenny.

'Agreed, but I really would like a shower after all the running around, Lover boy.'

'As would I' he said, starting to remove his shirt and heading for the ensuite. Jenny did not need any further encouragement and proceed to pull her jeans off before making her way into the bathroom.

*

The Perry Gene

Having not made the gallery, Billy and Jenny decided to have a glass of wine and watch the river go by before they braved the move across to Julia and Tony's.   It was now 7.50 and although they were both dressed to go out, neither was making a beeline for the door.   The bottle of wine looked inviting and Billy considered pouring another glass.   However, Jenny could see where his attention was and got up, scooped it off the table and put it back in the fridge.

'No, we are going to go to this event and get it over with.   You never know, they might be pussy cats when we get there.' Jenny said it confidently enough but there was definitely a sense of hesitation on her face.

'Pussy cats?   A cougar and an old Cheetah is more like it.' Billy beamed with this feline analogy.   'Ok, let's go then.'   Jenny had picked up flowers earlier and Billy took a bottle of champagne from the fridge in an effort to be congenial.

'Now be nice Billy.   You know what they say, *Least Said, Soonest Mended.*'

'You know I never really got that if I'm honest.   It's one of those bloody expressions my Mother would have used, you know, like *you know what thought did.*' Jenny walked over to him.   'Just like the film *Roadhouse.*   Be nice until it's time not to be nice.'

'And when will I know when it's time not to be nice?' Billy enquired. Jenny leaned towards him and kissed him long and hard.   When she pulled away, she held his face and simply said,

The Perry Gene

'I'll tell you when.'

*

The first hour had flown by and remarkably it was all going rather well. Surprisingly, when he was not menacing for the Southern Counties, Tony could be charming. He was still that brooding hulk that Billy had first spied from the window of the apartment, and this was reinforced by the barrel chest and rather squat physique. But with a classy designer shirt and Armani jeans he knew how to set the right tone. Billy also thought that the hair was a little too dark for his age, maybe a touch of dye to hide the grey?

Julia had introduced them around with enough *loveys* and *darlings* to keep a West End show in encores for months. The other guests at the party appeared to be affluent and amiable. Billy figured they were more about social climbing and acceptability than anything to do with Tony's business. Nobody had driven so Billy assumed they were all local residents of the area and he wondered if this was a regular occurrence. There had been no mention on the invitation of a special event to explain the rationale for the evening. After a while it became clear that this was something that happened infrequently but as a way of catching up. Tony and Julia appeared to be returning a few previous hosting invitations and this was also a way to introduce their new neighbour.

Julia had gone to more expense than trouble as the bubbles were flowing but the finger food looked more like it had all come from a high-priced packet than having been made fresh by her own fair hands. Billy thought he

The Perry Gene

might test the water on that point and ask about the catering, but he received a kick from Jenny as a reminder that he was to be on his best behaviour.

Over the next hour, two guests drifted away citing an early start in the morning, due to the horse racing at Ascot. This led to a fairly lengthy exchange on the subject with Julia getting more animated. It became clear that Tony had some part share in a race horse, although what was less clear was whether it was a leg or just a hoof. Tony went out on to the balcony for a smoke and left them to it as Billy guessed he had probably heard the stories about the pony once too often. Or maybe it was something else, he could not be quite sure. Julia was recounting a couple of the races where *Balcombe Tunnel* had won or been placed and how they had really enjoyed the champagne that evening. All the story telling appeared to make her thirsty as her rate of alcohol intake seemed to be increasing rapidly along with a noticeable slur.

Fifteen minutes later and the pair of accountants from the next building said their goodbyes to Tony and air-kissed Julia's cheeks. The man, Philip, shook hands with Billy and mumbled something about doing it again. Jenny on the other hand received the full treatment from his partner Fliss. She gave her a huge hug, kiss and then whispered something in her ear. With this they saw themselves out leaving just six now. Jenny could see the way this was going. As the evening wore on Julia was becoming rapidly intoxicated and with this her animation and volume level rose. Jenny was wondering if this might be a pattern, letting the guests know when it was time to make themselves scarce to avoid any awkwardness.

The Perry Gene

Although the light was now starting to fade it was still a beautiful warm evening so Billy walked out onto the balcony. The OCD in him was still strong and he was intrigued to see what differences there were in the view from his neighbour's apartment. The two residences did not quite mirror of each other and this apartment extended out slightly further than Billy's. Billy noticed immediately that if he leaned out, then he could actually see into his own lounge and this made him feel just a little uneasy. He decided he needed to be careful what he got up to in view of his neighbours and not to wander round half dressed. It also suddenly occurred to him that Tony could have actually seen his wife inside the apartment with Chris. The thought made him shudder physically and as he did so he heard someone walking up behind him.

'Someone walk over your grave Billy?' The way Tony spoke made Billy shiver even more. It felt full of menace. Something was stirring in Billy and he realised it was time for fight or flight.

'No, I was just thinking about your old neighbour Chris Deville' Billy paused and turned to look at Tony 'must have been a bit of a blow; especially for your wife.' Something flashed across Tony's face but Billy was not sure what it was. Recognition, a memory, a vision of seeing Deville with his wife possibly? But as soon as it appeared it was gone. Tony was not drinking heavily, unlike his wife, and Billy figured he was the one who liked to stay in control. Billy thought he must be the late-night whisky type. He could picture him waiting until everyone was gone; until his wife was sparked out in bed or on the sofa beside him and sitting there with an old single malt. A drink that cost real money, aged eighteen years or more; dark and peaty. A large measure, slowly consumed as a fire burned within him and the alcohol fuelled the flames. Now Billy could see that the regular pattern of the night for Tony and Julia was repeating itself and Tony was bracing himself for déjà vu.

'Why do you say that?' Tony turned away from Billy, lit a cigarette and blew the first puff of smoke out towards Tower Bridge. Billy followed his eye-line and watched in wonder at something he had failed he see in his entire time at the apartment so far. The roadway that ran between the two towers was splitting and lifting. The bridge was about to open. In the distance beyond Billy could see one of the sumptuous Russian pleasure cruisers that docked for a few days at a time in the Port of London. They could only get in and out at high tide and so this one had taken the chance to slip its moorings and head out to sea.

'Oh, I found Deville's diary. It just made reference to someone called J. I just assumed your wife was being a good neighbour. I guess you must be busy with work. In all the time I have been here, this is only the second time we have met, the first being earlier today. Although I have seen you keeping vigil from time to time. I thought it was nice they struck up a friendship and that she had someone to keep her company while you were away.'

'Well, yes, it was good that they got on. He was quite the little gossip and she loved that. He also had some fairly arty friends who turned up from time to time. Julia used to love that side of your Aunt's life. She was in her element when they all descended on the apartment for a party. Air-kisses and art; camp and camaraderie. It was all a bit false for me, not what I was brought up with.'

'So, it must have been a shock him committing suicide like that. She must have been upset?'

'Well, to be honest, I think things had cooled by then. I think she considered him a bit of a flirt and so stopped spending time with him.'

'Yes, the diary said as much.' With this Tony turned back to Billy, suddenly the bubbling anger erupting onto his face.

'What is it you're getting at Billy? You keep going on about this diary. What do you think you know?' Billy ignored the question and went to the edge of the balcony to look down.

'Bit of a long drop. What would you say, fifty feet or more? You could make a mess going over one of these. Makes you wonder doesn't it?' Billy paused, took a sip from his drink, and left the question hanging there in the air between them. 'So, you're in building construction I hear?' Carefully side-stepping the last two unanswered questions, Billy knew his window of opportunity of pulling the tail on the tiger was getting perilously small. Tony stopped and took another draw on his cigarette. The change of tack had obviously wrong footed him.

'Yes, that's right, building management and refurbishment.' The words toppled out like they lacked the support of scaffolding to shore them up. Billy assumed Tony must now be trying to work out what Billy was up to.

The Perry Gene

'You working on anything particular at the moment? Business must be good if you own a race horse; I hear they are money pits at the best of times.'

'Julia loves to talk big, especially after a few drinks. We owned a share in a horse. In fact, it was an eighth and even that had some tax benefits for me according to my accountant. Damned thing cost me more than I ever made off it. But yes, we have consolidated a lot of the portfolio into one main project.' Billy had heard Transon talk like this and he knew these were not Tony's words, but maybe his accountant's. He was a thug, he had learned the trick of parroting the right lines to the right people in order to obtain finance, but that was all. He was a wolf in businessman's clothing and Billy realised that North and South were right. However, he needed to hang in there for just a little while longer before getting away.

'Oh, that's interesting. Would you be able to tell me where this project is or is it a confidential business secret?'

'No secret. We are renovating a large apartment block down by the railway; just over a mile from London Bridge. It was full of down and outs and squatters, but they left when we started work. We are going to have a very nice set of apartments for rich city folk and Julia and I will retire on the profits with a bit of luck.'

'By the railway you say?'

'Yes, we are hoping the area will be the next Bermondsey in terms of property. Borough tube is close and there are great buses into the city; not that these city types take the bus.'

The Perry Gene

'So fairly close the Flag and Staff then?' At the point Billy said this, Jenny walked out onto the balcony. Tony stopped and stared at Billy. He knew he had walked into the biggest bear trap ever and Billy was watching to see what Tony did next.

'We thought you had got lost out here' Jenny said sensing the dead air that hung between the two men.

'Or jumped?' said Billy. Tony went to speak but Billy continued 'No, Tony was just telling me about his business and now he has finished his cigarette I think we were about to come in, is that right Tony?' Tony stared at him for about ten seconds and then stubbed out his cigarette and threw the end over the balcony towards the river.

'Yes, I think we are done here.' Tony pushed past Jenny and walked back into the apartment. Jenny looked at Billy, said nothing, but turned her head as if to question what was going on. Billy very briefly and discretely shook his head to say, not now and not here. She nodded and then she grabbed his arm and walked back into the apartment.

Billy could see a change immediately. The slightly loud Julia was now in full force drunk mode. She was flirting with the male of the last remaining couple other than Billy and Jenny. Billy had spoken to them earlier. Kevin was a Compliance Officer in a bank, fairly senior, his Spanish wife Maria was in Risk. It had not meant much to Billy at the time but he was now feeling his current course of action was fairly risky. He had little experience of

Corporate life but whatever Maria's work skill set was, he knew one thing. She was not good at hiding her body language when it came to her husband being dragged around the make-shift dance floor of the lounge. The music which had been little more than background earlier had been ramped up in volume and the easy listening mood had been replaced by seventies disco. Julia was currently singing along to *Dancing Queen* while proving in reality she was anything but. When the song finished, the brooding Maria made a rapid move to recover her husband. Tony walked over to Julia and had a quiet word in her ear. Julia's level of drunkenness could now be judged by the effort she made to act sober. Billy had seen this enough in the pubs and clubs when fixing machines. The late afternoon drinker who had not gone back to work after lunch but rather had continued with their libation. Eventually there comes a point when the bar staff refuse to serve on the manager's instruction. The act the drinker then goes into to convince them that they were sober in order to get another drink was now rather reminiscent of this. Billy saw Tony grip her arm and she pulled away from the pain he obviously inflicted.

Julia marched into the kitchen area to get another glass of champagne. By this time, the corporate couple were shaking Tony's hand and saying their goodnights. Billy knew it was the right moment to get out, but it was going to be awkward to leave at the same time as the other guests. Jenny had sensed the mood and was raising her eyebrows. He mouthed to her *'One more and let's go'* to which she nodded her head slightly. Julia approached them with a bottle of champagne and poured some clumsily into their glasses; in Jenny's case, over the glass and onto the floor and her shoes.

'Oh, look at me, so clumsy' she slurred 'let me clear it up.' She walked over to the sink and got a kitchen towel. When she returned, she got on her knees and started to wipe the floor. Then when that was clean, she started trying to clean off the champagne from Jenny's shoes. Jenny went to protest but Julia took her leg with one hand rubbed the shoe with the other.

'It's ok Julia, they're not damaged. I can clean them later.' Julia however was ignoring Jenny and now where some wine had splashed on Jenny's leg, she was wiping it dry. She looked up into Billy's face and then rubbed a little higher on Jenny's leg. 'Julia, I don't think there is anything left now, you can stop.' Julia licked her lips and rubbed above Jenny's knee.

'Maybe Billy likes it' slurred Julia. Jenny pulled away and walked over to Billy at the same time as Tony moved in and half lifted, half dragged his wife off the floor.

'Get up woman, you're making a fool of yourself, again.' Tony was holding back the anger, but it was obvious from the force he pulled her up that he was furious with her display.

'Billy, you're a real man, I bet you like a bit of girl on girl.' Finally, it was there, all trace of the lovey darling gone and now the Essex girl revealed. Working class and upwardly mobile, she said as much about Tony's roots as hers. Tony pulled her to him. 'Ouch, you're hurting me, you bastard.'

The Perry Gene

'Careful Tony, she bruises easily' Billy said. Jenny looked at him with eyes wide. She knew Billy was pushing Tony to see what he would say, but this was not a game they had agreed. Billy seemed to be singing to his own tune. Then she saw it, as if in an epiphany. Xavier, Mrs Granger, her boss, the good Doctor were all noticing it come to the fore; inside Billy was the inner Elspeth and her genes were now on display. This is the behaviour that had got her into trouble with ivory smugglers and gun runners and somehow it had surfaced in Billy. Something had appeared in him that was largely dormant until now. He was standing up to Bully. Not just ignoring it, but stepping in.

'What do you mean by that, you nosey little sod?' Tony had gone almost white with rage. Spittle was projecting from his mouth as he spoke.

'Oh, just something I read' Billy said, standing square on to Tony and holding his gaze. Julia has gone quiet and the tears were now silently beginning to roll down her cheeks.

'Well this has been nice' said Jenny trying to extricate them from the Mexican standoff without one of the gunfighters pulling the trigger. 'We really must do it again, maybe we can host next time.' Her words seemed to cut the air and her positive reaction left the room stunned in silence; she knew she had about thirty seconds before the situation bubbled over again. She walked across the room, kissed Tony on the cheek, brushed the tears away from Julia's eyes and did the same to her. 'Come on Billy, we have an early morning tomorrow.' Jenny grabbed Billy's hand and before the spell could be broken, she almost dragged him out of the door of the apartment and used her keys to get them inside his.

'We need to talk Billy' and now it was her turn to be angry.

'Ok, I'm listening.' But Billy was not, he was barely in the room and she could not work out where he was. Was it Tony's lounge, or on his balcony? No, Jenny could not see it, but Billy was standing, as if in an out of body experience, on the high railway line looking over the Flag and Staff. Playing through his mind were scenarios which led to Chris Deville's death. What he couldn't see right now, was who pushed him.

'Billy, look at me' she pulled him round and stared into his face 'I need you here and engaged, not dreaming.' With that, the moment was gone and he lost the image in his head. 'What the hell were you playing at in there? North and South told you to leave him alone. We agreed you would be subtle. In the end, you went out of your way to bait him. Why?' He went to hold her but she pulled back. 'No, argue first, make up after, that's the way it works.' He held his hands up in surrender.

'I'm sorry. It wasn't planned. The more he showed his hand, the more I realised what he is.'

'And what's that?'

'A bully. A monster. But worse.'

'Worse?'

'I could see all of those controlling tendencies of my Mother. I don't blame Julia for being the way she is. She is a victim of Tony's actions; like I was with my Mother.   But unlike in my case, when Julia found some love, and I think she did fall for Deville, even if it was one way, Tony had to get rid of him in order to get back control.'

'You have no proof.' Jenny was actually a little scared now. She had seen many sides of Billy but this was something new.

'Well then it's time I got some.   I will call Roger North tomorrow and set up a meeting.'

'Just be careful what you start Billy.   I don't want you disappearing too.'   Now Jenny moved in to hold him.   'I am falling for you Billy Perry and that man is dangerous. I would be devastated if anything happened to you.' Billy looked up at the portrait of Elspeth that now hung upon the wall and dominated the room.

'I'll be fine' he said and smiled. 'I'm a Perry, I am learning that we're quite tough.'

4.   Thymine

The Perry Gene

Chapter 16

Jenny slept uneasily after Billy's performance at the party. There were nightmares about Tony and every worst scenario of what might have happened to Chris Deville. When she awoke in the morning, unrested and wrapped up in Billy's duvet, the bed was empty. Her first thought was that she had imagined it all, but then realised this was not her bedroom and concluded it was all real. Jenny wondered where her boyfriend, and now lover, had gone. She got up and looked around for something to pull around her, not quite ready to prance around Billy's apartment naked. Walking into the ensuite bathroom, there was a towelling robe behind the door. She looked around and felt a little smile flash across her face. The room was pure Billy; organised, clean and tidy. What had happened last night to make him be so open and taunting of Tony? She knew there was still a lot to this man she was yet to get her head around.

Jenny wrapped the robe around herself and padded off down the stairs. As soon as she was half way down she could smell fresh coffee brewing. As she turned at the bottom of the stairs she could see Billy's head above the back of the sofa. It was then she realised that something in the room was different. She couldn't quite put her finger on it. As she stood there wondering, Billy turned his head towards her.

'Morning gorgeous, there's fresh coffee in pot if you want some.'

'Do you want a refill while I'm at it?' He nodded his head and held up his empty mug. Jenny strolled over towards him took the mug and went to the kitchen. 'There's something different about the apartment this morning and I can't work out what it is' she said as she filled the two mugs with steaming black coffee. Neither of them took milk and both took one sugar. Jenny liked the common things they shared, she felt an increasing closeness because of it. She took the two mugs and carried them back, handed one to him and stood to look out of the window at the sluggish Sunday morning river.

'I moved the sofa' Billy said, almost absentmindedly in reply. Jenny turned to look at him. He was sitting on the sofa in a pair of running bottoms and a running vest. By the look of things, he had been out on a long run, the vest was dark with sweat. His feet were bare, so he had obviously dumped the trainers and socks at the door on his return. It was at this point that Jenny looked across at the clock to see the time. It was still only half past eight, so Billy must have been up with the larks to go for his run.

'Should I ask why?' And then it dawned on her. 'You got angry at Tony being able to see into your apartment, didn't you?' Jenny could see that the sofa was now 5 feet further back in the flat. The view was still impressive but you could no longer see up or downriver as far as before. She went to the window and looked out. If you put your face almost against the glass, you could just about see the tip of the balcony railing from Tony's apartment. As Billy's balcony was further along the wall, it did not offer the same view in return so he had never thought about the fact he might be being spied on. 'I guess you have worked out how far into the apartment they can see and now...'

'I have moved the sofa far enough back that they cannot see me, sorry us, except by using some sort of Snooper's selfie stick.'

The Perry Gene

'And then you went for a long run to get it out of your system?'

'No, I went on a long run to think. You made it clear you were not happy last night. You don't want to aggravate Tony and make him the enemy. But part of me can't leave it alone. I know he had something to do with Chris Deville's disappearance and now I want to prove it.'

'I think this is taking the responsibilities of a being a landlord a little too far Billy.' She wandered back from the window and sat down on the sofa beside him.

'I'm serious' he said, the anger returning to his voice 'I can't explain it. I have a passion for organising and sorting. I like things to make sense not only in the physical world, but also in my head. Right now, one man is dead and Tony, that thug in there is walking around free as a bird. I don't know exactly what happened but I am going to find out.'

'And what then? What do you do when you find out, tell the Police?'

'I don't know. I haven't thought that far yet.'

'Well I suggest you do. If he finds out you are snooping, he is not going to win neighbour of the year award. He may even come after you.'

'I've texted Roger and I'm waiting for a response. I want to meet him later and get some advice.'

'Ok' she said 'Let's see what the two of them have to say. I'm coming with you though as I have questions.'

'Have you met them before, I guess they've been to the office?'

'Yes, Roger is the one who did all the talking. He is the one with the gift of the gab. Jerry sits quietly in the background.'

'I know what you mean. But it doesn't take long to see who is pulling the strings in that partnership.' Jenny went to snuggle into Billy and then thought better of it. He was still damp from the run. Billy saw her pull away and looked down at his shirt. 'I guess I need a shower or I will drive you away with the smell.'

'Well I need one too; I will jump in after you.'

'You could just come in with me. I could do your back.' The silly grin had returned to his face. Jenny however was not grinning but looked far away for a minute as if picturing something in her head.

'Sod that Billy, if we are having a shower together, I want you to wash my front, not just my back.' With this she got up, dragging Billy with her, then led him upstairs to the bathroom.

*

An hour later, Billy was making scrambled eggs and toast for the pair of them when his phone pinged to show a new message. It was from Roger; he was agreeing to meet up in the Boot at lunchtime. Billy quickly texted back that Jenny would be with him and then got on with the eggs. Jenny swanned down the stairs doing a good impression of a Hollywood starlet, her arms like those of a bird as she descended with grace and a lot of show.

'Roger has texted and agreed to meet up in the Boot & Flogger at lunchtime. I told him you were coming.'

'Fair enough, what do you want to do this morning?'

'I thought we might take a bit of a walk, it's a nice enough day.'

'Billy, it's dry out there at the moment, but's it's fairly grey. I'm not sure it's walking weather, what have you got in mind, the River, Greenwich Park?'

'Oh, nowhere in particular, possibly walking around Borough and Bermondsey, show you a few places you might not know.' Jenny took two plates out of the cupboard as the food was now ready to serve. She removed the toast from the toaster, spread it with butter and Billy heaped up the eggs on both plates.

'No, there is something else. I'm getting to know you very well Billy Perry, there is something you are not telling me. An ulterior motive maybe?' She took her plate, a fresh cup of coffee and sat at the breakfast bar. Billy had picked up newspapers on the way back from his run. This was something he knew she enjoyed but he had never bothered with in the past. It was another sign of the new and improved Billy. The world was no longer something foreign to him that he sat outside, he now was aware he had a place in it and could make an impact upon it. Jenny opened up the colour magazine and flicked through the articles while she ate. Billy opened the football section. The summer recess was over and although he had no match this week, from next Sunday he would be back wearing black and adjudicating South London football feuds. Billy was attempting to avoid the question with the food and the papers. After a minute of silence, Jenny looked up and prodded him with her finger. 'I asked you a question.   After last night I am not sure I want any more Billy-style surprises.   What is it that you are so keen to show me? The park you played in as a child?   Where you had your first snog? Come on Billy, I can read you like a book now.'

'Tony mentioned a housing development he was working on. It's down beside the railway, just south of the Flag and Staff.'

'I don't think I like where this is going.'

'I just want to have a look.   We can pop into the Flag for a pint and say hello to Shirley on the way back to the Boot.'

'Billy, seriously, Roger and Jerry told you to stay out of his way, didn't they?   Why are you so damned keen to kick that particular hornets' nest?' She closed the magazine, shut his sports pages and waited for him to speak.

'When we speak to them today, I want to be able to give them the full picture.   Last night, I figured if Tony is developing housing where he said, right next to the railway, then he probably has access to the track from his site. I just want to confirm that.   We won't do anything silly, won't get ourselves noticed.   He will never know.'

'Fair enough' said Jenny, picking up her coffee cup to wash down the eggs 'but stick to the script this time Billy, no surprises.   You were the man who used to hate them and now you seem to have turned into the conjurer who continually pulls them out of the hat.'

The Perry Gene

'One quick look and we are out of there.' Billy opened his paper back up and continued where he had left off with the football reports from the previous day's games.

*

It occurred to Billy only when they had got to the Flag and Staff that there was an awful lot of building in the area at that point in time. There were hoardings along large sections of the track side and beyond concealing both new builds and regeneration projects. Billy walked into the side door of the Flag asking Jenny to wait there for a minute. He found Shirley, but she did not have any real information on who was running which building project.

'There's a load of new apartment blocks being built around here, all out of our price range of course. Ted at the Nelson was telling me apartments in the Music Box are going to start at half a million. Not sure how anyone young gets on the property ladder these days.'

'This will be a refurbishment rather than a new build. Any ideas?'

'Oh, well now that's different, there are two big ones. The first is off towards Waterloo East and the second one is about a third of a mile down the road from here heading out of town. It's an ex-council block, had squatters and the like. It got cleared, not too gently from what I hear.'

'That'll be the one, do you know the address?' Billy took out a notepad from his pocket to write it down, but she looked at him blankly.

'Billy, I don't have the bloody address or postcode for your Satnav before you ask. It's a quarter of a mile straight down this road; next to the railway. You can't miss it. Think 1930's style housing with scaffolding around it. About thirty apartments in total.' Thirty apartments thought Billy, that's some nest egg he's sitting on.

'Thanks Shirley, I owe you one.' Billy went to leave but she grabbed his arm.

'I was looking outside when you came in. Who's the girl? You got yourself a fancy woman? You know I was always available.' With this she jokingly pushed up her cleavage in an attempt to show him what he was missing. Billy smiled, gave her a quick peck on the cheek and went to leave.

'A girlfriend, Jenny, if we have time we'll pop in for a drink on the way back.' As he opened the door he turned, 'But she can't replace you Shirl.' As the door shut behind him, Shirley stared at it for a few seconds. He had never called her Shirl before, as often as she had asked him to. What had happened to her Billy Perry? *I would love to see his Mother's face right now* she thought to herself.

As Billy left the pub, closing the door quietly behind him, he looked over to Jenny and pointed up the street.

'This way, about a seven or eight-minute walk.' He set off in the direction Shirley had suggested at a fair speed.

'Six or seven minutes at whose pace?' Jenny said racing to catch him up. She was never the fittest person in the world and had developed a bit of a wine waist a year or so ago, but since her time getting to know Billy, she had cut down on the large girly nights out. She had started going to the gym and realised how much better she felt for it.   It hadn't all been about trying to impress Billy, it was strange, but the more she saw of him, the more she saw in herself.   She wanted more out of life all of a sudden. She took on extra jobs around the office and also started looking at work emails outside hours.   It was like Billy was the catalyst for all the good things she had inside her, but for the moment she knew she just had to keep up with him.

Billy was a good judge of time and it took exactly six minutes, even if he did slacken the pace a little due to Jenny's footwear being more dance floor than running track.   But he liked that about her.   She wasn't all practicality, she was pretty too and he felt she was getting prettier the more he knew her. Billy had spent a lot of time on his own thinking about Jenny and he was really beginning to appreciate having her in his life.   It was not every girl that would put up with his ways.   The evening before had been a prime example.   Going in hard at Tony was never the plan.   Billy wanted to stay under the radar, but as he saw Tony's reaction to his questions, it was like Billy was a shark smelling blood.   His opponent had been caught unawares.   He was on the back foot and Billy knew it might be the only time he would get the chance to push him to his advantage.

Now the two of them stood across the street from a building that appeared to be in a cocoon. The roof was visible poking out of the top but the rest was shrouded in blue plastic which was wrapped tightly around the scaffolding.   The block appeared to be U shaped with the two forks of the U pointing out towards the road which left an enclosed courtyard in the middle.

The Perry Gene

The structure could be seen from the outside, but access in was blocked by a locked security gate. There was a fairly burly thug in a high visibility jacket sitting in a little Portakabin by the main entrance. Billy and Jenny surveyed the scene and pointed to a couple of potential ways to circumvent the main door. As they did so, Billy noticed they were attracting attention from the thug in the cabin. He appeared to be getting up from his chair and moving towards the door.

'Billy, let's go, we don't need any trouble.'

'Jen, it's fine, we are simply first-time buyers.' She looked at him and realised Billy was either getting very good at thinking on his feet or had planned for this eventuality. Rather than removing himself from the picture as he saw the thug exit the cabin Billy began to walk towards him. Jenny followed on behind and finally grabbed his hand as they approached the guard. The guard was about to speak when Billy raised his hand in a gesture of greeting. 'Hi, sorry to bother you but you don't know when these apartments will be ready do you?' The guard looked at him rather bemused; the trouble he had foreseen had vanished like morning mist and now he needed to be nice.

'I'm not really sure mate, I've only been here a few months. I move around the sites as they need me. The man scratched his head and looked like he was thinking. Talking and thinking at the same time were obviously a 'no no' Billy thought.

'Do you have any contact details of who owns the site? Is there a webpage or something?'

The Perry Gene

'Well now you're asking. I've got the foreman's details in case of an emergency but he won't appreciate being called for this. There might be a website though. I'll have a look in the cabin.' The guard jogged over to the cabin in an attempt to be helpful. Jenny came up close to Billy, she was still not comfortable being here.

'Can we go now? You aren't going to find anything else out here.' Jenny squeezed his hand and pulled but Billy wasn't quite finished. The guy was emerging from the cabin shaking his head.

'Nothing mate' he shouted across. Billy walked towards him.

'Any chance we can have a peek inside? Get an idea of what the apartments look like?' Billy moved purposefully towards the door to the site. The guard blocked his way.

'Sorry mate, it's a hard hat area. Even I'm not allowed inside.'

'What about a quick look through the window of your cabin, I guess you have a view inside? That can't break any rules can it?' Billy side stepped the guard and walked slowly towards the cabin. Jenny let go of his hand and waited at the kerb.

'Yeah alright mate. Watch the mess though, it's the cleaner's day off' he laughed. Billy walked into the cabin. On one side was a desk littered with paper and take away food wrappers. On the other was a window that looked onto the site itself. 'There you go, see, there's still quite a bit of finishing off to do, but you can get the general idea.' Billy wasn't sure what he was looking for until he saw it. Parked in the inner courtyard was a cherry picker with an extendable arm. He guessed this would allow the builders to do work on the roof and shift materials around easily.   Billy knew it could be used for other purposes.   He looked up and he could see the railway track above. It was a very common site around this part of the city. In the North the lines came underground or at ground level but from the East and South the commuter lines were all raised.   Now Billy realised how Chris Deville found himself on the track above the Flag and Staff.   He just didn't know who put him there and exactly why; but he had his suspicions.   'You had a good enough look? I don't want my governor turning up and seeing you here.' Billy walked out of the cabin.

'Your secret's safe with us mate.' Billy said, which appeared to go straight over the head of the guard.   Jenny looked relieved as Billy emerged. She didn't quite know why, but the whole episode had made her very anxious. She grabbed Billy's hand as he approached and dragged him in the direction they had come from. 'You look like you need a drink' Billy said to her as they go about a hundred yards away.   'Let's go in the Flag, we have plenty of time before we meet Roger.'

'Billy, I will ask you now, what I asked you last night, did you plan that?' Billy stopped and thought for a second. 'Plan what, how could I know that there would be a guard?'

'How did you know how to react? You seem to be completely at home with the deception.' Jenny let go of his hand and started to walk towards the pub. Billy grabbed hold of her gently and pulled her to a stop.

The Perry Gene

'It's not as simple as that.   You know I used to analyse things a lot, when I was in a bad way.   I would take a situation and cut it a number of ways in my head.   A bit like they say good chess players work.   I would think eight or nine moves ahead. My Dad used to say that all those years ago when he taught me to play.   Always think ahead.'

'So, you did plan it?'

'No, not exactly.   But while I was running this morning, I did go over every possible scenario I could think of that might happen when we got there.   One of them was a pretty low-grade moron as a guard and we needed a cover story.'   Jenny looked unconvinced by this.   Billy took her hand and placed it on his wrist. 'Feel my pulse.   I bet it's racing just as fast as yours?' She felt the beat and instinctively started to count under her breath, checking her watch. Billy looked confused.

'I trained as a first aider at work.   You didn't know that did you Billy? The trouble is, if you keep messing with the big boys in the playground, I think the medical help you will need will be a bit beyond my abilities. I won't say any more but talk to North and South and this time take their advice.'   She let go of his wrist and took his hand again. 'Now, how about that drink?'   As they arrived at the Flag and Staff the door was flung open and Shirley bounded out to greet Jenny with a hug.

'It's about time he got himself a girl.   I'm Shirley by the way, Shirl to my friends. You're actually lucky you snapped him up, I've 'ad my eye on him for some time now.   Anyway, good luck to you.' Coming close she whispered in Jenny's ear 'and don't 'urt him, or you'll have me to answer to.' Jenny pulled back, looked Shirley square in the face and nodded. Billy, seemingly oblivious to this, walked over to the bar to get served.

*

After two drinks and an hour spent with Shirley, Jenny and Billy headed over to the Boot and Flogger. Shirley had been the amiable host but had interwoven a lot of gossip while quizzing Jenny gently on her background and intentions. Once satisfied that she was good for Billy, they fell into a very comfortable rhythm. Billy knew he would now be interrogated about Jenny whenever he had business at the Flag and in the end, Shirley was making it clear to him that he had to look after Jenny too.

The walk to the Boot and Flogger was just over a mile, but with the nice warm weather, they took their time walking hand in hand. The beauty of this area was the number of interconnecting passages and cut-throughs. There was a multitude of ways of getting where they needed to go and they doubled back on themselves a couple of times when they saw something that piqued their interest. They passed the Island Café and the impromptu sounds pouring from the music school rehearsal rooms. Finally, turning into the small road on which the pub sat, thirty seconds later they were inside. Jenny went off to powder her nose and as Billy walked in, the same barman as last time, looked up and pointed in the direction of the snug bar. When he rounded the corner, Roger got up to shake his hand, but what caught Billy's eye was Jerry. He sat there hovering over a half-drunk pint. He had stopped reading and was quietly clapping his hands in the air in Billy's general direction.

'Drink Billy, I think you might need it by the time Jerry has finished with you.' Roger shook his hand as he spoke.

'Can I get a pint and a glass of white wine for Jenny?' Roger looked confused, trying to find Billy's imaginary friend. 'Loo' said Billy and Roger nodded.

'Of course. Now go and listen to Jerry for a minute. I think he wants a quiet word.' Billy walked over and pulled out the chair closest to Jerry.

'Applause, I'm guessing that's sarcasm' said Billy as Jerry drank from his pint. He wiped his mouth, then put the glass down slowly; winding up to deliver a well-prepared speech.

'Billy. Both Roger and I like you. You appear to be a decent bloke with good intentions. You are polite and respectful and most importantly you are Elspeth's nephew.' Billy saw him take a pause and thought how well that had gone, which meant there was a big *but* coming. 'But, what the bloody hell did you think you were doing winding up Tony Carruthers? We warned you what he was like.' Billy shrugged his shoulders and was about to speak. 'Hang on, let's wait until Roger gets back with the drinks, I think we need to hear it blow by blow.' Jenny appeared around the corner and Roger handed her a glass of wine as he came back from the bar. Much to Billy's surprise, the usually grumpy Jerry stood and greeted Jenny with a kiss on both cheeks. Once they were all seated he said quietly, 'Right, now, from the beginning, what happened.'

Over the next thirty minutes, Billy half narrated and was half quizzed about the night before. When he was finished, Roger asked if that was everything. Billy went on to explain about their trip that morning to the building site.

'So, you see, I was right, that's how they did it.'

'How they did what?' Roger was, as Billy suspected, not the brains here.

'They used the cherry picker to get up to the railway line and person or persons unknown, took either a living or already dead Chris Deville down the railway track a sufficient distance not to arouse suspicion. At this point, if he was not already dead, I would suggest his neck was broken and then he was hurled off. It would have been done late at night, after the trains had stopped, so there would be no witnesses.' Jenny and Roger now looked on as Billy and Jerry were locked in eye contact.

'Billy, you are in a lot of shit if he works out you know. You tied a bloody bell around your neck and stuck a label on saying *sacrificial goat* last night. If he is anything like we suspect, Tony is now someone you need to keep clear of.'

'Jerry, are you going to tell him the other part of the puzzle that makes sense now?'

'Do you know what Chris Deville did Billy?'

The Perry Gene

'No idea, I got the feeling he was some sort of civil servant.'

'Close. He was a local government official.' Jerry said. It was now Billy's turn to look confused. It was at this point that Jenny put her hand up. They all looked at her as if somehow, they had been transported back to school. 'Yes, feel free to share.'

'Was he by any chance in planning or building inspection?' Jenny asked.

'The lady wins a prize. Yup, he was the building inspector. Not for the complex you visited earlier, but apparently according to one of his colleagues he became very interested in it just before he died. Tony may be jealous but I suspect he's a ruthless businessman as well.' The four of them sat in silence. After a minute or so Jerry looked up.

'So, are you now going to stay away? Sell the apartment. At least move out.'

'No' said Billy 'I'm going to prove he did it.' At this point they all picked up their glasses, but Jenny's face had turned very pale.

The Perry Gene

Chapter 17

The week that followed was all about getting back to business.   Jenny had made her concerns clear after their meeting with North and South and Billy had promised to talk each step through with her first before doing anything more on the investigation.   Now it was time to concentrate on his machines, his customers and of course his staff.   On the Monday, Pete had told Billy that he had found a guy to work with him as an apprentice.   His name was Steve, he was eighteen years old and pretty much what Billy had suggested; a machine rat who had grown up around the arcades.   This was important for two reasons. First, he was aware of the technology required, but second and more importantly, he was used to dealing with the right sort of people.   Billy gave Pete the *thumbs up* to trial Steve for a week and said he would take him out one day to get the measure of Steve himself.

By Friday Billy had still not met Steve as he and Pete were very rarely in the lock-up at the same time. The feedback from Pete was nothing other than glowing.   Billy wasn't suspicious, he had no doubts about Pete, either his honestly or his logic. If Steve was no good, Pete would be back to square one, so if he said Steve was good, he probably was good.   But now Billy needed to see for himself, and then he and Pete could to make a formal offer.   Billy had left instruction that Steve was to be at the lock-up at nine on Friday morning to spend the day with him.   He had also organised a couple of beers that evening after work for the three of them. Billy figured he would know by then, and if Pete agreed they could seal the deal over a drink.

The Perry Gene

Billy arrived at the lock-up at eight thirty and got out of his car to open the doors. He was deliberately early as he wanted to prep a couple of surprises to test Steve and also do some paperwork. When he stepped out of the car he got a shock. Sitting on some packing crates by the door was a tall, thin youth with a shock of blonde hair in a pony-tail. What Billy was not expecting was the stranger to be wearing one of the new company Polo shirts. This was obviously Steve and he was very early. Already, there was something about him that Billy liked.

'Couldn't sleep or you been out night-clubbing until dawn?' Billy asked as he walked towards the youth with his hand outstretched. 'I'm Billy, Billy Perry.'

'T-Shirt gave it away to be honest boss and the fact that you and Pete could be twins. You sure you're not brothers or at least related in some way?' Steve smirked as he took and shook Billy's hand. Not a crushing handshake, or weak like a lettuce leaf. Just confident and trustworthy. 'I don't like being late' he continued 'and Pete said timekeeping is one of your things; bug bears he said.' Billy looked at him and wondered what else Pete had told him, but he realised Pete must have given Steve some idea of who he would be working for and what to expect.

'You are right about our similar looks, when we worked in the arcades as teenagers, we used to have a lot of fun with it.' Billy realised he needed to set the right impression and not sound too frivolous. 'Anyway, i've got some paperwork to do to start with and then we have four pubs to visit today, all long-term customers.　While I am getting on, I need you to do some cleaning and maintenance work on a couple of machine assemblies we are refurbing, you good with that?'

'If you mean the two old Jenson chassis on the workbench, I did one yesterday afternoon while Pete was updating the call logs and invoices.　If you want to check my work, I can start on the other one?' Now Billy could start to see what Pete had been saying about the keenness and intelligence of his new protégé. The guy was sharp, articulate, presentable and on-time.　Suddenly Billy had a warm feeling about how this was going to go.

'Alright then, I will have a quick look and let you get on.　Pete said you were keen.'

'Well I have never heard of an apprenticeship for what I want to do before so I'm taking this opportunity seriously.　I've been working on machines since I was thirteen as part of Saturday jobs, but you never get paid enough to live on working in the arcades themselves. This sounded right up my street and Pete said you were getting pretty busy.'

'Can you drive?　A van that is?'

'I have a clean licence if that's what you mean.　But I have never driven a van. Pete asked in the week, but he said I was not covered on the insurance.' Billy unbolted the doors of the shed, got back in the driver's seat and drove the car inside whilst Steve followed on foot.　Steve then went to the work bench and started to open up the machine assembly that sat there.

'Coffee?' asked Billy as he got out of the car.

The Perry Gene

'Oh, is that what you meant by apprentice?' said Steve defensively 'how do you like it?' He put down the screw driver he was holding and went to walk over to the sink. Then he saw Billy standing there, looking at him with the kettle in his hand.

'Do you *want* a coffee?' Billy looked at him as if to say *calm down*.

'Oh, ah, milk and sugar please.' Steve said sheepishly. Billy filled the kettle, plugged it in and grabbed a couple of mugs from the draining board where they had been washed up the night before. While the kettle boiled, he walked over to the bench and had a look at the assembly that Steve had worked on the night before. He checked the contacts. It was clear that the right alcohol-based cleaners had been used. He turned the tumbler assembly and listened to it click evenly. 'Is this where you tell me that the contacts are flat on rotor arm number four, just by listening to it?' Steve said.

'No, this is real life. From what I can see here, you do good work and according to Pete you know your stuff. Stop being so defensive. I'm not trying to trip you up. As long as you do your job, we'll get along fine.' He went back over to make the coffees and returned a minute later with the mug for Steve.

'Sorry, just nervous, I guess. I really like the idea of working here.'

'Fine, well you get on for an hour while I do some bookwork and then we can head out. Two this morning, lunch, two this afternoon and then a couple of beers with Pete later.' As he said that he heard a car outside. 'Talk of the devil.' About a minute later, Pete walked into the room.

The Perry Gene

'Morning gentlemen. Billy, how we doing on the van front, I'm going to have to start charging you for my mileage. You know I'm not insured for work in my car.'

'Wow, thirty seconds before you mention the van, that's a record. You normally wait until you've had your coffee.' Billy walked back over the kettle and as it was still hot, he made Pete a mug, black with three sugars. He handed him the drink. 'Sit down for a minute, let's chat.' Pete took one of the stools next to the workbench. 'You as well junior' he said to Steve, who narrowed his eyes as he dragged a stool over. 'First, the *bloody* van' said Billy. 'We have a second vehicle arriving on Tuesday. Same make and model as the current one and on Monday it is having the company transfers added to it.' Pete started to rub his hands together with glee until Billy stared at him and Pete knew it was time to stop. 'Second, estimate how many miles you have done and use forty pence a mile, send me an email and I will get it added to your payroll. But keep it reasonable. You know I appreciate you helping out with your car in the meantime, so next time you need a service, I will pick up the tab.' Pete was now beaming, this day kept getting better.

'Cheers boss, much appreciated. Buy you a beer later.'

'Done. Thirdly, junior here. From what I have seen of his work and what you have said over the last couple of nights, I am happy to make this a permanent arrangement, assuming, that is, that nothing goes wrong with the customers today. I have had a word with George about the apprenticeship scheme and apparently there are a few hoops to jump through, not least of which is formal day release to college.' Steve looked horrified. 'Yes junior, if you want the job you've got to go back to school one day a week. You still up for it?'

'Studying what?' asked Steve.

'Electronics and a basic business course. GNVQs will help you in the long run.'

'Oh, well, sounds alright, but what about pay? Am I going to lose a day's money a week? I'd be worse off than before.' Billy looked over at Pete and they both smiled at each other.

'We brought you in on a trial basis, but we needed to make sure you were interested in the business not just the money. The offer that Pete made is not the final offer. We are going to pay you a grand more a year and include the time off for college in that. In return, we need flexibility from you in terms of hours and on call outs. Does that work for you?' Steve was now the one smiling.

'If you are serious, then I am definitely up for it. I'm not great with the books, but happy to give it a go.' Steve stood up and held out his hand to Billy.

'I said as long as you don't screw up today, and you need to be able to hold your drink tonight.' They stood in a Mexican stand-off, Steve's face froze and then after fifteen seconds Billy and Pete burst out laughing. Billy shook Steve's hand and then Pete did the same. 'When the van arrives next week, you will be on the insurance to drive it. If you want to take it at the weekend and use it, then you are on call, ok? And be careful with it, it cost me an arm and leg to get you cover at your age.'

'Ok… Boss.'

'Now, it's about time some work got done today. We need to pay for all this coffee and laughter.' With that, Pete started to load some spares into his car, Steve returned to the bench to work on the assembly and Billy sat himself in front of the computer to work on some invoices. The system was higher tech now, with proper passwords, a firewall and back up to the cloud. The diaries on their phones also synced up with the jobs as they came in and they could order parts while out of the office. Pete was a handy man to have around and Billy started to think how long it would be until they needed to find another Steve.

'Billy' said Pete once he had loaded and was ready to leave, 'there's just one thing confusing me.'

'Yes Pete,' Billy looked up from the computer and picked up his slowly cooling mug of coffee.

'Earlier, you said George? You mean Mr Transon?'

'Yes, why?'

'I have never heard you call him George.'

'Well, then I guess it's about time I started using his name. He is after all one of Elspeth's pack of guardian angels.' Steve was looking over at the two of them perplexed. 'Tell you all about it over a beer later.' With that he made the motion of cracking a whip. Steve turned around smiling and got back to work.

'Have you seen Gordon lately?' Pete thought he would push the point to see where it led. He knew Billy only ever called the Doctor by his title and surname.

'Pete, you are not my analyst, I pay you to fix machines and hire staff. Now bugger off and earn us some money. See you at six in the Feathers.' Billy turned back to his books and heard the door shut behind him. Once Pete's car had driven off, Billy checked his watch to see how long it was before they would have to leave. 'Steve, check the registry sheets to find the machines we are going to work on and then suggest what parts we will need to load. Let's see how you do in the field.'

The day went well and Billy's belief that it was right to speak to Steve about the job so early in the day became more justified when he saw him with the punters and customers. He wowed Shirley who thought him to be somewhere between the long-lost Grandson she had never had, and the Diet Coke man. It was an odd mixture of protection and flirting which was funny for Billy to watch from afar. Now that she had met Jenny, Shirley was respectfully playing down the level of flirting in his direction and instead moved on to Steve as a target. Billy also liked how Steve dealt with the usual perils of working in a pub. When it came to a drunken customer late in the afternoon who wanted to engage a little too much with Steve while he was trying to work on a machine, the new recruit was both courteous and assertive. What could have been a difficult situation was diffused and Billy was impressed.

They didn't stay for more than a couple of drinks, Billy and Pete were both aware of the law and they had their vehicles with them, but they left Steve in the bar as he knew a few of the locals and wanted another pint. They walked out to the carpark together and as Pete was unlocking the van Billy put his hand on his mate's shoulder.

'You did well there Pete, keep an eye out for others along the way. If business keeps expanding like this, we will need more staff and you appear to have a skill at finding them.'

'Appreciate the trust boss,' he pulled at the arm of his tee-shirt 'even if I'm still not sure about the uniform.' But Billy could see Pete's face reflected in the window, so he knew he was smiling.

'I will be expecting you to run his work load at least for a few weeks. That's a bit more work for you in the short term, can you cope?'

'I think I can find time in my busy diary.' He turned to face Billy. 'I actually liked the challenge and have got a few ideas about how we could organise ourselves better if you are willing to let me try?' He seemed to hesitate before he carried on 'you seem to have quite a lot on outside of work these days; your Aunt and this exhibition thing. I can help more if you need it.'

'Pete, you are already doing more than you are paid for, and I appreciate the offer. I was going to speak to you about it next week, but since you brought it up, let's talk now. I was planning to give you an increase of another five grand a year. Also, up your commission slightly on any machine sales.' Pete looked taken aback as he hadn't seen this coming. 'You have kept the place afloat when we have been inundated with extra work from all the new machines and services. I just wanted you to know it's appreciated.' Billy stuck his hand out and Pete shook it enthusiastically.

'Thanks Billy. That would be amazing.'

'But the bloody T-shirts stay' said Billy defiantly.

'Done' said Pete as he got into the van 'I'll cover the on-call phone this weekend, have a good break boss.' He closed the door and Billy patted the side of the vehicle as it drove away.   In his mind he marked a virtual tick against his check list of things to do today, he was now ninety per cent complete. He no longer bothered with lists on paper, his confidence was boosted by every small victory in his life.   He still had the lists, but now they were just so many neurons firing in his mind. The last item, the final ten percent had been bugging him all week and now his task list elsewhere was done, he could get back to it. It was in fact Jenny who had brought it up.   She had asked if Chris Deville's diary held any clues as to why he had become interested in Tony's building site. The timing suggested by Roger North would have put it at around the breakup between Chris and Julia.   Billy had been so busy this week he had not had a chance to look, but now there was a bottle of wine with his name on it and a place on the sofa waiting for him.   He got into his car for the short drive home.

*

The Perry Gene

In the end it took him nearly two hours to find the three short passages he had previously missed. Obviously at the time, he had worked out the code for Julia and his mind was focused on the affair. So convinced was he that it was the cause of Chris Deville's untimely demise that he failed to see the other messages woven through the diary. The first clue was about two weeks before Chris finally dumped her.

> '*J was very tipsy today. Got in from site in the middle of the afternoon since the job finished early and she was waiting at the lift door when it opened. She almost fell over, so I am guessing she had been on the sauce for a while. She had a glass of wine in one hand, which she partly spilled, and a bottle in the other. It was the now fairly predictable drunken fumble, with her being noisier than normal. Always a concern that T will come back and hear.*
> *After we had finished and she laid there slumped on the sofa, I said she might want to keep the noise down as the last thing we needed was T finding out. She rambled on about T having a big meeting, hush hush, touching her nose, with some building guy. A problem with the new apartments. I didn't press her but figured she would let it slip later.*'

It got a little more revealing a few days later when Julia was back for more attention from her young lover. Billy was now doing mental gymnastics with what the text might mean.

'*We didn't get around to anything more than a quick grope as she said T was coming home soon. He was in a foul mood and had been showering loads. He had also thrown out some clothes. She said something about his face looking red and having red marks on it. It's then that I figured out he had been wearing a face mask. It's not unusual for the money men to visit site, but it is very unusual for them to don special protective gear. It got me wondering what they had found. It's not my patch, but I figured I would have a little dig. My run-ins with him have not been pleasant, so anything to land T in it would be good. As she left, she said something about T having put a fix in.*'

The next entry came after the acrimonious break up and was a little more coded. There was a sense that Chris was becoming nervous or anxious about his findings.

'*My enquiries have hit a brick wall in the office. The building is old enough to have had A in it, but the local inspector's reports show nothing. I am wondering about the fix J mentioned. Only way I'm going to prove it is by going there myself and checking. I drove past and security looks pretty lax. Need to find the right moment to go in.*'

The Perry Gene

There were only three more entries in the diary after that but they were unrelated to the site. Now Billy was kicking himself that he had not seen this earlier, or at least understood the significance. He needed to update Roger and Jerry but first he thought he had better let Jenny know. It was then he noticed the time, it was now nearly eleven and he finally realised his days of being ruled by the clock were long gone. More worryingly there were four texts on his phone from Jenny, He had not noticed the message indicator flashing. He started to scroll through them. The first message had been almost two hours before.

'Hi Billy, Billy Perry, you busy later, how did it go with Steve?'

An hour went by and the second text came in, still friendly, but shorter.

'You boys still in the pub?'

Half an hour after this, the tone was most definitely changing.

'Billy, mobile phones are mobile. You must have it with you, so you must be ignoring me.'

Finally, just twenty minutes earlier, there was a more frantic message.

'Billy, I'm now quite worried. Let me know you are in one piece. I'm coming over to check.'

Billy was just dialling Jenny's number when he heard the key in the lock and the front door burst open. He was up on his feet immediately and the sight was not pretty. Jenny rushed into the room, tears on her face, which appeared first as concern but then she became angry.

'Where the hell have you been Billy Perry, and why ignore my texts?'

'Sorry Jen, I didn't see them, I was reading.'

The Perry Gene

'Put the bloody volume on, I was worried.' She walked over and punched him in the arm. 'Don't scare me like that.' Billy walked across the room, closed the door behind her then led her over to the sofa where he had been reading.

'I was just reading Jen, I'm not in danger, I'm not about to fall off the side of the railway.' That comment did not impress her at all and she put her head on one side to stare at him.

'I didn't know. Just keep an eye on your phone in future. I worry about you; and that comment is also not appropriate.' He raised his hand to supplicate her but she pushed it away. 'I am serious Billy, I'm your girlfriend and I'm allowed to be worried.' She lowered her voice and said 'I would worry about you if things here were normal, but you are spending your time baiting a killer psycho, so keep in touch please.' Billy hugged her and gave a long kiss. 'Don't think you are going to get around me that way.' Billy kissed her again. 'But please keep trying.' Now the anger had ebbed slightly and her naughty smile was coming back. He kissed her once more.

'Better?' She nodded her head. 'Then grab a seat, let me get you a glass of wine and come and read what I have found.'

Twenty minutes later, having read the passages several times, Jenny looked over at Billy.

'Wow, this is gold dust, have you told the boys yet?'

'No, some psycho burst in before I had a chance to.' Jenny looked concerned again until she realised, he was referring to her.

'But one thing I don't get. The reference to A.'

'Oh, I do' Billy said 'the silent killer.' She still looked none the wiser.

Billy solved the problem with a one-word answer.

'Asbestos'.

The Perry Gene

Chapter 18

Over the next week, with all that had been happening with the business and the considerable amount of time Billy spent thinking about the demise of Chris Deville, the elephant in the room had been Elspeth's exhibition.   Xavier was persistent, but Billy was also very capable of stubbornly avoiding him when he had other things on his mind.   Apparently, this was also a trait common to Elspeth, as Xavier was only too quick to point out.   However, after a week of ignoring increasingly irate messages, Billy decided on the Friday evening that he would plug back into the world of art and respond to Xavier.   Billy dropped him a text and he guessed that the man must be hatching his phone as his response was instant.   A couple of quick sarcastic text messages later and Billy had invited Xavier over to the apartment that evening.   For moral support he also texted Jenny and asked her if she was free.   Billy was still getting the hang of the girlfriend/boyfriend thing and Jenny was often amazed by the texts he sent. Her response made Billy smile.

> Text: 'Of course I'll be there. It's Friday, I'm your girlfriend dummy, and where else do you think I want to be?   I will pick up food, tell Xavier we will feed him. He can bring the wine since that's all he seems to do.'

With this Billy dropped a text to that effect back to Xavier and got an equally humorous response.

Billy had a busy day ahead of him, so he put the breakfast dishes in the dishwasher.   There were some things about the old house he simply didn't miss and washing up was one of them. He could not see how he had survived so long without a dishwasher. But that previous life was almost completely gone as the old house was not only on the market, but it had two buyers and a property developer competing for it. George Transon was rubbing his hands with glee at the thought and talking in terms of Billy's investment portfolio. All that Billy knew was if he ever needed a kitchen fan, he could probably harness his Mother spinning in her grave at the thought of the sale.

A week into his new role and Steve was proving to be even better than expected. He was hard working; conscientious and savvier than the blonde ponytail would have you believe. The new works van had arrived and Pete was already letting Steve go to sites on his own, once he had been introduced to the management. This was doubling the effectiveness of the team and starting to take the pressure off again. Billy knew that he had a chance of further expansion and Pete was aware that this was part of the reason for the pay rise. As it was September, and the college courses had already started, George Transon had somehow managed to get Steve into the local Technical College. He was to start the following Wednesday as part of his day-release. When this was mentioned, it was probably the only time the surface confidence of the apprentice disappeared, as college simply reminded him of his lack of fitting in at school. Billy and Pete both reassured him, but made it clear it was a necessary evil he had to put up with in order to be an apprentice for them. Besides, going back to education when it was your choice and getting paid for it, was not the same as being a school child.   Billy guessed Steve would get into it after a month or so, but they needed to support him until then.

Billy decided they would repeat the end of week drinks from the previous Friday as it was a good way to catch up and close down any work issues early.   He figured he had an hour before he needed to get back to the apartment ahead of Jenny and then Xavier arriving.   However, to his surprise, both Pete and Steve turned him down as they were busy on a job.   It seemed that as it was Friday, Pete was introducing Steve to one of the bigger casinos in which they had the service contract.   Billy rather suspected it was so that Steve could stay on for a while (avoiding any awkward questions about age) and have some fun, which was fine.   It was never really Billy's scene, but he did realise that the more his team, as it was becoming, were present at client sites, the more chance there was of repeat business.   With an hour to kill now, Billy was going to drive home, but for some reason, rather than turning right out of the lock-up road, he turned left.   He wasn't quite sure what he was doing, but his mind had been mulling over Chris Deville's last few hours and there were some things he was trying to get straight.   He drove under the railway and down to the Flag and Staff.   He entered the car park and sat with the engine running as he looked up at the railway above. What would they do in the novels he used to read?   He simply didn't have the time to devour them like he used to; in the past he had been avid in this pursuit.   It seemed that the logic of problem solving fitted into the way Billy lived his life at the time; continually striving for order out of chaos. What was the clue that he was missing?   He looked across at the pub and then noticed the camera pointing at the car park.   That was it, surveillance, CCTV.   Was there any chance that the event had been caught on camera.   Surely that would be the first thing the police would look for though. He looked again at the camera, the angle on the car park meant there was no way it would pick up the track above, but did Shirley have any cameras?   Then it occurred to him; the thing that was nagging him.   He might not see the actual moment of the fall due to there being no camera pointing at it, but what about before?   He had surmised that Chris had in some way been manhandled, dead or alive, from Tony's site further down the track.   What he needed to see was if there were any cameras that would show this.   He was shaken out of his thoughts by a tap on the window.

'Billy, what the hell are you doing sitting in the car with the engine running?' It was Shirley, she had obviously seen him on the pub's CCTV of the car park.   He lowered the driver's window in order to speak to her.   Pointing at the camera that had alerted her to his presence he looked back at her.

'Evening Shirl. Is that the only camera you have?   Do you have one that looks out from the front of the pub?   Did the police ask for the footage from your camera?' Shirley looked confused, then turn in the direction of the camera and the penny dropped.   She knew Billy well enough to know that he didn't think like other people. She then counted off on her fingers as she answered.

'No, No and No.   I have a second camera at the back where the cellar doors are, but nothing out the front as I have no need.   It's a busy road, so normally nothing happens there.   The police did ask the question, but once I told them that they lost interest.   What's this all about Billy, you still obsessed with your tenant's death?'

'I think I know what happened but I need to see if I can find a camera that might capture it.   Sorry Shirl, I got to run.   Thanks, and see you soon.' Billy put the car into gear but then stopped.   He scanned the track side in the direction of Tony's building site, then looked across the road from it.   There was nothing at this point that he could see, so he dropped the clutch and pulled out, driving in the direction of the site.

It was nearly half a mile when the cocooned structure came into sight. So far Billy had seen nothing, but as he pulled up fifty yards short of the building he saw two office complexes on the other side of the road which looked promising.   Both were bristling with cameras and Billy knew he had a chance to prove his idea.   He parked at the side of the building site and starting taking pictures on his mobile phone camera of the buildings opposite him.   He knew he had no way to get hold of the data, but he was also well aware of a pair of gentlemen who could.   He noted the corporate names on the buildings and made sure he had them in the picture.   From what he could see there were three or four cameras that might give him the footage he needed.   When he was finishing up, the security guard from the previous week came around the corner.

'Oi, what you up to now?   Shouldn't you be taking pictures of this building if you want to buy an apartment' he pointed to the building site.

The Perry Gene

'Just checking on the neighbours and the view' said Billy quickly tucking his phone away before there were any misunderstandings. 'Well I think I got what I need. Good to meet you again.' Billy went to walk off. The guard called out from behind him.

''Ere, what's your name? My guv'nor is goin' to wanna know.' The thug called out.

'Sorry mate, got to run, got a meeting I need to attend.' The guard started to pursue him slowly but lost interest. Billy got in his car and was about to drive off, when he noticed the guard was speaking to someone who looked like a foreman. He was pointing to Billy's car and then at the buildings across the way. The foreman looked up and then appeared to catch on pretty quickly what Billy had been up to. He started to approach the car and Billy realised it was a very good time to get the hell out of Dodge. As he drove away he saw the foreman trying to read his number plate. Fortunately for Billy, it was slightly obscured with dirt as he had been too busy to clean the car and he managed to pull away before he felt the guy had got too close. Still, Billy didn't know if the foreman had enough details or in fact the ability to trace him based on a plate. What Billy did know was that he shared a garage with Tony. If the foreman mentioned the car to him, then the cat might well be out of the bag. Billy drove home in silence; he was not in the mood for music.

*

Jenny arrived with a flourish, which was much becoming the norm; she was a ball of energy and whenever she appeared, whatever his previous mood,

The Perry Gene

Billy felt energised.   What he didn't want to do was darken her mood or worry her, so he sent the pictures of the camera positions with an accompanying text to Roger's phone; Jerry still didn't share things like that.   With that mission accomplished, he went up to get a shower while Jenny prepared some pasta and salad.

When Billy returned twenty minutes later, Xavier was sitting on the sofa, which he had pulled back to the window (into Tony's view). He was drinking a glass of red wine and entertaining Jenny with what Billy assumed was a witty anecdote.   When Billy came down the stairs Xavier looked at him, paused and then carried on telling Jenny the story.   Billy guessed it would take a little while for the theatrical little monkey to get the snubbing out of the way. He wanted Billy to know he was hurt by being ignored.   Billy didn't have the time for it.

'I bet Elspeth didn't let you get away with that moody shit Xavier, so since you are so keen to point out I have her genes, I won't either.   Now cut it out and play nice or don't play at all.'   Billy took a glass of white wine that Jenny was handing him, looking suitably impressed at the new teeth on her boyfriend.

'My god, the puppy has grown into a hound. You so are Elspeth all over, even from that flounce down the stairs. And actually' he enunciated each syllable 'she let me get away with a fair amount.' Then he stopped and saluted in an American throwaway style 'but fair enough, I was being a bit petty. However, nobody likes being ignored.'

The Perry Gene

'Then just send one text and wait like any normal human. You are not the only game in town at the moment.' Billy looked at Jenny, he was trying hard to keep his cool about the site, but she could see he was tenser than he should have been at this point.

'Did something happen I should know about today Billy? Bearing in mind our previous conversations about mushroom management.' Billy looked completely confused until Xavier jumped in, gleeful that he had a way into the conversation.

'She means keeping her in the dark and covering her with shit.'

'Well to be honest' Jenny interrupted, 'I was referring to the former, not the latter. But still yes, tell me what has happened.' Xavier realised he was now in the middle of something juicy and sat there on tenterhooks. The look that Jenny gave him made it clear that it was serious. The problem was, with Xavier there, Billy's attempt to explain the significance of the event turned the story into a half hour epic. By the end of this time, Jenny got the now overcooked pasta onto plates and they sat in silence eating. When the food was done with and each of them had a full glass of wine again, Xavier took the opportunity to get back to the business in hand.

'We have an opening date for the exhibition if anyone is interested? I've identified a lovely little gallery under the Oxo Tower, on the South Bank.' Billy looked at Jenny who had already clocked that this was Billy's original suggestion and she raised her eyebrows but said nothing. 'It's close enough to the Tate to get the art crowd and has a huge footfall of diners and tourists.

The Perry Gene

Coming up to the Christmas season, you should get some present purchases as well. I've got a couple of regular exhibition art students who can man it and I've found a night for the press opening.'

'Press opening' Billy repeated 'aren't we getting a little ahead of ourselves Xavier, she was a photographer who retired, then became a bit of recluse when she fell ill? She has not produced any new work in years.'

'Two things, one, liar liar, she has done new work, you need to check those photo archives better. I have spent a lot of time on the data and she was working on a new project when she was diagnosed, not finished, but sufficiently advanced for our purposes.'

'On what?'

'Migrant workers, the ebb and flow of the Thames.' Billy stopped and thought for a minute.

'You said two things.'

'Yes, your input. Her nephew making biographical field notes.' Billy was shaking his head. 'Your pictures, you idiot.'

'I got what you meant, I just don't see who will be interested.'

'Well her old newspapers for a start. She worked for two of the heavy-weights. With a little word from me, they are fairly champing at the bit.'

'Fair enough then,' said Billy, starting to run out of questions and objections 'when and what do you need from me?'

The Perry Gene

'Well' Xavier exaggerated the pause and for a moment looked a little uncomfortable. He seemed to regain composure and then continued 'I love what you have sent me so far. The childhood photos from the old lady. We've had those blown up.' He paused again 'but there are four or five images I mentioned that we are still missing.' He stopped as Billy got up from his seat and walked over to the window.   As he got towards the edge he had the feeling of being watched.   He looked across towards Tony's balcony, but there was nobody there; he was imagining it.

'You want the bloody shot of the grave, don't you?   You want her last resting place photographed in her own style to include in the exhibition.'

'Yes, that and the school please. It's still there, I checked the records.'

'Are you sure you are ready for that?' Jenny went over to Billy and held his hand. Just at that moment Billy looked up, although he saw nobody, what he did see was a cloud of cigarette smoke. He felt his resolve harden.

'I will go on Sunday after football.' He paused as if he had forgotten something. 'Xavier, you didn't say when.'

'Four weeks tonight is press night.'

'Hell,' said Billy, 'I'd better get on with it then.'

*

It was already two o'clock once Billy had returned from football and showered.   He ached and after the long summer of not performing his refereeing duties he was starting to think maybe he was getting too old for it. He now found himself looking at the younger, fitter and altogether angrier players that were coming through the ranks and wondered if his days of playing peace-keeper were over.

He wrote down the address and postcode of the school and the cemetery in his notebook; a device almost redundant now. He couldn't remember the last time he had noted a question to ask Doctor Miles. In fact, now he thought of it, there was one thing to ask, do I really need to see you anymore? Thinking this through, he realised he should visit the good doctor one more time and close off the therapy sessions.

Jenny had offered to come with him today for moral support and if it had been just the school he was visiting it would have been ok, but Billy figured he had to go the graveside alone. It was now nearly eight months since Elspeth had died and ignoring Xavier's requirements, he knew this day was coming and he had been putting it off deliberately. He had no idea how he would feel or what he should do or say. In many ways it was all a bit surreal, but over the last few months of getting to understand a little of the Aunt he never knowingly met, he had developed some very strong feelings of family. The reinforcement from Xavier, Roger North and George Transon of behaviours he shared with Elspeth had exacerbated this further. But now the day had come, there was a genuine nervousness deep within him as he got into his car. It had been many years since he had visited his Father and Mother's grave. It was one of the first things Doctor Miles had encouraged him to stop doing as part of this therapy. They were always guilt filled times, where he was forced to think as much about his Father and his Mother.

The Perry Gene

It took Billy just over an hour to drive out to Brookwood on the Sunday afternoon as traffic was light. The cemetery was located about fifteen miles from the house that Billy had visited on two previous occasions. He parked the car and pulled a folded piece of paper from his pocket. It was an email from the cemetery superintendent showing the plot in which Elspeth was laid. The map was vital and immediately Billy knew why Elspeth had decided to be buried here; George had mentioned it was a specific instruction. The cemetery was like walking through an art gallery. According to the information in the email, Brookwood was a Victorian overspill cemetery when London's graveyards became full and at its height, even had its own railway service bringing the dead and mourners. Billy suddenly saw parallels of the link between railways and the dead with the way that Chris Deville had died, falling from the railway line. He mentally edited the last line and replaced falling with *thrown*. He tried to focus on the surroundings to remove the image from his mind. The graves from London's rich merchants were ornate and intricate. Mausoleums created for whole families to be brought together in death, something that would never happen to Billy. His grandparents were cremated and scattered, his parents shared a twin plot near the old family home in the local churchyard. When his time came, Billy already felt he would like to be here, with someone who even in death was caring for him in ways he could truly only now begin to comprehend and appreciate.

After another ten minutes of walking and searching Billy eventually found the plot. It stood out from the graves around it, but he wondered how

The Perry Gene

Elspeth would have been able to arrange this? This was not a new part of the cemetery, but the graves were in a very good state. Other graves around the area had the Verdigris of age upon their faces. Elspeth's plaque itself was simple, her dates, her name and a few brief words about her life, Billy read one line over and over and then out loud.

'Loving daughter and devoted Aunt' he repeated. After a minute he said 'You certainly were that Aunt Elspeth. I'm sorry I never met you.' Billy took several photographs of the grave alone, but then realised this was never Elspeth's way, she was all about context. He set up a shot with her gravestone in line with the stones around her and as he focused to get the other inscriptions clear, his eyes fell on the name of the closest one; Perry. He took the photograph and then looked at the other graves clustered around. They were all part of the Perry family, going back over one hundred years. Elspeth was buried here, because she was at last at peace with her own people; her family. No wonder she had been angry about her parents being cremated and the ashes scattered without consultation or approval by his Mother and Father. They had broken a family tradition. Billy needed to leave now, but from a carrier bag he had brought from the car he removed some cut carnations, a spray of varied colours. He had meant to leave them all on Elspeth's stone, but now he found himself dividing the bunch up into six equal groups and he lay one set of flowers on each family stone. Suddenly, as he walked away and retraced his steps back to the car, he felt an incredible sense of well-being and belonging. Now it was time to complete the required photographs for Xavier and then return to the important task of seeking justice for Chris Deville.   A task that Billy now knew Elspeth's keen sense of justice would approve of.

*

On Monday morning Billy thought about what he wanted to achieve that week and where best to focus his efforts.   After returning home on the Sunday evening he had chatted to Jenny for a while on the phone and though initially he thought that a solitary evening would be preferable after visiting the grave, he soon asked her to come over.   There were two reasons in his mind, the first of which was the good mood he had walked away from Brooklands in. Secondly, he realised how important his relationship with Jenny was becoming and as he looked at Elspeth's image hanging on the wall and dominating the room, he knew somehow that she would approve.

When Jenny arrived, he showed her the set of photographs he had taken and she made comments about which ones seemed most appropriate to send Xavier. Afterwards they went for a walk and had some dinner at a friendly little Indian restaurant on Union Square, just off Bankside.   Jenny was surprised how bright Billy was and although he tried to explain why, he found the reason and his rationale not really working or sounding right, so he dropped it and they just ate their shared curry dishes in a comfortable silence.   Jenny did bring up the subject of her parents and would he like to meet them, but then it got awkward again for a while as she thought she had yet again stepped on some sort of taboo subject.   When this occasionally happened, Billy found it very easy to be magnanimous about things as he realised she was only worried about offending him because she cared.   The walk hand in hand along the river was only spoiled when they approached the apartments and Billy saw they were being watched by Tony from his balcony.   He was smoking what looked like a cigar, but there was no pleasantry or wave or recognition.   Tony simply scowled directly at Billy and it occurred to him that maybe the Foreman had informed his boss, and his neighbour had put two and two together.   Jenny didn't notice at first, but realised Billy had gone quiet. She looked up and saw Tony and immediately dragged Billy down the side of the building where they could not be seen.   They entered through the rear door and walked the stairs to avoid calling the lift.

Jenny left early on the Monday and took the bus over to her office. Billy was doing a bit of paperwork in the apartment and was going to go to the lock-up a little later.   Already Steve was having an impact on the work load. While Billy was there, he called Doctor Miles' receptionist and asked if he was free that week.   After a few pleasantries she found a suitable time for both of them on the Thursday.

At just gone ten o'clock Billy headed out of the apartment and down to the garage to get this car and then from there set off for his workplace under the arches.   Certain parts of his make-up would never change and he instantly noticed that something was different.   He did a double take on his car and realised he had a flat tyre at the front.   No, not one, but two.   He hadn't remembered going through any glass. He walked over to take a look and the situation became clearer.   There was a clear slash mark in each tyre about an inch across. Billy guessed a knife or a screw driver. Well that was just petty.

Billy's initial thought was some squatter or local kids, but then it dawned on

him. Nobody could get into the building without a key-fob for either the main

door or the garage exit. Whoever did this had been able to bypass the obvious

physical security. It took a moment and then he realised what one answer could

be. Was this Tony? A little gentle threat to keep his distance from the site?

What happened next if he did not? No, he was just getting carried away, surely?

So, the ex-detectives were right, it was time to start watching over his shoulder

and also time to get some new tyres. Although lightning was unlikely to strike

twice in the same place, Billy also thought about installing a hidden camera in

the garage so that this didn't become a habit.

The Perry Gene

Chapter 19

After his initial difficulties on Monday morning, Billy was back on the road in the afternoon. The garage that supplied the vans had a call-out service and ignoring the obvious cost of a couple of tyres there was no real harm done. Pete managed to cover the work in his absence and Billy used the time to make a few calls, one of which was to Roger North. Although they were still working on the task, Roger thought they would have some information on CCTV availability by the middle of the week, so Billy suggested Wednesday night for a couple of drinks, somewhere quiet, but not the Boot this time. Roger mentioned that he and Jerry had a couple of quieter back-up boozers but they were a little further for Billy to walk to. After agreeing this was fine, Roger suggested the Blackfriars Wine Bar, which Billy didn't know. Roger told him where it was and asked Billy to trust him.

From the directions, Billy had no idea where he was going, but when he walked down the side street just across from Southwark tube, the reason became very clear. It was only a wine bar in name, in reality is was a quiet little boozer built into the railway arches, the kind of place you only found out about if someone tipped you the wink. When he walked in, he immediately saw Jerry in a booth with a laptop open. Roger was nowhere in sight. Billy raised his hand and made the sign of a drink but Jerry called over to the barman.

'Frank, can we have another bottle of the Rothschild and an extra glass?' This Billy guessed was not his first drink of the day. Jerry seemed genuinely troubled and Billy's perception was reinforced when he approached him, as he got up to shake his hand in greeting. 'You are something else Billy boy.'

'What have I done now?' Billy was concerned he had transgressed some unspoken rule, but why then the handshake?

'Your brain would have been good for police work, you know that? Good intuition. Good logical mind.'

'Did you find something?' Billy was now looking at the open laptop and he could feel his heart begin to race.

'Did we find something? Oh yes.'

'What?' Billy looked around again 'and where's Roger?'

'Dropping off a a few bottles of Scotch to a thirsty security guard. Payment in kind.' Jerry was taping his shirt pocket poking out of which could be seen a USB stick. The barman came over with an opened bottle of red wine and another glass for Billy. He gestured to pour but Jerry gently shook his head and waved him off. He quarter filled the fresh glass, topped his own up and handed the drink to Billy. 'We've had our own little success too, but more about that when Roger gets back, he will only be ten minutes or so.' Billy sat down and tried the wine; Jerry knew what he was talking about in many areas judging by how good it tasted. He looked fit to burst and he gestured Billy to come around and sit in the booth. Billy sat next to him and looked at the screen of the laptop.

'Well, what have you found?' he asked Jerry.

The Perry Gene

'You have two buildings both with cameras that might record the railway, but you have to remember a few things about CCTV; it's not like the movies. Firstly, whatever we pick up on these will not be what the cameras were set up for, this is incidental, so there will be blind spots. Secondly, at night and at that distance, the quality is likely to be grainy at best.'

'Ok, so we are lucky to catch anything and what we've got isn't great, is that the gist of it?' Billy wasn't in the mood for the slow reveal but he knew he couldn't push it as these guys were doing him a favour. He also guessed there was a bill for the Scotch coming his way at least.

'Oh, I haven't finished with the best bit yet. Thirdly, nobody is made of money, so they don't record and store forever. Most of the footage for what is more than six months ago has been written over several times, especially now that data is stored on hard drives and not tapes any more. The better the image, the more the storage, so conversely, the more likely the image is to help, the less likely it is to still exist at this stage.'

'And yet you are very excited about something' Billy snapped.

'Patience young grasshopper, of course there is something. The first building was a wash out, nothing left on their system older than a month. Fortunately for you the second building is a data centre for an insurance company. It not only has a lot of cameras, but they are good quality and more importantly, motion activated.' Billy was now lost.

'Meaning?'

The Perry Gene

'They turn on for about two minutes every time the motion sensor detects movement. That means since they are not recording continuously they don't use the storage as quickly and images are likely to be available for longer. It seems the company has some compliance rules it needs to meet and so we are lucky with the building we had available.'

'So' Billy said, trying to move it along, but not wanting to annoy Jerry any further 'what have you found?'

'Three clips, I have written down the time signatures to look at here.' On the table in front of him was a beautiful copper-plate hand written note with three sets of time codes on it. Jerry unlocked the screen and punched in the first code. 'See in the bottom corner, a car pulls up to the side of the building and someone gets out. Note that the time is showing twelve minutes past one in the morning. You can't see the face due to the quality, but you can see the driver enter the site at a very odd time.'

'Bugger me, what you show is enough. I can see that's Tony's car, I certainly know what it looks like from the garage in the apartments. And more importantly, the general shape also looks like Tony. So, the question is, who turns up to inspect their site at that time of the morning?' Billy looked at the rest of the still image, nothing else looked out of place. 'So, we know he was there, not exactly damning, from your expression when I walked in, you obviously have more.' Jerry punched in a second code, which then displayed the screen with a time fourteen minutes later.

The Perry Gene

'Now, look at the top right-hand corner. You can't see any detail of the bucket itself, but what you do see is…' Jerry waited for Billy to recognise what he was seeing before continuing his commentary.

'The arm of the cherry picker moving' Billy interrupted. 'Who would be doing that late at night? That tends to support my theory but as yet nothing here is proof of wrong doing, or how Chris Deville got up onto the railway, just supposition.' It was at this point that Roger walked in, beaming.

'You started without me, how far you got?' Jerry poured more wine into the other glass on the table and handed it to Roger.

'We are just getting to the interesting part, the third and final shot.'

'Excellent, this is where we find out the butler did it' chuckled Roger, but Jerry gave him a look and he stopped smirking. He punched in a third time code and the screen showed the scene two minutes later. Initially Billy saw nothing until Jerry pointed to the top left-hand side of the image.

'As we saw before, the cherry picker bucket itself is in a blind spot. Not intentional I guess as there was no way these guys knew about the CCTV, just unfortunate. But once they got the body up onto the track,' Billy looked at Jerry, who nodded his head, 'yes body, either dead or unconscious at this point. As I was saying, once up on the track, they needed to get the body away from the site before disposing of it.' Now Billy saw it, coming out from behind the shadow of the building edge, grainy, but sufficiently clear were two figures. One looked like the person who had been seen getting out of the car earlier and the second, a larger guy, had a body slung over his shoulder in a fireman's carry.

Billy could not be certain, but his best guess was that the person carrying the body was the foreman.   The clip cut off. 'That's all we have, but it's enough to prove your theory. Pretty cool Billy boy, you saw a crime that nobody else did.'

'Right, so what's the next stage, go to the police?'

'Nothing they can do with this Billy. The footage is poor quality; the logic is potentially so full of holes that a good lawyer would make Swiss cheese out of it.   Besides, what can you really prove about motive?'   Jerry took a drink from his glass. 'There is a little more though.'

'I thought you said that was all the footage?'

'Oh, it is' now Roger took up the story, 'but like in all good things, the way to find the truth is to follow the money.'

'Sorry, I don't understand.'

'That development will be worth well over twenty million when completed and sold off.   Tony is just not big enough to bankroll the whole thing himself, so we did some digging into his finances.'

'I thought he was loaded, Julia said something about owning a racehorse. Although he did make it clear that it was only part of a horse and he had got rid of it a while before we met him.'

'Yes, that's the point, *owned*.   They *owned* part of a racehorse, in the past tense Billy.   But Tony liquidated a lot of his assets to make this one big score.   He still came up short, so he borrowed money.   More accurately, people like him don't get bank loans, they are not good risks and don't like financial people or tax officials looking too closely at them. No this was very much an off the books loan and from people you don't mess with.'

'And in English? I am not following this completely. Why does this mean Chris Deville had to die?'

'Billy, do you know the time it takes to clear Asbestos from a building site, not to mention the cost?' Billy shook his head. 'We asked a friend of ours who is in the business and he reckons based on the building age and the size of the site, that it would take six months and cost upwards of half a million.' Billy whistled. He now started to see the issue that had faced Chris and may now be coming his way.

'So, as I said the foreman saw me taking the pictures and noted down my car as I was driving away' said Billy. Jerry stopped playing with the laptop and looked at Billy. 'It's possible that the Foreman mentioned it to his boss.' Billy stopped and was obviously thinking. In his mind he was linking the causal chain from the building site to his slashed tyres.

'Billy, anything we should know?' asked Roger.

'My front tyres were flat on Monday morning and I found holes that looked as if a screwdriver had made them.'

'Billy, why the hell didn't you say?'

'I thought it might just be local vandals.' He paused 'but I did wonder about the car being in a locked garage.'

The Perry Gene

'Any more trouble in the meantime?' Jerry had his hand on Billy's shoulder, but Billy was not sure if it was meant to reassure him or Jerry. In the end it was succeeding to calm neither.

'No, but then again I haven't seen Tony since. Although a couple of times now I have had the feeling I am being watched. Anyway, I stuck a camera in the garage to catch who ever does it, in case they come back.'

'Billy, it's a classic warning shot. Roger, we've seen this tactic from thugs like Tony before, haven't we?' Roger nodded his head in response. 'You need to consider leaving and getting away from him before this gets any worse.'

'Maybe I'm not finished.' Roger and Jerry both stopped and looked at Billy.

'What do you mean by that?' Roger nervously played with his glass and picked up the bottle for a refill.

'I mean, now I know what happened, I want justice.' Billy took the bottle from Roger and topped his and Jerry's glasses up. These were the professionals and yet Billy appeared to be the calmest man in the room.

'Justice or vengeance Billy? This is a serious game you are playing. Let's be clear, we are not police anymore, but we have principles. We don't want you going all vigilante on us as that is not what we are about. Justice is tricky in this case, as you don't have any real evidence. Vengeance is simple, but if something untoward happens to Tony, don't expect us to come running to your defence. You cannot do monstrous things and not become the monster.

Besides which, this is neither you nor Elspeth.' Billy wasn't sure if he should applaud the speech as it was so commendable and would not have sounded out of place at an awards ceremony.

'As long as he plays by the rules, I will too.'

'That's the thing about the Devil Billy, he never does play nicely.' Jerry finished his glass of wine. 'Right, keep us in the loop and don't do anything we wouldn't do.' Jerry gave Billy the USB stick. 'We have a copy in case it goes walkabout or in case anything happens to Tony.' Billy took it and shook Jerry's hand.

'What do I owe you for the whisky and wine?' He reached over to shake Roger's hand as he got up to leave.

'Just settle the bar tab, we got the whisky at trade from the landlord, but it's still going to cost you a couple of hundred.' This was less than Billy was expecting for the time they had put into the job. He had the feeling something else was coming. Roger turned away but Jerry looked and Billy. Billy opened his hand to gesture Jerry should share. 'Fine, the other thing is, if this ever goes to the press or gets written up in any way, we want exclusive publishing rights, done?' Jerry stuck his hand out again, Billy took it and nodded his head in agreement.

'Done.' The two ex-detectives walked slowly but purposefully out of the bar. Billy thought if that was them both playing good cop, he would hate to see either of them play bad cop.

*

The Perry Gene

Thursday morning, Billy again left the apartment later than usual as he had a meeting with Doctor Miles. He had the first appointment that day and the waiting room was empty when he arrived, but then again, he had only ever seen one other patient in there when visiting over the last few years as it was a specialist therapy and there were only two Doctors at the practice. Doctor Miles had brought on a protégé when his success started to be recognised and that was when he moved to the current premises. Billy remembered at the time how hard the upheaval had been for him, but now this was just a room like any other.

After five minutes the assistant at the desk told Billy he could go in. It was not someone he recognised, but then again, he had not been to see the Doctor in nearly three months. He had cancelled a couple of times, once through pressure of work, but the second time simply because he looked in his notebook the night before and saw precisely no questions. If there were no questions, why did he need to see his therapist? Billy had long since realised that his mental health was in his own hands now, the Doctor's work was done. It was time to let go of that particular safety blanket.

He sat down when Doctor Miles offered him a seat. The Doctor went to the fridge as usual and took out his poison of choice. He raised the can to Billy offering one to him.

'I can't abide the diet stuff; do you have a full fat one please?' The Doctor bent down to retrieve a second can from the fridge and then went to take a glass from the shelf. 'From the can will be fine,' Billy paused, enjoying how

his moment was going to go. He then continued with the bombshell 'Gordon'.
Doctor Miles turned his head so quickly to face Billy that by rights he should
have had whiplash.

'Billy, I see we have learned a new skill.'

'Not sure about you Doc, but I have.' Billy chirped.

'Doc, Doc? If I didn't know better, I would swear you have got
yourself a tame medium and have been chatting to Elspeth. That was the one
thing she did that really got up my nose.'

'According to my girlfriend and literary agent, I am channelling
Elspeth, although Xavier suspects it's just genetics.'

'Girlfriend, oh it's moved on a bit since my last chat with George'
Doctor Miles stopped and corrected himself 'with Mr Transon.'

'You can say George you know, I call him that now, although not to his
face I have to admit, but that's just because I haven't seen him for a little while.
Things have changed quite a bit since we last met. I thought we should meet
up to discuss if we need to meet up.'

'I am starting to think there is a touch of the Mary Shelley going on
here if I am honest' Gordon said as he realised, he was pacing and walked back
to his desk to sit down.

'Sorry I'm not sure of the reference? Meaning?'

'Frankenstein; look at the monster I have created.'

'I would hardly say monster, but a few things have been happening
lately and it has both helped me to toughen up a bit and also to see the world a

little differently.' Gordon templed his fingers and then realised Billy was staring at his hands so he placed them back gently on the arms of the chair. He suddenly felt like Billy had reversed the spotlight and that he was under scrutiny himself.

'Do you wish to share?' He paused and tried again 'would it help to talk about it?' Gordon realised the only way forward here was to sound less like a therapist and more like a friend.

'Well let's see, it's a bit like that Spaghetti Western; the Good, the Bad and the Ugly. Firstly, I am now in a relationship with Jenny and it's bloody marvellous. She is pretty, fun to be with and puts up with me, so that is a definite plus.' Gordon went to say something but Billy continued. 'Before you ask, she is the *Good*.'

'Well that's really positive, any problems around her you need to talk about?' Gordon tried to regain the doctor / patient model, but Billy was not falling for it.

'She does want me to meet her parents and every time family is mentioned she feels awkward, but I think that is her issue not mine. No, no help required with her, I'm doing fine on my own.'

'Right, shall we do the *Bad* or the *Ugly* next then?' Billy smiled and sat back in his chair, crossed his legs and templed his fingers to ape the usual pose of the doctor. Gordon scowled at him but he retained his position as he spoke.

'The *Bad* comes in the form of my interaction with Xavier. He is a little full on as I think you know from Elspeth? He is not bad in himself but this exhibition thing he has got me involved with does make me uncomfortable. I'm still trying to work out why I agreed to it.'

'Exhibition, George did mention something about displaying Elspeth's work, what's wrong with that? She was a fabulous photographer from the pieces I saw.'

'Agreed, it's just Xavier wants to use some pictures I have taken as biography. He also wants me there for a press evening. That really isn't my thing.'

'Billy, can I just remind you that most of what goes on in your life wasn't your thing ten or even five years ago. You are changing, growing, throwing off the yoke your Mother harnessed you with. That process has accelerated beyond all belief since you moved away from the family house. I thought it might, but not to this extent. I am extremely pleased but surprised by how rapid your progress has been. Just take the press event in your stride. Do you want support on the night? If you tell me the date, I can make myself available.'

'Doc' Billy stopped and put his hands down in contrition 'Gordon, I appreciate everything you have done for me and I know Elspeth would be happy. I do want you to come to the exhibition, but not as my therapist, but as a friend. You were one of my guardian angels that Elspeth put in place. It is only fitting you are there to see her final show.' Gordon smiled, didn't say a word for a moment and then nodded his head in acceptance. 'So now,' teased Billy, 'I expect you want to know about the *Ugly*?'

The Perry Gene

'I guessed since you used the phrase that we would get around to it. What are you referring to now?'

'Well now' Billy lifted his hand and started to count off points on his fingers. 'I have discovered my tenant Chris Deville was murdered by, or at the instruction of, my next-door neighbour, Tony. Chris was having an affair with Tony's wife Julia. Julia let it slip that Tony had a serious issue with his building project. While investigating it, Chris discovered that Tony was bribing a fellow building inspector to cover up the asbestos finding.'

'Woah; are you sure about this?   It sounds like there are some serious allegations here.'

'Hold on, not finished.' Billy had turned down three fingers while counting, he now went to lower the fourth. 'I have low quality CCTV footage showing a body being moved from Tony's building site along the railway towards the point where Chris's body *fell* from.' Gordon went to say something, but Billy raised his hand to stop him. He then lowered the thumb on his hand and closed it like a fist to signify the fifth and final point. 'Finally, as of Sunday, I am convinced that Tony knows I either have all the picture or at least suspects.' Gordon sat spellbound for a moment.

'What are you going to do?   I assume you have told the police?'

'Told them what?   That we illegally obtained grainy CCTV footage showing people messing about on a railway late at night?   That my demised tenant kept a diary where he mentions an affair and the husband of that woman in a bad light? That my tyres were slashed as a warning?'

'What? You didn't mention the last part before.'

'No, well like everything else, it can't be proved.'

'Billy, this brings me to the point of all our sessions, what are you going to do next?'

'I want to prove he did it of course. Not just for my sense of order and it being right, but also because it's what I think Elspeth would have done.   I've now had a chance to look at her work; the child labour, ivory, gun runners. Her new work when she died was about people smuggling into London up the Thames. I am convinced she would approve.'

'But she won't thank you for going the same way as Chris Deville.' Gordon reminded him.

'Then I need to be careful, Gordon.'

5.   Double Helix

The Perry Gene

Chapter 20

A week went by and there were no further issues with the Billy's car or in fact any other interference with his day to day activities. September gave way to October with a thump as the temperature dropped fifteen degrees and with it all hope of the Indian summer continuing. Billy only really paid attention to the seasons when it came to his role as referee at the weekend. The teams had played in snow before, sub- zero temperatures were not a problem, but the one reason that games were called off was water logged pitches. In reality less about health and safety and more about the damage imposed on the grass underneath. This weekend was an exception, Billy was home two hours early as one of the teams playing had got a flu bug that was doing the rounds and they could only field two players. He got to the pitch just as his phone was ringing from one of the captains to tell him they could not play. The other captain looked quite relieved in reality, as he was also down two players and had to call in favours to make up the numbers. Even Billy was not very disappointed to be heading home a couple of hours earlier than expected.

As Billy opened the door to his apartment, he sensed that something was not quite right. He thought he heard movement upstairs, but as he shut the front door it stopped. Was he imagining it? He wondered if recent events had made him jumpier. He relaxed a little but being Billy, he wanted to make sure that everything was where it should be. He checked the bookshelves, nothing wrong there, although two of the books looked like they had been swapped round. 'It must have been Jen' he thought to himself. He was about to give up the search when he again thought he heard a noise upstairs. Billy remembered the car tyres and the repeated warning of Jen, Roger North and Gordon. He went into the kitchen and looked for something to defend himself with. Scanning the available implements, he realised he was not that good with a knife at the best of times (there was a half empty box of blue plasters in the kitchen supplied by Jenny), so instead he plumped for the meat tenderizer that Jenny had brought round for use on their special weekly steak meal. It wasn't exactly ferocious, but Billy was caveman enough still to be able to wield a club without hurting himself.

He started to climb the stairs, slowly, trying not to make too much noise, then realised, it was his apartment; he was supposed to be here. Besides if there was a burglar, it would be good to let them know he was coming rather than startle them as then they might be more unpredictable.

'I know you're there, I heard you move. I am coming up and I have a weapon. Come out before this gets any worse.' Billy was saying the words but, in his mind, he felt foolish. There was nobody there, it would just be the wind blowing the curtains from a carelessly left open window. He took two more steps and stopped at the top of the stairs. 'Last chance before I get nasty. Come out now and we don't need to involve the police.' He took one more step and heard the rustle of movement in his bedroom. He rushed forward and threw open the door. Nothing. Was he wrong? He walked over to the wardrobes and looked inside each carefully. Again, empty. He looked around, focused on the bed and then thought to himself, surely not; nobody would try that. Well the easiest way to find out would be fun too. He bounded three steps and launched himself on the bed. As the springs compressed he heard a muffled scream. Hang on, it sounded like a female. 'Jen?' Billy asked.

'No, you fool' came the response from below. 'Get off so I can get out' Billy leapt off the bed and after a few seconds Julia emerged from underneath.

'What the hell are you doing here and how did you get in?' shouted Billy. Julia stood up and moved towards the door. Billy placed his body between her and the exit. 'Oh no, you are going nowhere until you explain what you have been doing in my apartment, my bedroom.'

'Finally, darling you want to keep me captive in your bedroom. I wondered how long it would take.' She wandered over to the best, laid down and held up his wrists to suggest she was ready to have the shackles attached.

'Stop changing the subject. Get off there and tell me what you're up to. To start with, how did you get in? Did you get another key cut?'

'But of course, darling, I never knew when you might be in need of some neighbourly TLC. I didn't think that little girlie of yours would last for ever, and a man has his needs. She pushed herself back up the bed and lay on the pillows. Her hands were now above her head next to the bedposts, cruciform. The implications were very clear but Billy was not at all interested.

'Get up and act your age. Even if I didn't have Jenny, I would not be coming anywhere near you. You are a poisoned chalice. Thanks to you Chris Deville is dead. Now tell me what you were looking for.'

The Perry Gene

'I wanted that bloody diary.' She stopped. 'Hold on, what do you mean Chris' death was my fault? He committed suicide.' She now got up from the bed, the playtime was obviously over and she looked worried.

'Well the diary is hidden and there is another copy elsewhere as well. It is evidence. Evidence of your husband having your lover killed.'

'Don't be stupid, he fell off the railway embankment. It was in the papers and the police interviewed us.'

'What I don't get right now, is whether your husband had him killed because of you or the asbestos. I honestly don't think he would care about you enough from the way he treats you. I am guessing Chris Deville died in order to hide the secret of the asbestos at the housing project.'

'How do you know about the building site?'

'The diary Julia. As I said you got Chris killed one way or another. Either for being his lover or for being the person who alerted him to the issue.'

'How could I, I barely knew anything at the time.' She was now starting to well-up; the tears were just seconds away.

'In one of your drunken afternoon rambles during the throes of passion. You let the cat slip out of the bag. When Chris investigated, he paid with his life for your big mouth.'

'I will tell Tony you know. Tell him all this. He will say it's all rubbish.'

'Too late Julia, I suspect he already knows. My car tyres were slashed. Not many people have access to the garage.'

The Perry Gene

'That's not proof. Anyway, why would he come after you?'

'Because I now know what Chris knew and Tony suspects I either have evidence or am looking for it.' Julia looked perplexed. 'No, I am saying no more, but if you fancy repeating this conversation with him, then feel free to mention I am going to make a case and then go to the Police. He is not going to get away with murder.' She pushed past and as she ran down the stairs she called back.

'You are wrong, but he is not going to be happy. You'll be sorry you stuck your nose into our affairs.'

'On the subject of affairs, don't forget to tell him you were in my apartment; that should help.' Billy shouted down after her. He started to descend the stairs as the door to the apartment slammed shut. 'Bugger' he said to himself, 'She's still got a key.' He walked to the chair where he had put down his bag from football and pulled out his phone. He sent Pete a text asking about the locksmith they used and if he had the number. After a few minutes the phone chirped a response and, in the text, Pete had sent the details. Billy pressed the call button with the new information.

'Hi, I'm in Butler's Wharf, how quickly can you come out and do a front door lock replacement?'

'Can be there in half hour. Broken is it?' came the response.

'No' said Billy 'there just appears to be too many keys in circulation. A throw back to my tenant.'

'You have some evidence you are the owner, right?'

'Yes, I can provide identification.'

'Right then, give me the address and I'll see you shortly.' Billy provided the information and then closed down the call. That was one issue out of the way but now he knew he was stuck in the apartment for a few hours. He dialled Jenny's number.

'Hi Jen, unexpectedly home early and I had a visitor, now I need to wait for the locksmith. You fancy me cooking you lunch?'

'Visitor, should I be worried?'

'No, tell you all about it later.'

'Oh secrets, excellent. See you in an hour. Oh, do I need to bring anything?'

'Only if you want to eat.'

'Oh, now I see, it's that kind of phone call. Do you have anything in?'

'Pasta, rice, soup…' Billy started to recite the contents of the cupboards until she stopped him.

'Shall I bring steak?'

'No, I think the tenderiser has been busy enough today. Surprise me.'

'I swear you get stranger by the day Billy, Billy Perry. Well then, see you as soon as I can.'

*

Three hours and three hundred quid later, Billy felt a little more secure in his castle. He realised asking for the key again was no guarantee that Julia had not made several copies and this could rapidly turn into a game of cat and mouse.   Additionally, the access she had to the apartment was also available to Tony.   When she had arrived initially Jenny had listened with incredulity about Julia being in the apartment and hiding under the bed to avoid detection, but she soon started to ask questions of Billy.

'What were you thinking?   He will now know what you know.'

'He already knows, remember, my tyres. With the price of a new door lock those two are becoming expensive neighbours.'   Billy took a key off the new ring of three he had been given by the locksmith and gave it to Jenny. 'Here, you will need this to replace the old one.'

'If you keep annoying South London gangsters, I'm not sure if I want to be spending too much time with you.   You are becoming a dangerous man.' But she took the key and smiled.   She loved the fact that he wanted her to have access to his place and after what had happened it meant all the more to her. 'Are you going to update North and South on your encounter?'

'I dropped Roger a text just to let him know, but I'm not planning on anything more.   I think they are going to keep out of this now, unless I do something wrong.'   She nodded her head, well aware that they had told him not to step outside the law with whatever he planned to get justice for Chris Deville. Billy picked up the plates from the table and took them to the kitchen.   The three hours elapsed had given Jenny time to get food in and they had cooked together while they talked about the visit.   Now having eaten, and without the exercise from the cancelled football match, Billy was restless.   In his mind there was a giant set of balance scales for calories in and calories out.   He fancied a run, but thought that Jenny would neither have the gear or the inclination for it. He thought about a walk and was about to suggest the river as usual but already Jenny was starting to read his body language.

'So, now you're restless.   You want to get out and let off some steam?'

'What have you got in mind?'

'I thought maybe grab a couple of Boris bikes and cycle down the river.'

'Are they still called Boris bikes?' Billy retained the facilities for pedantry.

'Let's just say it's a working title.   Why don't you bring your camera, you never know what you will see? We could set off in the direction of Greenwich, possibly then cross to the Island and up onto the canal towpath to Victoria Park.   It's cold and breezy out there but the rain has stopped. My Mother would call it bracing.' Billy loaded the plates into the dishwasher and washed his hands.   He turned to her as he dried them.

'Actually, that's not a bad idea.   I was looking at the images that Xavier was planning on using for the exhibition from Elspeth's final project. Might be nice to get some shots of the river and the canal, with people living on boats.   They are not all floating gin palaces, some are little better than squats.'

'Right,' Jenny responded, 'give me ten minutes to get changed. I have some trainers I brought over last week.'   Billy thought *trainers, we could have gone for a run after all*, but he said nothing and went to change his own clothes back into something more appropriate.

As they left the apartment, the door across the hall opened and Billy saw Tony standing there. Tony stared at Billy and it wasn't clear which one of them would speak first until Jenny broke the standoff. She walked over and pressed the call button for the lift.

'Looks like the weather is improving Tony' she said in an attempt to keep it light and get away without an argument.

'Yes' Billy said 'You don't want bad weather to create any more hold ups on the building do you Tony? You must be a bit behind already.'

'What do you mean' barked Tony.

'Why all that rain Tony, it must have delayed your work.'   Tony seemed to relax a bit as if he had thought Billy was referring to something else. 'And' continued Billy 'I'm sure it's tough to operate a cherry picker in the rain.' At that moment the lift went ping, Tony went puce with anger and Jenny bundled Billy towards the opening doors to get him away.   'Catch you soon Tony' was Billy's parting blow. He turned to face him and the doors shut in front of their faces.   Once the doors closed and the lift started to descend, Jenny turned to Billy.

'Now that wasn't too bright was it? You can't keep goading him like this.   You saw his face; he's going to respond.   It was just his tyres last time, but you know he is capable of more. Keep it up and I will stay away Billy.   I'm not keen on you or me getting hurt by that man.' Billy nodded his head in agreement, but his mind was somewhere else.   He was placing chess pieces on a board. The black king and queen had both just moved and he, as the white knight in the white castle had responded.   In his mind he was seeing the word check, but there were still too many possible moves to predict how the game would end,

*

With the weekend over the week ahead was busy.   Although work had eased off a little following the introduction of Steve on the payroll, there was still a fair amount of work to keep up with.   Billy had a call from Shirley about one of her machines that had gone bang in the pub over the weekend.   As Shirley was a long-term customer Billy thought a bit of personal attention was called for.   He arranged to go there later on Monday afternoon and to make it the last call of the day so he would have an easy journey home.   With the workforce growing and the vans being required by the boys, he was left to use his own car increasingly. The spread of his business was increasing and now some of the pubs and clubs were over fifteen miles away from the lock-up, which was no fun to get back from in London traffic.

When he got to the Flag & Staff it was quiet and he was almost the only person in the main bar.   Shirley was clearing up the glasses from the lunchtime session so left him to it for half an hour or so.   From the phone call Billy had guessed right, the power supply had blown, but it had damaged half the main processor board and it was going to take nearly an hour to swap out both and reconfigure the machine. He had the power supply in but was still working on removing the processor when Shirley came over.

'How's it going Billy?' she said and plonked herself own on the chair next to him.

'Busy lunch?'

'Surprisingly, yeah. Not sure what was going on but a couple of parties were in, think there may have been a staff announcement at one of the local firms, guys drinking their sorrows away.'

'Good for business though.'

'Yeah, mostly. But we also had an odd pair in, snooping around.'

'What do you mean, snooping around?'

'Well they were asking questions about who fixes the machines here.'

'What, asking about me?'

'No, that's just the thing. When they saw the machine in the corner was dead they started asking about who fixed them when that happened. One of them said they had some machines that needed sorting and were looking for a new maintenance company. Anyway, I gave them your business address and then they finished their drinks and left.'

'Well, that's not exactly suspicious.'

'It is when I tell you that I rang James up the road to talk about the local licensees' association and while we were chatting, he mentioned that two guys had been in earlier today asking him the same questions. When I described them, it was the same blokes.'

'Yup, that is a bit odd.' Now Billy's mind was racing, surely not something to do with Tony? Had he decided to call Billy's bluff? 'Did they looked like they might work on a building site?'

'Now that Billy is spooky.'

'Why?'

'Because when he paid for the beer, I thought to myself, those are a pair of hands that have seen hard work. You know, calloused and cracked.' *The foreman* Billy thought to himself. Billy took the circuit board out and started to fit the new one. 'You want a coffee or a beer while you work?'

'Yes, please Shirl, a coffee that is. Not really in the mood for beer right now.' Shirley walked back over to the bar and started to work on the complex coffee machine.

It took Billy thirty-five minutes more to install and configure the machine. It was a nice little bit of business and he was pleased with the result as this particular machine had been playing up for a while. He cleared away his tools, as ever carefully replacing them in the correct positions in the toolkit. Shirley was watching from the bar and smiling.

'Still the same old Billy at heart.' Billy closed and locked the case and then took it with the broken parts to the van. Steve or Pete should be able to either recondition or cannibalise them for parts.

'I'll email you the invoice for the work. See you soon Shirl.'

'Thanks Billy, great service as usual.' She went to pick up a glass cloth and then turned to shout after him. 'Don't talk to any strange men.' But the door

The Perry Gene

was already closing as Billy left for the carpark.   He loaded the car with the

parts and was just getting into the driving seat when a dirty white van pulled into

the car park.   He didn't pay it much attention save the fact that it looked like

the plates had been broken off, possibly in a little shunt on site or while

delivering.   Billy pulled out into the main drag of the traffic.   It was still quiet

as this was not a road that got snarled up at rush hour, but he had the main

intersection in a mile or so and he knew it would be pretty busy at that point.

After less than a minute, a flash of white caught his eye in the rear-

view mirror.   It looked like someone was overtaking but on this road that was a

little reckless. As the traffic built up towards the intersection, chances to pass

were scarce.   Billy checked his mirror again and the flash came into focus, a

white van.   With the way his mind worked, Billy looked to see the plates, but

they were not visible, because the van was too close to him.

'Jesus,' Billy said out loud 'any closer and you will be inside my boot.'

It was then the van revved and Billy felt the first contact. The car shuddered

forward. He felt the steering go light in his hands as the tyres lost traction due to

the shunt. Billy indicated to pull his car over so they could swap insurance

details. But as he slowed, the van hit him again, stronger this time and Billy's

head was flipped back against the head rest.   He put his foot down to get some

distance between himself and the van. As he did, he got a glimpse of the driver,

the recognition was instant; the foreman from the site.   'Jenny was right', of all

the things to go through Billy's mind, the first one bizarrely was about his

girlfriend's ability to predict Tony's actions.   The second thought was that he knew this situation called for either fight or flight. As the van revved its engine and started to gain, Billy realised flight was the only real option here. Looking in the other mirror of the car he now realised the passenger was also someone he recognised; the security guard. You had to hand it Tony, he liked to keep his business close to home and not to outsource.

The traffic was getting heavier which allowed the white van to have one more bite of the cherry, this time it was a much gentler tap as Billy saw it coming and managed to cushion the blow by accelerating at the last moment. However, the foreman was now upping the ante and started to pull alongside the rear of Billy's car on the wrong side of the road. Oncoming traffic was veering out of the way. Billy accelerated too; he knew that a tap on the rear quarter of the car would spin it and he would end up slewed across the road. The last thing he wanted now was to be caught by his two pursuers. He got the feeling there was a beating with his name on it.

Running through his head at analytical speeds which surprised even him, Billy was comparing the options. Drive to a police station? Impractical, he didn't know where the closest was and he wasn't sure how long he could keep out of these guys' way. Ram them back? Put their van out of commission; what if he damaged his own car? Yet again he was back to the fact it was two against one and to coin a phrase, Billy was a lover not a fighter. The lights ahead on the main intersection turned to amber and Billy saw his opportunity. Across the junction from where he was approaching there was a red London bus indicating to turn right across his path. As the traffic lights turned red, Billy flashed his headlights to encourage the driver to go. As the bus started to move Billy gunned the engine. Two things then happened at the same time. Firstly, the Foreman driving the white van, which had started to slow, also pushed his foot hard down on the accelerator. Secondly, the bus, based on Billy's invitation to go, began its turn across the junction. Billy knew for this to work it would be like threading a needle, with very little room for error. He aimed for the front of the bus and when he was no more than twenty feet away, he veered to the left just enough to steer clear of the oncoming vehicle. The bus driver slowed without stopping as Billy pulled round him, but as he squeezed past there was the sound of a long furious horn and the bus proceeded. Other cars started to vocally protest and Billy realised as he glanced in his rear-view mirror that his impromptu trap had been sprung. He gunned the engine even further to clear the lights now he had passed the bus.

The white van was not quite so lucky, the thirty feet that Billy had gained was just enough to ensure that the driver would not be able to execute the same manoeuvre. More than that, the additional speed he had put on when accelerating could not shed so easily. His brakes went on, but the van skidded on the slick surface. This was where the laws of physics came into play. Every action had an equal and opposite reaction and for the foreman, it was to implant a tonne of white metal into the front of a red London bus. The city soundscape now became a cacophony of car horns.

Billy guessed from the noise what had happened but could not see where the van had ended up as his view was obscured by the bus slewed across the junction.   However, he suddenly realised he had an opportunity for gaining

the upper hand.   He pulled his car into the next side road and found a space he

could slip into.   It was a yellow line, but he would only need a couple of

minutes so he decided to risk it. He took his phone with him as he locked the car

and jogged back towards the street corner.   He carefully turned the corner,

trying not to be too obvious and was greeted by a scene of utter chaos.   The

driver of the bus was out inspecting his vehicle and getting out of the white van

were two men who looked somewhat shaken up.   They didn't notice Billy but

were walking over to talk to the bus driver.   Billy took his phone and started to

snap the Foreman but more importantly the security guard who was with him.

Billy knew this would be useful for just one thing, leverage.   He was relieved

about one thing; it looked like nobody had got injured in the process, just a

small shunt in the van and a graze on the bus. He slunk back around the corner

before he was noticed by his pursuers and jogged back the twenty yards to the

car. As he approached it, he realised the white van had made quite a mess. There

was no way the back door would open any more, and he needed one new light

cluster, but apart from that, he was lucky that both he and it were in one piece.

He got back in, put his seat belt on and smiled at how this had helped him

survive the episode in one piece.   He started the car and realised his luck only

lasted so long.   On the outside of the windscreen was a parking ticket. In the

distance he saw a warden disappearing around the corner of the road.   Billy

rolled down the window, reached out and pulled it off, before he headed back to

the lock-up.

The Perry Gene

When Billy arrived back at base, Pete and Steve were loading a machine into the van and once completed, Pete came over.   He looked at the car and then at Billy, who was still fairly white in the face.

'Bearing in mind, I know you are a really safe driver, do you want to tell me what happened?   That looks like the back of the car was in a crusher.'

'Just a little bit of road rage' said Billy, not wanting to drag his friend into the fight.

'Bit more than road rage Billy, that's going to cost money to fix.' Pete started to investigate the damage further.   'Looks like they had more than one bite of the cherry too. Did you get their number?'

'In a manner of speaking' Billy replied almost absent minded. 'I got their number alright.'   As did the bus driver and more importantly my camera Billy thought.   'You delivering that tonight?'   Billy tried to steer the conversation back to work.

'Yup, another sale, you will have to start having awards.   Thing is, it was not me this time, but Steve.   He got on so well at the casino the other night with the duty manager, he got us an order for another three machines. That boy is a find alright.   This is the last one loaded and so we are off to deliver them now.   Anything you need before we leave?   Help to get into your car, I've got a can opener somewhere.'   Pete patted himself down as if looking for the tool he had offered.

'Very witty. No, you are good, you get off and make us some money.'
Pete walked to the van door, Steve was already sitting in the other side. Billy lowered his head to peer through.

'Good work Steve.' Steve smiled, slightly embarrassed. Praise was not something he was used to. As he got into the van Pete stopped and looked and Billy.

'Did that guy find you?'

'What guy?'

'Bloke phoned up this afternoon looking for you. He mentioned he had been given your name by Shirley and he wanted to do some business with you.' The penny dropped in Billy's mind. He could feel the bumps and the bruises from the van impacts and connected the dots.

'Yes' he said thoughtfully. 'He found me alright.'

The Perry Gene

Chapter 21

Arriving back at Butler's Wharf, Billy knew he had little choice but to make two phone calls, one to Jenny and the other to Roger North. In terms of the former, he knew it was more than his life was worth not to tell Jenny what had happened. From the latter, Billy needed advice. He was not sure what to do next and in reality, he was far more shaken up than the air of confidence he had projected at the lock-up would suggest. He pulled into his allocated parking bay and saw Tony's car three spaces along. Billy got out and locked his battered car. Walking around the back he inspected the damage for a second time. Looking across, he compared his old and now damaged car with the pristine motor that Tony drove. Dark thoughts went through his mind of maybe smashing one of Tony's lights or slashing his tyres, but he was aware this was wrong; it was not his way. He pressed the button for the lift, not caring any further if Julia was alerted and up there waiting. He knew after their little chat that she would not be bothering him again. With the apartment lock changed she was now just a nosey neighbour once more.

As the lift doors opened, standing in front of Billy was Tony. His face was calm, there was no visible sign of anger or aggression. Billy stepped aside to let him pass. Tony walked out of the lift, but when he was level with Billy he stopped and turned to face him.

'You still sticking your nose in my business or have you now taken a hint to mind your own?' Tony spoke slowly and in a low pitch. It was calculated, designed to scare. No histrionics, this appeared to be some form of affected malevolence and Billy was almost impressed. Tony had drawn close to his face and Billy could not only smell but feel his hot breath.   Billy was surprised that the volatile thug he had seen glimpses of at the party and read a lot about in Chris's diary, was actually holding it together and not going off bang.   But then Billy realised how scared Tony really was.   This must be his last roll of the dice.   He had slashed tyres and his hired help had tried to send Billy a different message. Now this face to face approach; it reminded Billy of the story recounted by Chris Deville of his altercation with the older man in this very car park.   It looked like this was a favourite place for him to threaten.

'Not sure what you mean Tony.'

'I mean…'

'I hadn't finished' Billy interrupted him.   He wanted him to lose his cool; to be put back off balance. 'Were you referring to your wife and her flirtatious attentions?' Billy held up one finger and then made the effect of counting off on it. 'The fact she has been trespassing in my apartment?' Billy counted a second finger.'

'Listen, you smart little bastard, I don't give a fuck what you do with my wife.'

'Ever the charmer Tony.   You really are a class act.'   Billy lifted another finger to count.   'Could you be referring to me looking into the fact that you have hidden the presence of asbestos at the building complex you are working on?' Now Tony's mask dropped and he pushed Billy in the chest.

The Perry Gene

'Shut your mouth if you know what's good for you.' Billy took a step back and raised another finger.

'Or the fact you are bribing a building inspector to ignore the problem and not fixing it. What's that saving you, about half a million? Do your business partners know? Be a shame if they found out, right?' Tony stepped forward again and pushed Billy in the chest once more, but harder this time.

'If you know what's good for you, you will walk away now.' Tony stopped, took a deep breath and tried a different tack. 'Or is this some sort of blackmail? You after money to keep your mouth shut?' Billy looked at him and shook his head. He raised the thumb on his hand to count off five.

'Or maybe you simply don't want me telling anyone that you had your neighbour, your wife's ex-lover, murdered because he found out about the asbestos.' Tony stopped and this time it was Billy who pushed the old thug in the chest and hard. Tony was obviously not used to people retaliating and he stumbled backwards four or five feet until he regained his balance. Billy needed Tony to say something now, anything incriminating. Although he had not planned this, he knew that in the corner of the garage was the tiny camera he had installed to watch his car and he was aware having checked the tapes that they were still standing in its field of vision. Tony however was not stupid. The push from Billy had been a wake-up call and Tony regained his composure.

'You don't know what you are talking about.' Tony now tried to turn the game on Billy. 'Elspeth said you were sick; she didn't mention delusional. Not sure where you get these weird ideas from? Have you been reading too many gangster books Billy? Is this the bit where the villain confesses and the hero gets the girl?' Tony now turned away from Billy and walked over to his car. On the way he looked at the rear of Billy's vehicle. 'You had an accident, you need to be careful out there. All sorts of lunatics around.' With this parting blow Tony opened his car, got in, started the engine and squealed away up the car park ramp. Billy pressed the button for the lift again. He needed to get back into his apartment and look at the camera footage. Now he had something else to share with Roger and Jerry.

*

On entering the apartment, Billy dialled Jenny's number but it rang without being answered. He guessed she was busy so he waited for the answerphone beep before leaving a brief message.

'Jen, Billy, couple of run ins with Tony today. I'm fine but wanted to let you know as I promised I would. Give me a bell when you get this please.' He quickly hung up the phone and powered up the desktop computer which now sat on his desk in the lounge. A waggle of the mouse and the sleeping monster came to life. Steve had proved even more useful than Billy had expected and had managed to install some scripts to make accessing the garage camera and downloading the images much easier, although Billy had simply mentioned the vandalism; no specifics about Tony. Billy followed the simple steps and transferred the file of his conversation to pen drive. He texted Roger to say that he had a video that might be of interest to him. In the text he used the phrase *video nasty* with a smiley faced emoticon. Roger texted back a few minutes later to say he would pop round that evening if that was ok as he had some other business in the area already.

While Billy sat there and waited for Jenny to call back, he decided to review the conversation with Tony. He wasn't sure how good the audio quality of the webcam footage would be, even though he was pretty convinced Tony had not said anything that would stand up in court. Failing to deny an accusation was not exactly proof. Getting aggressive and exploding when someone calls you a murderer could be considered the behaviour of an innocent man. But in Billy's mind, it was all part of a jigsaw and he was slowly putting the pieces into place. The corners and edges were complete, he now just needed to finish the tricky detail in the centre and see how the whole picture looked when the missing pieces were found. The phone rang and Billy answered immediately.

'Hi Jen, thank for calling back.'

'Billy, this isn't a business meeting, I was really worried when I got the voicemail. Are you ok?' She was breathless as if she had been running.

'You miss the bus? You sound like you've done a marathon.'

'Billy, let me explain to you how this thing works between us. I am sitting in the changing room of the gym in my workout gear. I was about to hit the shower when I noticed the missed call on my phone. As soon as I heard you had a run in with Tony, I wasn't waiting to shower.'

'So, you are sitting there smelly then?'

'What? Yes, oh bloody hell Billy take this seriously. What happened?'

'You remember the security guard from the site?'

'Yes, what about him? You said you would stay away from them, no more antagonising.'

'If you will let me finish, I will explain that I did nothing of the sort. The guard and that foreman I told you about tried to run me off the road in a white van.'

'Billy, are you being serious? This isn't a game.'

'Deadly serious. I had to drive really badly to lose them.'

'Badly?'

'I'll explain later. The car is bruised but functional; in fact, that's how Gordon used to describe me. It needs a couple of new lights on the back, but apart from that it's driveable. You coming over later? I need food and a drink after today.'

'Woah there cowboy, you said two run-ins with Tony. That is one run in with Tony's thugs, have you seen them again or have you bumped into him too?' There was a mixture of annoyance and sarcasm in her voice. She was still not completely sure if Billy was merely innocent in all of these interactions or if he was provoking them.

'Has anyone ever told you that you have trust issues young lady?' Billy mockingly put on the voice of Gordon for effect, but he realised this would go straight over Jenny's head as he assumed, she had not never met him. 'Since you asked so nicely, I can confirm that you are right. I did literally bump into Tony in the car park.   I was about to get into the lift when he came out and started to throw his weight around.' Jenny went to interrupt but Billy stopped her 'and before you say anything, I have the whole thing on video.   I have cut a copy for Roger and Jerry; they are coming to fetch it tonight.'

'Tell me now Billy, how did it end, this little chat with a bit of bumping.'

'Oh, the usual, I guess.   He called me delusional, implied I was still sick and mentioned I needed to take more care on the road as accidents could happen.'

'Shit Billy, you need to go to the police, this is getting out of hand.'

'Not yet, I can handle it.'

'Did Chris Deville think that too?'

'No, but Chris didn't have my secret weapon.'

'I hate to ask, but I'm going to out of concern for you. Secret weapon?' Even though she was the other end of the phone, Jenny knew when he spoke, that Billy was smiling.

'Elspeth's genes.   I am a Perry.'   She hung up the phone and Billy went back to looking at the video.

*

When Jenny arrived ninety minutes later Roger was just finishing up with Billy.

'You were right Billy, he is rattled and you are certainly pulling his strings, but there's nothing there that a court of law would accept as being anywhere near a confession. Did he know about the camera, or were you just unlucky that he did not say anything incriminating? He was losing control at the end there. He also doesn't do his own dirty work.   I guess you are right; his level of violence is directed at Julia only.   When you pushed him in the chest, he was not expecting it and did not know how to react.'

'That's one of the reasons I kind of feel sorry for her.   The guy is a user and abuser. Judging by the way she reacted the other day, I believe she genuinely had feelings for Chris. Her shock about his death and the circumstances around it was real.   She knows Tony isn't up to it, but I guess she also knows he has connections and thugs to do his dirty work for him.'

'Billy,' Jenny interjected 'remember this is the woman who deceived you and lied to you about the keys so she could let herself into your apartment when she thought you were out.' Billy was about to say something but Jenny was in full flow and counting off the infringements on her fingers. 'She then rooted through your personal possessions, presumably to get that damned diary back,' finally Jenny paused for breath.

'I know, I'm not going soft, I just think having been on the receiving end of bullying for years, maybe I see a side to her that is just as a victim.   She was still wrong.'   Jenny looked relieved. She ran her hand through Billy's hair and bent down to kiss him.

'If you're starting that, then I'm off' said Roger. 'I will take the pen drive and show Jerry. He might make more of it in terms of psychological feedback.' Roger grabbed his jacket from the back of the chair and went to leave. 'Billy, seriously now, this is getting dangerous. Watch your back, but remember what we said, it's got to be lawful, whatever you're planning.' Roger let himself out and Jenny slid into the chair beside Billy.

'Planning Billy. That's the word isn't it? I was trying to work out on the way over how much of this is you as a rabbit in headlights and how much is being orchestrated.' Billy held his hands up in surrender, but Jenny persisted. 'Show me that video please. I want to see what you and Roger were discussing. I need to understand what you said, because if it's anything like the last encounter with Tony I witnessed, then you are continuing to stoke that particular fire. The fact is, fires burn.' Billy got up and pulled her with him away from the sofa and over to the desk. He pressed play on the clip and she sat transfixed while straining to hear every nuance.

When it was finished, she walked into the kitchen, took a bottle of wine from the fridge and poured herself a large glass. She held the bottle up to Billy but he signalled he was fine. She got the idea he had already consumed a couple of glasses since their initial phone call and now and it bothered her that he seemed to be more concerned than he was letting on.

'You didn't exactly calm things down, did you? Do you know what you are going to do when he comes after you?' The pressure was building in her voice, Billy sensed a change. 'I keep saying it's not a game but you keep playing.' She walked slowly towards the window, the tears were seconds away and she knew she could not control them. She stared out the window at the river. The days were starting to draw in and with this there came a chill in the air.   She shivered or so Billy thought, it was a pre-shock for the earthquake that was to come.   'Billy' the words were strained now 'I'm in love with you and I'm so scared.' The last two words were so soft as to be almost inaudible. He could see her body starting to rock gently as the tears began to roll down her face.   In the reflection of the window Billy could see her pain. He walked up behind her and put his arms around her, but she pulled away.   She turned to him, her face was wet but these were not simply tears from being upset or scared, Jenny was angry too.   Angry with Billy for trying to pull his own playhouse down.   He moved to towards her, but she held up a finger of warning. 'This has to stop.'

'Not yet. Not until it's finished. Look, I will be careful. They are not going to try the car stunt again.   I need maybe two more weeks. I will stay away from him until then.'

'Two more weeks and then what?'   Jenny dabbed at her face with the back of her sleeve.

'Two more weeks and then I give what I have to the relevant authorities, isn't that what they say?' Billy moved towards her again and this time she acquiesced.   She gripped him tightly as he held onto her.   'It's all going to be fine. You asked me to tell you when things happened and I did.' She nodded her head but going through Billy's mind were different thoughts. What came next, he was not sure, he needed time to think but it was not something he could discuss with Jenny.

*

The Perry Gene

The following morning, the weather had turned fresh with a sharp frost having settled on the City. Jenny headed off to work and Billy went for a run. He was increasingly finding running was the only time he had to think.   Work and life were becoming complicated.   The company was growing, his staff were bringing in more business weekly and Xavier was still badgering him about the exhibition. The final touch was that the press launch was set for two weeks' time but Billy had not been made aware of its significance.   When pushed as to why they could not delay, Xavier had first mentioned the rental on the gallery, then the new staff he was bringing on board, but finally the truth came out.   All the rush for this date was something that if Billy had any normal upbringing, he would have been aware of.   Friday 16th, the night of the press launch, would have been Elspeth's 65th birthday.

Xavier thought Billy would have known, as he still didn't always get what a massive amount of new information Elspeth's nephew had been forced to assimilate in the intervening period since her death.   However, Billy had now fulfilled his end of the bargain and all the photographs were assembled.   On top of that he had provided Xavier with a few of the biographical details from the file and some small pieces of prose for the exhibition sales brochure.   Even now Billy found the idea that people would pay hundreds of pounds for his Aunt's photos to be a little strange.   Having said that, he had adorned the apartment with more images from her collection, swapping out some of the more squalid pieces for things he felt were more impactful and in keeping with the theme.

The Perry Gene

As Billy ran, his mind went back to the problem in hand. He wasn't violent by nature and although he felt Tony deserved to be treated no better than the fate which had met Chris Deville, it was clear this was something Billy could not do. Even if he could bring himself to deal physically with Tony there was the small matter of North and South making it very clear they would not tolerate any violence. Going through his mind was how best to hurt Tony. Julia was just a thing to her husband, a possession, something pretty on his arm. She was also just as much a victim as Billy, so anything in that direction was out. As he pounded the pavement his mind circled around and around. He still had to be certain about Tony's true motive for having Chris Deville killed.

He slowed down as he approached Westminster Bridge and stopped to stretch. As he lunged forward to extend his hamstrings, he held the pose and counted. While counting he noticed the amount of building work going on just in that part of the city. 'How much money is this costing' he thought to himself. As he went to swap legs and stretch the other, he was hit by an epiphany that almost knocked him off balance. It was so obvious; he could kick himself. The way to hurt Tony was through his wallet. According to Jerry he had sold his other property interests to pour everything into the one single building development, but it hadn't been enough. He had sold personal possessions such as his share in the race horse; still he had come up short. Finally, based on North and South's snooping, he appeared to have gone to the sort of money men who broke bones if you didn't pay them back. Then the asbestos was found and he was having to bribe people to keep the development on track. When Chris Deville found out, Tony had him killed. Still at the core of all this was money and Tony's need to complete the building project to pay his creditors and to secure his finances. Billy began the run back to the apartment secure in the knowledge that the only way to hurt Tony was through his finances.

After a few minutes Billy took a short detour from the route at the base of the OXO Tower to look at the exhibition space. Currently the windows were covered with whitewash to stop people looking in, but there was a poster on the wall advertising the event and a month-long opening of the gallery. Billy would concentrate his efforts on that for now and once it was over, he would figure out how he could deal the killer blow to Tony's wallet and so see his fall from grace, although not the type of fall that Chris Deville had suffered. He felt his pulse rate drop and a slight chill as he cooled. He needed to get back to the apartment to shower. The working days were getting longer and he didn't want the boys to think he was slacking. He had already found Pete still in the lock-up finishing off things at nine o'clock in the evening twice in the last week. 'Still', he thought to himself 'not bad having so much work on, it's good for cash flow.' He laughed out loud as he started to run, seeing the parallel between his own burgeoning business interests and his plan to wreck Tony's.

The Perry Gene

Chapter 22

Although he was keeping an eye on the other traffic around him and a watch for Tony when coming and going from the apartment, Billy found the next two days went by without incident.   Maybe standing up to Tony did the trick?   But with work being so busy Billy was quickly distracted by the calls coming in and jobs piling up.   On the Wednesday evening he also had a message from Xavier saying he needed a final meeting to discuss the gallery opening.   It was only nine days away and although the *urgent* issues seemed anything but that, Billy humoured Xavier as he was starting to get to like him.   He could see now why Elspeth would have put up with his little ways as he was certainly very talented when it came to organisation. He also appeared to be well connected as not only were the broadsheets interested in the exhibition, but a few independent art and photography magazines and at least one Sunday paper's magazine.   With this in mind, rather than work late to complete paperwork at the lock-up, Billy left Pete and Steve to finish off and went straight from his last call to meet up with Xavier at the gallery.

In the end, it appeared the most important thing to decide was on the choice of canapes and drinks to be served. Xavier was looking at funds available for the night and wanted to push the boat out a little when it came to wowing the press.   Champagne, not Prosecco, he insisted.   If Billy was honest, he still couldn't tell the difference.

'I need to finalise the guest list, we have already sent our invitations, but is there anyone you want to invite along Billy?'

The Perry Gene

'Pete and partner and the same for Steve. Mavis and Fred?'

'Who?'

'The couple who now live in my grandparents' house. I think Mrs Grainger would be too frail.'

'What about your neighbours? They knew Elspeth'

'No' Billy said rather too forcefully. Xavier looked at him with surprise. Billy noted the expression and thought about explaining, but then considered it better to keep it to himself. 'Just a bit of a falling out. It will wash over, but probably not the best timing.'

'Ok, you're the boss Billy.' Xavier stopped and surveyed the room. The white washed windows were now cleaned but brown paper sashes had been hung in front of them to block the view until opening night. 'So, what do you think?' Billy looked around at the stark whitewashed breeze block walls and the contrast with Elspeth's photographs. In his mind he compared it to the gallery / coffee shop where he had met Xavier with Jenny and it came out far better.

'I have to admit you've done a good job here my friend. The layout is good and the selection of photographs looks like it tells a good story.' Looking around the room he saw a timeline of Elspeth's life. At the start of the line were Billy's photographs and those he had recovered from Mrs Grainger. No, Billy's pictures were not the same quality or style, but the naïve biographical images almost helped to emphasise a progression of Elspeth's work. The first of her images were displayed in mock-ups of enlarged front-pages of national newspapers. 'I'm still not sure people will pay these prices, but here's hoping.

The Perry Gene

It would be nice to send her off in style and wish her happy birthday' Billy mused.

'Well don't forget, you are going to need to make a brief speech. And darling the emphasis here is on brief, no monologues or grand recitations. Something about you discovering Elspeth and thanking people for coming. If you're struggling, I can write something for you.'

'I will give it a go and let you know.' This was not something Billy had ever done before, but how hard could it be? Billy spoke to people in pubs and clubs every day. He would figure it out.

After half an hour of looking at the prints, checking menus and going over the same ground with Xavier several times (which appeared to be his way), Billy made his excuses and decided he was going to go back to the apartment and try and have an early night. He was not used to the relentless pace of work and the other commitments that now demanded his time. He had planned to get in a run and then straight to bed. Jenny was out with work mates, so it was a good opportunity to enjoy some quiet time alone.

*

They knew he was still inside as they could see the company van parked on the land beside the lock-up. Mason, the security guard, was jumpy, but Phil the site foreman scared him enough that he kept quiet. They had been watching the lock-up for over three hours and their orders were clear. Scaring Billy had not worked; it was now time to hurt him. They had seen the van pull up and two guys get out before entering the lock-up. One had a blonde pony-tail and the other was their target. Although it was getting dark, they could recognise the same guy they had chased in the van two days before. Short cropped hair, lean build, slim and fit. He had the same stupid uniform on. They were going to hurt him, but they wanted the other guy out of the picture first. Rather than just wading in and not being able to control the situation, Phil had held back.

'The young one looks like a junior. He won't work late. Let's wait until Mister Perry is on his own and then we will invite him to a little bonfire party.'

'It's a bit early for that Phil. It's only October.'

'You really are as thick as pig-shit, aren't you?' Phil shot his partner in crime a filthy look and went back to watching the lock-up.

*

Inside the lock-up Steve was finishing off the maintenance on a machine tumbler unit which kept sticking. He liked the fact the next generation of machines included video elements. These old mechanisms were getting more and more unreliable and technology was moving on. Apparently, this made him somewhat unromantic about his job according to his bosses, who both grew up with the electro-mechanical devices, but Steve knew about the future of their industry and it was all electronic. Easy to maintain, easy to upgrade, easy to sell. Pete sat across from him and worked on the diary and order book. The busier they got, the more admin was created, even though these days paperwork was more computer-based than anything. Pete was thinking about asking Billy for an office clerk to free him up do what he was paid for.   He would raise it next time they sat down for a beer.

'Right, I'm heading off boss, got things to do, people to see, you know what it's like.'

'Not sure I do Steve.   I'm going to ask Billy to install a bed here for me.'   Pete laughed, they both knew he loved what he did and the freedom Billy gave him to work.   'I'll be here for another hour.'

'Anything you need?'

'No, you head off Steve, you've done well today.' Steve didn't need telling twice; he grabbed his keys and jacket and headed for the door.   Pete got up from the desk, turned up the radio a little and put the kettle on to make a coffee.   No reason he couldn't have a coffee and enjoy his job, even if he was working late.

From across the road, Phil saw the younger of the two men leave the lock-up and get in the van to drive away.

'Right, he's on his own, let's give him five minutes and then we will go in.'

'You sure about this Phil, it's pretty heavy.'

'Grow a pair.   You wanted the job, it goes with the territory.   This nosey little bastard needs to learn to mind his own business.' Mason sat in silence. A bit of roughing someone up was fine but what Phil was suggesting scared him.

The Perry Gene

'Come on, that's enough time, go in the back of the van and get the can of petrol.' Mason opened the door to get out and Phil reached behind him and took a baseball bat off the back seat of the car, 'Get a move on' he barked at Mason 'we don't have all night.' As he got out of the car, he dropped his voice but when he spoke it was far more menacing 'and neither does he.' Mason took the petrol can out of the boot and slammed the back door. Phil glanced back and glared at him. He spoke very quietly now, 'without waking up the whole bloody neighbourhood.'

The two men walked across the road to the lock-up and checked to see if there was anyone around. As it was off the main road, by this time it was quiet and the area was deserted. It was now dark and there was not much illumination from the streetlights. Phil carefully pulled open the door an inch or two and the music increased in volume. He looked inside to see if he had been observed. Nothing, he was ok, their target had his back towards the door and had not heard a thing. Phil motioned to Mason to stay where he was while he crept forward making sure he did not make any noise or get into the reflection of the screen. As he approached Pete he raised the bat and Pete detected the movement. He began to turn but it was too late the bat was already travelling down in an unstoppable arc. It hit him a glancing blow on the back and side of his head. Pete slumped forward onto the keyboard and after a few seconds the computer started to complain at the repeat key entry from the dead weight laying on it. Phil lifted the body and pulled it back in the chair to stop the noise.

The Perry Gene

Phil turned and gestured Mason to come in.   Mason walked over and Phil pointed back at the door.

'Shut that bloody thing, we don't want anyone walking in.' Mason put down the petrol can, returned to the door to shut it.   When he came to collect it, Phil had already picked up the can and was liberally splashing petrol everywhere.

'We're not just going to leave him, are we?' Mason went over to move the unconscious body. 'I thought we were just going to burn the place? Nobody said anything about killing anyone.' Phil put down the can and grabbed Mason by the collar.

'Billy Perry hasn't been very good at learning lessons so far, this way there is no chance he will not get the message, now leave him and get out.   I'm about to light up and he's about to develop a serious smoking habit.' Mason took off towards the door, he didn't need telling twice and the sooner he was away from here the better.   The petrol smell in the air was already turning his stomach. For the rest of his life he would think of this moment every time he visited a petrol station.   Phil walked slowly after him carrying a rag which was dowsed in petrol. Mason stumbled into the fresh air and breathed deeply. Phil flicked his lighter, lit the rag and threw it back into the room.   It hit one of the patches of petrol and there was a whoosh of ignition.   Phil closed the door and then grabbed Mason by the arm.

'Help me with this' he said as he started to pull the large industrial waste bin across the entrance.   It was only half full so he didn't really need the help but in Phil's mind he wanted an additional hold over Mason. There had to be zero chance of the fool speaking to the police or his mates. His fingers were all over this and he would be in just as much trouble if it ever got out.

Once the bin was moved, they both jogged back over to the waiting van, got in and sat there for a minute until they saw smoke swirling above the door. Phil started the engine and slowly drove away turning left at the end of the road to drop the van off at the building site.

*

As Steve approached the turning for the lock-up, he saw a white van pull out and drive off under the railway bridge. He didn't think anything of it at the time. He was too busy kicking himself that he had left the on-call phone in the lock-up. He took most of the shifts with the phone for being the new boy and although it didn't go off very often, he didn't want to let Pete down. As he turned into the side street on which the lock-up sat he immediately saw something was wrong. Smoke was billowing out from the top of the door. He pulled the van over and hit 999 on his phone. It was answered immediately and he gave details while he got out of the van to see what he could do. He was told an engine was on its way and that they would send an ambulance too. When he got to the door, he could see it was blocked by the bin. It took a bit of effort but he managed to move it sufficiently to get the door open. It wasn't quite an inferno but the combination of petrol, solvents and wiring was creating a lot of smoke. He could just about see Pete through the smoke, but he wasn't moving. He didn't know much about first aid. On the TV they stressed not to move people but with the fire and the smoke he knew he had to do something. He ran in and immediately the acrid smoke was in his eyes and his mouth. It burned inside his nostrils and as it hit his throat he started to cough. If it was like this for him, what was it like for Pete? He took hold of Pete's slumped body under his armpits and dragged him towards the door. Pete had been low down, but Steve was in the middle of the smoke layer and now he started to choke on it. He continued to pull Pete back and got him into the fresh air. He could hear sirens but they were a way off. Pete had blood on his head but he was breathing. Steve was torn. He didn't know if he should stay with Pete or go and try to stop the fire spreading. He decided Pete was safe enough so he lay him down and went back in to grab the fire extinguisher. He popped the mechanism and started to spray foam on the two largest areas of fire. This had the effect of increasing the smoke but it seemed to at least stop the flames getting worse.

At that point two thing happened to make him leave the confined space and get outside. Firstly, one of the solvent bottles they used for cleaning machines exploded with the heat. Steve felt a piece of metal whistle past his face. Immediately after that he heard the sirens outside and saw the pulsing blue lights. He dropped the extinguisher and went out to get Pete some help. As he left two firemen were getting down from the truck in breathing gear and another was already putting a blanket on Pete while his colleague was on the radio checking on the location of the ambulance. After a few moments to get his breath back, Steve called out to one of the fireman emerging from the building.

The Perry Gene

'How is he?' Steve panted before bursting into a fit of coughing. The fireman with the radio next to him stopped talking into it and came over to adjust the foil blanket wrapped around Steve. He then checked the plastic oxygen mask over his face and began to take his pulse.

'Don't talk, save your breath. Your mate's going to live.' Steve slumped to the floor and thought of all the things he should be doing now. He coughed again and then sent a text to Billy.

Text: 'Fire at Lock-up. Pete injured. Fire almost out. Will text from hospital'

'First thing you want to do is text? I don't get you kids these days. Mind you it looks like you saved your mate's life tonight, so I suppose you have every right to tell everyone.'

'Telling my boss' Steve wheezed as he took the mask off his face. 'How bad is it in there?'

'You were very lucky. What you did with the fire extinguisher seemed to have stopped it getting any worse. There's some smoke and water damage from our hoses but mostly nothing that a lick of paint won't fix; nothing structural by the look of it. Insurance should cover your stock and tools.' An ambulance was pulling in behind the fire appliance. Its blue lights were on but there was no siren.

'Where are you taking him? Can I come too, I need to be able to tell my boss where he is' spluttered Steve. As he said this his phone kicked into life.

The Perry Gene

'They are not just taking him; they will want to take you too. You need checking over because of the smoke,' he looked at the phone 'is that his master's voice? If so, tell him you will be going to St Thomas's'. Steve looked at the display and confirmed it was Billy's number. He pressed the answer button and went to speak but his throat was sore. He took a sip of tea and then proceeded to update Billy. His voice was coming back but he kept it brief as he continued to break into brief coughing fits. He closed the call and put the phone back in his pocket. Pete had been brought around but was coughing heavily as the medic applied a triage bandage to his head. The fireman looked at Steve quizzically. 'The police are going to want a word.' Steve pulled a face and shrugged his shoulders. 'That cut on his head is not from the fire and the place reeks of petrol. This was no accident. Your boss; had any other little accidents recently? Business in trouble is it?'

'It's not like that at all. Business is booming. No way this is down to us, must be thugs or a rival.' But Steve was now thinking hard. The bin that had been used to block the door, he was not going to mention it to anyone until he saw Billy, but he knew there were questions to be answered.

It took the paramedics another five minutes to get Pete ready for the ambulance. With Pete on a stretcher and Steve in a foil blanket the scene looked like the end of an apocalyptic marathon. The police were on the scene talking to the lead fireman, who was directing his men to pack their equipment away. Their job here was done, but the investigation would now begin in earnest. As the crew shut the ambulance door, the last image Steve had of the scene was a uniformed officer examining the large bin that had been pulled away from the entrance to the lock-up by the fire fighters. He appeared to be discussing its location with the crewmen invovled. Steve then sat back on the seat and examined Pete. He was awake but his head was bandaged so heavily he looked like something out of *The Mummy*. He was in a fair amount of discomfort, but he was alive and with it. Pete tried to speak to him, but Steve focused his eyes on Pete's and slowly shook his head. This could all wait and certainly any conversation needed to be had with Billy first.

*

Billy arrived at the hospital about twenty minutes after the call with Steve. He looked for A&E as he figured Pete would be triaged before going to any form of ward. He still didn't know how badly injured Steve or Pete were and he was wracking his brain as to how a fire could have started. They were always so careful with the solvents. They had extinguishers. It must have been a major issue for it to get so far out of hand that a fire engine and an ambulance were required.

Billy saw Steve in the waiting room. His company tee-shirt was filthy and he looked dishevelled. He got up when he saw Billy coming.

'Christ are you ok Steve? Where's Pete? How is he? What happened?' Under stress Billy was reverting to type. A barrage of questions and no time to answer them.

'Boss, give me a chance. Pete is being seen by the doctor right now. They are checking him for concussion. Both of us are suffering from smoke inhalation, but he's got a gash on his head.' Steve took Billy by the arm and steered him towards the coffee machine. He opened his eyes wide and mouthed *Shush* to his boss. 'You got any change for a coffee' he said for the benefit of anyone listening. Then Billy noticed a police officer standing across the other side of the room. Steve took the pound coin and offered it to Billy who then turned and faced the coffee machine. While he pressed the buttons, he spoke slowly and softly to Billy, trying not to be noticed by the policeman. 'It wasn't an accident. Someone bashed Pete over the head, left him for dead and set fire to the lock-up. I forgot the on-call phone, came back and found the place on fire with a bin rammed against the door to stop anyone getting in or out. I also remember seeing a white van driving away but didn't think much about it at the time. The police don't know anything, but the firemen smelt petrol. People are going to ask a lot of questions. So am I boss. We can't talk here, but we need to speak and soon.' The machine dispensed the coffee and Steve stopped speaking.

Steve took the cup and returned to his seat; Billy went with him. As Steve sat down the policeman wandered over.

'Excuse me sir, are you Mr Perry?' Billy turned to the policeman.

'Yes, officer, do you know anything about Pete? I'm concerned about him. Steve has said he was fairly badly injured.'

'Smoke and concussion sir, but the doctor seems to think he will be ok after a day's bed rest. We need to ask you some questions about the fire. The Fire brigade seem to think it was no accident.'

The Perry Gene

'I understand officer, but I am more concerned with my friend right now. Can I come and make a statement and answer your questions in the morning? I haven't even seen the site yet.'

'If you let me have some contact details, I don't see how that would be an issue.' Billy pulled out a card from his wallet and handed it to the officer, who gave him a card in exchange. 'Thank you, sir, if you can come into Southwark police station in the morning, I'm back on at ten and we can talk then.' The policeman walked away and Billy took the seat next to Steve. They didn't say anything for a while.

After fifteen minutes, the nurse who had been examining Pete came over to speak to Steve.

'We're going to keep your mate in overnight because of the concussion. But we haven't got a bed for at least an hour. I suggest you have a quick word with him and then go and get some rest yourself.' Steve rose and Billy got up at the same time. 'Sorry are you family?' the nurse asked Billy.

'No, I'm his friend and their boss. I got here as soon as I heard.'

'Well just five minutes, he is still groggy and needs his rest.'

'Ok, and thanks for looking after him.'

Steve led the way to the cubicle. As they let themselves in through the closed curtain, Billy was shocked by the sight. Pete looked white and his head was covered with a rather large bandage which for some reason made Billy smirk. In the middle of all this seriousness, his friend and worker looked rather comical.   Pete opened his eyes and smiled at Billy, obviously trying to put on a brave face.

'You never said anything about working me to death Billy.' Both men knew humour would help them get through this, but Billy couldn't help feeling responsible. He knew from Steve's comments and the lump on Pete's head that this was another escalation of hostilities.

'Pete, I'm sorry. I'll make it right.   Just you concentrate on getting well.   Steve and I can keep the ship afloat in your absence.'

'Yeah' chimed in Steve 'we've got this boss. You just get better.'

'Steve, they told me what you did. Hell of a thing. Coming in and getting me out. Then going back in to try and put the fire out. The fireman talking to me said you might put them out of a job.'

'Anything to help, you know me.'   The nurse put her head around the curtain indicating it was time to go.

'I will call in the morning and see how you are Pete' Billy put his hand on his friend's shoulder 'get some sleep.'   Steve saluted as he left the cubicle.

'You need a lift back to pick up the van?' Billy asked Steve.

'Yeah, good idea. I'm not even sure I locked it.   It was all a bit mental at the time.'

'I'm sure it will be fine.'

Billy's car was parked in the local NCP car park which took them a couple of minutes to walk to. Billy paid for his ticket and they walked down to collect his car.   When they approached the car, Steve took more interest in the dents on the back.   The garage had replaced the lights already in order to make it legal, but the scars of battle still remained.

'Is this to do with the same thing as Pete getting attacked?' Steve asked. Billy stopped and turned to him.

'I can't be certain, but I think it is.'

'Billy what the fuck is going on?   Is it another firm? Have we stepped on someone's toes?'

'No, nothing to do with business. It's complicated and right now, I'm not sure how quickly it will get resolved. But I am sorry you and Pete got dragged into it.'   Billy opened the car and they both got in.   He started the engine and while he drove through the car park and used the ticket to exit the barrier, Steve was silent.   The traffic was quiet as it was now nearly eleven. The events of the evening had made both lose all track of time.   They made the turning for the lock-up in just over twelve minutes. As Billy signalled to pull in, they saw the van there left parked badly as Steve had pulled up in a hurry. Steve was right, the van was unlocked, but luckily nothing had been taken when he opened up the back doors to check.   They both looked across to the lock-up.   There was police tape surrounding the entrance.   Billy figured they would not get any access until after his interview and also any form of investigation by the fire service.

'So, am I out of a job?' Steve said, looking at the tape. 'It's not like we have an office anymore.'

'Well that's not strictly true. I will call George in the morning and get keys to the house.   It's up for sale and has been painted, but it will work fine as temporary work space. Do you have the on-call phone?'

'Yes, I grabbed it when I pulled Pete out.'

'Right then, can you field any calls for me tomorrow? Have a check in the van and see what spares we have and what we might need in the short term. When I'm finished with the police, I will let you know and by that time I should have got us access to the house.'

'Yes, I can handle that, but there is the sixty-four-thousand-dollar question.' Steve stopped for a moment and looked at Billy.

'What if they come back? Leave that to me. In the new place, they won't know where we are and I will have a word with some people to see what can be done. I am going to have to act dumb tomorrow as there is a bigger picture, but it will get sorted, I promise.' Billy offered his hand and Steve shook it but there was some reluctance. This was not the apprenticeship he had in mind.

'Fair enough' said Steve as he turned and got into the van 'let me know if I can help.'

'You already helped a hell of a lot tonight.'

Steve drove off in the van and Billy sat back in his car. He stared at the lock-up and the police tape for a few minutes, then started the engine to set off for home.   In his mind were two things, the promise he made to Steve and how the hell he was going to explain this to Jenny.

The Perry Gene

Chapter 23

Thursday morning came as a brutal shock to the system. Billy had sat on the sofa for hours in the dark, watching the river and thinking. He knew he had questions to answer, to Pete, Steve and Jenny. He had the initial issues of dealing with the police and making sure his company could operate, but after that he needed to conclude his business with Tony once and for all. He had finally dozed off at around 4.30am so when at 6.30am the light started to filter back in, he awoke with a start. He felt awful for the lack of sleep and had a crick in his neck and back from slumbering on the sofa. In front of him was his trusted notebook and the actions he had drawn up in the small hours of the night.

The first thing on the agenda was to start getting the pieces into place on the chess board. He texted Xavier, assuming he would pick it up later, but wanting to tick a few items off as soon as possible.

Text: 'Two extra guests, Julia and Tony my neighbours, please drop over a couple more invites to me and I will deliver by hand later today.'

He hadn't expected a response, but just two minutes later the phone buzzed a reply.

Text: 'Amazing darling, a week to go and you can't sleep either. Leave it with me, I will get it sorted, TTFN.'

Billy put a mark against the action on the list. He then knew the next call was going to be hard work, so first he went over to the kettle and switched it on, he needed coffee. Jenny would be up by now, possibly going to the gym or

The Perry Gene

getting ready for work. She was going to be angry and worried but he needed her to stay calm and stick with this for just a little while longer.

When the kettle boiled, he poured the water onto the instant coffee, added milk and piled in two sugars. He knew he would need some help getting through the day. He dialled Jenny's number and she answered on the third ring.

'Billy, Billy Perry' she opened with 'I thought you had forgotten my number. I normally get at least a *good night* text, but last night nothing. Did you get a better offer?' Her voice was mocking but playful. She liked having him on the back foot, but above all else she liked having him in her life. 'You didn't let that cougar in again, did you? She is a kitten that has most definitely turned into a cat.'

'Jen, I need you to listen for a minute.' The line went silent and Billy knew he had her full attention. 'There's been a fire at the lock-up. Pete got hurt and has been in hospital all night; Steve pulled him out and helped control the fire until the brigade turned up to put it out. I didn't call because I got home late from the hospital and didn't want to worry you.'

'Fire, oh my god. What happened?'

'I can tell you more later on, but I need you to do me a favour. I need to get the keys to the old house from George this morning. Can you arrange that if I drop by when he first gets in? The lock-up is going to need a lick of paint and an insurance claim.'

'Of course, Billy. Can you be there around ten?'

The Perry Gene

'Can you make it nine-thirty please? I have to make a statement to the police at ten and I want to get the keys to the house so Steve has somewhere to work from.'

'Police? Billy, what are you not telling me? How did the fire start?' As she spoke her speech got quicker and her voice more frantic. After a brief pause, she continued 'Has this got something to do with Tony?' Billy took a deep breath before continuing.

'I think it has. Steve went back to the lock-up having forgotten the phone and found the place in flames. He also saw a white van drive away. He didn't think anything of it at the time but afterwards we put two and two together. It looks like they knocked Pete out, doused the place with petrol and then blocked him in with one of the rubbish bins. Steve called 999 first. Then he saw the bin, pulled it aside and got Pete out. Once Pete was safe he grabbed an extinguisher and did what he could, but there was a lot of smoke from smouldering wiring.'

'I told you to leave Tony alone' there was now anger in her voice. 'It's ok for you to play pin the tail on the donkey, but now other people are being kicked. Honestly Billy, I could hit you.' Silence. They both sat there with the line open and all they could hear was each other's breathing, her now calming down from the tirade. 'So, what now? You said the police, you are going to tell them I suppose?'

'Tell them what Jen? Tell them that a south London property developer had two thugs set fire to my lock-up because I know he killed someone, but can't prove it?   That his building had asbestos but he is bribing the Building Inspector?'

'Well, now you put it like that, yes, that's exactly what I expect you to say.'

'But it's all circumstantial.   There's one thing I learned from all those crime books my Dad loved so much.'

'What's that, all police detectives are dysfunctional?'

'Very funny' his mind skipped to North and South and immediately he saw the humour in it, even at this time. 'No, I mean you don't show your hand until you are ready.   You keep your powder dry.   If we tell the police without sufficient proof, then Tony will simply find ways to prove it was all just my imagination.   Remember the car park; he is already suggested I'm sick. This will all be part of my diseased mind. That's what he will say.'

'Listen Billy, I will say this one last time.   We do it your way, but I am not sure how much more of this I can take. I am worried about you, what if he goes after the guys again?'

'I don't think he did go after them.   I think he sent them after me and they didn't get the right person. Look, I need a week. Give me to the weekend of the exhibition and it will all be over.'

'Ok Billy, but please be careful. I love you'

'I will, and I will see you at 9.30 for the keys.'

*

The Perry Gene

Billy jumped in the shower and had a shave to try and make himself look slightly better than the walking dead after so little sleep.   He didn't want the police to think he was anything other than an upright citizen, which indeed he wasn't at this point.   He grabbed another coffee to keep the flow of caffeine in his system at a nice point of reinforcement without wiring him too highly.

Billy drove over to get the keys from Jenny.   Fortunately, her boss was already in and available. Billy had the feeling she had pre-warned George of the issue as he was bristling when Billy arrived. He was standing at the desk with Jenny as Billy walked in.

'Billy, Jenny filled me in about the fire.   Is everyone ok?'

'Yes George.   I spoke to the hospital this morning before I drove over and Pete had a good night.   All things being equal he will be out today and fit for work after a day or two of bed rest.   Luckily there appears to be no lasting damage from either the smoke or the bang on the head. Steve is agitated by the situation but is ok.'

'Yes' said George 'the situation.   Jenny filled me in on the bigger picture.   You should have said things had got out of hand.'

'I spoke to North and South about it, I assumed they would keep you in the loop.'

'No, apparently discretion really is the watch word of those two.' George handed Billy an envelope which bulged and jangled. 'Jenny mentioned you needed to use the old house.   Do you know for how long; we are close to finalising the sale?   All the decorating is done but there is not much in the way of furniture.'

'Just long enough for us to get the lock-up cleaned and painted. Are you able to deal with the insurance and get that sorted for us?'

'The insurance will have to wait until the police have finished their work, but I will get the team from the house on it as soon as we are granted access. If it's anything like I suspect it is a week or more's worth of work to empty, clean and paint it. But as I say, access it crucial.'

'I'm going to drop the keys off with Steve and then the Police are my next port of call.' Billy looked at an unusually tight-lipped Jenny. This was not the girl he now knew, but it occurred to him that she was back in her work environment and had to be subtle about what she said and did. 'Jen, I will let you know the outcome from the police and maybe if you are free, we can catch up later?'   She looked awkward in front of her boss.   Billy didn't know if George was aware how far their relationship had progressed.

'Well, I had better get along to my office and prepare for my next client.   Billy, good luck and be careful.   If things get nasty, you are going to need to reach out to the police and tell them what you know.'   George took his mug of coffee that was sitting on Jenny's desk and climbed the stairs up to his office. Billy watched him touch the heavily glossed handrail and had a brief flashback of the moment he visited George's office for the first time all those months ago. So much had changed, but he could still feel that thick paint under his hand as he touched the rail.

'Billy, you know I am worried about you. I am not sure I want to be anywhere near that psychopath of a neighbour of yours, but I do want to see you later. Why don't you come to mine for a change? It's small, but it doesn't have hot and cold running henchman on tap. I think you could do with a night away from the apartment.' She stared at his face and touched it with her hand. 'You also look like crap. How much sleep last night?'

'About an hour. On the couch. I must admit I am tired and sore. I have got to get a few things done today. How about I come around about eight? You are right, I need a bit of space and distance from Tony right now.'

'That's fine, but please keep me in the picture today and let me know what the police say.'

*

Billy arrived at the Police station and looked for somewhere to park. There were some visitor spaces a hundred yards away from the main entrance. Billy made a mental note of this for future reference. He locked the car and entered the building looking for the front desk. Behind the safety glass a middle-aged woman looked bored and slightly harassed.

'I was asked to meet a' Billy looked at the details he had written down the night before 'a PC Emerson?'

'Your name sir?' the automaton asked almost by rote.

'Billy, Billy Perry.' Billy smirked to himself, he really did need to get out of that habit. The receptionist looked down a list in front on her.

The Perry Gene

'Yes, he is expecting you. Take a seat sir and I will let him know you are here.' Billy sat down and looked around the reception of the police station. Apart from the heavy glass screen and a few posters on the walls about crime prevention, this could have been any doctor's or dentist's waiting room; right down to the pile of out of date magazines. In the background, Billy could hear the receptionist speaking into the phone to alert the officer of Billy's arrival.

After five minutes there was the buzz of a solenoid which reminded Billy of the door to the apartment's complex. The door opened and PC Emerson walked out.

'Mr Perry, would you come this way please.' The policeman took Billy into a side room, offered him a chair and went to sit opposite. 'You want a tea or a coffee?'

'No, I'm fine thanks. I didn't sleep much and any more coffee would probably be bad for me.'

'Didn't sleep much?' the officer picked up on Billy's comment.

'Well yes, it's not every day your staff get injured and your business gets put at risk. I am glad to say that Pete is on the mend and Steve seems none the worse for his escapades.'

'Bright boy that one. We got most of the detail we needed from him in the hospital last night. He had a good set of eyes and is pretty clued up for a kid his age.'

'Yes, thank god he was there to help.'

'There are just a few things we need to clear up.'

'I understand that. I also need to know when I can get back into the lock-up. We have a business to run. I have my records in there and parts for the machines.'

'Yes, Steve mentioned you fix games machines. What we need to know is how and why the fire started Mr Perry. The Fire Brigade is suspicious that there may have been an accelerant used. Who would do that Mr Perry? Do you have any enemies? Business competition for instance? Cut throat game is it, Steve suggested you had expanded quickly recently?' Emerson was scribbling notes on his pad as he spoke.

'Absolutely not. Never had any issues like that. We have however had bits of graffiti before as you can see and the bins have been set alight once in the past. This was probably just local kids getting out of hand.'

'Local kids don't normally hit someone on the back of the head when they start a fire.'

'They must have discovered him there and then tried to cover up the attack in panic.' Billy stopped and looked at Emerson straight in the face unblinking. 'P.C. Emerson, this is the only explanation I can think of.' Emerson scrawled a few more lines.

'Well, we will do a little more checking, see if we can find anything on the local CCTV cameras, but I didn't notice any directed at your building so we may not get anywhere. I would suggest you install some.' Yes, thought Billy, CCTV evidence can be extremely handy. In his mind he was back watching the video of Tony and his thug carrying Chris Deville's body and had zoned out of the room. After a few seconds PC Emerson interrupted him, 'Mr Perry?'

'Sorry, I was miles away. Tired I guess. When can we get back into the lock-up? I have staff to keep employed and customers to service.'

'Scene of Crime Offices finished there this morning and the fire bridge investigator will be done later today. You should be able to get in there this afternoon sometime. If you think of anything else that would be helpful to our enquiry, please don't hesitate to contact me; you have my details.' Both men stood and they shook hands. P.C. Emerson showed Billy to the door.

*

Billy had lost about an hour going to the Police station and getting back to where he needed to be. He had sent a text to Steve giving him the post code and the address to meet him and when he got there, the van was already outside. Billy parked across the road, got out and beckoned to Steve to get out of the van. Billy looked suspiciously at the house, but the feelings of his Mother's presence seemed to have vanished. The painting crew had done a good job and the outside now looked twenty years' fresher. He hoped the inside would look as good.

'So, this was where you grew up?' Steve said, looking at the house as if trying to picture Billy within it, as some form of junior version of himself.

'Yes, but the painters have done their job. It's not looked this good in years.' Billy took the set of keys that George had given him and gave one to Steve. 'I know you have questions about last night, but you are safe here.

The Perry Gene

Nobody apart from people I trust know about this place, so let's keep it that way. It's going to take a couple of weeks to sort out the lock-up and after that time the problem will be sorted.' Billy unlocked the door and Steve followed him in.

'But why would someone attack Pete like that, it makes no sense?' Steve asked after the door was closed and the noise of the street was shut out. It was oddly quiet and echoing in the house. There was no furniture to speak of except the painters had put the old curtains back up to stop squatters getting the idea it was empty. They had power and water.

'They didn't attack Pete.' Steve stopped and tried to interrupt but Billy continued. 'They attacked me, or so they thought. Come on, even you have remarked how much alike we look. Peas from the same pod. Same hair, same shirt, from behind, at night, easy to mix us up. That's why firstly you need to understand, you are not in danger. Secondly, as I said, this is a blip and it is not going to stop us working and earning a living. I am going to lean heavily on you for a few days. Forget sales and new machines, just concentrate on keeping the balls in the air. I will make a few calls and let our bigger customers know. People are understanding, especially if I mention Pete getting injured and you being a hero.'

'I'm not sure about hero. Anyone would have done the same.' Steve interjected, but only half-heartedly. He knew the score.

'You don't believe that for a minute and nor should you. You did well, I'm proud of you, but now we just need some breathing space until things calm down. You up for that?'

'I've got a mate who knows his stuff, do you want me to ask if he wants some work?'

'Not on his own, but if you want to stick him on the van with you for lift and shift, plus a bit or moral support, I have no issues with that.'

'Money?'

'Work something out, don't go mad, I'm trusting you.'

'I spoke to Pete and he wants to come back.'

'Not until next week, he needs rest. He took more smoke than you did and he had the crack on the head. Can you cope until Monday?'

'As long as you pick up any slack boss, and as long as you tell me what's going on.'

'Right, take a seat.' Both of them sat on the kitchen counters. 'You know my car had its tyres slashed?' Steve nodded his head. 'Then I got the bangs on the car from that road rage incident?' Realisation crossed Steve's face.

'You reckon my white van from last night is your white van from last week?'

'Exactly. In fact, I have a photograph of the drivers. But they don't know that yet.'

'So, you just came back from the police station, why not tell them?'

The Perry Gene

'There are bigger fish to fry. I want their boss. Not just for intimidation, arson, bribery and building violations. I want him for murder.' Steve went quiet and very white. After a few seconds he stood up.

'You're not joking, are you?' Then he walked over, hands in his pockets, thinking. 'Who died?'

'It's complicated, but it's the guy who used to be the tenant in my apartment. I have a solution but I need a week. And I need your patience and your trust. I know I am asking a lot, but I can only see one way to resolve this and I need to do it right.'

'I know Pete trusts you and I trust Pete, so I can keep patient for a week or so, but it will be on two conditions.' He went to count off on his fingers and Billy nodded his head ready to listen. 'First is that Pete and I are not in any more danger.' Billy had to admit he was more impressed with this young man the more he had to do with him. Billy nodded agreement. 'Second, that you tell me the whole story when it's done.'

'Agreed to both. Right now, telling you the whole thing could put you in danger, so I will tell you both everything afterwards.' Steve put his hand out and Billy shook it firmly in binding consent. 'Now one last thing, practical matters. The lock-up should be accessible in a few hours. Let's get a bit of lunch and then check what we can salvage. Then we will secure it and leave it to the cleaning and paining crew that George is sourcing. After that we need to get the parts brought over here, see what we are missing and get additional spares ordered. All good?'

The Perry Gene

'All good boss, I'm starving, couldn't face breakfast this morning. But please, not smoked bacon?' He smirked. Billy winced and in that little bit of emergency room humour, he knew things with Steve would be fine.

*

The rest of the day was busy with trying to establish their temporary base of operations. George had a word with the insurance company and with a bit of wrangling had got agreement for Billy to remove parts required for the business as long as he photographed everything first. When they explored the scene, it was clear that although things were bad, the bit of makeshift firefighting performed by Steve had helped a lot. Billy had lost a couple of machines completely and some parts were unserviceable, but they managed to scavenge enough that a call to the suppliers was unnecessary at this point. The orders computer was also salvageable with a little bit of work and cleaning from Steve. The biggest issue was that everything stank of smoke. It seems to have permeated the very materials themselves. The other kit that was unusable was either damaged by foam or water. Billy, as agreed, would leave this for the insurance inspector to evaluate later. After three trips in the van, the house was filled with parts, kettle, cups and music from the slightly smoke tinged radio.

Billy was not really in the mood for a drink after work so he let Steve go, taking the on-call phone with him. Billy had made half a dozen phone calls to clients to keep them onside and to assure them business was 'as usual' as possible. People liked Billy and his honest approach in the past; this earned him a lot of leeway now. By quarter past five he was beginning to flag. He realised that the lack of sleep the previous night was catching up on him. Adrenalin had got him so far, but there were limits. He was due to be at Jenny's place in a couple of hours, but in the meantime, he had one final task he needed to perform; surveillance.

Billy drove to a quiet road that was about a quarter a mile from Tony's development. He walked the final distance looking for a place to watch from. He found a small side street which was at the rear of some shops on the main through road. It afforded a view of the main gate of the development. Builders were leaving the site as he started to watch. He was careful that he could not be seen and he spent a lot of time playing with his mobile phone. He then put headphones on and started to talk, simulating a call. He just hoped his phone didn't ring for real now. At six pm on the dot, the night security guard turned up; a face that Billy knew only too well. 'Excellent' he said out loud, then realising that his inner voice had become outer, he continued to babble an incoherent stream of words to keep up the pretence of being on the phone.

Billy sat and watched and by ten past six, the last of the workmen had left the site and the guard was left there on his own. He had locked the main entrance to the development; a large green painted plywood gate covered in razor wire above. *Nothing says welcome to your new home like razor wire* thought Billy. The guard then sat in the cabin that he had previously invited Billy into. There was no sign of him doing any form of rounds, but Billy figured that would happen every couple of hours during the night. The set up was perfect for what Billy needed. He would just need a couple of more days' worth of surveillance to check that this was a regular pattern to enable him to get his planning right.   Now it was time to get over to see Jenny.

Not wanting to alert Tony to the mistake his men had made attacking Pete just yet, Billy knew for now, he needed to keep a low profile.   He had brought a bag from the flat with a couple of changes of clothing and some toiletries.   He felt a bit odd as he drove in the direction of his girlfriend's place and then it occurred to him.   It was not just that he had not stayed there before, but rather he had not even been inside.   When he arrived, he rang her phone to see if she was home.   She answered immediately and told him to stay where he was.   Two minutes later Jenny appeared from the entrance to the flats, literally bouncing; to say she seemed pleased to see Billy would be an understatement. He got out of the car to greet her, at which point she threw her arms around him and kissed him.

'You know I have been worried sick about what is going on, but I also missed you.' She managed to say this only once she had disengaged from a long and very passionate kiss.   She pulled back from him and looked at the lines on his face and the bags under his eyes. 'You look like hell, tough day? No sleep, I guess? How is the lock-up?' Billy smiled for the first time since Steve's smokey bacon comment that morning.

'You are even starting to sound like me.   What is it they say about owners becoming like their dogs?' With this Jenny punched him playfully on his arm, but the tension was broken and with his bag in one hand, she led him into the flat by the other.

The Perry Gene

Entering the flat, Billy was filled with questions and observations. It was small, but tidy; clean and homely. There was a picture of her and Billy on the sideboard, Billy had no idea where it had come from, but he liked that it was there. There were also pictures of Jenny with her parents. Family was obviously important, no wonder she was keen for him to meet hers and also why she probably had felt so guilty about his.

'I have some stew on that I made in the slow cooker, is that ok? Glass of wine?' 'Just the food please. I am not sure I can handle booze at the moment.'

'Agreed, that's seems sensible. It will be about five minutes while I warm it up.'

Billy sat down on the sofa and looked to see if there was room in the flat to swing the proverbial cat. He knew even more now what a debt he owed to Elspeth for the setup she had provided. He could never have afforded anything as grand as the riverside apartment and that was before you took the money into consideration. He sat back on the sofa and considered the fact that he had been entrusted with the Perry family silver. Now it was time to pay the piper and act like a Perry in dealing with Tony. But not just like any Perry, like Elspeth Perry.

Jenny walked into the room with a tray and the bowl of hot stew five minutes later. The first thing she heard was the soft snoring Billy was making as he lay back on the sofa. In any other circumstance she would have been furious, but with what he was going through at the moment, she just smiled.

Dinner for one she thought.

The Perry Gene

Chapter 24

On the Friday morning, Billy awoke early on the sofa where Jenny had covered him in a blanket. He remembered sitting there with the offer of dinner and then nothing more. He guessed almost immediately what had happened and then smiled when he felt the blanket over him. It was still only five, but he needed to do a little something early so he found a pen and paper and scrawled Jenny a note. He said he wanted to freshen up but would return for breakfast in an hour and a half.

Billy drove back to the apartment and parked his car. He climbed the stairs and let himself into the room silently. 'No point in disturbing the neighbours' he thought. He got changed into his running gear; tracksuit bottoms, not just shorts, as he was going to be out for a while. He then left the apartment as quietly as he had arrived and headed off at a good pace, out of view of his neighbours' windows just in case. He ran for about twenty minutes until he neared Tony's building site. From the night before he knew where he could stand to observe without being seen for a short while, but it would look suspicious if a jogger stood on a street corner for too long, so he searched for a better place.

After a few minutes he found a bench upon which he could appear to be doing stretches and dips. It was slightly further away from the site, but still had the view that Billy required; the security hut. He could see the security goon was inside because light was spilling out. As Billy guessed from the night before and his previous observations, the guard didn't seem to do much guarding.

As six thirty started to move towards six forty-five, Billy was regretting not putting on a hoodie to keep warm.   The sweat of the run was cooling him down and he was beginning to feel the cold.   But then he saw what he needed.   The guard emerged and started to unlock the main gate. Billy noticed there were now three locks on it, where he thought he had only seen one before. Maybe Tony was beefing up security, was he concerned someone might come calling? Once the gates were open, the guard did a cursory check inside then returned to his security hut.   This meant the site was now open for the workers to enter, but there was still no way to get inside without the guard seeing.   No matter, Billy had seen enough and he just needed to check if this routine was the same every day.

As the first builders began to turn up around seven Billy knew it was time to make himself scarce.   Ensuring he was not seen, he jogged off back in the direction of his apartment and a warm shower.

Billy made good time and was away from the apartments before eight, dressed this time for work.   He stopped off at the local bakers to pick up fresh bread and arrived at Jenny's with just enough time to make her some toast and coffee.

'You shot off early this morning, I thought you might come and join me' she teased.

The Perry Gene

'I felt a bit groggy after a night on the sofa and thought a run and a shower would perk me up. On that front, sorry about last night, with the fire and not sleeping I was...'

'I know' she interrupted 'I could see that you were dog tired. Just don't make a habit of falling asleep on me. I may have wicked plans next time.' She kissed him on his cheek and then wiped away toast crumbs that she had planted on his face. 'Good run?'

'Yes, in fact I may try and get a few more in to pick my fitness up a bit, I have been so busy lately that I feel a bit stodgy.' He poked himself in his midriff, there was not a lot of give there, but when he puffed out his cheeks to make his face look fat she laughed.

'A girl likes to have something to get hold of. Don't go all super fit on me.'

'Never.'

'What have you got on today, still trying to recover bits from the lock-up?'

'Actually, we pretty much did that yesterday. I've got an insurance assessor coming later and Steve is busy trying to run the empire from the old house. Apart from the parking, I think he prefers it to the lock-up. It is a lot lighter and brighter after the paint job.'

'And how are you about being there? Is her ghost still in residence?' Jenny took a breath, looked at her watch and realised she was becoming late.

The Perry Gene

She was not used to this distraction in the morning. She gulped her coffee and got up to go and do her teeth.

'I think the painters may have scared her off. Besides, with all her stuff gone, she seems a lot less present.' Billy watched as she walked into the bathroom. 'Am I boring you?'

'Sorry lover, but you are making me late for work and you know what his nibs is like; I am listening though' she shouted from the bathroom. She poked her head round the door a minute later with her mouth full of foam and an electric toothbrush. She puckered up to give him a kiss and he smiled. He loved how comfortable this had become. It made him think what he had been missing for so long. Well this was one thing his Mother couldn't spoil.

'You need a lift?'

'No, I'll get the bus, it's quicker and probably safer than your car since you had a target painted on it.'

'Harsh, but true.' Billy said getting up. 'Come to mine for dinner this evening. I will cook. Is eight o'clock alright?'

'Sounds wonderful.' She came over, this time with an empty and minty clean mouth and gave him a long kiss. 'Mmmm, you still taste of coffee. See you later lover boy.' Billy took his leave and walked out to where he had parked the car.

*

Apart from the obvious work that would now pile up without Pete on board, Billy had two other things he wanted to achieve on Friday. First and most importantly was to check on Pete's condition. He discovered that his Man Friday had been released from hospital as planned the previous evening. He dropped round to Pete's house, but learned from his girlfriend Molly that he was sleeping. That would explain why Pete was not answering his text messages. Molly confirmed he was on the mend and all things being equal he would be back on the job next week. The fact that she didn't mention the circumstances of how the fire started made Billy think Pete hadn't gone into specifics. He decided it was best to leave her in the dark if that is what Pete wanted. No point him worrying her if Pete had kept it to himself and the less people that knew the better.

The second task was a little more convoluted but was vital to Billy's plan to ensnare Tony. He dropped in to see Xavier who was not his normal lively self but rather a nervous wreck in a bright yellow boiler suit, making him look like a cross between a stressed canary and Bob the Builder. He appeared to have the weight of the world on his shoulders, although there was no evidence of him actually doing anything other than directing people around.

'You look a little stressed my friend, all not going well?'

'It will all be fabulous' Xavier said through almost gritted teeth 'it's always the last-minute things.' He reached into his pocket and pulled out two pieces of paper. 'Like last minute additions to the guest list. These things don't happen on their own you know.'

'I know Xavier; we pay someone to print them. Now stop being a drama queen. Is there anything you actually need that I can help with or can I go deliver these?' Xavier appeared to calm visibly as he knew Billy was once again calling his bluff and gently ribbing him.

'Nothing I can't handle darling.' But it was a now much calmer Xavier who Billy left in charge of the almost completed exhibition space.

Billy went back to the house. He divided up the outstanding calls with Steve, sorted out the weekend cover rota between them and was finished around 5.30. On his way home, he stopped near Tony's site again and confirmed the timings. The gate was shut by six once all the workers were gone. By six thirty the guard was safely lodged in his little shack with his iPad, watching a movie of some description. 'Money for old rope' thought Billy. 'I wonder if your boss knows how little you care.' When he had seen enough he headed back to the apartment.

Jenny was due to arrive around eight, so he started the food prep and when he had it to a point it could be left, he took the two invites out of his jacket pocket and walked across the hallway. He rang the bell of Tony and Julia's apartment and waited. After a few seconds the door opened and Tony appeared.

'You.' Tony stuttered, 'I,' before he could finish the sentence Julia burst past him. She wrapped her arms around Billy and gave him a hug.

'Darling, we've been so worried. We haven't seen you in days. Is everything alright.' Billy hugged her back and then extricated himself from her grip, at which point she seemed a little disappointed.

'Well I've been snowed under with work' Billy looked at Tony 'since the fire.'

'Fire darling, what fire? She went to hug him again but he dodged.

'A fire at the lock-up. Pete my mate got injured.'

'Pete?' queried Tony. 'Who's Pete?'

'We grew up together in the arcades. We look so much like each other; simple people can get us mixed up.'

'How did the fire start? Was it a work accident?' Julia asked, obviously none the wiser to the larger conversation.

'No, it was arson, in fact Pete was attacked first from behind. A real cowardly way to go about your business.' Billy let the comment hang in the air. 'Wouldn't you say Tony?'

'Well, yes.' He replied slowly and quietly.

'Is he ok? Do they know who did it?' Julia was literally bubbling at the gossip.

'The Police have their ideas. A white van was seen leaving the site.' Julia fell silent.

'Means nothing. Thousands of them all over the city.' Tony said, trying to be matter of fact about his observation. All the while Tony knew where Billy was going with this.

'Yes, on building sites all over the country. But I think they have more to go on, mind you I can't say too much.' Billy tapped his nose as if he knew something. 'On-going investigation and all that.' Tony now seemed desperate to change the conversation or shut the door.

'Anyway, I'm sure you didn't ring the door just to tell us all this?' he glared at Billy.

'No' Billy said 'I rang the bell to apologise. Things have gone very wrong and I feel like I have let you, my special neighbours, down.' Tony said nothing and waited for the line that Billy was spinning to come off the reel.

'What is it darling' said Julia 'what's happened?'

'Yes, please share.' Tony followed up; the undertone of which was anything but interest,

'Well that excitable idiot of an artistic impresario, Xavier, somehow forgot to send your invitations for the opening next Friday. Honestly, I was so ashamed I had to come in person. I wouldn't want you to miss the press night for Auntie Elspeth's last show as you were obviously so close to her.' Julia almost exploded in a mixture of delight and excitement.

'Oh darling, what a thoughtful boy, think nothing of it. At least you found out in time. We're not doing anything are we Tony? Next Friday, we can go, can't we?'

'As long as I don't have to work and nothing comes up.' Tony was now fuming that he had been manoeuvred and he didn't even see it coming. Billy handed Julia the invitations and she planted a big kiss on his cheek. Billy returned to his apartment with Julia left standing still fit to burst on her own threshold. Tony had slunk inside quickly.

'Check' said Billy as he closed the door.

The Perry Gene

The weekend was spent on recovery and last-minute issues with the planning of the exhibition.   However organised and in control Billy thought things were, Xavier could put on a new histrionic spin and apply more pressure.   After meeting them a couple of times, Billy found he liked and easily trusted the guys Xavier had hired. They were experienced at this, despite being quite young. This wasn't their first rodeo apparently, according to them.

Billy managed to see Pete over the weekend; in fact, Billy and Jenny took both Pete and Molly out for lunch on Sunday to catch up.   Steve was praised for keeping the ship afloat, but with Molly around, Pete never mentioned the fire once. He was carrying a noticeable bruise on the side of his head, but other than that and the odd bit of coughing he seemed fine. Billy tried not to dwell on how different things might have been had they not been lucky with Steve's return.

'So, your old house is the new corporate HQ' said Steve slightly mockingly.   'You know I never got to see it as a teenager.   You were always too scared of your Mother to take anyone home.'   Billy thought about it for a while.   Pete was right.   All those years ago, it was like his life working in the arcades and even school never impinged on his home life.   In his mind he now had this image of a dragon, guarding the gates to the kingdom; a dragon with his Mother's face.   But as he continued thinking about the mythical monster, it started to morph, first into the foreman and then growing in size and turning into Tony.   It was time to stand and fight the dragon like a white knight.   He had gone silent and he realised they were all looking at him waiting for some kind of response.

'Sorry, I was miles away, what did you ask?'

'I was wondering what you were smiling at?   I just said I was sure it was not fond memories of your Mother.' Pete commented, but then wary that he might have crossed a line.

'No, I was thinking of slaying a dragon.'   Molly giggled and realised this was some private joke.   Pete and Jenny looked at each other and said nothing.   The moment gone, they got back to chatting about the trivia in their lives and ordered another round of drinks.   Jenny realised then just how hard she was squeezing Billy's hand; her knuckles had gone white.

'One more week' he whispered in her ear. She released her grip.   Pete looked across at the two of them.

'I think they do rooms if you two need a moment.' They all started to laugh and the tension was broken.

*

The next few days fell into a routine.   Every morning Billy got up and ran. He ran the same route to the same bench.   On the bench he stretched, did press ups, dips and crunches. He wanted his fitness back and this distraction was helpful.   While he used the bench as a makeshift multi-gym, he kept up the surveillance.   The detective novels of old, which he now barely looked at, always mentioned routine.   Look for patterns; where there are patterns, there are holes in security.   This guard was pretty much useless.   He did things at the same time every day, with almost Swiss timekeeping. Workers left, he locked the site. He sat in his office and amused himself. Next morning, he unlocked the site fifteen minutes before the staff arrived.

By Friday morning, Billy had seen enough and he knew it was time to put his plan into action. At six twenty, slightly earlier than usual, he changed his route and ended up at the guard's hut. He saw the guard inside and before there was a chance to react he burst in and shut the door.

'What the hell do you want? I thought... hang on' the guard was obviously not going to win a Nobel Prize any time soon.

'Stay sitting down, shut up and listen or I will call the Police right here and now.' The guard sat glued to the spot as instructed; he was obviously scared.

'And what you gonna tell 'em?'

'Shall we start with how you ran me off the road?' The guard went to get up. Billy pushed him back down 'Sit rover.'

'No idea what you are talking about. I'm gonna phone my boss.' Billy pulled out the small print of the photo he had taken of the white van when it had collided with the bus. It clearly showed the guard. He had carefully edited it, not to show the foreman. That was another matter. When blackmailing, Billy knew you had to manipulate the weakest link.

'You do take a nice photo.' The goon remained silent. 'Or shall we discuss how you tried to kill me and burn my lock-up to the ground?' Fear washed across the face of the guard. Somewhere in the back of his mind, he thought this day might come. 'Or even how you were so stupid you attacked my mate Pete from behind by mistake.'

'That's why' said the guard and realised he should shut up.

'Let me finish the sentence for you.' Billy paused for effect 'Sentence, now there is a good word. Hold that thought. We'll get to that in a bit. That's why I don't appear injured is what you were going to say I believe.' Billy let the last comment hang there in the silence. The guard now realised there was a big white light coming at the end of the tunnel. He didn't know if it was daylight or an oncoming train.

'So,' said the guard slowly 'what is it you want?'

'Well, I thought you were looking a bit peaky.' The guard was now confused. This was not a conversation he was equipped for. 'I think you need a night off.'

'I can't afford it' said the guard, 'I need the money.' He really wasn't getting it at all. Which was perfect thought Billy.

'No, there is no need for you to lose out. I know your routine now. You lock-up after the workers have gone, sit in here all night and then next morning you open up again before they arrive. Tonight, will be different. When you normally lock-up, you won't set the locks, but rather you will go home and get a good night's sleep.' The guard still seemed confused. 'And then in the morning, be sure to set your alarm nice and early. You need to be here to open up the gates at the normal time.'

'But the gates won't be locked.'

The Perry Gene

'Don't you worry about that; I will make sure they are.' Billy let the information sink in and then he knew he needed to add the frighteners. 'I will not call the Police on you for what you have done unless you do one of two things. Firstly, if you tell anybody about this conversation and secondly if the gates are not open tonight or you are here.' The guard looked blankly at him. 'This is the bit where you nod and agree.' Dutifully, he took his cue and slowly nodded his head. 'Remember, gone by six thirty, gates unlocked, tell nobody or you will feel Mr Plod's size nines on your neck.' Billy tried to stifle a smile as he turned and walked out of the security office. He had read the Mr Plod line in a detective novel five years ago. It had appealed to him then as such a clichéd threat, but he never thought he would have the chance to use it. He was really starting to like the new Billy Perry.

*

It was damp, dark and had the faintest smell of urine; for the life of him Billy could not work out why. The garage of his flat was locked to the outside world. Possibly passing revellers relieving themselves late at night, but either way it was not the most pleasant environment in which to wait. The only variable in his plan he could not control was the time at which Tony would appear. Billy figured he would have to get home early enough to get changed and then they would get a cab to the gallery, so Tony could have a drink or two. Now they were in the middle of October, it was already getting dark outside by five thirty and in the reduced light of the garage it was murky to say the least. Billy knew that the two strip lights would come on when the automatic door operated, but he had taken care of that with a judiciously removed fuse. As long as Tony was alone and Billy got the jump on him then he could handle this on this own. He didn't want to involve his team, partly so they knew nothing about his plans and secondly as they had already been inconvenienced enough by Tony's thugs.

At five forty-five the electric shutters started to roll-up and Billy heard the deep throaty growl of Tony's white Jaguar. It was a classic and in pretty good condition; clearly Tony's pride and joy. This appeared to be the only thing left of any value Tony had retained when he entered the transaction for the building project. Billy had played this out many times in his mind, like the good chess player he was. He had tried to think of every move and anticipate the reaction. He could move easily from his hiding place to where Tony would get out of the car. His eyes were used to the gloom, but with the lights out, Tony would be at a disadvantage. Although Billy had threatened Julia with a steak tenderizer when he found her in his apartment, he would never have hurt her with it. He was too much of a gentleman; but with Tony he would like to make an exception. However, this was not what was called for. In fact, he fell back to Elspeth for a solution. In her belongings he had found a small Billy club which she had obviously kept for personal protection. The irony of the name did not escape him,

As the engine from Tony's car guttered Billy crept forwards just behind the driver's door; still out of sight from his intended victim. Tony pushed it open and started to leverage himself out of the car. He was grumbling about the lights not working, but with one clean swing of the club to his head, the grumbling stopped. Tony's body slumped down onto the floor.

'Before we go any further, that's for Pete, you vicious bastard.' Billy spoke slowly and quietly, but his actions were not slow. From behind the pillar he pulled out masking tape which he wrapped tightly around Tony's mouth. Turning him over, he tied his hands and his feet and then popped the boot of the car. Inside it was almost empty, this was better than Billy expected and he heaved the body unceremoniously into the space. He shut the boot lid and took a look inside the car. As he had seen on the surveillance film from the previous nights, Tony had a laptop bag which doubled as a briefcase. Billy smiled, he was going to need that later. He slid the bag behind the back seat of the car, locked it using the keys and went up to the apartment to change. He had managed to get this completed in just eight minutes; two minutes ahead of schedule. He now had quarter of an hour to get ready for the exhibition before he had to leave. The main event would not start until seven but he and Tony had a slight detour to make; not that Tony would know much about it.

Seventeen minutes later, Billy was back in the car park. He was wearing a smart but casual suit and black leather gloves. He knew Xavier would be dressed as the usual Peacock, but he needed both practicality and a sombreness in his clothing tonight. They were after all going to celebrate the life and work of his Aunt, the woman who had set this whole tale in motion. He unlocked the car. He did not know how long Tony would be out for and he cared even less. Tied up and bound, he would stay wherever Billy put him. On the passenger seat rested a trilby. 'Yes' thought Billy, 'you are sort of arse who would wear a hat while driving, well let's make sure the world sees you leave.' He adjusted the seat, started the car and headed for the exit ramp. He knew where the CCTV was positioned and he made sure the only image it got was the top of the hat.

He had factored the driving time to the site into his plan and even with a hold up for the rush hour traffic he reached his destination by six thirty-eight. He could see the gates were closed, but the padlocks were undone. He got out, opened the gate, jumped back into the driver's seat and manoeuvred the vehicle inside. Billy drove the car to the most secluded spot within the compound, which was furthest away from the street, just in case Tony woke up and started to make a noise. He closed and locked the car, walked to the building site entrance and pulled the gate behind him. He secured the padlocks so they looked closed, but they were still unlocked. It would fool any passers-by until he returned in the early hours. He now needed to hurry, but the toll of the last few days was beginning to show. He was getting bags under his eyes and felt exhausted. It was a good twenty-minute walk to the gallery but he did not want any trail of taking a cab so he alternated walking and jogging. He arrived with a whole minute to spare and waiting for him was a slightly panicked Xavier standing alongside Jenny. The doors were already open and Billy guessed that this was the way things worked. Music was playing, there was a surfeit of alcohol being consumed and flashes from cameras were intermittently strafing the air like indiscriminate lighthouses. Billy entered his new kingdom and

The Perry Gene

Xavier started a ripple of applause that slowly grew more rousing. 'Jesus' thought Billy 'How long have these people been here?'

*

After half an hour or so, once the initial flurry of introductions from Xavier had begun to calm down, Billy actually started to enjoy himself. There was a constant flow of champagne in delicate glasses, but he limited himself to just one, which although he sipped at, didn't really go down. He spent time chatting to Fred and Mavis and also managed to talk to the good Doctor for a while on a non-therapeutic topic. In fact, it was good to see so much of Elspeth's support system in place on the night and he had vowed to bring Mrs Grainger to the exhibition one afternoon to give her some quiet time with the photographs. These people had become important in Billy and Elspeth's story and he intended to continue to celebrate them. The most amusing sight for Billy was to see George Transon and Gordon Miles together; both congratulating each other for the outcome of their endeavours.

Xavier was in his element and was having too much fun to notice Billy's personal guests. The journalists had a bunch of questions they wanted answers to, but the brief that Billy and Xavier had come up with was simple. Elspeth was something of an enigma in this context as Billy had never known her. There was an official Bio and of course the broadsheets which had used her pictures in the past had sufficient detail to pad out the review. Several times the idea of a follow up book had been mentioned and Xavier was visibly excited by this. More importantly for Billy, his own pictures were also going down a storm.

'They like the naivety of the images; no prepossession' Xavier said on a number of occasions. Billy didn't quite get it, but he didn't argue; this was a very nice distraction. Billy was also keeping an eye out for the next chess piece to materialise and finally at just before eight o'clock Julia appeared. She looked flustered as she came up to Billy.

'Billy darling, is he here?' she asked breathlessly.

'Who?' Billy said, acting innocent and confused.

'My stubborn husband. He appears to have disappeared.' She grabbed a glass of champagne from a passing waiter and slugged back half the contents before she came up for air.

'Sorry Julia, he may be here but I have been talking to Press men and guests all evening. Didn't he say he might have to work the other night?' Billy waved to a couple of photographers who were making their way out having got their required footage.

'Yes, but he is not answering his phone. His car is not in the garage. He does this from time to time; probably got tied up with something at work.'

'Yes' Billy said, you are probably right. He kept his thoughts to himself about where Tony was tied up and who had done the tying.

'Mostly I am just embarrassed darling. This is your big night for Elspeth and he is missing it. It's just rude. Elspeth would have been so proud to see what you have done here.' Julia finished her first drink and swapped the glass with one on the tray of a passing waiter.

'Sorry to be rude myself, but I must catch up with a few people, or Xavier will never talk to me again. Jenny is here, I'm sure she would like to see you. I promise to come and find you later.' Something in the way Billy said it pricked Julia's attention and the bubble of concern was suddenly burst.

'Oh, you are a naughty boy darling. Later it is then.' With this she took her glass and wandered off to look at the exhibition.

*

Ninety minutes later and the room was left with a few people making the best of the free flowing champagne. The main guests had gone and Xavier's boys had stopped serving. The maestro was preening himself as they had managed to sell a third of the prints in just one evening, red dots appeared across the room like a virulent strain of chicken pox.

'We are already in profit dear boy.' He cooed at Billy.

'We...hmm. Alright Xavier. But I think it's time to draw the evening to a close. Hopefully we will pick a some more sales over the next few weeks?'

'Billy, when the newspapers do their reviews on Saturday and Sunday, we will be sold out by the end of the weekend. If this goes the way I see it, the book deal will come next. Just leave it all to me.'

'How about we leave it a week and then let's have dinner and discuss where we are?'

The Perry Gene

'Billy, it's like telepathy, you read my mind.   Ok, I will get the boys to shut up shop.   Busy busy.' Xavier shot across the room like a Whirling Dervish and started to give orders. Billy saw Jenny chatting in the corner with Julia.   The third party in the conversation was the wall which was acting as a crutch for the now very drunk neighbour.   If Billy and Jenny had developed a Bat-Signal, it was now she would be using it.   Billy walked over.

'Did you find Tony in the end Julia or did he have to work?' Billy enquired.   Jenny shot him a look and he realised Julia had been crying and the tears restarted with his questions.

'He hasn't answered his phone' Jenny offered.   Billy realised Jenny had been chaperoning Julia as she had become more worried and maudlin. 'We' she emphasised 'think he might be sulking.' To Jenny's horror Billy put his arm around Julia's shoulder and gave her a squeeze.

'Never mind Julia, his loss is our gain.   We're heading off now, do you fancy a walk along the river or shall we jump in a cab together?'   Jenny was looking worried but realised very quickly that Billy was sober and not suggesting anything other than helping get Julia home.

'That would be lovely darling.   You are such a gentleman; not like that pig. I do like young gentlemen.'   She drifted in thought. As if remembering something vital, she softly said 'Chris was a real gentleman' more to herself than the room.   This was Billy's signal to start walking her to the door.   He waved to Xavier then the party of three, Billy, Jenny and Julia disappeared into the chilly night to find a cab home. It had just started to rain gently; mizzle. Maybe the weather had caught Julia's mood.

There were a few more tears in the cab. Billy had already convinced the driver that Julia was not going to throw up on the way. When they got back to the apartment they took the lift up to their floor and he and Jenny helped Julia with her keys to open her front door.

'A little nightcap?' she slurred 'or maybe you had something else in mind' she now looked at Jenny. This reminded Billy of the comments made at the drinks a few weeks before. The implication was obvious and also revolting to Billy.

'Not this time thanks Julia, besides Tony should be back and we don't want to wake him do we.' Billy knew damned well where Tony was, and it certainly was not in the marital bed. He and Jenny said their goodnights and opened the front door to Billy's apartment. Once inside, Jenny gave him a big hug.

'You managed that well. She is a handful when drunk.' Jenny stopped and thought for a moment. 'You said some things in the past about her being a victim and not being all bad. I think I see that now. Tony really is a bastard for not turning up, isn't he?' Billy could see that the strain of the evening and alcohol had also taken their toll on Jenny. She looked tired.

'Let's get you to bed. It has been too good a night to spoil by discussing him.' He kissed her and took her by the hand, leading her up the stairs to bed. He helped her out of her clothes and into bed. Five minutes later, she was out cold.   Billy turned off the light and walked down into the lounge.

He quickly changed his clothes into dark sportswear and headed out of the door.

'Time for the end game' he thought.

The Perry Gene

Chapter 25

The trip back to the building site, was uneventful, but involved a little bit of care. Billy needed not to be seen on any CCTV systems in case his activities were any called into question. This meant taking several detours on his run and it added between ten and fifteen minutes to the journey. When we reached his destination, the gate was unlocked as he had left it. He pushed through the gate and pulled it closed behind him again.

He Billy took a pair of gloves and Tony's keys from his small backpack. He slipped the gloves on and then unlocked the car; he was still remembering important little details from his beloved crime novels. As the central locking system whirred, he heard movement in the boot. He pushed the button and lifted the lid. Billy wondered how long Tony had been lying awake, scrunched up. He hoped the tethered man was claustrophobic. Billy cut the chords connecting Tony's arms with his legs; he was still tied securely but would at least be able to stand. Tony was making noise behind the gag. Dragging him awkwardly out of the boot Billy pulled him to a standing position. He held his finger to his lips, made a ssshhing sound and showed Tony the knife he was holding. Tony stopped making a noise and his eyes grew wide with increased terror. Tony wasn't to know Billy had taken this from the knife block in the flat that Jenny had recently bought him as a present.

Billy pushed and pulled Tony towards the other side of the site where the equipment was parked. Opening the gate of the Cherry Picker, he manoeuvred Tony inside and then got in after him and closed the gate.

The Perry Gene

'I thought we might go for a little trip' said Billy. 'Both physically and metaphorically.' He looked up in the air, almost talking to himself but making sure Tony got the message. 'A little trip down memory lane. You've been in the Cherry Picker at night before, haven't you Tony?' Billy looked at Tony and then once it had sunk in what was happening, he continued 'Silly me, you need that gag taken off or you won't be able to tell me what happened. Billy ripped the gaffer tape roughly from Tony's mouth. 'Just remember, you scream out, and I have this.' Billy held up the knife until it glinted in the street lights. Now with his mouth free, Tony finally had the chance to speak, for the first time in nearly 5 hours.

'I need a drink, let me have some water.'

'I have something better' said Billy, pulling a bottle of Tony's beloved Scotch out of his bag, and putting it to Tony's lips he poured a good measure. Tony spluttered as Billy poured in more than he could drink and the excess ran down his face.

'I just wanted a drink of water; you trying to drown me?' Tony said once Billy had stopped pouring.

'Suicidal men don't jump off buildings after drinking water. Cowards who do things like that always get loaded first.' Billy held Tony's head back and poured again. Tony tried to struggle, but Billy brought his knee up swiftly into Tony's stomach and left him gasping for air. He then poured more of the nectar down his throat. Billy put the bottle back in the bag and as he did so, unseen by Tony, he pressed a button in his pocket.

The Perry Gene

'Nobody will believe I jumped. I am a businessman, I am successful.'

'Chris Deville was successful too. He was good at his job; diligent. Apparently according to your wife, he was good in the sack too.' Billy knew he needed to goad Tony. A confession was not the only evidence he would need, but it would seal the deal. 'What was wrong, too much whisky? Too much pressure at work? Man, of your age, couldn't you get it up any more? Did Julia outsource her needs to a younger man? You must have been livid.' Tony was now struggling at his bonds trying to get free. He lunged forward into Billy in an attempt to push him out of the cradle of the crane, almost catching Billy unawares. Billy struggled to push him back to the other side of the cradle but Tony was disadvantaged with his hands tied and he eventually complied as Billy raised his hand in warning.

'When I get my hands on you; I'm going to fucking kill you.'

'Is that what you said to Chris that night? High up on the railway? Tell me, I'm genuinely interested. To set the record straight. Did you have Chris Deville killed because he porked your wife or because he found out you had asbestos in the building and you were bribing the Building Inspector?' Tony was now glowing almost incandescent with rage.

'Well, like those adverts say, it was twofer.'

'Sorry, imagine I am just stupid little Billy Perry, Elspeth's backwards nephew. What do you mean twofer?'

The Perry Gene

'Oh, for Christ sake, you really are a moron, aren't you?   Twofer; two for one. Either reason would have been good enough. It's not the first time that stupid bitch has shagged around, but he was about to blow the deal.'

'So, you killed him.'

'No.'

'I have the footage, you ordered it.   You were here when it happened and you went with the foreman as he carried the body from the Cherry Picker down the railway track where the body was thrown from.'

'You can't prove any of it. It's your word against mine. Now let me go and I might just let you live.'

'Oh now, I don't think so.   I think we should relive that night, blow by blow.' Billy turned the key on the crane's control and the cradle started to rise. He knew how far it could go up and still remain in the CCTV blind spot.   But Tony was not to know this.   His bravado was wavering and the fear returned. When they were ten feet off the ground, Billy stopped the cradle. 'Out of interest, did you kill him down here or up there?   I know Chris was dead before he fell; the fall itself was not enough to kill him; just badly injure.   Also, my friends had a word with the coroner and there was a blow to the head not consistent with the fall.   So, what happened?'

'I tell you what happened and then you let me go?' Tony moved into bargaining mode, ever the business man.

'I thought more along the lines of Crime Watch.   You tell me and we do a reconstruction.   Imagine I am playing the foreman.   He's a right nasty piece of work, isn't he? Did he strike the killing blow? Down on the ground? Did you catch Chris snooping, collecting evidence to reveal the scam? Was it meant to be a warning and it all got out of hand? Or did you see his smug face in front of you? The face of the man who had been fucking your wife. Did you lose it then and there? Did you kill him and then co-opt your poor innocent foreman to carry the body up to the track and throw it off?' Billy finished and looked at Tony, who was now red and sweating. Had he pushed hard enough?

'It was the bloody foreman. Stupid sod hit him too hard. We had to get rid of the body. It wasn't me. Now you know, let me go.' Billy reached for the controls, but rather than take the cage down, he took it up and other ten feet. 'What the fuck are you doing. I told you it was foreman. You can't do this.'

'We haven't finished yet. We have some work to do. Oh, by the way, can you get a network connection up here?' Tony stared at Billy and looked confused.

'What?' But as he spoke Billy pulled Tony's laptop out of the backpack. As he did this, he also clicked off the recorder in his pocket. The next bit was not for the police to hear. This was a nice 'fuck you Tony' that Billy was about to gift wrap.

'It's just we need to send an email.' Billy powered up the machine and smiled as the network indicator showed connected. 'Oh look, WIFI' he said almost gleefully.

'What email?' Tony had forgotten his predicament for a moment and wondered what on earth Billy could be up to.

'I am going to make the decision you have to make very simple.'

'Decision?' echoed Tony, 'What decision?'

'The fact that you are going to go to the Police to confess your crimes.'

'You must be even more stupid than I thought it you think for one minute I am going to implicate myself in anything.'

'But you already have. I taped our conversation' Billy said, pulling the thumb drive recorder out of his pocket.   Yes, Billy knew he might be heard on the tape as well.   But if he kept just the parts, he needed it would be pretty damning.   Tony lunged forward again, but Billy was ready for him this time and was in far better shape than a man who had spent the evening bundled in the boot of a car.   He pushed him back against the cage and then brought hit foot hard against the top of Tony's knee making him collapse down. The laptop was still safely in Billy's other hand.

'That will never hold up. Is that all you have?' spluttered Tony.

'This is not my case, your honour.' With this Billy put the laptop down and placed his thumbs behind his collar aping a barrister. 'This is just one exhibit of many. We also have the CCTV footage of you and the foreman up on the track.   The pictures of your foreman crashing his van into the bus after trying to run me off the road and lets not forget the fire.   Then there will be the email, which brings us nicely back to your computer.'   Billy knew this bit should have been tricky, but he had already looked at the laptop earlier and realised the password was written on a slip of paper in the laptop bag in case Tony forgot it.

'You keep going on about email, what the hell are you talking about.'

'Well now Tony, my old mate. In your remorse at the death of Chris Deville and the needless attack on my employees and myself, you decided before you killed yourself that you would come clean in your suicide note; or in this case email.'

'I thought we had dispensed with this game now. You are not me; you won't throw me off or you become what you hate. You are powerless. Anyway, you said just now I had a choice, what is it?'

'Confess to the police or bear the consequences.'

'You really are a stupid little sod. What consequences?' Tony almost spat the words out, so sure was he of victory. The surge of the whisky in his blood stream and the adrenalin of the fight was making Tony even bolder.

'Well you see, that depends what's in the email and who I send it too, doesn't it?'

'Nope, no idea what you are getting at' said Tony, but the edge had come off his menace all of a sudden. Billy actually had him worried.

'Let's talk content. First off, you are going to say about the asbestos you found in the walls.' Tony was silent. He had not seen this coming. He assumed this was all about Chris Deville. 'Next, you are going to confirm that you are bribing the Building Inspector to make the issue go away until you can sell the apartments. Any health issues after that will not come for years and you will be long gone.   Finally, you are going to mention the foreman hitting

and killing Chris Deville and you two dumping the body.   We can dress it up a

bit to make the foreman look worse than he is.' Tony was now looking

decidedly ill.

'You are going to send that to the council and the police, I guess?

Nobody is going to believe it.   I will say I was hacked.   You got my machine.

You are sick, demented.   I bet you're sleeping with her too? Go on admit it.

Nobody will believe you, they will believe me, the business man, and the pillar

of the community.'

'You know Tony, I was worried you might think that, so a couple of

friends of mine did a little digging. I know you are broke. You've thrown

everything into this.   Your apartment is mortgaged to the hilt, you sold the race

horse, no new car just that classic vehicle which you adore and all your other

properties liquidated.   Still you came up short, didn't you?   I don't think, no

sorry, I know you didn't go to the bank.   You went to some very unscrupulous

people in the East End.   Through this building project, your silent partners are

trying to launder a whole bunch of dirty drug money to make it nice and

wholesome and clean.'

'Prove it.'

'I don't have to.   I have their email addresses.   I'm betting you didn't

tell them about the asbestos, did you?   If the Building Inspector blocks this site

due to asbestos, you are going to be six to nine months and half a million over budget.   You can't afford it, because you have to pay back the piper.   I have added them to the mail addresses.'

'You're bluffing.'   Billy lowered the laptop to show Tony the screen. 'You can't send that.   I will be dead in days.'

'Which is why you are going to confess.'

'No, as soon as I leave here, I am having you arrested or worse, I might just let the foreman have some more fun. You aren't going to be able to send that.'

'Oh, sorry' Billy said.   'Didn't you realise?   I was showing you the sent items folder.   The email went was sent when we first starting talking.   By now, my case officer from the fire, the council housing office, your financiers and several national newspapers have received this email. You my old china have a snowball in hells chance of getting out of this in one piece unless you act fast.   Ok, what will it be?'

'I'll see you in hell before I help you.   I'm not going to admit anything to you; I'm not going along with this bollocks.'

'Do you know' said Billy 'I rather hoped you would take that approach. You now need to have another little sleep.'

'You're going to hit me again? Just try it.'

'No Tony, I only hit you before because of Pete.   I have a much better way of putting you to sleep.   Elspeth was a photographer.   A dark room is a wonderful place when it comes to chemicals.   I can't quite manage chloroform, but this is close enough.   Billy reached into the bag, pulled out a rag and held it over Tony's nose.   It was not a pleasant smell and it did not act that quickly,

but after about 30 seconds, Tony went limp. 'No' said Billy out loud. 'Effective,

but not nearly as satisfying.' He now started to lower the cage to the ground.

'Check, and mate in two moves' he said as he manhandled Tony into the

passenger seat of his own car.

*

Billy left the site as he had found it and as he shut the gate, he clicked

the lock shut.   If the security guard did not turn up the site would not look like

anyone had been there. Luckily Tony was too cheap to have installed CCTV and

this was a bonus for Billy; one more thing he would not have to fix. He was

wearing Tony's hat and long raincoat that he had retrieved from the back seat of

the car, to obscure him from the cameras across the road.   He got in the driving

seat and set off for the ten-minute drive to Southwark police station.   Tony was

out cold in the seat next him, but Billy was not sure how long it would last. He

needed to be quick but not to attract too much attention.

Pulling up to the parking space he had used the previous week when

visiting the station, Billy parked the car and then dragged Tony across from

passenger side into the driver's seat.   From his backpack he poured the rest of

the bottle of Scotch over Tony's face and jacket.   He left the spent bottle on the

passenger seat.   He took off Tony's coat and hat and placed the hat on Tony's

head.   The laptop was slipped back into Tony's briefcase and Billy was set.

Now he just needed a little attention. He rammed Tony's head into the steering

wheel making the car horn go off.   As soon as the noise started, he slammed the door and ran to the side alley which he had parked deliberately near.   He needed about thirty seconds to get away from the scene, using a route which would not appear on any cameras.   He knew the police would be out shortly.   Before breaking into a jog for the two miles home, he pulled off his two neoprene gloves and threw them into a dog-toilet bin.   In all the time in Tony's car, the cherry picker and using the laptop, he had not left a single print.

Billy arrived home around 1.30 in the morning.   He rolled under the security gate which led to the garage having left it partially open earlier by blocking the sensor.   There was no record of his electronic key fob operating the door to the apartments. He now quietly climbed the stairs and let himself in with his Yale key.   He knew he needed to get back into bed so that Jenny was able to provide him with his alibi, but he needed a drink first. Tonight, that was not Billy.   It was not even Elspeth.   It was scary, exhilarating but most of all it was not without a lot of personal risk.   He realised his heart was still pounding.   Before going up to have a shower, he poured himself a brandy.   There was no way he wanted to smell whisky any more tonight. He took the glass and looked out at the river. He loved this city, but even more so at night. When it was quiet, it became almost like another planet, filled with strange alien creatures that the tourists never saw.   Billy thought of the folk that Elspeth had been photographing on her last project.   The immigrants, the casual workers, the abused and misused, but that was the story of this city.   There were always users and abusers; victims and villains.   He turned and looked at Elspeth's portrait.

The Perry Gene

'We would have made a great team Auntie. No. We DO make a good team. You would have been proud of me tonight.' He drained the glass and headed up the stairs into the spare bedroom to shower so he wouldn't wake Jenny. He let the water run for a good fifteen minutes, feeling like he needed to wash away all traces of Tony and the yard from his skin.

When he finished, he dried himself off, but his hair was still damp. He crept into the bedroom where Jenny was gently snoring. Billy guessed she must have had a fair amount of alcohol too as she was minding Julia at the gallery. He snuggled against her and she stirred half awake. She kissed him and pulled him into her. Within two minutes, there were two slumbering bodies wrapped around each other snoring in unison.

*

Billy rose early considering his late-night excursion. Jenny had a little bit of a hangover so Billy suggested to her that maybe the gym or a run might be a good way to get rid of it. He just needed an hour to complete the final task, then he was free of this whole episode. Jenny dressed in her running gear and tried to convince Billy to join her.

'You coming with me?' Jenny asked as she did some gentle stretching in the lounge. Billy was looking out the window having made a coffee.

'I've got a bit of a calf strain, so I will give it a miss.' He bent his leg up and rubbed his calf to reinforce his excuse. 'Besides I want to check in with Xavier to see if there is any feedback from last night.

The Perry Gene

'Getting old lover boy?   The strain taking its toll? Your executive lifestyle?' smiling she dug her fingers into his ribs, kissed him on the neck and whispered in his ear 'are they love handles I can feel?'

'Just go, I will have plenty of energy to deal with you later.' Billy smacked her gently on the bottom and she walked to the door to go for her run.

Once Jenny had gone, Billy pulled the thumb drive from his track suit pocket. He plugged it into the computer and uploaded the track.   It took him about twenty minutes to isolate the key passages and transfer them into a clean file with his voice removed.   He copied this new file on a USB drive along with the footage from the CCTV camera and the shots of the foreman and security guard after the bus accident.   The white van could be clearly seen. He printed a note to the police officer who had interviewed him after the fire at the warehouse, and then added this to an envelope stapled to which was the policeman's contact card that he had been given.

When Jenny returned, she went up for a shower and Billy popped down to the riverfront and into the local paper shop to pick up the large Saturday editions.   Xavier thought this might be the first place they may see a review of the exhibition, but it might not appear until Sunday due to the timing. Billy took the papers back to the apartment and without thinking used the lift.   As he exited at his floor, the door of the opposite apartment opened.   An unkempt looking Julia emerged.   It looked like she had just woken up from a heavy night.

The Perry Gene

'Billy, it's you. I thought it might be Tony.' Julia said as she came towards him.

'Is he not home? Maybe he went drinking with the lads at the site?'

'He's not answering his phone.' Billy knew exactly where the phone was, sitting at the bottom of a cement footing with the battery removed.

'Maybe you should call the Police? He might have had an accident' Billy thought the police would be able to enlighten her. He didn't want to hurt Julia any further but this was no longer his issue. This woman's alcoholism and philandering had been a contributing factor in Deville's death.

'Oh my god, do you think something's happened?'

'I couldn't say, probably not, but it might put your mind at rest. You know what they say about bad pennies; they always turn up.' Julia screwed her face up. She didn't like the implication of her husband being bad, but deep down she knew he was no angel. It's a pity she didn't realise just how dirty the face of her angel was. 'I need to go as Jenny has breakfast on, but please let us know when he turns up.' Billy walked quickly into his flat, killing any further chance of communication.

Jenny was sitting downstairs waiting for the kettle to boil; she was dressed in a big white fluffy bath robe.

'Did I hear you talking just then?' she asked as he walked in.

'Julia, hungover and looking for her husband.' Billy said putting the papers on the counter. 'No obvious evidence of Xavier's grand publicity plan in the papers from my initial review.' Jenny stood up and walked up to him and spoke more quietly.

'You changed the subject; are you saying Tony has not turned up? Billy do you know anything about this?'

'Let's just say Tony may be helping the police with their enquiries. On that front, if you want to get dressed, I will take you out to breakfast. I need to drop something off on the way.'

'Are you going to tell me anymore?'

'I promised you this would be over in a week. Today is the last day. Trust me, and I will explain all, but I just need to complete the last move.' She hugged him.

'Right, I'll be quick. I didn't eat much last night and now I need some food after the run.'

*

Twenty minutes later, the two of them were sitting in the car along the road from the Police station and Billy had the envelope in his hand. He needed to get it to the investigating officer but wanted to do it anonymously. He had thought about asking Jenny to do it, but again, he wanted to leave no trail. They sat there in silence for a couple of minutes.

'Breakfast Billy, remember? My stomach is rumbling.' Jenny held her tummy as it literally gurgled in protest to prove the point. Billy was about to answer when he saw the answer in front of his face.

The Perry Gene

'Jen, I'm getting out. I need you to drive the car around the corner and meet me there.' Jenny pulled a strange face but realised with Billy it was best to nod and agree. He would explain when he was ready. Billy got out of the car and Jenny slid over. 'See you in five' he said and sauntered off. Billy had seen a postal van pull up close to the police station. Now it was just a matter of timing. He put headphones in his ears, turned on his phone's music and started to run towards the station. As the postman took the mail from the van, Billy timed his run. At the point the postman crossed the pavement Billy bowled into him. They both went flying.

'What the bloody hell you doing?' shouted the postman, his mail knocked out of his hands and lying on the floor.

'I am so sorry; I was in another world' said Billy as he removed the earphones. 'Here let me help you.' Billy bent down and started to collect the spilled letters. He slipped the envelope into the pile and handed them back to the postman. 'Sorry again mate.' He started to jog off and popped his earphones back in to stop any further conversation. As he rounded the corner, he saw Jenny waiting. He got into the passenger seat, belted up and she drove off.

'Where are we going?' Jenny asked.

'Anywhere you like. Breakfast is on me. But make it somewhere quiet, we need to talk.' Billy smiled, a smile that was going to last a long while. In the corners of his eyes were traces of Elspeth. Traces of the Perry gene.

The Perry Gene

Epilogue

The rain fell as a fine mist on the grass as Billy walked across the cemetery. He was not to know how similar conditions were to the night when Chris Deville died, but today was something different. Currently there was no sign that Chris was buried here. Billy had first sought out any relatives, and then when finding none, had tried to find the grave. Even Jen had questioned why nobody had ever claimed Chris Deville's personal effects. It all made sense now and it drove Billy to one final act of remembrance. The story that Gordon had recounted about Elspeth looking after her Cameraman's daughter financially after he died struck a chord. Dealing with police, mortuary and local authority he followed a paper trail to get here. Breadcrumbs that ran from the flat, to the railway line and finally to the piece of unmarked soil. Today that was to change.

As the two workmen first dug a small hole and then manhandled the granite headstone into place, Billy watched on. By now the rain was soaking through his thin coat, but he was too engrossed to notice. No, this was not the old Billy of *petite-mals* and silences, but a new more determined and thoughtful Billy. There were still lose ends. A trial had been scheduled for Tony and the foreman and Julia no longer lived in the flat next door; it was up for sale, but today, one thread would be tied off. When the workmen finished, they nodded to him and walked away carrying their tools. Billy was finally alone with Chris Deville but found he had nothing to say. He read the words of the inscription in silence.

'Chris Deville, A good man, in a poisonous world.'

The Perry Gene

Billy knew he owed much to the episode with Chris, for it was through this that Billy had finally come alive. But the true thanks would always go to his Guardian Angel. He had one final stop of the day which was to visit Brookwood. Flowers and a little quiet moment with Elspeth and the Perry clan. He knew in his heart she was watching and she was proud. He had truly proved himself to be worthy of his genetic heritage.

Printed in Poland
by Amazon Fulfillment
Poland Sp. z o.o., Wrocław

53872899R00219